IN A WORLD IN WHICH BODIES AND SOULS ARE FUELED BY OBSESSION...

KATE PALEY—A woman who's always believed ambition is a tightrope one must walk alone...until she opens her eyes and her heart.

ADRIAN NEEDHAM—The roguish Cockney director shuns Hollywood and all its artifice and greed—and the hold it has on the woman he loves.

SYLVER CASSIDY—A teenage superstar whose life in the fast lane takes her on a crash ride that nearly leaves her for dead...until one man shows her the way out.

RILEY QUINN—An ex-cop writing the great American detective novel, he finds inspiration in Sylver—and perhaps salvation from the demons tormenting him.

NANCY CASSIDY—Her daughter Sylver was her ticket to the *in* crowd and she'll do anything—with anyone—to get there again.

DOUGLAS GARRISON—Studio head and golden-boy puppet, he's been riding Kate's successful string of blockbusters—until the ax falls.

"Elise Title makes her mark in this exciting behind the scenes look at Hollywood."
—*Romantic Times*

Also available from MIRA Books by
ELISE TITLE

OUT OF THE BLUE

Elise Title

HOT PROPERTY

MIRA BOOKS

ISBN 1-55166-012-1

HOT PROPERTY

Copyright © 1994 by Elise Title.

Printed in U.S.A.

To all my pals at PAGE

Prologue

Beverly Hills, California
Spring 1993

"You're not nervous, are you, Suzanne?"

"Moi? You mean just because this is my first time, Don?"

"No, Suzanne. Really? Your first time? And you've picked me? I am truly honored. No, I'm humbled. Moved. Touched. Hell, baby, I'm hot."

"Whoa, Don. I hate to burst your bubble, but I didn't exactly pick you."

"Suzanne, I'm crushed."

"I do think the committee made a very good match-up, though. Does that make you feel any better?"

"That depends. What are you doing after we give out the next award?"

"Speaking of awards, Don, don't you think we ought to... Well, you know...."

"Grab the Oscar and hightail it back to my place for a cozy dinner for two by candlelight, Mantovani playing in the background...?"

"Mantovani?"

"Okay, Barry Manilow."

"I think we'd better just go ahead and announce the nominees for this year's Academy Award for Best Supporting Actress, don't you?"

"You mean right now, Suzanne. And then afterward...?"

"Right now, Don. And we'll talk about afterward, afterward."

"Okay, folks, the nominees for this year's Academy Awards for Best Supporting Actress are..."

As the scene on the big-screen television switched from the podium of the glamorous awards gala at the Dorothy Chandler Pavilion to "candid" close-ups of each of the nominees as they were announced, the man in the black tux sprawled on the king-size bed across from the TV wasn't paying any attention. Neither were the two detectives, the three uniformed cops, the forensic boys, the photographer, or the coroner and his two investigators who were working the room. It was a virtual policemen's convention in there.

Lieutenant Al Borgini, Beverly Hills homicide chief, a lanky man in his late forties with a military crew cut, pointed to splatters of blood and brain matter on an antique Chinese calligraphy hanging above an ornately carved rosewood headboard. "Is that a brushstroke or what I think it is—blood?" he asked one of the forensic boys, who immediately gave the scroll a closer look.

"Blood," the expert said matter-of-factly, carefully taking a scraping with his knife, then depositing it into a plastic bag and scribbling an ID notation on white tape and sealing it. The photographer snapped a shot of the hanging, then several more of the dead man on the bed.

Borgini's assistant, Hank Salsky, a bulky man in his late thirties, dressed in a rumpled Columbo-style trench coat, was giving the opulent bedroom a three-hundred-and-sixty-degree survey. He'd been with the L.A.P.D., Beverly Hills Division, for only a few months, his previous beat the mean streets of Detroit. This was his first introduction to the lifestyles of the rich and famous, and he was behaving like a star-struck kid.

"Man-oh-man," Salsky muttered as he took in the enormous bedroom with its electronically-operated raw silk teal drapes, the sumptuous crystal chandelier hanging from a ceiling draped in sky-blue damask like something out of an Arabian pasha's palace, the pristine marble-topped dressing table above which was a gilt-framed mirror, a huge chintz chaise longue, and, snugly housed in an oversize antique armoire, a giant-screen TV that he would have given his eyeteeth for.

"I'll lay you odds," Salsky said, "that my whole three-room apartment over in Pasadena could fit into this bedroom and there'd still be plenty of space left over, say, for a family room."

"Salsky, this isn't a homes-of-the-stars tour," Borgini grunted impatiently. "Check around, huh?" He turned to the coroner. "What do you say, Doc?"

"Clobbered with something heavy at the base of his skull. Can't be sure yet, but I figure death was instantaneous or pretty damn close to it," the coroner declared. One of his investigators rolled the dead man over, muttered that it sure would make life easier if they could find the murder weapon. Borgini's gaze fell on the victim who was now lying on his stomach. The poor bastard looked a lot worse from the back, where the blow had struck him, than from the front.

"Somebody really didn't like this character," Salsky deadpanned from across the room.

"Can you fix the time of death, Doc?" Borgini asked, ignoring, or at least trying to ignore, his assistant's irritating asides.

"I'd say somewhere between 3:00 and 4:00 p.m. Looks like he was getting ready to go to the Academy Awards shindig." He held up a ticket he'd found in the inside pocket of the tux.

"What a waste," Salsky said. "I bet those are the hottest tickets in town tonight," he added with a grin.

Borgini shot his assistant a look. "Salsky, go interview the housekeeper. She says she found him like this at five-twenty. Claims this was her day off, but she came back to make herself some dinner and get ready for a night on the town with her boyfriend." He hesitated. "Go easy with her. She's pretty shook-up."

"Maybe he still owed her this month's salary. You think she did him in, Chief?" Salsky asked. He was over by the electronic drapes, which were drawn shut, trying to figure out how to operate the gizmo that opened them.

"Why don't you ask her?" Borgini said caustically just as Salsky pressed the button that activated the opening of the drapes. Early-evening light drifted into the bedroom. A beam of light shot off an object lying on the finely oiled walnut floor behind the drapes, drawing Borgini's and Salsky's attention. It was a gold andiron, one end of which was covered in blood.

Salsky grinned at his chief.

Borgini rolled his eyes. "Hey, will someone turn off that damn TV?" he barked, the background drone starting to get to him.

One of the uniformed officers, an earnest and attractive new female recruit, hurried over to the cabinet to obey the homicide chief's command. She reached for the Off button when Salsky called out, "No. No, wait a sec. I think they're about to announce the nominees for best actress. I'm rooting for Emily Chapman. Did any of you guys see her in *Sign of the Times?* Man, she is one hot number."

Borgini gave the uniformed cop a "your ass is on the line" grimace and she quickly shut off the set just as the announcement was about to be made.

Salsky shrugged. "Okay, okay. I'll go chat with the housekeeper." As he started across the room, he glanced over at the body on the bed. Something shiny on the cuff of the dead man's black trousers caught his eye. He moved to the bed.

"Salsky, what the hell—" Borgini snapped, stopping midsentence as his assistant pulled out a pair of tweezers from his raincoat pocket, which he used to remove the small silver object clinging to the cuff. He held the item up with the tweezers for examination. It was a silver earring in the shape of a star, a diamond chip flashing at its center.

"Could be a clue. What do ya think, Chief?"

The corners of Borgini's mouth started to twitch, a sure sign he was getting stressed out. "What do I think? I think we'd better treat this homicide with kid gloves, take it nice and easy, not jump to any conclusions. This is no ordinary stiff. And something tells me there aren't going to be any ordinary suspects. Which means we're going to have the media crawling up all our collective asses on this one and we don't want to make any mistakes and get shafted.''

As he gave his little speech, the chief's bloodshot brown eyes never wavered from his assistant. Salsky, for all his luck—and okay, talent—impressed Borgini as a real loose cannon. Once upon a time, before he'd made it to chief, Borgini had been teamed up with another loose cannon—his old partner, Riley Quinn, who was, for it all, one hell of a cop. Salsky could have learned a lot from him. Borgini was man enough to admit he had. Then again, he'd taught Riley a few things, too. Not to mention having saved his life.

Salsky carefully dropped the shiny silver star-shaped ear-ring from the tweezers into another plastic bag and cere-moniously handed it over to one of the forensic boys. Then he winked at his chief. ''Hollywood. Don't ya just love it?''

PART ONE

Fall 1992

One

"So Fielding says to me if I don't like it I can always go independent," Greg Coffman complained to Kate Paley over lunch at La Scala.

Kate speared a piece of leafy red *radicchio* from her salad plate. "And you're surprised? You've been with Fielding for over a year now. Don't tell me you still haven't figured out what a monumental ego trip he's on."

"No one likes being browbeaten," Greg countered in his high-pitched reedy voice. "Especially in front of a roomful of your colleagues. And then comes his big speech, the basic gist being that my supposed problem is believing I have the Midas touch, and that I'd better wake up and realize making movies is nothing more than roulette."

"Personally, I think a crapshoot is a better analogy," Kate said with a wiseacre grin. "What a game, though, when those dice roll your way." She'd had a hot hand this past couple of years, but at the moment she had nothing in development that was really getting her juices flowing. She needed something big; something that would make the old-boy network take notice. What burned her was that if she weren't a woman, she'd already be where she felt she deserved to be. Some days she felt like she was making real progress. Other days she felt like she was swimming against the current.

"Fielding cut me off before I even got going with my pitch. 'I'm against it,' he says. Period. Fini," Greg whined. "I was speechless. I didn't even think it was going to be a hard sell. And just last Sunday, I'm playing golf with the big man and he's treating me like I'm his golden boy. Not that

I'm tooting my own horn, but *Making Millions* was pretty damn close to being a runaway success.''

"*Making Millions* was also right up Fielding's alley,'' Kate reminded him. "A nice, simple shoot-'em-up action flick.''

As Greg droned on about the indignities and gross injustices he faced at every turn over at Avalon, Kate grew bored and discreetly began sizing up the room.

One-fifteen and the heavy hitters—most of them men, naturally—were settled in at their usual tables, wheeling and dealing in between swallowing down tasty morsels of Chef Leon's fine Italian fare. La Scala, with its subdued dark wood walls, amber mirrors, soft lighting, and red leather booths, was still one of the "in" eateries for Hollywood's movers and shakers.

Kate got a warm nod from Fred Meisel, head of distribution at Cinebar, as she spotted him and Don Hunt, a head honcho at Beekman Pictures a few booths away, having what looked to be a serious schmooze over steaming plates of mussels marinara. Kate wasn't a fan of either man. She viewed Hunt as a guy with a calculator for a brain. Everything with him was numbers. He pinched pennies better than her mother used to pinch fruit at the supermarket. As for Meisel, back when she was getting started in the business and looking for a break, she'd applied for an associate producer's job at Cinebar. Meisel was doing the interviewing. He'd been real smooth, chatting her up, tossing out a slew of compliments. Even though she was a novice at the time, she sensed she was being played along—especially as he kept arranging more interviews. When she confronted him at their third little get-together, he sheepishly confessed that he thought a beautiful young woman like herself might prove too much of a distraction in the workplace. He was so dense, he couldn't even understand why she got pissed. The jerk actually thought he was paying her a compliment.

In a booth across the room, Kate saw Bill Kelso, the Richard Gere look-alike who everyone was saying would be up for an Academy Award nomination for his star turn in *Calling the Shots*. The actor was fawning over a gorgeous brunette. Kate couldn't place her because she was half hidden by one of the faux orange trees, the signature motif of the trendy eatery. One thing was for sure. It wasn't Aileen, his pristine blond Aussie wife of little more than two months. Hey, for all Kate knew, two months could be some kind of record for Kelso. Hollywood relationships weren't exactly known for their longevity. Most of them were short but deliciously torrid. Come to think of it, most of them were also short and pretty messy. Kate had done her best to avoid those sorts of brief, messy entanglements. She'd only really slipped up once, and that was a long time ago.

When Kelso's dining buddy, the willow-thin brunette in skintight black leather, leaned forward to take a bite of her cheesecake, Kate recognized her. The flavor-of-the-month starlet, Stacy Allen. Kate felt a stab of envy as she watched the piece of cheesecake slip past her lips. Once upon a time when she was twenty-three or thereabouts, she, too, could have sucked down a two-thousand-calorie dessert like that with impunity. Now, at thirty-six, every one of those bites would go straight from her mouth to her hips. Wouldn't it be nice, she sometimes thought, to eat everything she wanted, never again set foot inside a gym, and simply let the fat fall where it may?

The lean, sinuous starlet caught Kate's eye and smiled prettily. Not even any smile lines to mar that disgustingly flawless ivory skin. Kate decided it was the kind of skin that wouldn't age well, then wondered if she was being catty or merely terrified of being thought a relic even before she hit forty.

After giving one of her imperial "Aren't you lucky I've even deigned to notice you" nods, Kate willfully stabbed a piece of crisp endive from her salad plate sans her favorite vinaigrette dressing, and turned her attention back to her luncheon partner. "Did you say a Lerner script?"

"What do you think I said? Artie Matthews at ICA brought it over to me. I'd bumped into Lerner at the Bistro Garden last week and we got to talking about it. As soon as I left him, I called Matthews and convinced him this was a project made in heaven for Avalon," Greg said, a bead of sweat punctuating the tiny mole just above his lip. At thirty-nine, the craggy-faced, athletically built Greg Coffman, vice president of Avalon's motion-picture division, was considered by most to be a heavy hitter at Avalon. Kate knew better. Greg had a major problem—a surefire kiss of death in La-La Land—he had a need to be liked. A fatal flaw if you intended to have any staying power in this crazy business. Trying to win friends left you far too vulnerable to giving in when you shouldn't.

It was an insane profession. Having more than her own share of woes and frustrations as VP of Paradine's motion-picture division, Kate at times seriously questioned her own sanity. Was it worth all the aggravation and grief? Damn straight!

Greg dabbed at his mouth with his linen napkin. "Don't look now, but Ron Bruer just walked in."

"Showing his face so soon after the debacle," Kate mused.

"He spotted us. Yup, he's coming our way."

"Head drooping slightly? Shoulders a little slumped?"

Greg smiled cattily. "So astute. As always, Ms. Paley."

Ron Bruer, a bear of a man who reminded Kate of Robinson Crusoe, had the unenviable distinction of being the writer/director of NewMark Pictures' most expensive, most highly touted and biggest flop of the season, *On Her Own*. A couple of years before he'd almost convinced Kate to back the film. She thanked her lucky stars that she'd passed on the project.

"Kate. How are you? Looking gorgeous as ever." Bruer placed his beefy hand on the sleeve of Kate's suit jacket in greeting, flashing her a natty kiss-ass smile. Kate was quick to note the twitch in his right eye.

She felt a flash of pity for the writer. One flop and everyone—including her—was starting to write him off. What was his crime? That he was fallible? Like the rest of them weren't? Ron Bruer was a nice, bright, talented guy. Just like she was a nice, bright, talented gal. Unfortunately, that alone would never cut it.

Bruer gave Greg Coffman a nod of homage before focusing back on Kate, his expression earnest. "I hear the sneak of *Breaking Legs* went over the roof. Looks like you got another winner on your hands." He hesitated, sagging a little, his smile wilting on his face. "Look, I know you're busy as hell, Kate, but I would love to sit down with you...."

She could hear the pleading note in his voice. Didn't the guy have any pride? Or at least enough smarts to know it was considered a breach of Hollywood manners to admit you were feeling needy. It embarrassed people. Worse still, it made them uncomfortable and all they wanted to do was steer clear of you, afraid that what you had might be catching.

"With your people, that is—sometime soon and..."

While Bruer was grappling for the right words, an elegant man in a British-cut navy pin-striped suit was shepherding an exquisite redhead in a Norma Kamali white silk dress over to their table.

"Kate. Greg. I had to stop by and introduce you to my wife, Lisi." Stan Geller, a senior VP at Filmways said, callously edging Bruer out of the way.

Kate and Greg greeted the sixty-two-year-old Geller's wife with brief handshakes as Bruer skulked off to his table—not one of the six power booths in the front room, that was for sure. Poor guy, Kate thought. If he struck out again, he might find the place booked next time he dropped around.

"Stan tells me, Kate, that you're one of the cleverest and shrewdest women in the business," Lisi drawled.

Was this Geller's fourth wife or his fifth? Kate had lost count. One thing she did know—they always got younger. She guessed that lovely Lisi was somewhere in the below-twenty-five range. In a business where boy or girl wonders, in that order, were forever being glorified as if somehow youth and wisdom were joined at the hip, Kate, at thirty-six, was more than a little sensitive about the age thing. God knows, her medicine cabinet was becoming a veritable gold mine for keeping the creeping monster at bay—number thirty sunscreen, the finest French moisturizing emulsions, special night creams, exotic morning oils purloined from tropical plants, unique herbal pastes to prevent tiny brown spots, skin enrichers to apply under makeup. She already had selected the plastic surgeon she'd go to when the time came.

"Word's out *Breaking Legs* had the best opening week-end of any of Paradine's movies so far this year. Nice work, Kate," Geller was saying to her with a mix of deference and envy. Powerful men like Geller might rave about her to their wives, but Kate knew how difficult it was for these guys to swallow when a woman in the business scored big points. Hard for their male egos to digest.

"Listen, any time you want to jump ship. . ." Geller pan-tomimed the rest of the sentence, extending his hands in an offensively paternalistic "Come to Papa" gesture.

"I'm happy on my ship, but I'll store your invite in my Rolodex for a rainy day, Stan," Kate said airily.

Stan took hold of his wife's arm and headed off to join kingpin agent, Len Burke, at an even more prestigious booth than Kate's.

"I remember a time not so long ago when Geller wouldn't give me the time of day," Kate said snidely. "Now, if I asked him, he'd gladly take that gold-and-platinum Rolex watch right off his wrist and lay it at my feet."

"So, tell me, Kate, how does it feel to be one of the most influential women in La-La Land?" Greg asked, only half facetiously.

"Not as good as it's going to feel when I'm heading the pack," Kate quipped. Beneath the surface, she was dead serious. What was it her mother had always said? *Never get mad. Get even.*

"By the way, did you catch that look the luscious Lisi Geller gave me?" Greg said with a grin as he cut into his succulent chicken cacciatore. "I think she's hungry for my body."

Kate had caught the look, as well as the designing smile Greg had tossed back at her. Being drawn to married women on the make was another of Coffman's fatal flaws. He'd made enemies of some influential husbands around town.

Kate took a sip of her San Pellegrino. "I guess the hon-eymoon's over."

They both laughed, but then Greg sobered up. "Maybe I'm the one that should be jumping ship. If Fielding doesn't budge on the Lerner script. . ."

"What's it called?" Kate asked nonchalantly, but her wheels were starting to spin.

Greg's eyes sparkled. "*Mortal Sin*. Don't you just love it?"

"What's not to love?" Kate said with a grin.

"Matthews is in a position to put all the key elements together for me—a nice, neat package. He's already got Dan Mills biting at the bit to direct. And he's assured me any one of a half-dozen A-list actors in his stable would gladly sign on for the leads. And what does Fielding do when I tell him I've copped the coup of the year. He bitches and moans and ends up throwing it in my face."

Kate smiled sympathetically. She knew that the legendary studio chief, Hal Fielding, was renowned for his volcanic rages and the positive glee he took in humiliating his staff. A couple of years back, staffers at Avalon were jumping ship faster than a candidate's team in a losing presidential bid. In these lean Hollywood times, however, people on the "in" were too afraid of finding themselves permanently out in the cold if they took a voluntary hike. Kate knew that Greg Coffman was no exception. That was another of his fatal flaws. He lacked daring. And he'd never learned the fine art of manipulation.

"You still don't get it, Greg. You don't hand Fielding anything, especially if it's perfect. It makes him feel inadequate. And if there's anything someone like Fielding hates to feel, it's inadequate." Kate knew all about avoiding that particular feeling like the plague. *Eau de* insecurity. Let anyone sniff it on you and you were a goner. Especially if you were a woman, you were constantly being tested.

Kate vividly remembered her first solo executive-producing deal at Paradine—a sweet little suspense thriller called *Deadline*. It had been her chance to prove she could take charge of a production—not an easy task since she was working with a first-time scriptwriter. She'd known the film would be a tough sell, tougher still to get made, especially as she was adamant about taking complete charge of the physical production. Not only hadn't this sat well with the money people, she'd had one hell of a time getting her director, Adrian Needham, to cooperate. The two of them had argued over how they interpreted the film, whom should be cast, how much location shooting was needed. He'd wanted to film it in black-and-white; she'd insisted that without color there'd be no appreciable payoff at the box office. Adrian hadn't cared two hoots about anything so mundane as how many tickets got sold. Kate had accused him of having no ambition. He'd accused her of selling out. He'd walked off the set twice, swearing a blue streak, and vowing that he was through.

Then there was their huge, embarrassing blowup in the tony Polo Lounge of the Beverly Hills Hotel, two-thirds of the way through filming. They'd gone there for a conciliatory drink. Instead, halfway through their first round, they'd got embroiled in a dumb argument over the interpretation of one of the monologues at the end of the film. Kate, who prided herself on never losing her cool no matter how angry she got, had ended up throwing her martini in his face. Then it was tit for tat. Only Adrian had been drinking a Bloody Mary. One of the waitresses had caught sight of her after the drink had landed, saw all that red liquid streaming down her white silk blouse, thought she was bleeding, and phoned for the paramedics. Kate had never been back to the Polo Lounge since.

Adrian had blamed the fighting on her, claiming she deliberately instigated most of their battles as a way of keeping him from getting too close to her. He accused her of being afraid of intimacy; went so far as to tell her he believed she equated intimacy with weakness. His analyses of her made her see red—half the reason being she was scared that he was right; the rest of the reason had to do with the fact that they happened to be enmeshed in a heated and very intense love affair. This gave them the opportunity to have endless fights about their personal relationship as well as the movie they were making together.

The only night they hadn't fought was the night of the premiere of *Deadline*. Kate could still picture the two of them clutching each other in their rented limo, Adrian having to ask the chauffeur to pull over three blocks away from the theater so she could jump out and throw up at the curb.

Never before or since had Kate been so scared, worked so hard, felt so desperate or so exhilarated. Never before or since had she had a relationship to match the one she'd shared with Adrian. And to the disappointment, envy and venom of all those sharks eager to see her fail, *Deadline* turned into a surprise box-office smash. It won an Oscar for best script and Adrian Needham was nominated as best director. The best thing about it for her was that she'd faked them all out. The worst thing was that it had marked the end of one of those short, torrid, but oh-so-messy relationships she'd been avoiding like the plague ever since.

"I tell you, Kate, I'm not giving up on *Mortal Sin*," Greg said so emphatically, it drew her back to the present. "No way I'm letting this package slip through my fingers. I only wish Fielding wasn't such a hard-ass egomaniac."

Although Kate readily agreed with Greg that his boss was a son of a bitch, secretly she respected Fielding; even thought that below the skin, she and Avalon's studio head were a lot alike. Driven. Pursued by demons. Always using their varied emotional arsenal—everything from menace to charm to calculated candor—to their best advantage. Kate liked to think she was not only subtler but more decent than Fielding about the way she used her weapons, but sometimes she wondered. She felt an uncomfortable twinge in her chest. Heartburn, she told herself. Otherwise perfectly fine. Never better. Maybe if she wrote it one hundred times on the blackboard...

"Did you hear the latest?" Greg injected. "Fielding pitched his car phone out his open window on his way to the studio yesterday and smashed the windshield of the Porsche he claimed was trying to cut him off."

The buzz around town was that Fielding's outrageous behavior would ultimately lead to his downfall, but Kate knew that any studio chief who could boast more than a billion dollars in grosses since he'd begun his reign, didn't have to worry. What a contrast Fielding was with her own boss, the overanxious and increasingly ineffectual Douglas Garrison. All Douglas could boast about lately was that he was in the enviable position of having a father-in-law who was CEO and the largest stockholder at Paradine. And of having her, of course. Now, if she were truly running the show...

"At least he didn't shoot him," Kate said dryly, Greg having once told her that Fielding carried a .38 in his glove compartment for protection. They both had a little chuckle.

A minute later, Greg leaned over to Kate. There was a glint in his eye. "Uh-oh. An old chum of yours just walked in on the arm of Sid Gandel."

Kate's spine stiffened. "Don't play games, Greg. Who?"

"Nancy Cassidy. God, it's hard to believe that hag could have produced a daughter like Sylver. Not that Sylver's looking her best these days, either, from what I hear."

Kate cursed under her breath. "Maybe I can duck out before..."

"Too late," Greg muttered with a wicked smile.

Kate felt a hand on her shoulder. She looked up at the tall, middle-aged woman whose leathery skin and bleached-blond hair had both seen far too much California sun. Nancy Cassidy was wearing a too-bright red, low-V-necked jersey minidress, red mesh stockings, and black cowboy boots. A walking fashion faux pas. Kate caught Greg's eyes lingering on the older woman's ample cleavage. Nancy always did like to show off her new acquisitions.

She shifted her gaze to the man beside Nancy. Gandel, the short, stocky middle-aged agent in a custom-tailored suit that seemed like it had been tailored to a leaner body, looked decidedly uncomfortable. A man who knew his place. You couldn't be just anyone to schmooze with the power players. Nancy Cassidy, however, was deliberately oblivious—as always—to protocol. Kate had to admit the woman had nothing if not chutzpah.

It had been nearly a year since Kate had last run into Sylver's mother—rumor was that she'd gone off with some Italian count to Milan—but her reaction to the woman was the same as it had always been in the past. Nancy Cassidy repelled Kate. The ultimate backstage mother. Single-minded, demanding, overbearing. And Kate considered those Nancy's finer qualities. The ones that really made Kate's stomach turn were the woman's possessiveness and utter insensitivity, especially where her own daughter was concerned.

"You're looking good, Kate," Nancy said in a forced voice. Giving praise had never come easily to the woman.

Still, it was the ultimate compliment. Looking good—as they both knew only too well—was what it was all about. Unlike Nancy, Kate vowed that she'd never let how she looked or dressed become the subject of ridicule. She'd continue to work at her appearance with the same vigilance she applied to every other aspect of her life.

Kate caught Nancy enviously eyeing the René Brunaud windowpane-patterned gray-and-black man-tailored jacket and trousers she was wearing. The French designer, still undiscovered except by a select few, had a unique style, so there was never any mistaking a Brunaud for something whipped up by one of the established designers. Kate always took great pains to dress well. She believed clothes made the woman even more than they made the man, particularly in this business. You got scored by *who* you were wearing as much as *what* you were wearing. Kate got a small degree of pleasure seeing that Nancy had all she could do not to crassly check out her label.

"You know Sid Gandel, don't you?" Nancy added after a strained pause.

Kate gave the agent an impersonal but not-altogether-perfunctory smile. She felt some pity for Gandel—if only because he was saddled with Nancy Cassidy for lunch. Back some fifteen years, Gandel had been Sylver Cassidy's first agent until her blockbuster hit at age eleven, at which point Mama blithely dumped him for one of the big shots at ICA, then the top agency in town.

Gandel shook hands with Kate and gave a half smile of acknowledgment to Greg Coffman. After a nudge from Nancy, Gandel introduced her to Greg.

The minute Nancy heard that Greg was director of production at Avalon, she grabbed his hand, literally pressing it to her ample siliconed bosom. "Sylver almost did a film for Avalon a couple of years ago," she gushed. "*Always a Bridesmaid,* I think it was called. But it wasn't really the right oeuvre for her."

Kate rolled her eyes. Only Nancy would use an affected word like *oeuvre*. Not to mention that Kate happened to know that Sylver's name had never come up for that part, even though Nancy had launched a vociferous campaign to get her daughter an audition.

Greg Coffman managed to disentangle his hand from Nancy's. "The right oeuvre. Yes, that's important."

No one in the small group missed the sarcasm behind Greg's remark even though his tone was quite polite.

Nancy's mouth sagged a little more at the corners as she focused back on Kate. Despite herself, Kate felt a flash of sympathy for the woman. Nancy must have picked it up, because she brightened a little. "Have you been in touch with Sylver lately, Kate?"

"We've had some brief correspondence." Namely, Kate had put her signature on a few checks that she'd chalked off to charity. Or at least she tried to tell herself that it was charity and not guilt. What did she have to feel guilty about? Not only had she produced every one of Sylver's hits for Paradine, making her a household name by the time she was twelve, she'd also done plenty for her that went above and beyond the call of duty. She'd given Sylver the love, affection, guidance and support she hadn't gotten at home, her mother always being too busy cutting deals for her and making sure she was getting the "proper" star treatment. Not that Kate had ever minded. The truth was, she'd been crazy about the kid. Once upon a time they'd been real close. Sylver had looked up to her—like a big sister. There'd been some good times, some happy times. Still, there was no erasing the bad times.

"She's really pulled herself together, you know," Nancy said earnestly. "Put on a few pounds, started exercising. She looks great. Doesn't she, Sid?" They could all hear the pleading note in Nancy's voice.

Gandel looked down at his polished Gucci loafers. "Well, I haven't actually—"

Nancy quickly cut him off. "Sylver's ready to get back to work. This time she's really looking to stretch. No more ingenue parts. She wants to show the world that she's more than a pretty face. We're looking at some very promising

projects. Sid's going to be representing Sylver again."
Nancy gave the gray-haired agent an eager look tinged with
desperation.

"Well, we're going to be discussing it over lunch," Sid
amended, clearing his throat.

"Not that there aren't dozens of agents calling daily
who'd give their right arm to represent Sylver. And scripts.
We're positively flooded with scripts. But as I keep telling
Sylver, she's got to be very selective. Don't you agree, Kate?
I mean, you used to give Sylver that very same advice."

"That was a long time ago," Kate reminded.

"Too long. The two of you simply must get together.
Maybe we can all have lunch? Sylver does speak so fondly
of you, Kate. She's never forgotten all you've done for her.
All you . . . could do for her again. Sylver really is eager to
get back in the swing of things."

Eager was the operative word. The question was, Who
was the eager one, really? Sylver or her mother? For a long
while, Sylver had been Nancy's primary meal ticket. Still,
for all her contempt, Kate could feel for the woman. It had
to hurt seeing your daughter—your own flesh and blood—
living in some seedy West Hollywood rattrap, wasted on
drugs and booze. Kate even thought that Sylver should feel
lucky that there was someone out there who stubbornly refused to give up on her. Then she reminded herself that
Sylver wasn't a child anymore. And she might not want to
be rescued. Especially by "Mommy dearest."

Gandel, looking more and more uncomfortable with each
passing moment, took Nancy's arm. "I have a meeting at
two. We really should get to our table."

To Kate's relief, Nancy nodded reluctantly and allowed
the agent to steer her off.

"So who do you think is going to be picking up their
lunch tab?" Greg asked Kate with a wry smile when the pair
had moved on to a table practically on top of the waiting
line.

"Three guesses. And one of them isn't Gandel."

Kate pushed her unpleasant encounter with Nancy Cassidy from her mind as she left the restaurant and slipped

behind the wheel of her shiny new gunmetal gray BMW 300si sports coupé. She pulled out from the curb and headed back toward the studio. It was one of those steamy days, hot and smoggy even by L.A. standards. Off in the distance, the Santa Monica Mountains were nothing but a faint smudge. Kate turned up the air-conditioning. Never let 'em see you sweat.

As she drove down Canyon Drive to Sunset Boulevard, whizzing past Beverly Hills' most affluent neighborhoods—those mansions with their lush tropical foliage and manicured blankets of green lawn that were on every tourist's walking and bus tour—Kate focused on business; namely, her conversation with Greg Coffman about the Lerner package. An enthusiastic fan of suspense thrillers, Kate had always particularly liked Ted Lerner's work. He was one of the few scriptwriters she'd ever come across who never sacrificed honest psychological depth while at the same time keeping you on the edge of your seat chewing on your nails. Lerner's characters always had layers to their personalities and believability. Flawed but intriguing.

True, his films had never raked in big bucks, but Kate believed that was largely the fault of the directors and the studios who treated his scripts like low-budget art films. As would Fielding, if Greg were ever to talk him into the deal. Which Kate knew he couldn't. Not that that would soften the blow if she waltzed off with the Lerner project, which she was confident she could do by guaranteeing a big-budget treatment. Greg would feel that she'd screwed him. She would feel . . . crummy, but justified. What logic was there to letting the project go down the tubes? Or worse still, letting some other studio snatch it up—and botch it? In her hands *Mortal Sin* could turn out to be Paradine's biggest blockbuster hit in what was looking so far to be a lackluster season, in no small part thanks to studio chief Doug Garrison's less-than-sterling leadership.

So where did that leave her? A phone call away from Paradine Studios' coup film project of the year.

She frowned, realizing that it also left her miles past the entrance to the freeway. She'd been so deep in thought she hadn't paid any attention to where the hell she was going.

Her frown deepened when she realized she was driving right through shabby West Hollywood, Sylver's not-so-happy current hunting ground. This downtrodden neighborhood, with its tawdry shops, downscale eateries, and faded, peeling, pink and mint green stucco bungalows and apartment complexes, was a far cry from Malibu, where Sylver had grown up.

Kate had deliberately never committed Sylver's West Hollywood address to memory. She didn't want to think of Sylver living in squalid surroundings. Okay, so it was painful.

Kate knew that work was her best cure for pain. She snatched up her car phone. "Eileen, get me Artie Matthews over at ICA." Kate liked Matthews. He was politic, pragmatic and a great deal maker with a top-notch clientele. He also happened to have a thing for her, which never hurt.

Eileen called back a couple of minutes later. "He's tied up in a meeting. Should I leave a message?"

"Yeah. Say I'm very interested in the Lerner package he offered to Greg Coffman over at Avalon. *Mortal Sin.*"

Matthews phoned her back ten minutes later.

"No grass ever grows under your feet." There was clear admiration in the agent's voice.

"I'm interested, Artie."

"You haven't seen the script yet, have you?"

"I will as soon as you send it over."

There was a brief pause. Kate knew the agent was wrestling with his conscience. Just like she had a few minutes ago.

"It'll be our secret," she coaxed.

"Avalon's got till Monday. Coffman swears he can turn Fielding around."

"Next thing you'll tell me you believe in the Tooth Fairy, Artie." *That's it, Katie. Keep it cool. Keep it light. Amuse him.*

He laughed on cue.

She deliberately waited a moment before delivering the zinger. "We're willing to reach deep into our pocketbooks on this one, Artie. Put the kind of money into the project it deserves. Let's start with Lerner. What's the most he ever got for one of his scripts? Three hundred thousand? Half a million? How does an even million sound?"

Artie Matthews laughed. "Not as good as a mil five."

"If I like what I see, you'll be able to hammer out the details with Phil Rossman, our legal eagle, on Friday."

"Monday. Just to be on the safe side."

"We won't sign till Monday. But it would be stupid to waste time."

"You're really something, Paley. If I were you, I wouldn't be expecting any birthday cards from Greg Coffman this year."

Kate felt another of those twinges in the vicinity of her heart, but quickly quelled it. Wanting to be liked was Greg's problem, not hers. "He'll land on his feet. Anyway, I'm doing him a favor. Next time he won't be so quick to give away his advantage."

"You sure you can swing this package with your boss?" Artie asked. "We're talking a pretty hot script. Mills wants to take it to the limit. Could end up NC-17. Garrison's pretty conservative when it comes to sex." He laughed. "On the screen, that is. What he does in his private life..."

"Don't worry about Garrison."

"You're getting pretty cocky in your old age, Paley."

"Hey, getting old's gotta be good for something."

"How about dinner Monday night? To celebrate."

"No can do. I'm speaking at some Producers' Guild function. Talk to you Friday," she said as she turned into the Paradine lot.

"I'm gonna keep trying. One of these days, I'm gonna catch you in a weak moment."

Kate was approaching Paradine's gates. Tully, one of the old-timer security guards, gave her a respectful nod, tapped an invisible hat brim and pressed the electronic button. Funny, but no matter how many times she saw those gates part for her like the Red Sea, she felt this delicious flutter of anticipation and exhilaration. And the sense of being one of those lucky ones. The thing about luck, though—it always had a way of running out. Well, she'd just have to run faster.

"One more thing, Artie. About Mills directing *Mortal Sin*."

"Quite a coup, right?"

"I don't want him."

"You don't want Mills? Come on, Kate. He's the best."

"No. He's in the running, but he's not the best." And Kate knew for a project like this, only the best would do. Now the question was, could she get him?

The gate closed behind her and she drove onto the sprawling lot past the cushy offices, the charming landscaped bungalows, the curved road lined with swaying palms, the soundstages. Three seventeenth-century courtesans crossed the street. A little farther up, a cluster of Indians were having a smoke and shooting the breeze. Modern-day men and women, looking both efficient and official, whizzed around in motorized jitneys. Paradine Studios. This was her world, her universe.

The charged-up feeling that had been clinging to her all day faded into at least temporary oblivion as she pulled her purring BMW into the privileged parking space reserved for VIP Kate Paley. She felt her spirits rise; felt herself being lifted out of imminent danger. She was still young, right on the cutting edge, and she had just lucked onto a project that could be her entry into the really big time. No, she thought as she stepped out of her car. It wasn't a matter of luck. It was a matter of being able to think big. It was vision. And that, no one could take away from her.

Two

He doesn't often buy her things, but when he does he always chooses something red. He remembers the first gift he sent her. A bright red pinwheel, gift wrapped with colorful animal paper. He enclosed a painstakingly neat handprinted note—"With everlasting love from your truest fan."

His heart races and his hands get clammy whenever he thinks back to that rainy day he first discovered her....

He wakes up with a cold that morning and feels rotten when the alarm clock goes off, so he calls in sick. He starts the day with a couple of shots of Jim Beam—strictly medicinal. A few more and he has a nice buzz on. Enough to jump-start him.

His mood that day matches the bleak rainy weather. The little drive he takes does nothing to lift his spirits so he swings into the twelve-screen cineplex out on La Cienega. The movie he decides on, *Crying Will Get You Anywhere,* is marked PG. Good, clean entertainment. He likes that. There's enough R-rated stuff happening all around him. When he goes to the movies, he wants something wholesome, something with those "family values" the politicians are always mouthing off about.

He's immediately drawn to the poster advertising the film—a picture of a cute little girl with ringlets of honey blond hair falling to her shoulders, a few glistening tears trickling down her cheeks, a big, brave smile on her pretty red lips, and one of her azure blue eyes cocked in a wink. The credits read—Introducing Paradine Studios' Newest Child Star, Sylver Cassidy.

He can't take his eyes off her. She seems to be smiling right at him. Such a brave little smile. "Lost your way, princess? I know all about that.'' He places his palm lightly, gently, on her tearstained cheek. A couple walk by under a big black umbrella, the tall skinny guy mumbling something, the fat woman in tight white jeans responding with a shrill little laugh. Laughing at him. He pulls his hand away from the movie poster, feeling an urge to go after the guy, have it out with him. And fatso. Who the hell is she to be laughing at him?

He clenches his hands together, his gaze drawn again to the poster of the little girl. The rage starts to recede. Instead he feels this overwhelming urge to wipe away those glistening tears. *Don't cry, princess. You don't have to be scared. Nothin' breaks my heart more than seeing a pretty little thing being scared.*

Like that adorable redhead he used to watch in the ice-cream shop. Every Saturday afternoon. Sitting in a booth with her momma. Looking so frail, so lonely, Momma never saying more than two words to her. Whenever he would catch her eye, he'd smile at her, letting her know she wasn't all alone; getting it across to her that he understood what it was like to have a momma who didn't care two hoots for you; a momma who thought she could buy you off with two scoops of chocolate ice cream once a week when what you really needed was holding, cuddling, being told how beautiful you were, how much you were treasured. The pretty little redhead was getting the message. He knew she was. Until Momma caught him smiling at her. The jealous bitch grabbed up that sweet little thing and whisked her off. The next Saturday, they didn't show up. Sitting in their booth, instead, was a cop. He never went back, never saw that pretty little redhead again.

His eyes fall back on the poster of Sylver. She's a lot prettier than the little redhead, a lot sweeter looking. And her big blue eyes stare right out at him. His mouth curves into a smile. His momma always used to call him a sour-puss. When she wasn't drunk out of her gourd and calling him worse. ''Maybe if you learned to smile a little, girls would like you better,'' she'd say. And he'd think to himself—*What the hell is there to smile about?* Now, he's smiling.

"Show's starting," the cashier in the box office calls out to him. "Hey, the kid's a real winner. You'll love her."

He nods, feeling like fate has finally stepped in and is lending him a helping hand for a change. He buys his ticket and takes a seat up front. The theater's almost empty. He's glad. He hates crowds. Especially crowded movie theaters. Movies for him are such a personal experience.

From the moment she appears on screen, he's a goner. Everything about Sylver is perfect. Those innocent, trusting blue eyes, that impish smile, the way her blond curls bob as she runs, the strikingly melodic voice. There are other little girls in the movie—playing her schoolmates—but Sylver stands apart from all of them. And what is she? All of ten? He can't take his eyes off her. Alone with her in that darkened theater, he can feel his dreariness and loneliness disappear.

Sylver. Even her name's perfect. He lets it play over and over in his head as he sits there drinking her in, savoring every movement, every gesture, every sound she utters. In the climactic scene where she cries because her best friend died and her father gathers her up in his arms, his own arms reflexively cross his chest. He's the one holding her, comforting her, stroking her silken hair, murmuring soft, soothing words. "I won't let anything hurt you ever again, princess." Someone clears their throat in the row behind him and he swallows hard, coughs, and drops his arms into his lap.

He sits through every showing of the film that day, feeling the thrill of being able to watch Sylver without someone catching on to their budding relationship and dragging her off. He leaves the theater in the dark of night. He sways when he gets out on the street, oblivious to the pounding rain. He feels dizzy, elated, reborn.

On the way home he stops at a newsstand and buys every movie magazine and tabloid he can find. Alone in his apartment, he goes through each one, searching for any pictures or articles about her. Every time he finds even a mention of her name, he carefully cuts it out, pasting it tidily into a newly purchased red leather-bound scrapbook. He has always been partial to red. He is overjoyed when he discovers in one article that red is Sylver's favorite color, too. A bond between them. And there are more links, convincing him that fate truly has brought them together. They are both only children raised by strong, powerful mommas, no daddy in the picture. Like him, Sylver, offscreen, is quiet and shy. She doesn't feel comfortable around most people, interviewers write. She does have a temper, though, some of them note. One article refers to a temper tantrum she threw on the set. He knows better. Sylver just kept things in, like he did, until there wasn't room inside for one more hurt, one more disappointment. Until you just had to explode. No other choice. The others can't understand that, though. People don't understand sensitive creatures like the two of them. Think they can be pushed around, made to toe the line. Can't see they need special care and tenderness. Can't understand the thing he understands so well: the desperate yearning to be loved. He and Sylver—they are soul mates.

He pulls down all the shades, clears the wall of his bedroom facing his bed, taking down several religious paintings and a print of a clown he purchased at a flea market. Soon, the wall begins filling up with pictures of Sylver he cuts out of the magazines. Then he begins sending for publicity shots of her. Later come the candid shots. Sylver coming out of a gala movie premiere, Sylver attending a charity baseball game, Sylver shopping on Rodeo Drive. He becomes quite a good photographer over time. Or maybe it's that Sylver is the perfect subject.

He sends her presents—always something red. That pinwheel first, then a fuzzy red sweater, a red leather diary for her to write her secret thoughts—maybe one day she would share them with him. When money's tight—which it usually is—he sends her a red rose. What matters is that she knows he's always thinking about her.

Then comes *Glory Girl,* the film she makes when she's seventeen. Sylver Cassidy's first on-screen romance. It's also the first and only movie of Sylver's he doesn't like. Not that she isn't wonderful and beautiful, as always. Even more so now that she's growing up. What he hates about the movie is seeing that greasy, muscle-bound, egotistical jerk kissing her like she's cotton candy or something. Worse still, the press are all writing about how Sylver and this jerk, this Nash Walker, are a hot Hollywood item offscreen, too. He doesn't believe it for an instant. Sylver could never love a dumb, insensitive slob like that. Actors. He knows all about actors. You couldn't work in this town and not know. They are all the same. Self-involved, stupid, selfish bastards with about as much sensitivity and depth as a thimble.

Still, after the movie, he sends her a dozen red roses. And a note. "Never sacrifice yourself for someone beneath you, princess. When it's right, you'll know. And I'll be there. All of my love, always, your everlasting fan."

It's soon after *Glory Girl* that his whole world collapses. Sylver vanishes. For weeks, months, there's no sign of her. The tabloids have a field day fabricating hideous rumors—stories about her alleged drug abuse, getting arrested for drunk-and-disorderly conduct, supposed eyewitness accounts of all sorts of sordid activities. Lies. All dirty, stinking lies. Every time he comes upon one of those filthy articles he tears it to shreds, then burns it. The one thing he doesn't do, can't do, would never do, is forget about her. *I'm with you, princess. Wherever you are, I'll find you. I'll make it all better. I know what it's like to run scared. I know what it's like when it all gets too much for you. Just hold on. I'll be there.*

Desperately, he begins roaming her neighborhood in Malibu, searching but never catching sight of her, finally having to face the fact that she must have moved. But where? At night, he comes home to his empty apartment, staring at his wall of photos. He can't get her out of his mind for a minute. He can't sleep nights worrying about her. She haunts his thoughts, his dreams. He can feel her loneliness, her need. It's his own. There are no boundaries between them. They are two aching hearts in the same body.

The months drift into years. Finally the tabloids stop writing about her. Yesterday's news. Hollywood's such a heartless, fickle town. Either you're somebody or you're nobody. There's no in-between. Lots of times he thinks about packing up and leaving. If it wasn't for Sylver, he would.

I won't forget you, baby. I won't leave you. How many times did I tell you I was your guiding angel?

He never stops looking for her, and then finally, he strikes gold. He comes upon an article in one of the film magazines—one of those "Where are they now?" pieces. There's a small photo of Sylver, too blurry to make out her features clearly, and a brief paragraph mentioning how she'd been recently spotted having a chili dog at Benny's Hot Dogs in West Hollywood.

He hangs out at Benny's every day after that, calling in sick at work, saying he has a real bad flu. He knows he's taking the chance of getting fired, but he doesn't care. He doesn't care about anything but finding Sylver. It doesn't even matter that he hates hot dogs. He stuffs down a dozen of them over the next week and a half, because he can't just sit there and not order something. As long as he's eating, they can't toss him out.

Then it happens. He's in Benny's, sitting by the window, trying to swallow down a bite of the rank, rubbery meat, staring out at the street, and she walks right by him. His palm slaps the window and she glances his way for the briefest of moments before walking on. She looks pale and drawn, her eyes vacant, haunted, but he sees the faint smile. It's enough. It's all he needs. He tosses out the rest of his hot dog, feeling reborn, bursting with new energy, as he follows her down the street, hanging back as she slips inside a decaying apartment complex called Fairwood Gardens. It hurts to think of her living in such a broken-down joint, but the joy of finding her erases everything else. Then he heads straight down Melrose Street in a daze of happiness. . . .

"Can I help you, sir?"

The question brings him halfway out of his reverie. He gives the pudgy, middle-aged saleswoman a blank look. When her gaze drops to the red silk teddy edged with lace across the bodice that his fingertips are lovingly tracing, he feels a flush spread across his face.

"For your wife?"

He can't speak.

The saleswoman smiles knowingly.

She thinks he wants to buy the teddy for his mistress. She
doesn't understand. She cheapens love just like all those
others. The teddy's completely wrong for Sylver. What's he
even thinking? He hurriedly walks away. Then he spots a
beautiful red silk kimono on one of the mannequins. Yes,
this is more like it. Soft and sensual, yet demure, elegant.
Perfect for Sylver. He has to buy it for her—even after his
eyes flick on the price tag. What does he care that it will be
canned soup and crackers for a week? He doesn't give a
damn about what he eats. Sylver has hit hard times. He saw
how she looked; how she was living. It tears him up inside.
He can picture her in the kimono; see the bright smile light
up her face; the tears in her eyes when she reads his note,
sees that he hasn't forgotten her. "I'll get you out of there,
princess. I'll rescue you. All my love forever, Your everlasting fan...."

Later, the gift-wrapped package in hand, he's hurrying
down Sunset Strip, sticking close to the awnings of the tawdry shops, trying to stay dry. He's passing by a run-down
theater that specializes in soft-porn reruns. A made-on-the-
cheap B flick called *Desperate Attraction* is playing. The
poster by the ticket booth grabs his attention like a blow to
the groin. It's all he can do to restrain himself from smash-
ing through the glass and ripping the poster off the wall.

He can't believe it. Sylver. His pure, innocent, once-
radiant Sylver. Oh, when he saw her earlier that day, he
knew she was going through hard times, but he never
dreamed it could have gotten this bad for her. Not that he
blames her. She was driven to it—victimized by the lechers
that swooped around her like prey, the moneygrubbers, the
soul peddlers. They took advantage of her suffering. He
knows what it's like to be kicked when you're down and
hurting, desperate for a lifeline. He's been kicked around all
his life—by his mother, the kids in his neighborhood, bul-
lies at school, his bosses at work, even the woman he once
thought he loved. Before he knew what true love was. Before Sylver.

Now look what they've done to his princess, his baby.
Revulsion and anguish sweep over him at her attire, or lack
of it—a filmy black negligee that leaves little to the imagi-

nation. Her eyes are closed. Not in ecstasy, as her pose means to make you believe. He knows better. Her eyes are closed to shut out her shame. Her shame is his shame. It's his fault. He's let them do this to her. His temples pound, his lungs have difficulty taking in air. Sylver. Poor Sylver. My princess. My love. His fists clench. He wants to kill the bastards who made the film; kill everyone who forced her to do it.

Even as he vows to walk right on by, a force greater than himself sucks him into that seamy picture house. A shiver of repulsion shoots down his spine as he breathes in the vile, rancid stench in the lobby. The smell gets worse as he steps into the theater proper. The floor's gummy, his soles stick as he walks. There are creaking sounds from the torn, rickety seats as assorted lowlifes get comfortable. He feels sick to his stomach, wanting to spin around and run out. Then he's ashamed. How can he desert Sylver in her greatest hour of need?

He stops in the aisle and stares at the screen. *No.* His hands jerk up instinctively to cover his eyes, but they freeze midway. He feels rooted, immobilized as he stands there, unable to look away. Horrified, he watches Sylver, topless, in skimpy black bikini panties, slowly, provocatively walking toward a muscle-bound cretin sitting on a sofa. She climbs right onto his lap, her firm, high, perfect breasts inches from the monster's face.

Bile rises in his throat. His legs buckle. He collapses into a seat, feeling tortured as he watches the cretin maul her, suckling her nipples like an overgrown infant. Sylver writhes in his lap, looking convincingly aroused. Always the consummate actress. Smiling on the outside, crying on the inside. He can feel her tears and her shame. They are mingling with his.

When he sees the cretin draw her bikini panties down over her smooth, creamy buttocks and begin working his hand between her thighs, he feels a wave of nausea. They're really going to do it. Right up there on the screen for everyone to see. Right in front of him. He leaps from his seat and runs from the theater like he's fleeing a fire. *I'll kill them.*

I'll kill them for doing this to her. I'll do something. I've got to do something.

He escapes down Sunset in the rain, sneakers splashing through the puddles, panting hard, fighting down the vomit, then losing the fight as he turns onto Vine where he up-chucks in the middle of the sidewalk. He ducks into an alley, dropping to his knees as sobs erupt from him. Clutching himself, he rocks back and forth on his heels, hatred consuming him; and what he hates more than anything is that watching her on that screen acting like some two-bit whore, turned him on. He is sickened by his own weakness. His love for Sylver was pure....

Only when he gets back to his apartment, soaked, disheveled, stinking of vomit and sweat, trembling, does he realize he's left the gift-wrapped, two-hundred-and-thirty-nine-dollar red silk kimono back in the theater.

He can never go back for it. He'll have to settle for another red rose. It's the thought that counts. That's what his mother always told him.

Three

Nash Walker tossed his black leather biker's jacket on a straight-backed chair as he stepped into the tiny bedroom, sparsely furnished with a white Formica-veneered bureau, an art deco-style armchair upholstered in a putrid shade of chartreuse vinyl and a double bed shoved against one wall—otherwise you couldn't swing the door open all the way. The shade over the one window in the room was drawn, but shafts of dusty sunlight beamed through the torn slits. The air had the stale smell of cigarettes and booze. The window air conditioner was on the fritz, as usual.

Leaning against the bureau, Nash plucked a joint from the pocket of his black T-shirt, then smoothed back his peroxide-streaked blond hair.

"That fruitcake again," he sneered, glancing over at the standing TV tray that doubled as a bedside table.

"That's not a fruitcake, darling, it's a rose." Sylver said, giving him a crooked smile. Sprawled on the rumpled bed, she stretched her hand out for a toke of his joint, but he ignored her, crossing the room and slapping the bud vase off the TV table with the back of his hand. The cheap white porcelain shattered on the bare wood floor, spraying water on the bed. Nash stomped on the rose.

"Feel better now?"

He glared at her. "Wasted and still the comedian. Maybe you should try stand-up. Or can't you stand up anymore?" He grabbed the covers and pulled them off her. She was wearing the tattered sheer black nightie she'd worn on the set of *Desperate Attraction* a year back. The hundred grand she'd made for doing the cheapie thriller had long ago been spent on booze, coke, rent and fast food.

Sylver pulled the cover back over herself and gave him a hostile look. "Why stand up to make a few bucks? Aren't you the one who's always pushing me to lie flat on my back?"

"For chrissakes, you talk like I was your pimp. Ted Reed doesn't make porno flicks. He's a perfectly legit independent producer. He makes art films. You ought to be down on your knees licking his boots, thanking him for wanting you in his flick."

"So I can limber up for his *art* film?"

He threw up his hands and stormed over to her purse on the bureau. He had to dig for it amid the clutter of dirty clothes, ashtrays overloaded with cigarette butts, cheap cosmetics and a couple of empty bottles of J&B.

"Why can't you get it through your head that I don't want to act anymore?" Sylver shouted at him, her voice laced with despair. "I wouldn't care if Cecil B. DeMille dropped down from heaven and wanted me to star in *The Ten Commandments 2* for three million bucks...."

"If all you want to do is lie around here all day, you could at least clean this crummy dump up once in a while," he snapped back. "This floor hasn't been swept in a year. You have more clothes thrown around the place than you do in the closet. Not that this whole apartment isn't about the size of a closet to begin with. At least you could dust and clean out ashtrays, put the laundry away, make the joint tolerable."

"I thought that was the maid's job. Or is this her year off?" Sylver said facetiously.

"Very funny." He flipped open her wallet only to find the billfold empty.

He spun around and gave her an accusatory look. "Where the hell's that fifty?"

Sylver stared blankly up at the cracked, yellowed ceiling.

He stormed over to her and yanked her by the shoulders to a sitting position.

"You selfish bitch. You copped some coke, didn't you? And blew it all while I was busting my hump going out on auditions."

"Maybe you were busting your hump," she said in a flattened voice, "but not from auditioning."

He gave her a desultory smile as he finished the joint. "Gotta get it somewhere, babe."

She knew he got a kick out of taunting her. Once upon a time, remarks like that had cut her to the quick. How long had it been since he'd wanted her? Or since she'd wanted him, for that matter? She couldn't even remember the delicious rush of desire she'd once felt when he took her in his arms. Now, on the rare occasions when they made love, it was like Nash was playing it strictly for the camera. All form and no substance. And she wasn't really even a player in the scene. Strictly an extra. A walk-on. Only she just lay there.

Had Nash really ever been her gentle, tender lover? Her knight in shining armor? Had she imagined it, or was it another role he was playing? He'd been sweet and tender when they first began filming *Glory Girl*. So patient and understanding. That was when he'd stolen her heart. That was when she'd had a heart to steal. Love was so much less complicated on celluloid. You got handed all your lines, all your moves. You knew exactly what to do. And what not to do.

In real life, she and Nash seemed to do everything wrong. They'd grown so used to lashing out at each other, neither one of them even winced anymore. Maybe she'd just stepped into the wrong movie; gotten miscast in the "victim's" role. *Could somebody please tell me how the hell to get out of my contract?*

Nash cupped her chin roughly. "Did you score? Did you blow it all, Sylver?"

She shoved his hand away and gave him a weary look. Sometimes she wondered what it was that held them together now. Mutual despair?

"I gave the money to the landlord. It was either that or..." She shut her eyes and let her head fall on his shoulder. "I need a drink."

"Only this morning you were preaching to me how we should both go cold turkey."

"Never listen to me when I'm in a momentary state of sobriety." She manufactured a smile, not wanting to admit to Nash or to herself how much she wished she could pull herself together.

He grinned. ''We need cash to buy booze, baby.'' His voice was softer now, more coaxing. He smoothed her tangled blond hair away from her face. ''You look like hell, Sylver. You're wasting away. At least go down to the beach once in a while and get a tan, for chrissakes.''

''Don't you know too much sun causes skin cancer?'' she quipped.

''Right. If you're gonna kill yourself, why leave it to chance.''

''I wouldn't kill myself, Nash. Just to spite you if for nothing else.''

He glared at her.

''That was a joke. Okay, so I still have to work on my routine. I was only trying to get you to smile. You look so damn sexy when you smile, Nash. It makes those big brown bedroom eyes of yours sparkle like diamonds.'' She fell back against her pillows, feeling that it wasn't fair that she looked so lousy whereas, even though he'd sought as much solace for his misery in drugs and booze as she had, Nash had somehow managed to retain his chiseled, almost-girlishly beautiful features—save for that virile, sexy week's stubble that never seemed to grow. Poor Nash. Once upon a time, every teenyboppers' favorite teenage movie heartthrob. Now just another faded star in a faded galaxy. A has-been and not yet even thirty.

''Did you call Paley like you promised?''

Sylver pulled the covers up under her chin. ''She's not in town.''

''Bullshit.''

''I can't keep asking her for loans, Nash. We're never gonna be able to pay her back.'' She didn't tell him that she hadn't called to ask Kate for money this time. He'd only make fun of her if he knew she'd called Kate to ask for her help.

Back in the old days, Kate had always been the first one she'd turned to when she was hurting, lonely, keyed up or scared. Kate had been the big sister she'd never had. Kate was the one who took her to Disneyland on her eleventh birthday, having the makeup and costume people at Paradine disguise her first so she wouldn't be mauled by admiring fans. Even her mother hadn't recognized her. It was one of the best days she'd ever had.

Most of her "best days" as a child had been spent with Kate. One time when she was heartbroken because she had never once been to a slumber party, Kate threw a humdinger of an overnight for her at her house in Bel Air, inviting a half-dozen girls that Sylver had never met before or seen since—and doubted that Kate had, either. She must have rounded them up from a nearby private school. It didn't matter. That night was a dream come true, all of them staying up the whole night, laughing, telling dirty jokes, eating popcorn, going through dozens of cans of caffeine-juiced soda pop—something her mother forbade at home. The next day, before she left for the studio, she'd thrown her arms around Kate and told her she loved her more than anyone in the world—even more than her own mother.

Kate had almost never failed her. Except the one time she'd needed her most. Sylver shivered. She almost never thought about that time anymore. She'd willed it into nonexistence. With the help of drugs.

She focused back on Kate, the only friend she'd ever had. Okay, Kate wasn't perfect. As if she, herself, was? Or anyone else she'd ever known? She still could think of no one to turn to for understanding but Kate. And she needed someone on her side. She couldn't do it on her own. She was too weak, too desperate for escape, too used to grabbing on to whatever got her through the nights. And the days. Anything to keep her numb. At some point Nash would wear her down—he'd tell her he owed some dealer big time who was prepared to break his jaw, his beautiful jaw, if he didn't come up with hard, cold cash—and she'd end up giving in, making another one of those disgusting, humiliating films. She was hanging by a thread, her last vestige of dignity and sanity up for grabs.

Nash placed his hands on either side of Sylver's pale, drawn face and stared into those incredible azure eyes of hers. Even dulled by booze and drugs, her eyes still had the power to mesmerize. "You could ask your mother...."

A flash of anger brought a spark of color to her face. "I won't ask her for anything."

"You agreed to meet her for lunch tomorrow, didn't you?"

The color faded. "Only to get some peace," she said dully. "She's been driving me crazy calling every goddamn hour pleading with me just to sit down and have one stupid meal with her. I liked it better when our phone was shut off."

"I know how you feel about your mother, baby—"

"No, you don't. You don't know how I feel about anything, Nash." Her tone wasn't angry or accusatory. Those kinds of emotions took too much energy. She was drained, wiped out. She felt like her whole life was spinning out of control and there was no way to slow it down, nothing to grip on to. No one. Certainly not Nash. He was spinning as fast as she was. He just did it with more style.

She was oblivious to the tears running down her cheeks until Nash eased her back down on the bed, stretching out beside her. "Don't cry, baby. We'll figure something out. We always do, don't we?"

She could feel her body break out into a sweat. A tremor shot through her. "I hate this. I hate when I stop feeling numb."

He pushed up against her. He was hard. She groaned silently. The last thing she wanted right now was sex.

He began stroking her, her knobby shoulders, her bony arms. He rolled her onto her side, curving his groin around her buttocks.

"Don't you have anything? Some ludes? Anything?" she whimpered.

He cupped her breasts, kneading them. One hand slipped down her concave belly, between her thighs.

She pressed her legs together, but she knew that Nash wouldn't take the hint. Anyway, it did feel okay, his touching her. If he could turn her on, she might forget, at least for a short while, that she needed to get high.

She rolled onto her back and circled her arms around his neck. He kissed her roughly, his teeth gnashing into her lips. She could taste blood. It didn't matter. She tried to pretend it was like it had been for them in the past when they were young and innocent and in love.

Nash wasn't giving her time to work up the fantasy. He was shoving her nightgown up over her hips, unfastening his jeans but not even bothering to take them off. He was still wearing his cowboy boots.

Then he was on top of her. She could scarcely breathe, he was so heavy. *Forget the fantasy.* He pried her legs apart with his knee. She steeled herself, willing detachment. Better that than sorrow and that awful emptiness even as he was filling her.

His hands were under her, moving her to his own rhythm, his breath heavy with the smell of booze and cigarettes fanning her face. His eyes were closed. Once upon a time he'd kept them open while they'd made love, wanting to look at her, watch her face as she reached orgasm. She was never more beautiful, he would tell her. Now when they made love, he never said a word.

It was mercifully quick. He came with a series of long, low grunts and then rolled off her. He no longer showed any concern that she didn't climax. Par for the course. He arched his back and zipped up his jeans.

She pressed her head to his shoulder and smoothed back his hair from his face. "That was nice," she lied. Not that she had to. Nash didn't expect it or even need it. She said it because she wanted it to be true. She wanted what they'd shared to be an act of love. She wanted to stop feeling so disconnected from Nash—worse still, disconnected from herself.

He sat up, swinging his legs off the bed. "I've got a few bucks. Get dressed and we'll go over to Murphy's Bar and chug down a couple of shots. You need to get out of this crummy pigsty, get some air. You're white as a ghost."

She started to protest. Why couldn't he go and buy them a bottle that they could drink up in the apartment? She hated going out, dreaded anyone recognizing her. Not that it happened much anymore. Still, the few that did recognize her always gave her such pitying looks. As her mother had exclaimed—in her inimitable fashion—the last time she'd seen her, she looked "like death warmed over." Did her mother think she was offering up some brilliant revelation? Like she was blind? Like she didn't know she was wasting away? Like that every time Nash touched her with his eyes sealed shut, she wasn't reminded that she was little more than skin and bone? It wasn't even that she didn't give a damn. She did. She just felt powerless to stem the tide. Sometimes—so help her, God—she tried. It was like struggling against the onslaught of a typhoon. A speck of dust blown around in a storm. Her whole life seemed consumed with feelings of helplessness, loss, humiliation, shame.

Not that Nancy Cassidy didn't have a solution for everything that had ever ailed her little girl. No sirree. Nancy would fix it; Nancy had all the answers. Nancy always knew what was right for her. Once upon a time Sylver had even been naive enough to buy that crap her mother dished out. Once upon a time she'd made it so easy for Nancy to use her—the dutiful, compliant child; the stupid child. She'd smartened up, though. Times had changed. God, how they'd changed. Just being near her mother now made her feel twisted with rage—one of the reasons she always got stoned before their get-togethers. She didn't have the strength for a major blowup. She didn't have the strength for much of anything.

The day after their last less-than-joyful get-together, Nancy had phoned her, informing her that she'd signed her up at a health club and made appointments for her with her dermatologist, her nutritionist, her hairstylist and her manicurist. An early birthday present, with an added rejoinder that she should never look a gift horse in the mouth.

Sylver didn't set foot in the health club. And she never had any intention of keeping those appointments, even in the unlikely event she could have remembered the dates.

Sure, her mother wanted her back in shape again. Not because of any great maternal concern, though. Sylver had stopped believing long ago that her mother had her own interests at heart; that what she did she did out of love. Nancy wanted her to make a comeback so she could fill the coffers again. Sylver knew all about how Nancy's bad investments and even worse choices in men had cut deeply into her savings. Nancy wanted to recapture the old glory days when money was flowing like champagne. She'd made it clear to Sylver every chance she got that she would pull all the necessary strings—if it killed her—and Sylver would play the dutiful puppet—if it killed her—in order to put the name Sylver Cassidy back up in lights. Nancy refused to concede that those days were over for good. Nor would she concede that Sylver wanted it that way. Would have it no other way.

Reluctantly, Sylver let Nash drag her out of bed and help her get dressed—a black turtleneck jersey, a pair of worn jeans. He had to make another notch in her belt. It got him angry.

"Look at you," he said in disgust, like it was a surprise to him; like he hadn't been stroking her body less than five minutes ago. "No waist, no hips, even your boobs are starting to shrink. You're wasted, Sylver."

"No parts for skeletons in Ted Reed's 'art' films?"

He gave her an angry shake. "I'm running out of steam with you, Sylver. If I get that part in the flick Ben Samson is doing at Avalon, I'm outta here, baby."

Sylver wouldn't say it, but she knew Nash didn't have a chance in hell at that part, or any part in a "reputable" movie. It wasn't only a matter of his being a lousy actor or having been out of the limelight for too many years; he was simply too desperate, and it showed. In Hollywood, anyone who was desperate was treated as a pariah. Still, even the possibility that he'd walk out on her one of these days and she'd find herself all alone, made Sylver panic. She clutched his shirt. "You can't leave me, Nash. You're all I have."

"And what's that, baby? Your own personal pimp?"

"No, no. I didn't mean it, Nash."

"Hey, you'll still have your secret admirer. Let him take some of your abuse for a while. Maybe it'll be a turn-on for him. It sure as hell isn't for me." He shrugged her off and started for the door.

"Hold on. I gotta find my shoes. Wait for me." She searched for her sandals but couldn't find them amid the newspapers, clothing and bedding strewn on the floor.

Nash was already out in the dank, seedy hall, the only light coming from a couple of bare low-wattage bulbs and the glowing red Exit signs over the fire doors at either end. He headed past the elevator, which was busted yet again. Sylver ran after him, barefoot, catching up with him by the stairs.

"I'm sorry, Nash. Please. Please, don't be mad at me." She wrapped her arms around him from behind, trying to halt his progress. "Wait, Nash. Just let me go inside and get my sandals. You know they won't let me into the bar barefoot."

He shook her off. "Forget it. I need some space. You're really getting on my nerves, Sylver."

The door to the apartment next to theirs opened as Nash was starting down the stairs and Sylver was shouting for him not to go.

"Anything I can do?" her neighbor asked.

She shook her head, not even turning around, watching Nash race down the three flights. "Damn you, Nash!" she screamed.

"You sure?"

Slowly, she glanced over her shoulder at the tall, dark-haired, well-built man in jeans and a white dress shirt rolled at the cuffs who stood at the open door, the sunlight from inside his apartment forming a weird kind of glow around him. She squinted at him. "You're not Mrs. Rosenberg."

"No. Never was."

Sylver gripped the banister for support as she turned to face him. "What happened to her?"

The man leaned against the doorjamb, unabashedly observing her. "I guess she moved on or died. I moved in yesterday."

Sylver suddenly felt dizzy and disoriented, swaying a little, but when her new neighbor started toward her she held up her hand. "I'm okay."

"Sure you are."

They continued assessing each other silently. "I don't suppose you've got any Scotch or bourbon unpacked yet."

He shook his head.

"Beer? Wine?"

He continued shaking his head.

She was holding on tight now, the dizziness escalating. The hall smelled of Mexican food and cigarette smoke. She felt nauseous. "A joint?"

"Dope's illegal."

A chill zigzagged down Sylver's spine. "Don't tell me you're a cop?" Just what she needed—the fuzz for a next-door neighbor.

He folded his arms across his chest. "Not now."

"You mean...you're off duty?" She kept one hand on the stair railing for support and wrapped the other across her stomach in an attempt to quiet the ache and the demons that were beginning to claw their way to the surface.

"I mean I'm retired."

She observed him more closely. He couldn't have been much over forty. If that. "You look too young to be put out to pasture."

He smiled. "I wasn't exactly put out. Kicked out would be more apt."

Enough of the neighborly chitchat. Her legs were feeling rubbery. She needed to crawl back to bed, but she might literally have to crawl to get there. If only she could get a little something in her to perk her up. Or at least prop her up.

She gave him a beseeching look. "Come on, neighbor. We should toast..." Her eyes closed and she could feel her legs start to give way.

He scooped her up a split second before she would have gone tumbling down the flight of stairs. She felt too sick and too weak to protest as he carried her into his apartment.

"Same as mine," she mumbled, giving the furnished living room a bleary sideways once-over. "Only neater."

He set her down on the threadbare orange couch. When he went off, she felt strangely abandoned. He returned a minute later with a tall glass of what looked like plain orange juice.

She grimaced when she took a long swallow and realized that's all it was. "Aw, come on. You've gotta have something around here to liven this up. Vodka? Gin?"

"Sorry, Sylver. I'm on the wagon. Drink up."

Sylver stared suspiciously at him. "How do you know my name?"

"The landlady told me."

"What else did the bitch tell you?"

He sat down beside her. "That you're two months late on your rent and if you and your scummy boyfriend don't come up with the dough by the thirtieth she's booting you both out."

Sylver sank wearily against the cushions, clutching the glass with two hands. "The story of my life in a nutshell. What's your name, neighbor?"

"Riley Quinn."

"And what's your story, Riley Quinn?"

"I'm a writer. That is, a would-be writer, if I had the courage to face my typewriter more often."

"Whaddaya write?" she asked groggily.

"Police stories. Write what you know, right?"

Her head lolled. "Right."

He extracted the glass of orange juice from her hand. "I think you ought to lie down for a bit."

Her eyes shot open. "Forget it."

"I wasn't planning to join you."

As he started to rise, she grabbed for his sleeve. "If you could just loan me a few bucks..."

"For your rent?"

She shook her head.

"You that bad off?"

She gave him a wry smile. "Don't I look that bad off?"

"You'd look better if you cleaned up your act."

She jabbed him in the arm and pulled herself to her feet with effort. "I don't need any sermons from you. My mother's already cornered that market, buddy."

"Riley."

"Really, Riley." She staggered across the room, hoping she'd make it to the door.

She was almost there, and feeling real proud of herself.

"Wait."

Not now. She had some momentum going.

A few long strides and he intercepted her at the door, stuffing a bill into her hand.

She didn't check out the denomination until she got into the hall and had heard her new neighbor's door shut.

Slowly, nervously, she unclenched her fist and looked at the crumpled note. Twenty bucks. She brightened as she staggered into her apartment and made a beeline for the phone. She knew she could count on Johnny, the delivery boy down at the Melrose Liquor Store, to get her order over on the double.

Four

Eileen Moss rapped on her boss's closed door, waited for the okay, and popped in. "Guess who's no longer the flavor of the month?"

Kate glanced up at her slim secretary. A former Miss Vermont, no less. Still, she was top-notch at her job. Beauty and brains—the perfect combination. It was never far from Kate's mind that one day, the bright Miss Vermont or Miss Some-other-state, could be sitting behind her vast chrome-and-glass desk dealing with the chaotic mix of scripts, memos, treatments, mail and messages. Which meant that she would either be sitting someplace a lot better or a lot worse.

"Jason Ritchie," Kate replied with an "I gotcha" smile.

As always, Eileen was duly impressed. "You've been gone all day. How did you hear?"

"It was a good guess," Kate said calmly, but inwardly she was positively electric with excitement.

"He certainly didn't last very long," Eileen reflected. "What's it been? Nine months?"

"I didn't expect him to last this long."

Eileen's phone rang in the outer office. When she left, Kate leaned back in her swivel chair and smiled.

She hadn't been smiling nine months ago when her boss and longtime paramour, Douglas Garrison, told her over a candlelit dinner at her place that he was bringing Ritchie on board as the new president of the motion-picture division.... He saved the news until after dessert—probably because he was worried that she would shove the *crème brûlée* in his puss. She certainly would have been tempted.

When he dropped the bomb, she stared into Doug's faintly pockmarked, angular face—first with incredulity, then fury. The imposing, gray-haired fifty-two-year-old studio chief, elegantly dressed in a blue cashmere blazer and gray slacks, squirmed uncomfortably under her scrutiny, unable to muster his traditional polished suaveness. His broad shoulders slumped a little. His dark brown eyes couldn't quite meet hers. This man—who had once been her role model and hero with his brilliant focus, his drive, his ambition and his insolence—looked more like a nervous deer caught in a car's headlights than the mighty head of one of the largest independently owned studios in Tinseltown.

She watched him strain for the right expression, then shake his head, at a loss for what it might be. He looked down at his perfectly manicured nails, seemingly fascinated by them. "There are reasons, darling...."

She didn't blow up. There would be no big, explosive scene. One thing she'd learned over the years—keeping cool under fire always worked to her best advantage. "Let's get one thing clear right now. No way am I reporting to Ritchie," she said in clipped, no uncertain terms. "If I can't continue to go directly to you..."

She saw the relieved smile pop up on his face. "No problem. Ritchie isn't going to interfere in our routine in any way. Think of him more as a...partner, not a boss." He offered up a patronizing smile.

"Except that he gets the title and the big bucks," she countered, pausing briefly before jabbing with a solid undercut. "We have very different ideas of what a partnership is all about, Doug." Once upon a time, he'd talked about the two of them being partners, too. Partners at work and on the home front. She'd even gone so far as to buy some bridal magazines. Hard to remember ever having been so young and naive. Hard, anyway, to acknowledge the memory.

Doug flushed at her jab and quickly stuck on his solicitous "You mean everything to me" look. "I know how you're feeling, Kate. Don't you think I wish things could be different? But honestly, I think Ritchie's going to make us all look good. I feel very positive vibrations about him.''

Kate rolled her eyes. No. This was too much. The man really was losing it. "Oh, God, Douglas, you didn't..."

She'd hit a nerve and knew it. The studio chief immediately went on the offensive. "Just because you don't have a spiritual core..."

"Give me a break, Doug. You picked Ritchie because your wacko New Age psychic told you to?" She later found out that Jason Ritchie also sought spiritual guidance from the very same psychic. Coincidence? Not!

"No, that's not what I'm saying. Shanda merely supported my decision," Doug retorted with barely suppressed rage. He was very sensitive about his "quest for spiritual salvation," which Kate knew translated to a "quest to save his ass as much as his soul." Over the past few years, as Paradine revenues began their slow descent, the studio chief's panic had escalated, and he began leaving a trail of psychologists, herbalists, and spiritualists in his wake. When the chips were down and the pressures were mounting, Doug inevitably sought a quick fix by someone he believed had a direct line to the gods. The gods of success, that was.

Doug produced a hurt, little-boy look. It didn't play well. "I'd hoped you would support me, too, Kate."

"I'd hoped that when that slot became vacant I'd be stepping into it," she retorted tightly. Hoped, nothing. Doug had all but promised it to her. And she'd been all but dumb enough to believe him. Why were some lessons so damn hard to learn? Because she had worked her butt off to prove the presidency of her division belonged to her; because she and Doug both knew she damn well deserved it; because in her expert hands the studio would finally have a chance to reclaim its former glory, not to mention profitability? Dumb, dumb, dumb. Things in Hollywood didn't work that way. Not when you were a woman and there was still one living, breathing member of the opposite sex left on the planet to recruit.

Doug smoothed away an invisible crease in his blazer. "You will step into it, Kate. In time. You just need a little more... seasoning."

She was finding it harder and harder to maintain her cool. "How seasoned is Ritchie? What is he? Twenty-seven? Twenty-eight?"

Doug rose, backing away from the table, clearly anxious to defuse a potential scene. Kate knew how he hated scenes. If it had been anyone but her, she was sure Doug would have sent a subordinate to hand her the bad news. He was a great believer in the old "shoot the messenger" theory. If Douglas Garrison was going to stab you, you could bet good money it would be in the back. Kate just never fully accepted that it would be her back.

He pulled out a perfectly pressed and folded linen handkerchief from his trousers pocket and dabbed at his forehead. "I'm feeling a lot of pressure right now, Kate. My illustrious father-in-law isn't happy with the studio's lackluster performance of late. And when Charlie Windham isn't happy, you know what happens to my blood pressure."

"My blood pressure isn't doing too well right now, either," she said dryly. "Maybe I should pay a visit to your brilliant Shanda and see if she'd support my decision to pack my gear and walk out." She was feeling sorely tempted to hand in her walking papers. Plenty of other studios would grab her; would be happy to offer her a position equal to the one she had at Paradine, probably with some added perks. Anger gave way to depression. Perks weren't what she wanted. Nor would any other studio ever really feel like home to her. Paradine Studios was in her blood. This was the empire she wanted to rule.

Doug hurried over to her, drew her up from her chair, clasping her shoulders tightly. "Don't even talk like that, darling. You know how important you are to me. To Paradine. Neither of us would survive without you." There was real desperation in his voice. Followed by another failed attempt to placate her. "It's just that I thought bringing in some new blood would juice things up. The two of you together—a one-two whammo. Ritchie brought Dekka a lot of hit-making productions."

Kate freed herself from Doug's grasp, but she gave him a level look. "When was the last one?"

Doug was quick to defend his new boy. "Not Ritchie's fault. Dekka's had its management problems. You know that."

She'd lost. She knew it and she knew that Doug knew it. What was the point of belaboring a done deal? She'd made it clear where she stood; how she felt. On his part, Doug would go out of his way to appease her in any way he could. He was too scared she'd bolt. It was a small victory at best. Patience, she told herself. The big victories would come.

She did get the satisfaction of getting in the last word. "What do you want to bet he'll be out of control before his first movie's in the can for us?"

Now, nine months later, she also had the satisfaction of having been right on the money. Too bad she hadn't pressed that bet with Doug. She would have won. Nine months on the job and *A Dangerous Woman*, Ritchie's premiere production with Paradine, was still in postproduction. There'd been problems all through the shoot—two changes in directors, a grumbling cast and rampant spending that was threatening to almost double the budget. Then there were the rumors about the kinky favors Ritchie regularly requested from the young, innocent and desperate-to-get-ahead women on the set.

Kate rubbed her hands together. Actually, Ritchie's short reign might very well turn out to have been a blessing in disguise. His abysmal failure as president of the motion-picture division could be her big break. With Ritchie out, she was the most obvious and qualified person to slip into the soon-to-be-departed studio exec's shoes. Doug wasn't likely to go reaching outside Paradine again for recruits. And if he stayed in-house, there was no way he could overlook her and bring in somebody else. Even he knew that a move like that would be tantamount to forcing her to resign. Besides, her track record over the past nine months had been stellar. And then there was *Mortal Sin* moving onto a front burner.

Kate pressed her intercom. "Could you try that call to London again, Eileen?"

"I just did. Left another message."

Kate frowned. "Anything pressing?"

"Mr. Garrison wants you to join him at three-fifteen in screening room seven. Roberts at Cinetrex says he has a hot tidbit for you, but he'll save it for when he sees you at the Bellman banquet Friday night. Frank Zimmer from TAA called twice. Says it's important."

Kate checked her watch. "Anything else?"

Eileen cleared her throat. "Sylver Cassidy called again. That makes four times—"

"You know the procedure," Kate cut her secretary off briskly.

"She says it isn't a loan this time. She just wants to talk to you. She sounded pretty... desperate."

"She and a half-million others," Kate said sardonically, but her gaze did stray across the row of framed eight-by-ten glossies of the studio's illustrious stars, past and present, adorning one of her caramel-colored walls, coming to rest on the photo of Sylver Cassidy. Sylver at seventeen. Not only beautiful but with an offbeat quality that had convinced Kate and a lot of others back then that the ex-child star turned teen starlet was destined for world-class superstardom. Despite herself, Kate felt a flicker of something in her gut. Frustration? Anger? Sorrow? Guilt?

She quickly averted her eyes from the photo, summarily dismissing those disruptive feelings. They were always lurking in dark corners like grisly vampires ready to spring for her jugular and suck the drive and determination right out of her. Steering clear of dark corners was the only solution. Sylver Cassidy was definitely one of those dark corners.

"Phone Sylver back and tell her I had to fly out to Phoenix. Problems on a shoot. You know the spiel."

"Roy Bates just walked in for his one-fifteen. Are you ready for him?"

Kate sighed. "Give me a couple of minutes." She punched up her afternoon schedule on her monitor. "Get a message to Mr. Garrison and tell him I'm going to be tied up this afternoon."

Kate heard her secretary's small intake of breath. "You mean you won't be able to join the chief in the screening room?"

Kate merely smiled. "That's precisely what I mean, Eileen. Oh, and if that call comes in from London while I'm with Bates, cut in," Kate said, checking her watch. "Even if it doesn't, ten minutes." Ten minutes was all Kate could take at any one sitting of Roy Bates, Paradine's director of development.

A minute later Eileen buzzed her.

"I have Mr. Windham's personal assistant on line two."

A small explosive charge shot through Kate. The CEO's personal assistant calling her? She got right on the line.

"Mr. Windham would like to meet with you on Thursday, Ms. Paley. One o'clock."

Kate confirmed without checking her schedule. It didn't matter what else was on the books.

"Your place, Ms. Paley."

"My office? Fine." Kate couldn't believe it. Windham was coming to *her* office. A flash of panic overwhelmed her, but she told herself that CEOs never fired vice presidents in person. A simple pink slip...

"No, Ms. Paley. I mean your home not your office."

For a moment, Kate was speechless. "Yes...fine. My home. One o'clock."

Something was up and Windham was taking no chance of the two of them being spotted together in public. A private little tête-à-tête with the crown head of Paradine. This was getting "curiouser and curiouser."

Kate held Roy Bates off for a few more minutes while she composed herself. Thursday was three days away and she knew if she wasn't careful she could drive herself nuts second-guessing what was up. She couldn't take her own advice. It was impossible not to contemplate what this visit by Windham meant. It had to be either something very positive or very negative. Definitely one of those two extremes. It wasn't every day the CEO paid a visit to a VP's home for a private little schmooze. In fact, Kate couldn't name a single time.

So what was it? Good or bad? It had to be good, she told herself. She'd done Paradine proud. These past few months, especially. Maybe he wanted to reward her for her efforts on *Breaking Legs*. Another possibility. Had he decided to step around his son-in-law and personally offer her Ritchie's ex-job?

Why the secrecy, then? It didn't make sense. Everyone would be expecting her to take over the ousted division president's reins.

She felt sick as a new scenario nudged its way into her mind. What if the fifty mil the studio had recently borrowed hadn't been enough to get Paradine out of the credit crunch and Windham was selling the studio? To a Japanese or German conglomerate? To a multibillion-dollar soft-drink company? With a takeover would come a very likely across-the-board sweep. Out with the old, in with the new. And the young. Was the deal still in hush-hush negotiations and Windham had decided to tell a select few; give them a head start on looking for new positions elsewhere? Would he expect her to accept the news graciously, and feel grateful besides?

She got up, went over to her Louis XIV cherry-wood credenza and poured herself a stiff glass of Scotch, straight up. She never drank hard liquor during the day, but if there was going to be a day to break that tradition, this was it.

Eileen buzzed to signal her that she was sending Bates in. Kate finished off the drink and slid into her sumptuous butterscotch leather chair behind her desk as the director of development appeared at her door. Bates was a small man in his early thirties with a pudgy face, oversize wire-framed glasses, and a stringy goatee. He was wearing a plaid shirt, a bolo string tie and black jeans. A cowboy from Queens.

He stood in her doorway as if he were in the presence of royalty. Kate pretended to be reading a fax, allowing herself to regroup.

When she looked up from the fax and glanced over at Bates, Kate saw the mix of envy and appreciation on his face as he took in her redecorated office. Even though she certainly didn't hold the director of development up as a paean of good taste, it always gave her pleasure to know her sense of style and class was appreciated. The office had turned out even better than she'd anticipated. Glowing with sponged caramel walls and decorated with an eclectic mix of modern, classic and folk furnishings, the large airy space had both weight and presence—like the woman who occupied it. Then the sickening thought came to her: For how long would she be occupying this office? It was one thing to move up to Ritchie's even more spacious and luxurious quarters, quite another to be forced to pack up and move out.

Kate vowed not to keep second-guessing herself and gave a brief nod, setting Bates in instant motion. He strode across her eighteenth-century Aubusson carpet looking like an overeager insurance agent desperate for a sale. There was a thin bead of perspiration across his upper lip. Kate knew she made Bates nervous. She intimidated a lot of men. It was one of her talents. With Bates and those of his ilk, it took no effort.

Kate remembered how, five years back, Bates had been the hot, happening youngster on the staff. Like so many of Douglas's choice picks—Kate excluded herself—Bates had proved disappointing. Some of that had to do with his penchant for getting stoned in the middle of the day. The rest had to do with his lack of vision and abject bad taste. Both he and Kate knew he'd gone as high as he was going to go at Paradine. Not that a lot of people wouldn't have given anything to be in Bates's place. In Kate's eyes, though, he was just another Tinseltown loser, and she had little patience with losers.

She rose and walked over to her window, broadening the distance between them, as if the lack of ambition he was suffering from could be contagious.

"Pitch me your five best shots, Roy. And keep them each to two minutes, tops."

He riffled through a stack of papers. "What a week. I've really got some good stuff. Of course, I've had to weed through plenty of crap. There was this one writer came in yesterday who pitched me a story about this guy in a coma who wakes up in another dimension and suddenly he's a tribal African chief on Mars—"

"One minute gone, Roy."

Roy flinched. Kate knew he was thinking that she was arrogant, rude, unyielding. She also knew that if she were a guy, he'd think she was dynamic, aggressive and powerful.

Her gaze remained fixed on her watch. She didn't have to look up to know that Bates was sweating even more.

"Okay, I think I got a real hot one here. Costello from VM Productions brought in the script. There's this guy, Alfredo, a Joe Pesci type, who loses everything—his home, his business, his girlfriend, his—"

"I think I get the idea," Kate intoned dryly.

The muscle in Bates's jaw twitched. "Right. The thing is, this is a real character piece. But with plenty of comedy and action," he quickly added, knowing Paradine didn't greenlight soft dramas. "See, this loser, Alfredo, wants to commit suicide because he feels so hopeless and inadequate, only he doesn't have the nerve. So he advertises for a hit man in the personals. This Sam answers the ad, Alfredo mails the hit man twenty thousand bucks along with instructions, and the deal is set. Only who shows up to do the hit but this gorgeous dame. Stacked, voluptuous—you know, a Dolly Parton type. And Alfredo falls head over heels in love with her. At first Afredo doesn't get it—that she's Sam, the hit man. This is her first job and she's real earnest about it, see. She keeps trying to do him in and he keeps trying to stay alive. Meanwhile, this relative of his dies and he inherits two million—"

Kate raised her hand to stop him cold. "An inheritance? Give me a break, Roy. What's your next one?"

"We could work around the inheritance. He could win the lottery. There's a real good arc to the story. Let me tell you the first-act bump."

Kate was eyeing the phone. Sometimes ten minutes could feel like a lifetime. "Leave the script. I'll give it a read." She wouldn't, but if she simply nixed the idea, Bates would waste her time trying to convince her she was wrong, challenge her reasons or try to change her mind. None of which he'd be able to do, so why bother.

"Okay, I got another hot one...."

Kate finished up her meeting with marketing early. There was still time to make it to the last half of the screening, but she opted instead to use the time to read through the Lerner script. What if it wasn't all she hoped it would be?

Her anxiety proved unwarranted. *Mortal Sin* was a great read—sizzling, all right. And hard-edged. She was sure the movie would be one of Paradine's biggest hits ever. Especially with the right director. It would leave blockbusters like *Basic Instinct* in the dust.

As hot as she was on the project, Kate felt edgy and agitated all through the read. What if she couldn't get Adrian Needham to direct it? Had he gotten her messages? Was he playing games? If Eileen had left any name but hers, would he have returned the call by now?

She chastised herself for being too sensitive—not a trait she allowed to surface very often. Nor was it constructive to dwell on the past. Or imagine that a man like Adrian would. Their love affair had been short and anything but sweet. In hindsight, Kate knew it was crazy to imagine they could have pulled it off right in the midst of their ferocious battles over making *Deadline*. He'd simply demanded too much from her, expecting her to leave their clashes on the battlefield and not bring them into their bed. She couldn't split herself in two—any more than she could handle all the soul-searching and cerebral angst that were as much a part of Adrian as the air he breathed. He was always going on about emotional integrity while she was busy losing sleep over budget worries and break-even points.

For all their differences, she had been captivated by Adrian. Not only was he brilliant. Not only did he have drive and energy to match her own. Adrian was the only man who had ever refused to take her at face value. He saw beneath her steely finesse. He made her laugh, even at herself. And when she laughed, she stopped feeling so empty. He saw her passion, her tenderness, her sweetness—what he teasingly called her "childlike qualities." This was odd to Kate, who felt she'd never really been a child. She'd grown up with so much responsibility—having to look after her wheelchair-bound mother, taking charge of the household chores, dealing with irate bill collectors, fending off the advances of her father's sleazy pals who would drop by to "see how Mikey's pretty little girl was doing."

Adrian was the first person in her life who had ever made her feel cherished, despite the flaws, the imperfections, the vulnerabilities. Still, as much as she had adored him, as alive as he'd made her feel, she'd never fully been able to drop her defenses. Ambition was something she knew; something she'd grown up her whole life believing in. Love was another thing altogether. Being loved so openly, so expansively, was entirely alien to her. And, yes, terrifying. There were times when she'd felt, if she wasn't very careful, she would be swallowed up by Adrian's love. The idea of reconciling love and ambition seemed insurmountable to her.

And now? How much of what Adrian had seen in her eight years ago—the warmth, the tenderness, the sweetness and passion—still existed? What if what he'd always viewed as the best in her was dead and gone? Sitting there in her sumptuous office, Kate realized it had been a long time since she'd truly laughed; a long time since she hadn't felt empty inside.

She picked up a recent *Film Mark* magazine, flipping it open to an article on "renegade filmmaker, Adrian Needham, epic cockney poet of the common man." In the years since Adrian had returned to London, he'd made one brilliant and controversial independent film after another. None of them had garnered him big bucks, but big bucks had never been what it was about for Adrian Needham. In the article Adrian gave a scathing indictment of Hollywood's lack of creativity, its reliance on sequels, and the outrageous budgets that made it so hard for American filmmakers not to eventually sell out.

She smiled. Adrian hadn't changed much in that regard over the years. He always did have an uneasy relationship with Hollywood money, arguing that it interfered with his "creative spirit." Was that what was keeping him from returning her call? Or was this more a case of his uneasy relationship with her? She frowned, realizing she'd come full circle back to the spot she kept trying to avoid. Well, when she did finally hear from him she'd make it clear from the get go that there was nothing personal in the deal; simply a fantastic script—a chance for Adrian to be not only brilliant and poetic but receive the international acclaim he so rightly deserved. Now all she had to do was convince him of that.

Her eyes lingered on his picture. His appearance hadn't changed much, either, over the past eight years. The trademark tangle of thick black hair, the dark brows that shot off at different angles, those intense aquamarine eyes, the jutting, defiant jawline. There was an insolent, brooding aura about the man, even when he was half smiling as he was in the photo. Adrian Needham angry was an impressive sight. Even more impressive was Adrian Needham in lust.

Kate felt an uncomfortable surge of arousal and quickly flipped the magazine closed. Her agitation returned full force. Adrian Needham, Charlie Windham, Jason Ritchie... So much up in the air; plenty enough reasons to feel on edge.

And there was more. Although Kate had done her best to put her recent encounter with Nancy Cassidy at La Scala from her mind, the numerous calls from Sylver that morning had made the whole incident impossible to ignore. Plus the lead part of Beth in Lerner's script would have been a perfect vehicle—or as Nancy would say, "oeuvre"—for Sylver. Not that Kate would even consider passing up a current big-name box-office draw for the lead. Had Sylver stayed in the business, though, she would have spun cartwheels around almost any actress in town.

Was it possible Sylver had turned her act around? Was that what her calls had been about? Was Sylver desperate to convince her she really was on the mend this time? Off the booze? Off the coke? Off her low-life boyfriend, Nash Walker, Paradine's one-time heir apparent to Warren Beatty.

Sylver Cassidy had once had everything it took to make the leap into stardom. Except maybe the stomach for it. Here was all this talent oozing from every exquisite pore, and all Sylver seemed to want was to be "ordinary."

When Kate first discovered Sylver and resolved to make the child actress a household name, she'd found her endearing, sweet-natured, and oh-so-eager to please. Sylver's almost-instant attachment to her was a definite ego boost, especially coming on the heels of the surprise announcement of Douglas Garrison's marriage to Julia Windham. Sylver, with her warmth and adoration, helped Kate over a very rough time. Never picturing herself as a particularly maternal type, Kate was surprised by the depth of genuine affection she developed for Sylver. And, thanks to her many fun-filled outings with Sylver, she discovered a newfound playfulness in herself. Having fun had never been on her agenda before.

Occasionally, Kate would be hit with a pang of conscience. Sylver was being shoved into stardom by her overbearing mother and she was helping make it happen, but the kid was so damn talented. What did kids know, right? Kate was positive—or told herself she was—that Sylver would come around in time. When she got a little older, a little more savvy; when she was better able to appreciate the rare and wondrous gift she had.

Only it hadn't turned out that way. Once again, Kate found her mind being nudged involuntarily down memory lane to that late-summer evening nearly seven years back when Sylver had shown up at her Malibu doorstep in tears. It was during the middle of filming what turned out to be the young starlet's last movie for Paradine—or any major studio—*Glory Girl*. It was touted as Sylver Cassidy's first "adult" role and the film ended up being a slam dunk, Sylver's biggest grosser ever. And Paradine's.

Kate was flying high during the filming, just knowing it was going to be one of the studio's biggest hits. Her high spirits were unassailable even from complaints by *Glory Girl's* director, Nick Kramer, that Sylver had been acting up on the set. Sylver was a teenager. What did he expect? A little rebellion, she told him, was healthy. Sylver had been almost too compliant a child. Secretly, Kate liked seeing Sylver generate a few sparks. Maybe the kid would even get up the courage to sever those apron strings that Nancy had tied so tightly around her neck.

Nothing quite prepared Kate for the scene that July evening when she opened her door to see Sylver standing on her doorstep. The slender girl was wearing a pair of pegged black jeans and a bright blue chambray shirt that matched her incredible blue eyes, which were now filled with pain. She was struggling to fight back tears, her whole body trembling with the effort.

Kate stared at her in alarm. "Sylver, it's almost eleven-thirty. What's wrong? You look like you lost your best friend."

Sylver's lips quivered, and then she fell into Kate's astonished arms, the tears bursting like an eruption in a dam. Kate was dumbstruck and frightened. She'd never seen Sylver in such a state. "Okay, baby. Take it easy. We'll fix it, whatever it is."

Kate ushered her into the house, her first thought being that somebody close to Sylver must have died. Sylver's mother? Not that Kate would have shed many tears. But then she felt instantly guilty. However Kate felt about the woman, Nancy was still Sylver's mother. Hadn't Kate and her mother had enough of their own problems over the years? She'd still felt devastated when she died.

She gently smoothed Sylver's tangled hair from her face. "Talk to me, baby. You know you can tell me anything." Kate honestly meant that. There'd been many times when Sylver had confided in her. And Kate had always done her best to offer help and guidance.

Sylver tightly clasped her hand like it was a lifeline. "I can't...Kate. I just...can't...take it anymore," she gasped. "You've got to...help me, Kate. There's no one else...I can turn to. I tried to talk to my mother, but she...just got angry. Gave me her usual speech...about how I'm so unappreciative and selfish, and...spoiled."

Kate scowled. Just what the poor kid needed to hear. Kate made a mental note to have a few choice words with Nancy Cassidy the next day. How insensitive and out of touch could the woman be?

In the meantime Kate could see she was going to have her hands full with Sylver. She led her to a sofa, then poured them both some sherry. Sylver made a face as she took her first swallow. Probably her first taste of alcohol. Nancy Cassidy watched over Sylver like a hawk. No way was her starlet daughter going to go the way of so many others—drugs, booze and debauchery before they were even old enough to vote.

Kate sat down beside Sylver who immediately clutched her hand again, desperation etched on that perfect, China-doll face. Kate was sure she had no idea how utterly beautiful she was, even with her eyes red, her nose runny.

"What do they think I am, Kate? A robot without feelings? Being ordered around, pushed, prodded, manipulated. Laugh, Sylver. Cry, Sylver. Stick your tits out, Sylver. I don't even feel . . . human. I don't want to be an actress. You've got to get me out of this contract, Kate. I can't make this movie."

"You've just had a bad day, that's all. I'll talk to Nick, tell him he's got to put on his kid gloves. He won't hound you anymore, baby. You have my word. If he doesn't behave himself, I'll go down to the set myself and personally punch him in his nose." She kept her tone light and cajoling, but she could see it wasn't having its hoped-for effect. Sylver kept shaking her head, her long blond hair flying every which way.

"I've had nothing but bad days. Now . . . now they're getting worse. Don't you understand?"

"Of course, I understand," Kate said, but she was lying. She didn't really understand. Or maybe she simply didn't want to. Didn't want to see Sylver's despair, her vulnerability. Kate shut it out, just as she'd always shut out seeing those very same qualities in herself. Sylver had to be talked through this crisis. Kate saw no other choice. Sylver was Paradine's hottest property. The studio, and she herself—as the executive producer of Sylver's new movie—had too much riding on *Glory Girl*. Sylver Cassidy was *Glory Girl*. Without her there was no movie.

"How about this?" Kate said brightly. "As soon as the film wraps up, we'll go on a trip. Just the two of us. The Grand Canyon. You've always wanted to go there, right? We'll even rent donkeys and camp out."

Kate got no response. She stroked Sylver's cheek. "Hey, come on, kid. We're talking real sacrifice here. My idea of camping out is a suite at the Ritz. For you, though, I'll do it up right. Knapsacks, sleeping bags, tents, the whole nine yards. In two days, you won't even remember what you were so miserable about. That's a promise."

Sylver didn't respond. Kate chose to interpret her silence as compliance. She rose and went over to the phone. She did

what she thought was best for all of them—what she persuaded herself was best, anyway. She phoned Nick Kramer,
the director of *Glory Girl,* and made it crystal clear to him
that he was to treat Sylver like she was made of delicate
porcelain from now on. During the phone conversation,
Sylver sat on her couch, eerily subdued, sipping the sherry,
the tears drying on her face.

When Kate hung up, she took hold of Sylver's hands, as-
suring her that everything would be fine from that point on.
Only she couldn't quite look her in the eye. And they never
did make that trip to the Grand Canyon.

That year, the Academy Awards coincided with Sylver's
eighteenth birthday. Nancy threw her daughter a big bash
following the Oscars. Everyone who was anyone showed up
for the gathering, which turned out to be part celebration,
part commiseration. Sylver had been up for an Academy
Award for Best Actress for her role in *Glory Girl.* Nancy had
been absolutely convinced her daughter would walk off with
the award, even though Kate and most other insiders knew
Sylver was a long shot. When she didn't win, Sylver seemed
fine about it, but Nancy had been livid. No amount of telling Nancy that even getting nominated was a big deal, con-
soled her. Kate watched Sylver make every effort to keep her
spirits up that evening, but her mother's disappointment
was palpable. Kate was glad she had another engagement
and had to leave early. Before she left, she took Sylver aside
and told her she was very proud of her. Sylver had hugged
her tightly, thanking her. Some of the guilt Kate had been
feeling all those months for having talked Sylver into finishing the film, eased.

And then came the morning after—a morning Kate had
tried her best for years to push from her memory. The desperate call from Sylver, rushing to her side, the sight of her
in Nick Kramer's bedroom in the Hollywood Hills. It was
as if aliens had come in the night and stolen off with the real
Sylver Cassidy, leaving a lost, broken, damaged clone in her
place.

That was the beginning of Sylver Cassidy's inexorable
downward spiral. Or had it begun earlier? That very evening Sylver had shown up at her doorstep? In each in-

stance, Kate had been forced to choose between Sylver and Paradine Studios. Ultimately, Paradine won out both times. The question was, What did Kate lose in the process? She reminded herself that there was always a price. Paying hurt.

Kate's intercom buzzed, startling her from her disturbing stumble down memory lane. She immediately pulled herself together, but she couldn't quite shake the edginess, the sense of something unsuspected in the air. What was the matter with her today, anyway? It wasn't like her to drag out old, unpleasant laundry.

"It's Mr. Garrison on line 4."

Kate checked her watch. It was nearly five. He would just have finished screening *Rainbow Ridge*—was probably still in the screening room. She'd seen some of the rushes and guessed Douglas wasn't going to be too happy with what he saw. She'd tried to warn him the movie was a dud. Now he'd be in a total panic and she'd have to listen to him rant and rave for a good twenty minutes, after which she'd have to calm him down and get him to accept that they were going to have to scrap the theatrical release. It wouldn't be what the anxious head of Paradine would want to hear.

"Tell him I'm out, but that I'll be get back to him."

There was a brief hesitation before Eileen said, "Should I give him . . . a time?"

"No. That's all right. He'll understand."

"Okay, but I'll bet he won't be too happy."

Kate smiled. "Let him down gently."

"Don't I always," Eileen said.

Actually, Kate had planned to stick around the office for a while on the chance that call would come through from Adrian, but now she decided to "unwind" over at the Beverly Hot Springs. A shiatsu massage and a dip in the neighborhood spa's steamy hot-spring waters followed by a plunge in their icy pool was exactly what she needed to help her relax. As she stuck Lerner's script into her briefcase, and slid in her PowerBook 170—whose hard drive was loaded with the private fax numbers of Hollywood's movers and shakers and that went wherever she went—Kate decided she'd give her secretary a raise.

Five

Nancy Cassidy positioned herself at a corner table at the front of Harry's Bar and American Grill on the plaza level of the ABC TV Center. The European-style restaurant, with its rich oak wainscoting, studded with posters, paintings and tapestries from Italy, was an authentic namesake of the original Harry's in Venice, and one of Nancy's favorites. That wasn't, however, why she chose it for her luncheon with Sylver. Her selection had been carefully calculated to provide her daughter with some exposure, but not with anyone in the business who counted. After all, there was just so much that she could expect her daughter to get out of a onetime make-over and a month at a health club.

Sylver was already a half hour late. Nancy was scanning the menu, trying to keep her growing agitation under wraps. Sylver was always late—a star's prerogative.

Nancy's anxiety was getting the best of her. What if she didn't show up? All the effort and planning, the schmoozing, for nothing. Did Sylver think she actually liked pushing herself on people, suffering their annoyance, their irritation, their disinterest? She was still smarting after that brief encounter with that rude bitch Kate Paley at La Scala. Well, she'd show her. She'd show that snot-nosed Coffman, as well. She'd show them all. Sylver would be the reigning box-office queen again if it killed her. And everyone would know Sylver owed it all to her mother.

She smiled to herself, the fantasy of reclaimed fame and glory soothing her as always, putting her in good spirits. Sylver would show up. And she would look presentable enough at this point to bring her by Sid Gandel's office after lunch. To convince him that Sylver had gotten her act together this past year, Nancy had plied him with recent photos of her daughter. Photos carefully, and brilliantly, doctored by a photographer friend of hers. It was amazing what an airbrush could do. Sid, however, remained dubious and insisted on having a face-to-face meeting with Sylver before he'd even consider representing her again. Well, she'd show him, too.

When Sylver entered the restaurant, Nancy's mouth dropped open and her heart sank. If anything, her daughter looked worse than she had when she'd seen her a month ago. And that god-awful outfit—a frayed, grungy flannel shirt open to reveal an oversize yellowed T-shirt, worn, shoddy sandals, and a pair of jeans that were swimming on her.

Nancy pulled herself together quickly, rose from her chair, hurried across the restaurant and steered Sylver right back out the door. Raging at her under her breath, she hustled Sylver over to her pink Mercedes, unceremoniously shoving her into the passenger seat.

Once she settled in behind the wheel, Nancy glared at her daughter. "How could you do this to me? How could you, Sylver?"

Sylver gave her mother a benign, stuporous look. "What did I do now?"

"Look at you. You look like a reject from the Salvation Army. And you reek of rotgut."

"J&B is not rotgut. And I only had a little swallow. I was out of mouthwash." She omitted mentioning the line of coke she'd done to give her the courage to make it to the luncheon.

"You're disgusting."

"Why, Mother, I do believe that's the nicest thing you've ever said to me."

"You're a disgrace," Nancy muttered, tearing into the oncoming traffic.

"Now, now, Mom, don't keep trying to top yourself."

Nancy continued hurling abuses, but Sylver was feeling pleasantly numb and decided to simply enjoy the drive, mindless of where they were heading.

Nancy frowned, then immediately stopped. She needed more lines on her face like she needed a drug addict for a daughter. She tried a new approach.

"You know what you're doing, Sylver. You're wallowing in self-pity. And what you have to feel so miserable about is a mystery to me. It's just plain selfish. You're not a child anymore, Sylver. Responsibility comes with growing up."

Sylver started to nod off. Nancy took one hand off the wheel and shook her. "Don't pretend you're sleeping. I want you to listen to me, Sylver. Oh, I know what you think. You think I'm only trying to help you for my own gain. Well, you're wrong. You've always been wrong about me. And that's what hurts the most. No one wants to be misunderstood. Especially by their only child, their flesh and blood. We'll never recapture our lost years, Sylver." She dabbed at her eyes with the back of her hand.

Nancy's voice softened. "I love you, Sylver. Maybe I haven't always shown my love in the way you wanted, but I've done my best. I tried my best. I wanted the best for you. I still do. And this time around we're both older and wiser. This is our chance—our last chance—to do it right. One thing's for sure. I won't be naive enough to trust characters like those slick operators who managed your money before. Right into their own Swiss bank accounts. Everyone said they were the best. What did I know? I was too trusting. That was my crime, Sylver. And you seem bound and determined to keep making me pay the price. Everything I ever did for you, I did out of love. How can I make you believe that?"

Sylver stared up at the roof of the car, saying nothing. She'd heard it all before. Did her mother really think that saying it over and over again would make it true? Did Nancy really think she had any illusions left? About either of them?

An edge of frustration crept back into Nancy's voice. "I don't know how to get through to you. I never did. You've never been willing to meet me halfway. Is that so much to ask? Halfway, Sylver."

Sylver's head lolled to the side. As the pleasant numbness started to settle in and Nancy's voice receded into a murmur, she saw they were whizzing along the freeway past the tony restaurants and neon-lit beach-party shops of Malibu. Her old turf. The glitzy Day-Glo world of the privileged, get-back-to-nature, movie-crowd elite. For a moment, Sylver got lost in a time warp, remembering that first trip into Malibu—the drive to the small but chic beach house that Nancy had bought with the proceeds of her first hit, *Crying Will Get You Anywhere.*

Nancy had been aflutter with excitement. "Wait until you see it, Sylver. It's right on the beach. You can practically hop out of bed and land in the ocean. Of course, you must never go swimming unless someone's around."

All during the drive, Nancy had kept up a steady gush of patter about the place. When they finally arrived, Sylver was baffled. All she saw was a small house wedged between a row of other small, crowded-together houses on the side of a busy highway. *Two million for this?*

"Wait until you're inside. You won't even know that the traffic or any neighbors even exist. Not that I'm poohpoohing our neighbors. Jennifer Lynn, the actress, on our right. Todd Miller, the producer, and his . . . friend, on our left."

Inside, the Mediterranean peach-stuccoed beach house had been incredible. Low-slung and modern, one whole wall of the entire place was virtually an enormous window on the Pacific, which, true to Nancy's word, was practically outside their door. The decorating had clearly been done in deference to the sea. The floors, the walls, the furnishings—all the pieces beachy modern—were in shades of the seascape, from pale, milky blue to deep azure. Seaweed-like mats served as scatter rugs. Luxury and light oozed from every nook and cranny, but the house always felt more like a stage set to Sylver than a home. Everything was on display there. Including her . . .

Sylver was rudely awakened from her dream by a rough shake. She reluctantly opened her eyes, then quickly closed them again when she saw her mother's hostile face peering down at her.

"Get up, Sylver. Do you hear me?"

Sylver wished her mother would go away. At least long enough for her to take another toot. Coke was absolutely the only thing she knew that could get her through a session with her mother.

"All right," Nancy said, slamming the car door.

Sylver saw her chance come and go. Instead of walking off and leaving her in the car, Nancy stood right there in the driveway of her Malibu beach house and began shrilly shouting, "Pete! Pete, come out here!"

A couple of minutes later, a brawny, muscle-bound kid in black trunks who looked no older than twenty was dragging Sylver bodily out of the car.

"Don't be gentle with her," she heard her mother say angrily.

Pete, her mother's latest "houseboy," hoisted Sylver roughly over his big, broad shoulder, fireman fashion.

"I know, Mom. Don't tell me. You're doing this out of love, too," Sylver slurred sardonically. The little packet of coke she'd stowed in her shirt pocket fell to the ground. Nancy stooped to pick it up, gave a grunt of disgust and tossed it into the shrubbery. Sylver tried to mark the spot, but Pete, the pretend fireman, was moving too fast and she was being bounced around so much that she felt completely disoriented.

"Carry her into her old room," Nancy ordered as they stepped inside the house. "And get those disgusting rags off her."

"What should I do with them?"

"Burn them."

"I have to go to the bathroom," Sylver interjected.

Pete looked over at Nancy.

"Okay, put her down."

Sylver swayed a little until she got her bearings. She looked around the familiar beach house, which had virtually been untouched since she'd lived there with her mother until shortly after her eighteenth birthday. "Lunch at home. How cozy."

Nancy slapped her across the face, then shook her head sadly. "I won't let you smart-mouth me, Sylver. I'm still your mother. Maybe that doesn't mean anything to you, but it still means something to me. Now go to the bathroom."

Nancy turned to Pete. "Go find something in Sylver's closet for her to put on."

Pete hesitated.

"Do as Mommy dearest wants, Pete," Sylver said coyly, "or she'll start slapping you around, too. Or does she do that already? Maybe you like it."

Pete threw Sylver a look of revulsion and strode off. How to lose a potential fan in one fell swoop. Sylver started to call out an apology, but Nancy grabbed her by the shoulders, her long, expertly manicured nails digging painfully into her flesh.

"Now, let's get something straight here, Sylver. I've had it with your self-pity, your self-destructiveness. Do you have any idea what it took for me to talk Sid Gandel into giving you a second chance? I'm not going to let you throw everything away. This is your last hope, Sylver. You're twenty-six years old. If you don't make your comeback now, it'll be too late."

"I don't want to make a comeback."

"You're in no state to know what you want. So, I'm deciding for you. You're getting into shape whether you like it or not. I'm going to keep you here, under lock and key if necessary, until I decide you're presentable enough to appear in the outside world. No more drugs, no more booze. You'll eat what I tell you, sleep when I tell you, and watch your mouth from now on."

"Mother..."

"No arguments, Sylver. I know you think I'm the Wicked Witch of the West, but whether you believe me or not, I have your interests at heart as well as my own. We used to be a team."

"Like Sonny and Cher?"

"You're unstable, Sylver. If I decide you're too unstable to make the progress I expect, I'll have no other choice but to have you committed. And since money's tight these days, you can forget about some nice little stay in a swank Beverly Hills 'spa.' I'll have to put you in a state mental institution. It would hurt me more than I can say to do it, but I would. I mean it, Sylver. This is your last chance. What do you have to say now?''

"I'm going to throw up.''

A minute later, alone in her mother's plush bathroom, Sylver sat shaking on the cold Mexican-tile floor, feeling sick and trapped. She had no doubt her mother meant what she said. Sylver knew her mother felt cheated. All that work she'd put into grooming her daughter for fame and fortune, and Sylver had let her down. It didn't matter to her mother why. Nancy had never asked questions or offered up any understanding. She simply had to have things her way. Her way was the right way. The only way.

Sylver struggled to her feet, fighting the panic as much as the nausea churning in her stomach, trying to black out her fear, the indignity, the cruelty of her fate.

There was a sharp rap on the bathroom door. "Sylver."

"I'm... a mess, Mama. I'm going to... take a shower. Okay?'' Without waiting for a response she turned the shower on.

Nancy popped her head into the bathroom. She saw Sylver pulling off her flannel shirt. She'd already kicked off her sandals.

"Good idea,'' Nancy said, waiting until her daughter had stripped off her jeans, as well. Then she gathered up the discarded clothing as if they were covered in vermin and walked out.

Sylver quirked a defeated smile as her mother turned to give her one last look from the door. The door shut. Leaving the shower running, Sylver grabbed the terry robe hanging on the hook behind the bathroom door, slipped it on and threw open the window. She started to climb out, stopped, hurried over to her mother's medicine cabinet for a quick check. Her eyes brightened as she plucked a bottle of sleeping pills and a vial of Valium from the shelf.

She climbed out the window. Too bad she didn't have time to hunt for the coke her mother had so heartlessly tossed into the bushes.

Six

Kate had just stepped out of the pool at her Bel Air home when she heard a car pull into her cobbled driveway. She glanced over the fence, catching sight of Douglas Garrison's familiar yellow Lamborghini. She could tell by the way his tires squealed to a stop inches from her garage door that he was in one of his states. Nonetheless, she finished toweling off with unhurried care, then walked barefoot across the patio.

Stepping into her vaulted two-story living room, Kate smiled, thrilled by its recent redecoration—the earlier Art Deco style having grown stale, out-of-date.

The three months she'd put up with Jarrett Craft, interior designer to the Hollywood elite, had been well worth it. He'd transformed the place into a balmy island retreat, an exotic haven, inspired by Gauguin's languid Tahitian paintings. With no formal plan, the designer had mixed patterns and furnishings styles by instinct. Woven raffia covering the floor. A Bernini-designed sofa was dressed up with bright purple and gold cushions of Thai ikat silk. The pristine painting of a pool over the sofa was a David Hockney original. A few Hawaiian wicker tables, a pair of gilt antique chairs and a chinoiserie chest were all thrown into the mix. The overall effect of a tropical paradise was abetted by a vast bank of windows that looked out over fruit trees and newly planted island shrubs.

Kate was already pouring out a couple of martinis when she heard Lucia greeting Douglas Garrison at the door. Doug frequently teased her about having hired Lucia to be her maid, then ended up footing the bill for the Guatemalan refugee to go to college, thus having to hire a second woman to do most of the actual cleaning. He liked the story because it showed that Kate really wasn't as tough-as-nails as she presented herself to the world at large. He liked thinking that he had the "real" inside scoop on her—only she was always surprising him.

On this particular occasion, however, Doug looked more angry than surprised when he strode into the living room and set eyes on her.

She was standing over by the bamboo bar wearing a skimpy white bikini, still damp from her dip in the pool.

"What the hell's going on with you, Kate?" he said abruptly as she crossed over to him and handed him his drink. "*Rainbow Ridge* is a disaster. Where the hell was Hawthorne's head at? The whole damn thing's got to be re-cut. And even then . . ."

She smiled sympathetically as she shook her head. "You'll only be blowing more money on a lost cause. Go straight to video with it, Doug. At least you'll recoup some of your losses."

Lucia popped in, backpack slung over her shoulder. "I'm going now, Miss Paley. I have your dinners ready on the counter. Cold chicken and salad."

"Fine, Lucia. See you tomorrow."

"I will be here by eleven. I am having my chemistry final at nine."

"Right. Good luck."

"Good night, Mr. Garrison."

He gave a faint nod in Lucia's direction, then continued scowling at Kate. "What's with these cat-and-mouse games? Am I supposed to start sending you gold-plated invitations to screenings? You think, just because I didn't make *Premiere's* top twenty most powerful people in Hollywood list this year, I can be written off? Well, guess again, sweetheart."

"How many guesses do I get?"

He scowled at her.

"Come on, Doug. What's happened to your sense of humor?" She slipped her arms around his neck.

"Christ, you're soaking wet."

"Do you want to take a dip?" she asked, stepping back from him.

His eyes trailed her body in a long, lingering look. Anger, then laughter, now provocative interest. "New suit?"

"Like it?"

"I don't know yet. Let me see how it feels."

His fingers were running lightly over the tiny patches of cloth covering her breasts when she asked him about Ritchie. He dropped his hands to her ass. He wasn't pleased by her question, but he was clearly already too aroused to get angry again. "Who told you?"

"The question is, why didn't I hear it from you first?"

His hands began to knead her smooth, firm butt. Kate knew he was hoping to elicit compliance, just as she knew he wasn't really expecting it.

"Come on, Kate. Let's not mix business with pleasure."

She gave him a playful peck on the cheek. "Business *is* my pleasure, Doug. You know that."

"Don't play games with me, Kate." There was a hint of warning in his voice—also, an edge of concern.

She began unbuttoning his shirt. "Take a dip. You'll feel better."

He caught hold of her hand, pressing it to his groin. "That's not what will make me feel better."

"Later, Doug. I'm still wired from work."

She edged away from him and took a sip of her martini, observing the lines of frustration on Doug's face as he shrugged off his suit jacket, tossed it over a chair and sank into a slinky gold *pareo*-cloth-covered chair.

He let out a weary sigh. "I work my ass off and nothing ever seems to get done. Or when it does, it's crap. Okay, so I made a mistake with *Rainbow Ridge*. And with a couple of others this past year. On the other side of the coin, we've had twelve of the fifty top-grossing pictures in the last ten years, eight of them released while I've headed the studio. Three grossed more than a hundred million each. So this year the figures are dropping off a little—simply the nature of the game—and suddenly I'm cast as the bad guy."

Kate didn't remind Doug that she'd been directly responsible for all three of those blockbusters. She found herself feeling a wave of pity for the man who had once seemed almost like a god to her. He looked worn down. While he still worked out, she could see that he no longer put his heart into it. He wasn't winning the battle of the bulge any more than he was winning the battles raging at Paradine. Somewhere along the road, he'd grown too cautious, become too easily intimidated, lost his killer instinct.

Was it really only ten years ago that she'd seen Douglas Garrison as a supremely confident, creative, dynamic man? Not handsome even then, but devastatingly attractive. Maybe it was that aura of success he wore so well. Back then, he'd been a gutsy go-getter on the rise, second in command at Paradine.

She remembered the day they'd first met. There she was, a lowly reader at Paradine, fresh out of U.C.L.A., with a degree in film studies and fifty bucks in the bank....

"You the one that did this coverage?"

Kate looked up, stunned to see the eminent Douglas Garrison himself standing before her, script in hand. He tossed the script on her cluttered desk. Attached to the top was a typed half-page of coverage. Hers.

"Did you like it?"

She detected a faint smile before he answered. "The script, no. It was atrocious. The coverage, yes. It was..." He paused for a moment, like he was searching for the right word. Kate knew otherwise. He was evaluating her. From the way his smile grew more pronounced, she figured she was doing okay. He finally finished the sentence. "Smart."

"Thanks," she said, careful to keep her tone light. Her heart might have shifted into overdrive, but if she was going to score any points with a man of Garrison's stature—and she was going to try her damnedest to score as many points as possible—she decided to follow her instincts and act like she got compliments from big-time studio execs all the time.

His interest definitely seemed to heighten. He was studying her more closely. "You don't look surprised."

Score one point. Kate leaned back in her swivel chair and gave him an insouciant smile. Her dark eyes were deliberately blank. She knew better than to give the game away. Or her advantage. "Surprised that I'm smart? My mother always told me I was smart."

"You believe everything you're told." He was playing with her. Enjoying himself. Enjoying her. Score two points.

"When my mother said it, yes. She never lied." She crossed her bare legs, her short white linen Donna Karan skirt that she'd bought with a whole week's salary, creeping up her shapely thighs a few inches. She saw Garrison's eyes waver for a moment, but he managed to keep them on her face. Not a pushover. Score one for him. And another point for her, as well. She liked a man who wasn't obvious.

He perched himself on the corner of her cluttered desk. "You're new."

"Not too new to have greater aspirations."

When he laughed, she knew she was filling up her score sheet. She took time out to note that he had a very sexy laugh. He was altogether a very appealing man. He was also rumored to be very fickle. Kate knew she wasn't the first nice-looking reader he'd shown a brief interest in.

She saw him drop his gaze to her legs, but only briefly. A quick sample of the merchandise. "How about dinner tonight?" he asked, obviously liking what he saw.

Kate gave him what was to become one of her infamous no-nonsense looks. "I meant business aspirations, Mr. Garrison."

"Okay, we'll make it a business dinner, Miss Paley."

It would take her a while to persuade him she was serious, but she was confident that he would get the message. Not so confident that he would appreciate it. That was a risk she knew she had to take.

"And what will we discuss at this business dinner?" Her serious tone belied any suggestion of coyness.

She caught a whiff of very expensive musky cologne as he leaned closer to her. "You can set the agenda."

Within a few months of that fateful meeting, Douglas Garrison had become both her mentor—releasing her from underling hell—and her lover. In that order. Doug did get the message. In frustrating, but no uncertain terms. Kate was not going to sleep her way to the top. She didn't go to bed with Doug until he was already truly convinced of her value to Paradine. For a while their romance had been quite lovely. For a brief while, she even imagined she was hearing wedding bells....

She looked over at the studio chief, thinking now that, had they married, they probably wouldn't have lasted more than a year. She would have known him too well, and he would never have known her well enough.

Doug sighed. "I'm afraid I can't stay, Kate. Julia's having some damn dinner party tonight. I promised her I'd be home by eight. She sprang it on me as I was going out the door this morning."

"It's okay, Doug. I've eaten alone before."

"Once upon a time, you would have looked disappointed."

She gave him the look he wanted.

"And meant it," he muttered sullenly.

She could see where this was going. "Don't start, Doug."

He stretched his hands out toward her, his expression imploring. "You're driving me crazy, Kate. I need you. Now, more than ever. You know how much I rely on you. Without your support..."

Kate could hear the panic in his voice. It troubled her to see a man she'd once so admired, coming apart at the seams. Somehow, when it came to Doug, it wasn't so easy to be cynical about it all. They had been lovers off and on for nearly ten years. The romance had faded early on. Eventually so had the passion. At least for her. After her brief affair with Adrian Needham, it had never been the same for her with Doug. Once you had the real thing, you could accept no substitutes. Even when you could no longer accept the real thing, either.

What did that leave between her and Doug? Another kind of passion that they continued to share down through the years. A mutual and intense passion for the studio. It had never sat completely well with her that she was having an affair with a married man. On the other hand, Kate believed that Doug's wife was actually grateful to her for keeping her husband off the streets while she was otherwise engaged. Julia understood her husband's needs as well as she understood that she had her own "personal" needs.

Needs that got fulfilled on a regular basis with a medley of young, virile men—actors, writers, tennis pros, pool men. Julia was an equal-opportunity lover. There was no love lost between Julia and Doug. Which was probably why their marriage was so successful. Love merely mucked things up.

Kate felt that she and Doug had established an easy rhythm and a comfortable routine over the years. There were no surprises, no feelings of obligation. It never got too heavy. Lately though, Kate had been picking up a disturbing shift in the relationship. Doug was growing increasingly more demanding and needy. There was a panicky intensity about some of their recent sexual encounters that disturbed Kate more than she wanted to admit. She tried to give him a wide berth, however, knowing how much pressure he was under at Paradine.

On the edge of her thoughts about Doug and what he was going through at the studio, another more selfish thought lurked in the shadows. There was that terror, never far from the surface of Kate's mind: Could this be her in ten years? On the downslide? Getting pitying looks from new moguls on the horizon? Having to face the handwriting on the wall? The possibility was utterly horrifying, and she immediately countered it with—*never!*

She backed away from Doug, her expression inscrutable, composed, sipping her martini. That hadn't changed about her. She still never gave too much away.

Doug dropped his hands to his lap in defeat, leaning forward in his chair. "Okay, damn it, Kate, you're right about Ritchie. I guess I couldn't bring myself to tell you he was being ousted because you were the one who warned me in the first place...."

She came and knelt down in front of him. "I wouldn't have rubbed it in," she said playfully.

He broke into a smile, cupping her face and kissing her peach-tinted lips. "I do adore you, Kate. And it's not that I don't want to shift you up into Ritchie's slot, it's just..."

She pulled away, the playfulness gone. "Don't give me that crap about my needing more time, more seasoning, Doug. I'm ready. You know it and I know it."

"Look, we'll talk about it later, okay? Ritchie's body isn't even cold yet. I've got so many headaches right now...."

"Maybe I can help." She started to tell him about *Mortal Sin*, but he didn't want to talk business. He pulled her roughly into his arms, his mouth coming down hard over hers.

Sex was Doug's answer every time she pressed him. She knew the real story. He felt threatened. Not only was she outgrowing her mentor and lover, she was outshining him. Kate knew Doug was afraid he'd start feeling completely obsolete if he moved her up. She had to make him believe that she was the one who could help him recapture the glory that had been his. She had the vision, the fire and the guts to make Paradine sparkle again.

Doug was crushing her against him. She picked up the potent scent of his need, his fear, his confusion, his arousal. Once upon a time, she'd been, if not in love with Doug, certainly enamored of him. They had a history together. She still cared about him. And he was so desperate, she didn't have the heart to turn him down.

"Let's go to bed," she coaxed, more out of pity than desire.

They didn't make it to her bedroom. He was too eager, a little too desperate. Not much time for foreplay. He grabbed the scrap of cloth that comprised her bikini bottom and yanked. Then the bra. He flung the damp garments to the floor. Tomorrow she'd have to see if Lucia could mend the damage. Probably not. Too bad. She'd only worn the suit a couple of times. Still, she knew it gave Doug a lift to play he-man. And he needed a lift.

"God, you're so beautiful, Kate." He dropped to his knees, planting a random series of moist, insistent kisses down her well-toned body. His breath came in quick, shallow pants, his hands grabbing at her flesh, his fingers feeling fiercely for her. There was nothing artful or tender about his seduction. He was more like a clumsy, overzealous college linebacker scoring under the grandstand. Once upon a time it had been different.

He was still fully dressed when he took her crudely, roughly on the sofa, climaxing before Kate was even breathing hard. Afterward he fell back, panting, against the cushions.

"There's no one like you, Kate. There never will be. You're as irresistible to me now as you were when I first set eyes on you ten years ago. You look even better than you did back then. Success agrees with you, baby."

As Doug lay there, passive and blissfully happy, Kate experienced a letdown that had less to do with sexual frustration than with that feeling that had been nagging her for a while now: *Is this all there is?*

What more did she want? Or need? Power and success were right in her grasp. She could feel it, taste it. For so long, that had been the real turn-on for her. Far more than sex. Or at least, sex with Doug. It had been quite a while since that aspect of their relationship had given her much erotic satisfaction.

When Douglas was in a contented state of afterglow she snuggled up against him, lightly stroking his chest, putting aside girlish fantasies and getting down to business.

"I just read the script of a lifetime. *Mortal Sin* by Ted Lerner."

"Lerner? Mmm. He's done some good stuff...."

"None of it compares to this one." She let her palm rest on his chest over his heart. It was still beating overtime.

"None of his movies have ever grossed over forty mil."

"This one will go off the charts. That's why I want to budget it at forty mil."

Douglas shot her a look like she was crazy.

"Matthews at ICA can bring in major stars. I was thinking of Jack West and Laura Shelly for the leads. Between the two of them we're saying goodbye to nine mil."

"Forget it, Kate. We can't take the chance of—"

"Doug, this *is* our chance. Your chance. The chance of a lifetime. You never get anything in this world without taking some risks. You told me that yourself a long time ago."

"Yeah, well, there are risks and there are risks. Times have changed, babe."

She began to massage his temples. "I can do this, Doug. *Mortal Sin* will top two hundred mil. Your name will be golden. Trust me."

"I don't know, Kate. What's my father-in-law going to say?"

"When the profits start rolling in, he's going to say you're brilliant."

"I don't know, Kate," he repeated nervously.

She let her tongue slide lightly across his pursed lips. "I know, Doug."

"Money's so tight right now, Kate. A big budget like that... If we start playing for stakes we can't afford, we could go under."

"You've got it backward. If we don't play for big stakes, Doug, we won't survive."

They argued some more, but all she managed to get out of Doug was that he'd take it under advisement. *Under advisement.* He was undoubtedly going to run it by his latest guru-psychic. Doug was beginning to drive her crazy. If only she didn't have to rely on him for a green light. Even if she did step into Ritchie's shoes, Doug would maintain hold of the purse strings for any big-budget projects.

Kate debated whether to mention the Lerner project to Paradine's CEO at their private get-together on Thursday, on the chance that she could go over Doug's head and get a green light from the big man himself. She decided it would be wise to wait and see if she was being bumped up the ladder or being knocked off. Her gaze fell on Doug. Did he have any idea what his father-in-law had up his sleeve? Kate was pretty sure he didn't. Not that Doug had to worry much. As long as Windham remained at the helm, and as long as Douglas remained the dutiful son-in-law, his position as head of the studio was as secure as any job in Hollywood could be.

Her phone rang. Excellent timing. A perfect excuse to cut off the protracted goodbyes from Doug.

All he said was "Hi" and she recognized his voice, even though a lot of years had gone by since she'd last heard it. She had the oddest sensation, almost as if her stomach had slid out of her body. Her palms were clammy. She was glad when she heard the door shut behind Doug.

"Hello, Adrian." Her voice, unlike the filmmaker's inimitable cockney lilt, didn't sound quite like her own.

Seven

The trucker who picked Sylver up on the road a couple of houses down from her mother's place didn't even comment on her attire. In L.A. anything went. He tried propositioning her until she told him—"regretfully"—that she'd gotten a rotten case of the clap from her boyfriend.

The trucker dropped her off in front of her apartment complex, Fairwood Gardens. There were no woods—fair or otherwise—and no gardens. Just a couple of tired-looking palm trees that went nicely with the worn-out, peeling, putrid pink buildings. A poor excuse for a pool, emptied long before Sylver had moved in three years ago, filled the space in the center court.

As Sylver walked down the hall to her apartment, she considered stopping by to say hi to her new neighbor. Maybe he'd take some more pity on her and slap another twenty in her mitt. After all, she had been abducted by her ruthless mother, had all her clothes stolen, had to fend off a lecherous trucker's advances....

As she embellished her hard-luck story, she listened at Riley Quinn's door. She could hear the rhythmic clicking of typewriter keys. The "would-be writer" was writing. She sighed. *Some of us have courage, anyway.*

Unlocking her door, she prayed that she'd find Nash home. He never had come back last night. Not that he hadn't done that before. There were still lots of women eager to take him in. Fortunately, he usually tired of them within a day or two.

The apartment was empty. No sign that Nash had shown up and gone off again. The message light was flashing on her machine. Maybe he'd called and left a message. Better still, maybe Kate...

She would have clicked off the machine when she heard her mother's shrill voice, but she was struggling to get the cap off the Valium. All she wanted to do was take something to numb her up. So many feelings. It was just too hard.

"That was the last straw, Sylver. You've gone completely off the deep end. I've called Dr. Dumar and I'm having him draw up commitment papers. He agrees with me that you're a danger to yourself and others, grounds for involuntary commitment. Maybe a few months in a state psycho ward is what you need to bring you to your senses...."

The cap finally popped off, some of the pills scattering on the floor. Sylver stared at them.

Her eyes shifted from the pills to her phone. If she called Kate... But Kate wasn't there. Kate was in Phoenix. And Nash—he was probably drugged up, lying naked in some starlet wannabe's arms. Not even a red rose today from her one faithful fan...

Her gaze drifted back to the scattered pills, one hand gathering them up, her other hand digging into the pocket of the terry robe for the vial of sleeping pills. Mix and match. Telling herself she'd only take enough to forget about the sheer hell of life for a little while, she reached over to the bottle of J&B on her bedside table. Just enough left to wash the pills down. How lucky could a gal get?

In the minutes before the knockout punch registered, Sylver flipped on her radio and danced wildly around her cluttered bedroom to the raucous, funky music of the Grateful Dead....

He took a close look at her. He knew others were looking, too; even knew what was going through their jaded minds. Cops. They'd seen it all before. For most of them, being around death was more normal than being around life. Death was something they understood. They knew all the right procedures, all the right moves to make. It was routine. A snap.

Life was something else altogether. Life was compli-

cated, messy, no easy answers, one wrong move after
another, after another. Sometimes he wondered—hell,
he knew every cop in that room wondered—whether it
was worth it.

He kept looking at her, slowly twisting his neck back
and forth to work out the kinks that had settled in
without his knowing. Had she given up? Or just gotten careless? When it came down to it, was there really
any difference?

She looked so young. A kid. A lost, scared, lonely
kid. No sign of any troubles now, though. History.
Nothing left to be scared about, he supposed. Then
again, what did he know? Nothing at all about what
this was like for her. Only what it was like for him. Only
that it hurt, and he hated the hurt. Not the pain of it;
the piercing guilt that hung in its wake. He could have
done something. He could have stopped it.

He lit a cigarette, blew the smoke at the cracked ceiling. "Hey, would one of you bozos kill the music?"

A shrill rocker's voice kept screeching out unintelli-
gible lyrics over the speakers. His head was pounding
to the caustic, atonal beat. "Hey, turn it down. I can't
even hear myself think...."

Riley pounded down on his typewriter keys like a mad
musician—*dkrntelstjla'tkajtajgaep4ut/*. He couldn't hear
himself think, was right. Finally, after all these months, the
muse finally visits him and she's accompanied by some
screeching rock group going at full volume next door.

Shoving himself away from the table, he strode across the
living room and pounded on the paper-thin connecting wall
between his place and Sylver's.

"Hey, give me a break. Turn your stereo down."

He waited a minute. The music kept blasting. He pounded
again—hard enough to make a dent in the wall.

"Great," he muttered, trying to decide whether to call it
quits and go out for a bite to eat or go next door and have a
neighborly little word with Sylver. Or with that loser boyfriend of hers. He didn't much care for Sylver's taste in
music or lovers.

His features were etched with frustration as he stared across the room at the folding table that served as his makeshift desk—home to his typewriter, the one sheet sticking halfway out of the carriage, a nice pile of about fifty typewritten pages on one side, and that seemingly monumental stack of virgin white paper on the other side.

A little peace and quiet, that was all he wanted. That wasn't asking for too much. He'd been going great guns, writing clear through the night. He could easily go for another five, six hours, if only he didn't have that racket to contend with from next door.

He decided to deal with the racket, pushing up the sleeves of his blue knit jersey like he was readying for a fight. If the boyfriend came to Sylver's door and started to give him some lip, Riley had to admit he'd take some sincere pleasure in stuffing the guy's lip down his throat.

By the time he got to her door, Riley was itching for the boyfriend to open it. Maybe he wouldn't even wait for any lip. A creep like that, who would take advantage of someone as out of it as Sylver, deserved at least a solid uppercut to the jaw.

He scowled, looking down at his clenched fists. Slipping right back into his old patterns. Coming out of his corner of the ring swinging, explanations later. Or not at all. Who did he think he was, anyway? Some knight in shining armor? Hell, his armor was so beat-up and tarnished at this point, it was ready for the scrap heap.

He unclenched his hands, rapped hard on the door with his open palm. Maybe the boyfriend wasn't even in there.

No one responded to his knocks. Probably couldn't hear them over the blasting music. He banged louder, thinking about the twenty he'd reluctantly given Sylver the day before, knowing full well what she was going to do with it. Still, it wasn't enough to carry her through a two-day bender. Unless the boyfriend had come back with refills.

"Sylver? Sylver, are you in there?"

A woman's bloated face, her gray hair wrapped in curlers, popped out of a door across the hall. "You get that damn music turned off or I'm callin' the cops, buddy."

"Yeah, yeah," Riley muttered, jiggling the door handle, feeling a flash of surprise when it gave way. No one in L.A. who had any sense at all kept their door unlocked. Then again, if Sylver Cassidy had any sense at all, she wouldn't be in the mess she was in. Not that she probably didn't have a list of people a mile long she blamed for her current condition. Riley used to have a list, too. He reached a point where he was blaming everyone under the sun—everyone but the one person who was driving the nails in his coffin: himself.

He stepped inside to a carbon-copy layout of his own living room—or at least how his own living room would have looked if an earthquake had struck it. Sylver might have been a lot of things, but tidy wasn't one of them.

Riley took in the mess with one sweeping look. Dirty dishes, haphazard piles of laundry, and newspapers—mostly *Variety*—tossed everywhere—on the bare wood floor, across the threadbare brown-and-beige tweed couch, on the one derelict brown Naugahyde armchair, completely covering the pinewood cube that served as a coffee table. The windows were closed, the shades drawn, and the room was stifling hot. And smelled more like a drunk tank than he cared to remember. The whole slovenly scene brought back old, painful memories. He'd been here.

The music—now a blaring rap song with a Latin beat—was coming from behind the closed door of the bedroom. Riley hesitated, not relishing the possibility of finding a stuporous Sylver and her doped-up boyfriend entwined in each other's arms in bed, doing a horizontal cha-cha-cha to the rapper's chant.... *"Take it down the dark side. Hit your stride. Glide, baby, glide. You know what it takes. You know how to make it happen...."*

He got to the door, put his hand on the knob. A bead of sweat broke out across his brow. Something didn't feel right. A cop's sixth sense. Okay, an ex-cop's. Some things stayed with you, with or without the badge. He knocked cautiously on the bedroom door. "Sylver. Sylver, it's Riley. Riley Quinn, your next-door neighbor." He had to shout in the hope of being heard over the rapper mouthing off a mile a minute.

His hand slowly turned the knob. "Hey, I like music as much as the next guy, but..." He cracked the door open. "Listen, your front door was unlocked. I knocked first...." He went to open the door wider. It wouldn't budge. Something was blocking it.

Riley stood there for a moment, swaying slightly with the rapper's rhythm. Instinct garnered from close to a dozen years on the force told him it wasn't a piece of furniture that was keeping the door from opening.

He didn't shove hard, just enough to squeeze inside.

It was like she'd popped right out of the page stuck in his typewriter; like somehow he'd made it happen. The power of words. Was it Sylver who had been his fictional dead girl as well as his muse?

He blinked against the sight of her, feeling suddenly dizzy. There she was, curled up on the floor, still as death, her long blond hair falling every which way, one strand captured between her closed lips, her white terry robe open. She was naked underneath save for a pair of black bikini panties, her hipbones jutting out of her skin above the elastic band. As were her ribs. Skin and bones. He averted his eyes from her small but still shapely breasts, a grimace sweeping across his face. Years back, he'd seen her in a movie. Some gal he'd been fixed up with had dragged him to some dumb romantic comedy called *Glory Girl*. He wasn't much of a moviegoer, and he certainly wouldn't have picked some dumb love story to pay six bucks to go see. Yet that movie had stuck in his mind all these years. No, not the movie, really. The girl who starred in it. There was something about her—she lit up the screen, lit him up. She was so beautiful, radiated a heartrending innocence....

He shook his head quickly to erase the image of that girl-woman on the screen. His cop's instincts took over. This wasn't the movies. This was real life. He gave the room a fast scan. The boyfriend or an intruder could be lurking in the shadows, although there was no sign of a struggle having taken place. His hand went reflexively to his holster for his gun. Only there was no holster, no gun anymore. He wasn't here as a cop; just an irate next-door neighbor.

As he knelt down beside her, he saw the empty vials of pills on the floor. And an empty bottle of whiskey. So much for her having been attacked. An overdose, probably washed down with all the booze she'd bought, thanks to his generosity. Gripped by guilt, he cursed himself as he pressed his finger against the side of her milky-white throat, hoping against hope that he wasn't too late.

A pulse beat. Faint, but a pulse beat nonetheless. He couldn't believe it at first. Then he shifted into high gear, gathering her up in his arms. "Hold on, baby. You're gonna pull through whether you like it or not."

As if saying it out loud would make it true.

He forgot all about the blasting music—*"You can move me. Move, girl. Swirl those hips. Make it happen for me. Lose me in your eyes, in your sighs, in your bittersweet goodbyes...."*

Kate slowed down and pulled her BMW over to the right-hand lane to let an ambulance with sirens blaring pass by. A little red Mercedes coupe behind her beeped. She picked up speed again, merging back into the busy Wilshire Boulevard traffic.

A block later, distracted, thinking about every possible way this meeting with Adrian Needham could turn into a disaster, she almost went through a red light, slamming on her brakes at the last second. Her slowed reflexes got her a symphony of honks from cars whizzing across 3rd Street.

She dropped the visor, checking herself out in the mirror. A little more lipstick? Too much lipstick? Should she have gone with a redder tone? Was her nose shiny or was it the way the sun was hitting her face? She reached into her purse for her comb and ran it through her hair. She was wearing it loose to her shoulders, parted on the side. The way he used to like it...

She stalled out as the light turned green, suffering another medley of disgruntled honks. When she got the engine purring again, she cut back over to her right and pulled to a stop at the curb.

She dropped her hands from the steering wheel. Damn it, she was trembling. Like some dumb schoolgirl about to go out on her first date. This wasn't a date, she reminded herself sharply. This was strictly business.

So why the hell was she checking herself out in the mirror again? Dabbing more rouge on her cheeks? Checking to make sure she, too, hadn't changed much in nine years? Right!

Once again she went over last night's strained—at least on her part—phone conversation with Adrian Needham. If Adrian was also feeling uneasy, his voice hid it well. Maybe if she developed a cockney accent . . .

She was thrown off kilter right from the start, learning he wasn't in London after all, but right there in L.A.

"What are you doing here?" she'd blurted out, then flushed scarlet, grateful, at least, that he couldn't see her.

"At the moment, I'm returning your call, love."

His tone was light, teasing. She listened hard for an edge of hostility, anger, bitterness, but she couldn't detect anything negative in his tone. Still, she wasn't reassured. After all, they hadn't parted on exactly the best of terms, and this was the first time they'd spoken since their breakup eight years ago. She expected that convincing him to direct *Mortal Sin* would be a hard sell. Not that it was going to stop her from giving it her all. She remembered the director, Hal Jamison, once teasing her after she hounded him relentlessly for months until, exhausted from the pursuit, he finally agreed to helm *One Last Time*. He laughingly told her she must be dyslexic and stubbornly kept reading "no" as "on."

The line was silent on the other end. The ball was back in her court. Kate's palms were sweaty. For a woman rarely at a loss for words, she didn't know what to say to Adrian; how to get back on track—her track. Adrian wasn't one for small talk. That wasn't his style any more than it was hers. If she started raving about some of his last films, he would simply get bored. He already knew they were damn good. One thing Adrian didn't lack was self-confidence. His was the real McCoy. Unlike hers, although she put on a damn good show. With everyone but Adrian Needham. He had this way of getting under her skin, slipping right past her carefully guarded defenses. Just hearing from him again after all this time, triggered instant self-consciousness, not the least reason being that she was shaken by the physical reaction she had to his voice. Some things really didn't change—even after eight years.

She decided she'd better get right to the point before she started babbling and making even more of an idiot of herself.

"I have a project you may be interested in," she said briskly. Well, she didn't exactly have the project tied up yet, but she was damn well going to pull out every stop to get that green light, even if she had to go over Douglas's head. Nothing was going to keep her from making *Mortal Sin.* And nothing was going to deter her from getting Adrian Needham to direct it.

She held her breath, preparing herself for one of Adrian's typical diatribes on Hollywood films; preparing herself to counter each point. *This film was right up his alley. No one but he could ever do it justice. She was willing to give him as wide a berth as possible on budget and creative control. This wouldn't be a typical Hollywood deal....*

"Bring it on by," he said simply, pleasantly.

She was stunned by his casual, cooperative response. What? No tirade about Hollywood? Not even an inquiry about what this hot property might be? This definitely didn't sound like the Adrian Needham she had once known, loved, and been driven crazy by.

Kate felt a rush of panic. What if he was sick? He never had taken very good care of himself. He never ate right, never followed any exercise regime, and she had never known him to sleep more than four hours at a stretch. Had he finally worn himself down? Did he have a fatal disease? She really had to get a hold on her vivid imagination. Save it for the movies. Besides, Adrian certainly sounded robust enough.

When she finally found her voice, she mumbled guardedly, "Great."

"Say one o'clock, tomorrow? Do you still like smoked salmon with capers?"

Kate frowned. "Uh ... yes." She hesitated. Adrian?

"Yes, love?"

"Is something wrong? You aren't...sick or anything? You're not here in L.A. because of some...illness?"

He laughed—a throaty, sexy laugh. "I've never felt better. But your concern is very touching."

Kate's smile was thin as a razor. He was baiting her. A sign that he was as healthy as he proclaimed. Also a sign that there was some bitterness lurking. Okay, as long as she knew what she was dealing with. Adrian wanted to get in a few licks. Then, hopefully, he'd settle down. Hopefully she would, too.

"One o'clock. Where?" she asked in her all-business voice.

"Oh, didn't I tell you? I'm staying up in Topanga Canyon at Cassie Durham's place. You remember where it is, don't you?"

Kate went cold all over. She remembered where Cassie's place was, all right. She remembered Cassie, too. Cassie Durham had been an unknown eight years back when Adrian picked her for the female lead in *Deadline*. A pretty little redheaded vixen with a body straight off a *Sports Illustrated* swimsuit-issue cover, Cassie had worked on a daytime soap and done a series of forgettable bit parts in a string of B movies.

Kate had been less than impressed by the actress's credits and acting range. It was Adrian who convinced her that Cassie just needed the right vehicle to showcase her talent. Adrian had been right about Cassie, but Kate wasn't sure that it was strictly the actress's acting ability that had swayed Adrian. Before Kate got intimately involved with him, Cassie had been the one keeping the sheets on Adrian's bed warm. Adrian never had told her why he and Cassie had broken up, or who had been the one to call it quits. The whole time she and Adrian were together, Kate had never quite trusted that it really was over between him and Cassie. And now he was staying at her house....

It was ten minutes to one. She was going to be late. Why hadn't she at least suggested to Adrian that it might make more sense to meet at her office? Or on some neutral turf like a restaurant? The thought of possibly having to sit down to a lunch of smoked salmon and capers with Cassie Durham as well as Adrian, was already giving her a serious case of indigestion.

Another ambulance was whipping by as Kate started to pull back into the traffic. She almost got sideswiped. Maybe she should pretend she did. A good excuse to cancel. No. She couldn't back down before she even got going. Adrian's current living arrangements—temporary or permanent—had nothing to do with her. Nor did his love life. Her only interest was in getting him to direct *Mortal Sin.* Whatever "mortal sins" he cared to indulge in on his own time were of no concern to her. Or so she kept telling herself.

The ambulance jerked to a stop at the emergency entrance of L.A. General. Sylver, almost as white as the sheets covering her, was rushed inside the E.R. Riley broke into a run to keep up with the gurney. All around him was a sea of misery—kids bleeding from gunshot wounds, sobbing young women whose faces looked like they had collided with bowling balls, old people moaning in pain and fear, sick children clutching their mothers in terror, accident victims of every variety.

Sylver's gurney was one of many. The paramedics pushing her through the crowded space had to maneuver in and out of the traffic like motorcycle cops. An E.R. nurse, middle-aged, harried, took one look at Sylver and motioned the boys wheeling her in to get her behind one of the curtained-off areas. As Riley started to follow them, the nurse grabbed his arm.

"Who are you?" she demanded.

Riley thought fast. He knew the nurse wouldn't let him go in with Sylver unless he was a blood relative. "I'm . . . her brother. She was staying with me for a while. Look, if somebody doesn't get to her fast . . ."

A shadow of sympathy crossed the nurse's face. "I know." She turned and motioned to a resident working on a young boy on a gurney in the hall. The resident, small, thin, his glasses slipping down the bridge of his nose, didn't look much older than the boy.

Riley was in no position to be choosy. He knew that every minute counted. He followed the resident behind the curtain, watching silently as Sylver was given a quick, cursory check. The doctor might be young, but he'd been around long enough to know the score. Riley saw him turn to the nurse.

"We'll have to pump her out."

Riley caught the doc's look. It wasn't exactly full of promise. The nurse nodded. She knew the score, too. Win some. Lose some. Routine.

The resident was prepping Sylver. "What's her name?" he called out.

Riley hesitated. He knew if he told the doc that the woman he was about to treat for an OD was the onetime film star, Sylver Cassidy, the news would leak out and be all over the tabloids by the next morning. Sylver didn't need that kind of lousy publicity. Nobody did.

"Her name's Sylvie. Sylvie Quinn."

The doc motioned to the nurse, who shuffled over to assist him.

Riley wanted to shake them both. The pair of them looked so beat, half dead on their feet themselves. He was almost tempted to blurt out the truth. Maybe they'd work harder trying to save Sylver if they knew who she really was—or at least who she once had been. No. That wasn't fair. He knew they'd give it their best shot either way.

The nurse gave him a sympathetic glance. "You'll have to wait outside. It'll be a while." She couldn't quite meet his gaze. "You might want to call your folks."

Riley gave her a blank look. His folks? Then he remembered. He'd told her Sylver was his sister. He shrugged. "There's only the two of us." His eyes fell on Sylver, looking so small and frail on that gurney. *Just you and me, babe. Us against the world. Don't you go and leave me stranded here by my lonesome.*

The resident was inserting the tube down Sylver's throat as Riley slipped out from behind the curtain. He was shaken. Two years ago, the first thing he would have done if he was feeling this way would have been to head as fast as he could to the nearest bar. Now, he headed for the coffee machine down the hall. He didn't really want the coffee. It just gave him something to do.

Holding a cup of stale black java, he leaned against the wall across from the curtained space where Sylver lay fighting for her life. What scared him was that she might already have given up the fight. There hadn't been much fight left in her yesterday back at his apartment. A few sparks, though. And something else—a poignant clinging to some fragment of dignity. Like when she'd mistakenly thought he wanted to jump on her bones. Plenty of women in her straits would have tried to strike a bargain for a few bucks. Not Sylver.

It was crazy. He hardly knew her. Yet, she had touched him, inspired him, even. He'd walked into her path. *Stumbled* was more apt. Someone had been there to stretch out a hand to him. And now it was his turn. His gaze fell on the white curtain and he found himself doing something he hadn't done for more years than he could remember. He found himself praying. *Please, God, let her make it.*

Eight

As Kate's car snaked around a curved pebble-strewn driveway, Cassie Durham's sprawling mint green bunga-low, nestled in a woody canyon grove, sprang into view. Kate took in the house and the landscape with a critical eye. Cassie hadn't made a movie of any note in the past couple of years and whatever money she'd made, none of it looked like it had been spent on refurbishing. The stuccoed walls of the one-story bungalow were flaking badly, the tiled front patio was in need of a complete overhaul, and huge-leafed bird-of-paradise shrubs were running riot over the un-kempt grounds. Not, Kate knew, that Adrian would either notice or care about the woebegone condition of his host-ess's place. He was beyond such mundane concerns. How much notice, she mused, would he take of her?

She switched off the ignition, jangling the keys in the palm of her hand as she did a last quick check in her visor mirror, rubbing off some of her lipstick with her fingertip and massaging it into her cheeks for a bit more heightened color. She had struggled most of the morning with what to wear to this little get-together. In the past, Adrian had pre-ferred seeing her in worn jeans and plain, oversize man-tai-lored shirts. High-fashion designer duds left him cold. He liked her fresh and natural. Eight years ago, she could af-ford to go around ''unadorned.''

After trying on a dozen outfits, she'd finally settled on a pair of trim black jersey slacks and a V-neck slate gray cot-ton cardigan held closed with a bright off-center black silk bow. Underneath the cardigan she wore a white silk teddy with an edging of the lace that showed at the base of the V.

She slipped off her sunglasses as she stepped out of the car. Adrian had a thing about sunglasses. A Hollywood artifice, he claimed, to keep everyone from ever knowing anything about everyone else. "The eyes mirror the soul," he used to say to her all the time. Not always a comforting thought if you weren't all that keen on the condition of your soul.

A beat-up red Jeep was parked off to the side of the bungalow under a corrugated plastic-roofed carport. The hood of the Jeep was propped up and Kate caught a glimpse of a tanned, well-muscled masculine back bent over the engine. It was a back she'd know anywhere.

She stood by her car, embossed leather attaché case in hand, about twenty feet away from the Jeep wondering if Cassie was on the far side of the vehicle, out of her line of vision, serving as the "mechanic's" assistant.

What am I doing here? For a moment or two, the actual reason for this get-together fled Kate's mind.

"Don't just stand there. Start this bloody monster up for me" came a familiar roar from under the hood. The hairs on her neck prickled with nervous anticipation. She waited for Cassie to follow her master's command and scoot behind the wheel.

Only Cassie didn't appear. Kate frowned. Who the hell was he talking to?

Her? She realized, then, he had to have heard her pull up. Tentatively, she started toward the Jeep.

"Come on, love. Move your fanny. I'm wilting under here."

Kate arched a brow, a smile flirting on her lips. She hopped into the Jeep, but instead of switching on the ignition she gave the horn one loud blast.

Adrian Needham, his face smeared with black oil streaks, sprang up, cursing, hitting his head against the hood in the process. A grimace of pain was etched on his features, which were nonetheless as strikingly appealing as ever. As he stepped away from the Jeep, arms planted on his hips, Kate's eyes dropped of their own volition to his broad shoulders, down his dirt-streaked tanned chest to a still-flat, hard stomach. The snap of his jeans was undone, giving him the hard-edged sexy look of a male model in a Calvin Klein jeans ad.

Seeing him standing there, Kate felt like she'd gotten caught in a time warp. A feelings warp, too. Old emotions that she'd hoped no longer existed, or that were at least dead and buried, flared up like a sudden fever.

"Sorry," she said, sounding less flippant than she would have liked. "An accident."

Adrian glared at her. "An accident, my foot."

Kate grinned. "Do you still want me to start it up?"

He cocked his head in an old familiar gesture, the scowl still planted on his face. "And accidentally shift into gear and bloody well run me over? No thanks." He snatched a grease-stained white towel from the fender and began wiping his oil-caked hands. Without saying another word, he turned from her and headed toward the back of the bungalow.

Kate hopped down from the Jeep. Not an altogether-auspicious beginning to their reunion. Still, she felt a little better than she had a moment ago. If Adrian thought, even for a second, that she, of all people, had become a pushover during their eight-year hiatus, she was pretty sure she'd set him straight.

When she walked around to the rear of the house, she saw Adrian cutting across the water of Cassie Durham's heart-shaped pool. The pool area, like the rest of the property, was in need of repair.

Kate's gaze fell on the pair of smudged, threadbare jeans Adrian had been wearing. They now lay in a heap by the side of the pool. As she got a little closer to the water's edge, she saw that he was swimming stark naked. Irritation warred with almost-instant arousal. Casting a nervous glance around for Cassie, she was relieved not to find the hostess in sight. Adrian was making this awkward enough for her as it was.

Kate knew if she turned away or acted in any way flustered, he'd consider it a point in his favor. No one—not even Adrian—could score points off her that easily. Okay, so he was naked. And after eight years he still looked annoyingly terrific. And she was turned on. Hell, she was human. When she let her guard down. Which she wasn't about to do now. Win or lose this one, she had to set the tone right from the start or she'd lose her edge completely.

She stood by the side of the pool, both hands wrapped around the handles of her attaché case, unflinchingly watching him swim toward her. His form was as good as ever, damn him. She forced an air of bravado, convinced Adrian was deliberately trying to intimidate her in an attempt to cut her down to size. She decided he was really the one who was feeling intimidated. He might be an acclaimed independent filmmaker, but she quickly reminded herself, that she was the one with the power.

He swam right up to her, shaking his head rapidly back and forth so that water sprayed from his dark hair all over her.

"You look hot, Katie. Come on in."

Adrian was the only man who had ever called her "Katie." That, despite her often telling him it made her feel like he was talking to a child. He'd simply tell her that he wanted to bring out the child in her, arguing that she took life too seriously. The man was impossible. That hadn't changed about him, either.

"I'm quite comfortable. And I've got to be back at the studio in an hour." A lie. She'd freed up her schedule for the whole afternoon. Worse still, she sounded like a prig.

He smiled insolently. Like he didn't believe her. She remembered that smart-ass smile of his from way back. She could lie like a trooper with anyone but Adrian.

"Want to dig up a towel for me?"

She was glad for the assignment, as it gave her an excuse to turn away from him when he started to climb out of the pool. She spotted a blue-and-white striped beach towel draped over a shabby plastic chaise. She tossed it to him, deliberately squinting into the sun so that she didn't have to get too good a look at him. Ditching her sunglasses was coming in handy, after all.

He draped the towel sarong-style around his waist, taking his time, surveying her the whole while. Kate couldn't help wondering, *Does he like what he sees?* She ended up a little weak-kneed worrying about it, and sat down on one of the patio chairs near a table shaded by a striped Cinzano umbrella. She set the attaché case on the table, opened it efficiently and drew out the Lerner script, the whole time telling herself she didn't give a damn what he thought of her. Who was she kidding? The only person other than Adrian she couldn't lie to with impunity was herself.

"Here's the script I told you about. I was hoping you'd have time to look at it over the next couple of days." She spoke briskly, her eyes resting somewhere past Adrian's right shoulder. To make things worse, this ridiculous insanity she was putting herself through could all be for nothing. She knew it would have made more sense to have this get-together with Adrian following her meeting tomorrow with Windham, after which she felt strongly that her fate would be sealed. Either she'd be out and there'd be no point in even showing Adrian the script, or she'd be moved up and have enough added clout to battle Doug for the green light for the project. Only after that was accomplished, would it have made sense to try to rope Adrian in. So what was she doing here now? Why had she accepted his luncheon invitation so precipitously?

Kate forced the question from her mind because none of the answers she could come up with pleased her. Stick to the concrete. Adrian was the soul searcher. She was the pragmatic one. She had accepted his invitation, so now the challenge was to use the time to her best advantage.

So why was it she kept feeling like the advantage was all Adrian's? Hadn't she learned anything in eight years, after all? Wasn't "wiser" supposed to go automatically with older?

She clicked her briefcase shut and forced herself to give her ex-lover a cool, composed look. He was standing there smiling at her. A decidedly supercilious smile.

Her expression hardened. She was not about to let herself be the object of his derision. "What's so amusing?"

"Am I amused?" He observed her thoughtfully, his smile shadowed now by an expression that Kate couldn't quite define. All she knew was that it made her uneasy. Everything about this reunion was making her uneasy. She was beginning to think that maybe she should have gone with Dan Mills as director of *Mortal Sin,* after all.

Then she got angry with herself. *This is ridiculous. It takes two to play these little mental one-upmanship games. Cut straight to the chase. And then clear out before you lose any more ground and won't be able to recover your losses.*

"Look, Adrian. I have a terrific script here by Ted Lerner. It's going to blow you away. I want you to direct it. I know how you feel about working for a Hollywood studio, but I promise you I'll see to it that you have carte blanche. Or as close to it as we can humanly get. I'm talking a forty-million-dollar budget, here." Why complicate matters by mentioning that this wasn't a done deal yet?

Adrian ran his fingers through his wet hair, smoothing it back from his face, while Kate scrutinized him closely, looking for a clue to his reaction. He broke into a smile. Kate's heart started to beat faster.

"Are you hungry?"

She couldn't have heard right. "What?"

"I'm starved," he announced blithely as he turned and headed for the house through an open sliding-glass door, leaving Kate with the script dangling from her hand.

She sat there stewing for about five minutes, then crossed the patio and stepped through the slider into Cassie's living room, giving the small, compact space with its out-of-fashion Danish modern-style decor a desultory glance.

"I suppose I should have planned a barbecue," Adrian called from the kitchen. "It's the California thing, I know. But I brought over this incredible smoked salmon from Edinburgh. I was up there filming...." He appeared at the archway between the kitchen and the living room. Kate was relieved to see he'd thrown on a pair of faded military green walking shorts. No shirt, though, and still barefoot, his damp dark hair curling every which way. He looked like some incredibly vital Greek god, charged with energy and life. In contrast to all that brimming verve, Kate suddenly felt drained, exhausted, hollow inside. This wasn't at all how this meeting with Adrian was supposed to go.

"Come give me a hand with the salad, Katie." His tone had a new softness in it, but Kate didn't trust his shift, thinking he was being deprecatory—not to mention effectively deflecting any discussion of the Lerner script, which she was still holding in her hand. Would he even agree to read it?

"Where's Cassie?" she asked, not budging.

"In Italy somewhere. Filming some god-awful spaghetti Western, I believe. She left me the keys and her Jeep. Now all I have to do is get that blasted vehicle running again." His smile was incorrigible. "Maybe after lunch I'll have regained enough of my trust in you, Katie, to let you give me a hand with it."

Before she could toss back a snappy retort—something like "over my dead body"—he blithely turned and went back into the kitchen. "One thing I will say about California. The fruits and vegetables are truly delectable. Ripe, juicy, succulent...."

Kate moved to the archway of the compact white-and-peach European-style kitchen. Adrian was rinsing off a huge head of lettuce at the sink, which overlooked the pool. The counter was strewn with brilliant red tomatoes, oversize Spanish onions, a basket of strawberries, bananas and a platter of smoked salmon, all set off against the stark-white tiled surface. Adrian had clearly cared enough about this luncheon to do a considerable amount of shopping for it. He must have bought out the Farmers Market. Kate was immediately wary. What was in this for him? She refused to believe he was trying to impress her. Or woo her. Surely, he didn't still have a thing for her after eight years. No. He must want something from her. Maybe his views on Hollywood had changed. Maybe he was tired of running himself ragged trying to find independent financing for his films. Maybe he was ready for a switch from London fog to L.A. smog.

She eyed him suspiciously. "What are you doing here in L.A., Adrian?"

He reached over and tossed her a Spanish onion. "Here, slice this for me, love. Bloody things always make me weepy."

She caught the onion. Good reflexes. She laughed out of frustration. "I never was able to get a straight answer out of you."

He turned off the tap, shaking out the lettuce as he looked her way. "Not true, Katie. You simply didn't always like the straight answers you got."

She swallowed hard. *Damn the man.*

He gestured to the onion. "Here, toss it back. I don't suppose you want me to see you all teary-eyed, either."

Her lips compressed. She tossed her hair back. "Where's a knife?"

He picked up a small paring knife, holding it up in front of him.

A standoff.

He grinned. "How about we meet halfway?"

This was getting increasingly ludicrous. She strode purposefully across the room and snatched the knife from his hand.

She started cutting up the onion on the wooden board built into the tiled counter, vowing that if she shed so much as one tear she'd stab herself right in the chest.

They both worked in silence for a few moments, five feet apart, she dicing the onion, Adrian ripping up lettuce leaves and tossing them into a large wooden salad bowl.

"I'm here to receive an award."

His voice, barely more than a mumble, startled her. She was concentrating hard on blinking back threatening tears from the onion.

"An award?" She looked at him, amazed to see him actually blush. She forgot all about those tears she was fighting and they just started slipping unnoticed down her cheeks.

He grew intensely interested in his lettuce leaves, his brows knit together. "I donated some money from my last film for the Feast or Famine campaign and now they're making some bloody banquet honoring me. If I'd known what was in store for me, I'd have made the donation anonymously. I foolishly never thought..." He looked over at her and smiled.

"What?"

"I don't think I ever saw you cry before, Katie. Always the brave, stoic soldier. No matter how much you hurt, you never would let anyone get wind of it. Unless they were one of the lucky few to get close enough. For a time, anyway."

She looked away, snatching a piece of toweling from a roll on the counter. She folded it over and blew her nose with it. "It's the damn onion." The crazy thing was, though, she did feel like crying. And for the life of her she couldn't figure out why. Maybe it was the unexpected feeling of intimacy she was experiencing—she and Adrian working side by side in a kitchen fixing lunch together, just like old times. Or maybe it was hearing about the award he was to receive and remembering how deeply he had always cared about those less fortunate than him. Honorable, compassionate, tender, generous—Adrian was all of those things.

What good deeds had *she* done lately?

Sylver was being nudged. Someone was shaking her shoulder. She brushed off the hand, or tried, not quite hitting her mark. Her arm wouldn't cooperate.

"Leave me alone, Nash." She heard the words play in her head, but she wasn't sure her lips were moving.

"Miss Quinn? Sylvie? Can you hear me?"

Not Nash. A woman's voice. And she wasn't even talking to her. Who the hell was Miss Quinn? And why were they bothering her?

"Can I try to talk with my sister for a minute?"

Another voice. Male. Not familiar. *Go away. Talk to your sister someplace else. Can't you see I'm trying to sleep?*

Her head was throbbing. And her throat. It felt like sandpaper. Every swallow was agony. Come to think of it, her whole body felt like it had come apart at the seams. And she was burning up. Had she finally landed herself in hell?

A cool hand lightly stroked her fiery forehead. "It's okay, baby. I know you feel like you've been run over by a bulldozer, but you're going to pull through."

The man's words weren't fully penetrating, but she liked his soothing, gentle touch.

Slowly, she opened her eyes. An attractive man's face, etched with concern and tenderness, was looking down at her. She didn't recognize him, but tears immediately sprang to her eyes. It had been so long since anyone had looked at her in that way.

"What...happened?" she croaked.

"You swallowed a few too many pills. Not a good mix, especially when you wash them down with J&B."

She was having a lot of trouble focusing and she felt like she might wretch. "Where...am...I?"

"L.A. General." He took hold of her hand. That felt nice, too.

"Did you...bring me...here?"

He smiled. "Yeah. Like I told the nurse, you were staying with me and...well, what's a big brother for if not to look after his kid sister?"

She gave him a dazed look. Something was definitely cockeyed. This guy thought she was his sister? A clear case of mistaken identity. No wonder he was being so nice to her. "I think...you saved...the wrong gal."

Riley smoothed back her damp, tangled hair. "No way. Just sleep now."

Her vision was beginning to clear. The man talking to her looked vaguely familiar, but she couldn't quite place him. "You aren't the guy...who sends me red roses...are you?" Her eyes started to close. Everything was getting muted again. And now she was feeling cold. So cold. Her teeth were chattering. She felt the covers being drawn up to her chin, and then that soft, soothing voice again.

"Shh. Sleep, Syl."

She felt his hand start to move off hers, but she found the strength to grab hold of it. "Don't...go." She was scared. She wasn't sure what was happening to her. Her mind was spinning with terrifying thoughts. Only this guy's tender voice and gentle ministrations kept the terror at bay.

"I won't go. I'll stay right here."

Tears slipped past her closed eyelids. Memory was slowly beginning to filter back. Her mother's attempt to kidnap her, the message on her answering machine, all those pills. "I didn't mean it," she whispered in a lost voice.

Riley wrung out a washcloth in a basin of cool water and placed it on her damp forehead. "I know, baby."

She slept for nearly four hours, during which time Riley didn't budge from her side, except to make one brief call. Shortly before Sylver woke up, a second visitor arrived.

Sam Hibbs, ex-Green Beret and ex-heroin addict turned drug counselor, wore a smile of relief on his blunt-featured face as his eyes fell on Riley. "Had me a little worried when I got the message you'd called, man. Well, I'm glad anyway you're not the one in the bed." He eyed Sylver co-cooned under a pile of blankets. "Got me a new candidate?"

"I hope so," Riley said, doubting it would be easy talking Sylver into voluntarily signing herself in for residential treatment, but knowing it was her only chance.

Riley vividly remembered how he'd fought against admitting himself to Sam Hibbs's drug program two years ago. His partner on the L.A.P.D. back then, Al Borgini, now Beverly Hills homicide chief, did everything he could to talk him into getting treatment, but Riley was damned if he was going to admit he needed outside help to handle his problem. Hell, he wasn't even ready to admit he had a problem. Besides, he was tough. He didn't need anyone. Or so he kept telling himself.

Al wouldn't give up on him, though, even after he'd been summarily kicked off the force following a disastrous off-duty encounter with a drug dealer that had left him with a bullet in his thigh, and had nearly cost the lives of three innocent people caught in the cross fire. After Riley turned in his badge, he sank even deeper into a hazy blur of booze and pills, his only goal in life to forget—forget all the pain, the agony, the guilt, the fear. Most of all he wanted to forget Lilli. Lilli. The only decent thing to come out of a lousy ten-month marriage. The only decent thing in his whole life. Lilli had been the light of his life. A light brutally snuffed out by a vengeful low-life drug dealer he'd once put behind bars. It was as if he'd killed her himself. Getting drunk was his only escape. He kept at it for years.

It never did work. He couldn't escape his conscience any more than he could escape Al. Every time his ex-partner showed up at his door to check on him, he'd tell Riley about this terrific guy, Sam Hibbs, a pal of his from Vietnam, who ran a top-notch private drug-treatment center out in West-wood. Riley kept saying, "No way."

Having no luck getting him down to the treatment center to meet with Sam, Al finally arranged a meeting for the three of them at a Westwood coffee shop, a few blocks from the center. Sam and Al both worked on him—a familiar good-cop/bad-cop routine that rang all too obvious. Riley knew exactly what game they were playing, but he got won over anyway, mainly because Sam Hibbs had his number down pat.

As slick and crafty as he liked to think he was, Riley discovered in short order that there was no hiding from the drug counselor. Sam Hibbs saw right through him, because he'd been there himself. He'd made all the same excuses, told all the same lies, built up all the same walls of defense.

Five cups of coffee later, Riley found himself signing the admission papers Hibbs had brought along—even feeling relieved to give in. Not that there weren't plenty of times, those first few weeks especially, that Riley hadn't cursed both Al and Sam out for getting him into what he saw as his descent into hell. Like Sam said, though, he wasn't climbing downward, he was climbing upward. "Direction, man. Direction is everything. Pretty soon you're gonna see the light." It took a while, but Sam had been right. Now, Riley hoped Sam would be able to help Sylver see the light, too.

Sam came closer to the bed and peered down at Sylver. "She don't look so good. She gonna make it?" Sam never had been one for pulling punches.

"Yes," Riley said, the answer coming way too quickly and way too emphatically. Like the doc had told him earlier, Sylver was far from out of the woods. And even if she did pull through this time, there was no guarantee that she'd be so lucky next time around. All the more reason to get her into treatment now.

Sam put a hand on his shoulder. "Girlfriend?"

Riley flushed. "No. I . . . hardly know her." What he was feeling wasn't easy to explain, even to himself. "Then again, I guess you could say I know her like the back of my hand. Kindred spirits, I guess." That was part of it, anyway.

Sam nodded like he knew it was only a part of it, too.

Sylver moaned weakly, drawing both men's attention. Riley wrung out the washcloth and placed it on her forehead again.

"Did she try to off herself?" Sam asked bluntly.

"I don't think so. Not . . . consciously." He looked up at Sam. "But we both know, don't we, that when we go messing with drugs and booze, we're buying a ticket on a suicidal carpet ride."

Sam grinned. "You learned the program well, Riley."

"You were a good teacher."

The drug counselor's gaze shifted again to the semicomatose patient in the hospital bed. He studied her thoughtfully. "Damn, if she doesn't look a little like—"

"She is," Riley said quietly.

Sam's eyes widened. "Sylver Cassidy? You're kidding." Sam wasn't much of a moviegoer himself, but he'd seen a couple of Sylver's movies years back. The kid had a quality about her that made her hard to forget. The camera loved her. So did millions of adoring fans. He'd been taken by her himself. Hadn't seen her for years. Understood why, now. From the look of her, she'd been on the skids for a while. Even so, she still had something. If you had a keen eye. Which he did. And which his pal Riley obviously did, too.

Sam watched Riley take hold of Sylver's limp hand. "How the hell did you two . . ."

"We're neighbors. Look Sam, to keep the media off her back, I told them here that her name's Sylvie . . . Quinn. . . ."

Sam's bushy brow arched. "Your wife?"

"My sister."

Sam smiled crookedly. "Didn't think you'd take the plunge again."

The whole time he is sitting there in the emergency room, he can't get the image of that ambulance pulling up at the Fairwood Gardens out of his mind. The moment it draws up to the curb, he knows they've come for his baby. He knows in his gut something terrible has happened to her. He'd been standing on the street corner for hours, hoping that she'd come out. And then she does. On a stretcher.

He goes cold all over when he sees them putting her into the back of the ambulance. Jesus, they shove her in there like they're handling a slab of meat or something. Slobs. Cretins. And who the hell is that character who's come out with her, jumping into the ambulance with her for the ride to the hospital?

He jumps into his car, cursing its lousy acceleration, risking going through a red light not to lose sight of the ambulance.

Is it already too late? Is she dead? No. No. She can't be dead. His own heart would have stopped beating if hers had. He truly believes that.

As he races to the hospital, staring straight ahead through his windshield at the back of the ambulance with its sirens blaring, his mind keeps shifting back and forth between panic about Sylver's condition and consternation over the man riding with her. Who is he? He's never seen him before. Is he Sylver's boyfriend? Is this all his fault? He doesn't even know for sure what's wrong with her. All he knows is that if Sylver doesn't survive, he'll kill the bastard. He will. He swears it. And then he'll kill himself. Life without Sylver wouldn't be worth a plug nickel.

Nobody comes up to him or asks him any questions when he races into the crowded emergency room. He melts right into the swarm of sick and wounded. A chorus of screams, wails and curses punctuates the fetid air. The smell reminds him a little of that porno movie house and he feels sick to his stomach. It doesn't help his condition any when a kid a few feet away from him starts puking.

He tunes them all out. They don't exist; their pain and suffering is of no concern whatever to him. There is only Sylver. Only her pain, her suffering matter. If only he knew what was wrong with her, or how bad off she was. The not knowing is driving him crazy.

He longs to go to her, just to see her up close. He wouldn't even touch her. Just so she would know he was there for her. And she would know.

He thinks of all the bad things he's done in his life. All his life, he was always making the wrong moves, the wrong decisions. His mother was always angry at him, accusing him of being lazy and selfish. For so long he hated everyone, himself included; himself most of all. When Sylver entered his life, that all changed. She was the magic he'd been searching for. At last, someone to cherish and love. A perfect little girl. Saving her made him feel whole for the first time. Now he might lose her. Is he being punished for all his old sins? Or is it for that heinous unbidden lust that consumed him that night in the porno house? *Never again,* he vows. His love for her will be pure...pure...pure...

He sees the boyfriend step out from the curtained-off alcove where they've put Sylver. At least they had the decency to separate his princess from the riffraff.

He watches the boyfriend leaning up against the wall, drinking coffee. His baby could be lying there dying and the bastard's taking a coffee break.

The hair on his arms bristles and he breaks out in a cold sweat. He wants to slam that cup of coffee down the bastard's throat.

The doctor and nurse are still in there with her. What the hell is taking them so long? What are they doing to her? *You pull her through, Doc. Or you'll be sorry.*

His fists press into his eyes as the enormity of it all detonates inside him. *Don't leave me, Sylver. You're all I've got. You don't know it, princess, but you fill my whole world with sunshine. Everything will turn black without you. Don't be afraid to live, princess. I won't let anything like this ever happen to you again. I won't let any of them ever hurt you again.*

He stops his silent incantations as the doctor steps out from behind the curtains and goes over to the boyfriend. "Mr. Quinn, you can go in and see your sister now."

Quinn? Sister? Wait. What the hell's the doc talking about? Sylver doesn't have no brother. What con is this bastard trying to pull off?

He sees the nurse follow the doctor out. He watches her walk over to the desk, scribble something on a sheet of paper. He rises from one of the putrid green plastic chairs; an elderly woman clutching her gut claims it instantly.

Sweating profusely now, he walks over to the nurse. She's still writing.

"Excuse me."

She doesn't look up. She doesn't even stop scribbling. "We'll get to you as soon as we can," she mutters.

He clears his throat. He has a thing about talking to strangers. He isn't much of a talker under any circumstances. He learned long ago that people never really heard him, never really listened, never gave a damn what he had to say.

"Just hold on to your number and wait your turn," the nurse says irritably when he doesn't obediently shuffle off.

He regards her with pure hatred. The thought that this fat, nasty slob of a nurse is even in the same universe with his beautiful princess, much less has touched her, makes him want to curl his fingers around her big, flabby neck and squeeze the life out of her. She reminds him of the nurse over at County who took care of his mother years back— letting her rot in a crummy bed in a crowded ward, her sheets soaked with her own urine, writhing in pain, begging for something to put her out of her misery. Not that the nurse gave a damn. None of them did. His hand jerks into his trousers pocket. As his fingers touch the cool metal of his .22 he calms down a little. And stands his ground.

"No, it's not me. It's the girl...."

"Yes, yes. We're working as fast as we can...."

"No. I mean ... how is she? The blond girl ... Sylver..."

"The OD case? Don't know yet. Talk to the doctor." The nurse scoops up another chart and calls out a name.

He sways as she takes off, having to grab onto the desk for support. He fights for breath. An overdose? His baby? His princess? And that scumbag who brought her in, who is in there with her this very minute, holding her precious hand, is probably the low-life pusher who sold her the dope.

Quinn. Quinn. He repeats the name over and over so that it's indelibly imprinted in his mind.

She dies, Quinn, and you'll get yours. I promise you that.

Nine

Kate was getting ready to go out. She was due at nine o'clock at the opening of her old friend Marianne Spars's new restaurant venture, Stars and Spars, over on Bedford Drive in Beverly Hills. If this place was even half as successful as Marianne's other two restaurants in town, her pal would have another surefire winner on her hands.

Kate took great pleasure in her friend's success. Although she was close to few women, she'd hit it off with ebullient, straight-talking Marianne right from the start five years before. She'd known *all* about Marianne and Lou Spars, the multimillionaire film investor and art collector, even before she'd had the chance to meet them. For twenty-three years, the couple had been the president and first lady of Hollywood high society. Kate had gone to many functions at Moonrakers, their splendid estate in the Hollywood Hills. There was probably more important art at Moonrakers than at many museums. Then Lou dumped Marianne for the sexy French screen siren, Yvette Girard. Which stunned just about everyone in their crowd—none more so than Lou's unsuspecting wife, who just happened to have adored her sleek, charismatic cad of a husband. Marianne started to come apart at the seams. It didn't help matters any that the breakup resulted in the most intimate details of their lives becoming juicy fodder for the trades and tabloids. Lou's scandalous liaisons throughout their marriage, Yvette Girard's kinky proclivities, even Marianne's two miscarriages and the sordid details of an alleged brief affair with a Latin American polo player, courtesy of the polo player's former mistress—all their dirty laundry, much of it embellished or utterly fabricated, was dished out for public consumption. Desperate not to be treated as a pitiful object of ridicule, Marianne became increasingly reclusive. Kate and a few other good friends saw that she was close to mental collapse and managed to quietly get her into a private psychiatric clinic in Arizona. Now, almost two years later, Marianne had not only pulled herself together but had managed in very short order to become a celebrated restaurateur and an esteemed member of the Hollywood inner circle in her own right.

Until today, Kate had been looking forward to attending the opening of Stars and Spars. She hadn't seen Marianne in months; both of their schedules were always so insane that neither of them was ever free at the same time. Now, she was procrastinating about getting dressed to go out.

She sat on the edge of her bed, in her lacy black bra and matching panties, an elegant violet silk sheath strewn across her brightly patterned Tahitian quilt cover. She wasn't at all in the mood for a noisy gathering packed with all the beautiful and important people gossiping, laughing, talking business, dissing everyone who wasn't there. The only reason Kate was going at all at this point was to see Marianne, although she doubted she'd get more than a few words in edgewise with her eminent friend. Still, she knew Marianne would be disappointed if she was a no-show.

She reached for her dress, managing only to place it on her lap. She felt drained of energy, uncharacteristically lethargic. What was the matter with her? As if she didn't know. Seeing Adrian that afternoon had knocked her for a loop. She didn't even know if she'd gotten anywhere with him as far as the Lerner project was concerned. Naturally, she'd done her best to talk it up, but she hadn't been able to get any response at all from Adrian on whether he would consider directing *Mortal Sin*. He wouldn't even commit to reading the script. But then again, he hadn't said he wouldn't, either. By the time they'd sat down to lunch, Kate realized her sales pitch was starting to have a ring of desperation about it, and immediately gave it up. As for Adrian, he grew quieter and more aloof—or was it merely disinterested?—as the meal wore on. Kate hadn't stuck around for dessert. After the main course, she'd charged out of there like she had a fire to put out. In a way, she did. She was burning up inside with more emotions than she cared to examine. She did leave the script behind, though. Ever the optimist.

She reached for her glass of Chardonnay, which she'd poured earlier for herself and then forgotten about. She was so wired up. And for the first time in ages, she felt something she'd thought she'd all but extinguished—sexual frustration. She was disgusted with herself. Adrian dives into a pool naked and she's reduced to a quivering mass of raging feminine hormones. How could she even think about sex when she was so angry with him for the way he'd behaved toward her that afternoon. He'd been deliberately provocative, evasive, and downright rude. Besides, she had other worries. Until she had her chat with Windham tomorrow she felt like her whole future at Paradine was in question.

She tried to make sense of the emotions Adrian had triggered, but for once in her life, her analytical mind refused to click into standard operating procedure. She was just too damn horny. And what made it worse was that she was sure Adrian had picked up that haunting scent of desire—a scent she hadn't worn in a long, long time.

Wanting Adrian was crazy; getting emotionally involved with him was even crazier. She'd been that route before, the result having been a messy head-on collision with him in the end. Kate still bore scars from the impact, even though she hated to admit it. Did Adrian still bear scars, as well?

He'd been so angry at her when they broke up. So bitter. He'd wanted her to marry him. Only there'd been conditions. Like leaving Paradine; leaving Hollywood altogether. He wanted them to go to London, start up their own independent production company; make movies that had heart and soul rather than "special effects."

He'd been asking her to give up everything at a time when the doors were starting to open wide for her. Her success producing Sylver's early blockbuster films finally gave Kate her first real taste of serious clout. And it tasted good. Like an elixir of the gods.

She made one vow. If Adrian did agree to direct the Lerner script, she was going to keep their relationship strictly business.

Her phone rang. She thought about not answering it, but then she thought, What if it was Adrian? What if he was calling to give her his answer about the script? Okay, there was more to her expectations than just that.

"Are you okay, Kate? You weren't in all day. I was worried."

Kate was sorry now she hadn't let the call go. "I'm fine, Doug."

There was a long pause, like Doug was waiting for further explanation. She wasn't about to tell him the truth about her day, and she didn't have the energy to make up a lie.

"You're still mad about the other evening, aren't you? Don't dig your heels in on this one, Kate. Look, if you want to consider, say, twenty mil for the Lerner project, I'll give it a read."

"With that kind of budget there'd be no point in making the movie, Doug."

"Okay, okay, let's not get going on it, again. The real reason I called was to see if you wanted to fly up to Lake Tahoe with me this weekend. I need to get away, and there's no one I'd rather get away with than you, Kate. What do you say?"

"No, Doug. I can't."

There was another pause. "Can't or won't?"

Kate recognized the note of challenge in Doug's voice. That note had been in his voice a lot lately. The tougher things got for him at the studio, the more possessive he became toward her, the more demanding the needs he wanted—no, expected—her to fulfill for him. She wasn't happy about it, to say the least. Doug was changing the terms of their relationship, trying to direct it in a way that Kate most definitely did not want it to go.

At that moment she knew with absolute certainty that it was finally time to end her affair with Doug. Her decision had been building for a while. It was a culmination of events—the thoughtless, selfish, pitiful way he'd taken her the other night, and so many nights before that. Sex without intimacy; without tenderness; without passion. Doug didn't love her any more than she loved him. She doubted he was capable of truly loving anyone. He lusted after her; he wanted to possess her; he wanted the security of knowing she was there to satisfy his needs. He used her. And being honest with herself, she knew that she'd used him, too—to feel some sense of connectedness; to relieve the tension, the loneliness. Only it wasn't even doing that for her anymore. And she wasn't sure that whatever it was she was doing for Doug was all that good for him.

Of course, she knew that Adrian had something to do with this decision to end it with Doug. Seeing Adrian again that afternoon had made her remember what sex could be like—had been like. With Adrian, it had been the real thing. Better never to have sex again, she decided, than to have it for all the wrong reasons with all the wrong men. Surely, this sexual frustration she was feeling was strictly temporary.

"I can't go to Lake Tahoe with you. I'm busy this weekend, Doug." She couldn't callously end her relationship with him on the telephone. She'd let him down gently, face-to-face, after she knew where she stood at Paradine.

Doug's voice took on a whiny tone. "Kate, don't be mad at me. You know it drives me crazy when you—"

"I'm not mad. Go to Lake Tahoe, Doug. It'll do you good to get away for a few days. You looked so beat the other night."

"It isn't easy, Kate. The business with Ritchie..." There was a pregnant pause. "It could get ugly."

Kate sat up a little straighter. "What do you mean?"

"I got a letter this morning from some two-bit lawyer. Some hot little number who was an assistant producer on Ritchie's movie is pressing charges against him for sexual harassment. Her legal eagle's calling it classic, quid pro quo casting-couch shenanigans. They're going for big bucks, claiming that Ritchie's putting the moves on her caused her 'serious emotional disturbance.' That's a quote."

She took a swallow of her wine, not for the taste but because her throat had suddenly gone dry. "Does your father-in-law know?"

Doug gave a sharp laugh. "Charlie? Oh, he knows, all right. He got a copy of the same letter. He wants me to see to it that every top exec at Paradine gets scheduled in for a refresher course on the studio's policies against sexual harassment."

Kate was only half listening, trying, as Doug talked, to figure out the ramifications for her of this news flash. One thing was for certain: Windham would have to find a fall guy—someone at the studio would have to be called on the carpet for bringing a lech like Ritchie aboard. If Doug were anyone but Charlie's son-in-law, he'd be made the scapegoat and fired, his career very likely flushed down the toilet. Under the circumstances, however, some other company guy would have to take the fall for Ritchie. Or some other gal. . . .

"Kate, are you listening to me?"

She felt her stomach clench. "Yes, Doug. I'm hanging on every word." Hanging by a thread was more like it. Had Windham known about those charges against Ritchie when he had his secretary arrange his meeting with her for tomorrow? Was he coming out here to let her know that she was going to have to take the fall for the Ritchie fiasco? Well, the old man had another thing coming if he thought she'd go down without kicking and screaming.

". . . reason for my wanting us to get away to Tahoe. I don't need Julia hurling abuse at me all weekend for upsetting her precious father. Like I did it on purpose. Like I wanted to put a stain on the great Paradine name. I'm telling you, Kate, Julia's driving me up a wall."

"Maybe they'll settle out of court."

"Yeah, that's what I told Charlie. Hell, I don't care what this dame's lawyers say. Enough money always talks."

"Right."

"The problem is she's already gone to the press with the story. It'll be all over the trades by tomorrow. Not exactly the kind of publicity we need right now. Damn, I can't believe this is happening." He paused. "You're not saying much, Kate."

"What's there to say?" she muttered distractedly.

"I could use a little support. Some sympathy and understanding. You know as well as I do that Ritchie looked good on paper."

Kate had to smile. Doug had a talent for rewriting history.

"Look, I've got to go to the symphony with Julia and some of her insufferable friends tonight, but if I can get away afterward for an hour, I'll zip by."

Right, Kate thought. Long enough to unzip his fly. "No, Doug. I'm just about to go out. Marianne Spars's new restaurant, remember?"

"Oh, right. You won't hang around there too late, though. Make it home by midnight and I'll have a nice dry martini waiting for you."

"Not tonight, Doug. I feel crummy. I just got my period and as soon as I get home I'm going to climb into bed, take a painkiller and conk out," she lied. Chances were, she wouldn't be able to sleep a wink, thanks to Doug's news. He'd done her one favor, though. Got her mind off Adrian. Now, instead of fighting off visions of Adrian's beautiful body all night, she'd spend her time scheming, trying to figure out all her options, what her next moves might be, depending on whatever bombshell Charlie Windham dropped. When Windham showed up tomorrow, she was going to be ready for any pitch he threw her.

Doug let out a long, disappointed sigh. "Yeah, all right," he said reluctantly. "Think about the weekend, though. It will be good for us to get away from all this craziness. We've got to stick together through this, Kate. Support each other."

Kate muttered that she'd think about Tahoe and hung up, his last words captured in her mind. So Doug thought she needed his support as well as him needing hers. A slip of the tongue? Did it mean he guessed—or knew, for a fact—that his father-in-law was going to ask her to be Paradine's scapegoat? And if that was the case, what would Doug do? Kate was a realist. Besides, she knew Doug like a book. He could give all the lip service he wanted to supporting her, but when push came even to "tap," he wouldn't lift a finger to save her neck if it meant endangering his relationship with the Windham dynasty in any way.

Kate felt scared. A real, little-girl scared like she hadn't felt in a long, long time. With excruciating clarity, she remembered how it had once felt to be small and insignificant; powerless, dirt-poor, her father off screwing around, her mother sentenced to life in a wheelchair, thanks to a drunk driver. She remembered all those years working her butt off to win that scholarship to U.C.L.A. film school so she'd have a shot at making her dreams come true. She remembered her first apartment after getting out of school—a room, really—with damp patches on the walls and ceiling, rust-stained tub and sink, the crummy Salvation Army furnishings. She'd come a long way since those days, and she'd earned every bit of what she'd achieved.

Suddenly Sylver flashed into her mind. Sylver in a shabby apartment in West Hollywood, probably not very different from the one she had started out in. That was the difference. For Sylver it was the end of the road, not the beginning. Kate felt a shiver of fear streak down her spine. For all her smarts and her fierce determination, was she going to end up right back where she'd started?

Adrian Needham kept himself busy all afternoon—working on the blasted Jeep and finally getting it running, taking another swim in the pool to cool off from more than the L.A. sun, going on a long hike through the canyon—but he couldn't get his mind off Kate. Afternoon faded into evening and it was only getting worse.

What really threw him was that he'd thought he was fully prepared for their encounter, had even been looking forward to it—telling himself with an uncharacteristic mean-spirited stab of satisfaction that he'd get a real kick out of putting her through some hoops. The only thing he hadn't taken into account was how he was going to feel when he saw her. She was even more beautiful than she'd been eight years ago and he was so instantly turned on, he had a hard time remembering his own name. It was like taking a blow to the stomach. Oh, he kept up a good front, but that's all it was. A front. He was a fraud. Eight years ago, Kate Paley had sent him into a tailspin. Eight years later, her effect on him was exactly the same. In all this time, no woman had fired him up as Kate had—and, damn her, still did.

It was just lust, he told himself. She still looked terrifically sexy, better than ever. She was still turned on by him, too. Oh, she did a bloody good job keeping her arousal under wraps, but there were some things she couldn't hide from him. There was a certain heightening of color in her cheeks, the covert glances, the forced coolness. Yes, he still could set her juices flowing.

He didn't have to do much soul-searching to know that while lust might be a part of what he was feeling, it wasn't all of it. The hurt and the bitterness for what might have been but for Kate's damn ambition—that hadn't abated these past eight years, either. He'd merely suppressed those emotions, keeping away from her to avoid facing them. Seeing Kate again brought all the pain of what they'd had and lost right back to the surface. Nor had she changed. She was as ambitious as ever, her drive and determination having taken her to a top rung at Paradine. Adrian had no illusions. He knew Kate wouldn't be satisfied to stay where she was. She wanted more. And she wanted to use him to get it.

So, what was he going to do now? Get through that bloody award dinner and catch the first flight back to London? The safest bet, but he knew himself too well to imagine he could merely walk away. There was too much unfinished business here, too many unresolved feelings. And yes, a small voice whispered, too much lust.

What if he stayed for a while, set about to seduce Kate, tried to win her back, make her face up to what she'd missed out on all these years—the love, a family, the opportunity to make their own personal kind of movies that came from the heart instead of the bank?

And if he did manage to seduce her, then what? What was the point? Revenge? Make her fall in love with him again so he could hurt her as she had hurt him? Or was he so pathetically romantic that he actually envisioned a typical Hollywood-movie ending where they went off hand in hand into the sunset? No. A romantic though he might be, he'd never been one for trite, feel-good Hollywood finales. That wasn't the way it went in real life.

If only he could get a fix on his feelings. There was such a jumble of anger, pain, fear, confusion, and arousal kicking around inside him. He walked into the kitchen. The script Kate had left him was lying on the counter. He stared at it, but he didn't pick it up, wasn't even sure yet whether he was going to read it. He didn't know what the hell he was going to do. He never had been much of a planner. That used to drive Kate crazy about him. He operated almost solely on instinct, whereas Kate plotted and strategized every move. They were opposites in so many ways, but they both had the same rare gift of vision, the same fire in their bellies, the same yearnings. They understood each other as no others had understood them. They brought out the best in each other and the worst. Some of their fights had been real humdingers. Oh, but the making up...

Again his eyes fell on the script. He had no doubt it was as good as Kate had said. Taking it on meant a chance to work with Kate again. Fight with her again. Get both their juices flowing again. Carte blanche, she'd said. Oh, she would try to give him as much free rein as possible, but Adrian was far from naive as to how the Hollywood system worked. He and Kate could deal with their differences, but Kate wasn't running Paradine Studios yet. Adrian was well aware that, if he took on the project, he would end up butting heads with Douglas Garrison over the making of a big-budget movie. And Garrison was likely to be particularly troublesome—not the least reason being he'd feel threatened as hell at the idea of another Needham-Paley partnership and what it might lead to on a personal level. Adrian had stolen Kate from Garrison once before. Garrison was definitely not above being vindictive if he even thought it might happen again. It was no secret in the industry that Kate and Garrison had resumed their "discreet" long-standing affair.

Adrian saw the prospect of deep trouble all around if he took on the Lerner project. Then again, he was the kind of guy who frequently went looking for trouble.

It was getting dark. Adrian grabbed up the script, hurried out of the bungalow and climbed into the open Jeep, telling himself he didn't know where he was going as he roared down the canyon.

When her doorbell rang, it took a moment for Kate to register the sound and then translate that it meant someone was at her door. She stared down at her cocktail dress still on the floor and frowned. It couldn't be Ken. She'd arranged with Ken Cook, publisher of *Architectural Review* and her escort for the evening, to meet at the restaurant.

She snatched up her pale yellow silk kimono from her chaise and slipped it on as the doorbell rang insistently several times in a row. She felt a twinge of anxiety as she crossed to her bedroom window that looked out over her front drive. What if Doug had decided to stop by for a quickie before heading off to the symphony with his wife?

When she looked out the window, it wasn't Doug's familiar yellow Lamborghini she saw in the drive. It was, however, another familiar vehicle. A red Jeep. Instantly, all thought of her evening plans, even her anxiety over her crucial meeting the next day with Windham, fled Kate's mind.

She felt her heart drop to her feet, taking her stomach along for the trip. The blood drained from her head. She shut her eyes, but that only heightened the dizziness.

Clutching her robe closed, she somehow managed to make her way through the house to the front door. Still, as she reached for the knob, she hesitated. *Oh, God, what am I in for now?*

As she pulled open the door, she stepped back, staggering slightly. Adrian was framed in the light of the doorway—thumbs hooked in the belt loops of his faded jeans, one shoulder jutting aggressively forward, his thick dark hair all windblown, those intense blue-green eyes not looking at her but lasering right through her.

Neither of them made a move. It was as if they were caught in a freeze frame.

Finally some voice in Kate's head yelled "Action." Her hand, which was clutching her robe closed, dropped to her side. The kimono fluttered open in the California night breeze.

Taut as a bow, Adrian let his eyes cruise her supple, creamy flesh bisected by two flimsy patches of black lace lingerie. It hurt to look at her. He felt a physical pain in equal measure to his arousal. Why did you let what we had go, Katie? *Why did you hurt me so much?*

Kate felt like there was a chasm of time and space separating them; a chasm that had been subjected to years of erosion. Why was she standing here like this, exposing herself to his scrutiny, willingly allowing herself to be so vulnerable?

Because she wanted him. And then she said what she'd wanted to say to him at least a hundred times that afternoon, but hadn't had the nerve. "I've missed you."

Her words were borne on the wind like a faint whisper, but they reverberated in Adrian's head like a grand opera. His lips parted slightly, but no sound escaped. He made no move—neither to turn from her and drive off or to draw closer, take her in his arms, wrap himself around her as she so desperately wanted him to do.

She could feel the strain and wariness radiating from him. It was like standing in front of a high-tension wire. She tried a smile, but her lips were quivering so much she couldn't pull it off. "How about . . . we meet halfway?" The knowledge that this man—more than any other man in her life—could hurt her, terrified Kate, but she fought back her fear. There were other feelings possessing her, feelings more powerful than fear.

Silently, she went to him. He didn't meet her halfway. He didn't move, but he didn't take his eyes off her for an instant as she came and stood before him.

Slowly, tentatively, her hand reached out until her fingertips just barely touched his forearm. Still, it was a connection. That afternoon they hadn't touched at all. She only realized now how excruciating it had been to spend time with him and not touch. Touching had been so vital in their relationship in the past. They'd communicated so much with their touches—affection, tenderness, fear, passion, love.

Adrian was stunned to realize that he was on the verge of tears. "What am I doing here?"

Kate didn't know how to answer him. Adrian didn't know the answer himself. All he knew was that his life would be unbearable if he hadn't come there tonight.

Kate stepped a fraction closer, letting her fingertips and then the palm of her hand slide down his arm to the back of his hand. He continued to make no move to touch her. Even so, she felt the fragile connection, although she was afraid even the gentle Pacific Coast breeze would wipe it out. Or worse still, that Adrian might.

"I'm glad you're here." Her voice was tremulous, her longing for him so intense, she felt that she would break apart into a thousand fragments if he didn't touch her back. In a panic, she searched his face for clues to what he wanted from her; what she could expect from him. Had he come here like this to torment her? There were so many confounding messages etched in his features; so many feelings accumulated over eight years. How was she to sort them out? Could she even begin to?

In the end, it was her hand that dropped away, breaking the connection, so vulnerable at best. She couldn't do this alone. She needed something back from him—the faintest gesture, anything to let her know there was more inside him than just anger, pain, and spite. How about unbridled desire? That would suffice.

Damn you, Adrian. Take me in your arms. Hold me. Make love to me. Don't you remember what it was like? Our rhythm, our special beat.... I'm burning up inside. Can't you feel my heat?

His inaction was driving her crazy. What was the use? She'd tried to reach out to him.

"I was . . . getting ready . . . to go out," she muttered and started to turn from him.

His hand darted out. He grabbed her shoulder—so abruptly, so fiercely, a small cry escaped her lips. His touch was like fire, searing through the silk of her kimono, burning her already inflamed skin.

"I've slept with a lot of women these past eight years, Kate."

She flinched. So he had come to torment her. This was why he was here.

"But once I was inside each and every one of them and they would call out, 'Yes,' or 'Please,' every voice I heard was yours. Always yours. Only yours."

His hand dug into her shoulder harder and harder, but Kate welcomed the pain. She moved into him and he pulled her kimono down over her shoulders. Then his hands touched her flesh—her shoulders, her throat, the back of her neck.

They stared into each other's eyes until their faces were so close they couldn't focus any longer and then, at last, his mouth was on hers and they were kissing feverishly, right there on her front step, fully illuminated by the light streaming out from her house, fully exposed to the traffic whizzing by on the road.

Kate didn't care. She let her arms drop long enough to allow the kimono to fall to the ground. Then she circled his neck, lifting one leg and wrapping it around the back of his calf.

Adrian inhaled her scent deeply. It was always her scent, too, that he smelled, obliterating the scents of the other women he'd known intimately. He felt terrible guilt for letting those women believe it was them he wanted, even though he had tried to make himself believe it at the time, as well. He'd lied, cheated, shortchanged them and himself. What he'd truly wanted the whole time was constancy. What he'd wanted was Kate.

He drew her away with the same abruptness with which he'd first touched her; with the same fierceness. *This is a setup.* He believed this even though it was as much his own making as Kate's. He knew it would turn out badly, just as he knew it wasn't only lust and revenge that he was feeling. He couldn't keep his heart out of it. That bloody ticker of his betrayed him. He shut his eyes. *Grab that award and then get the hell out of town. Get away from this woman.*

Then his eyes opened and fell on Kate, standing there in her skimpy lace bra and panties right out there on the front step of her lavish Bel Air home, her arms crossing her chest like a shy young girl, her face such a candid study in anguish. That look was his undoing. Exposed, vulnerable, her true feelings so honestly displayed, she was irresistible.

"Katie," he whispered, lifting her up in his arms, his lips against her hair as he carried her into the house. She clung to him as if her life depended on it.

Inside her bedroom he laid her on the boldly printed quilt of her bed, trampling the evening dress she should have been wearing at that moment. For the briefest instant Kate thought about Marianne's disappointment over her not showing up at the restaurant, but then she knew that, under the circumstances, Marianne, of all people, would understand. Marianne had been one of the few people Kate had shared her secret with—the secret being that Adrian Needham had been her one true love as well as her one true male friend.

Adrian stood at the bed staring down at Kate, then leaned over, lifted her buttocks and slipped her panties off. Then he attended to her bra.

He smiled down at her sleek, creamy body. Every curve, contour, line, and swell of it was so much the same as eight years before. "You've taken good care of yourself, Katie."

She smiled self-consciously, embarrassed by his close scrutiny of her thirty-six-year-old body, not quite sure how to take the remark. Was he mocking her daily ministrations at the gym in an attempt to stop the ravages of time from taking their toll? Or was he truly pleased that she hadn't grown lumpy and soft and middle-aged?

He leaned over her again, the flat of his hands pressed on the quilt on either side of her waist. Then he dipped his head lower, the tip of his tongue darting out to the pulse beat at her throat, then making a deliciously sinuous trail down over her breasts, licking, tasting, sucking at her hardened nipples until she arched up toward him, gasping with the pleasure he was giving her as much as the pleasure he seemed to be taking from her. At that moment, she felt so open, so expansive, she would have given him anything.

This was what making love was like. She'd almost forgotten. No. She'd never been able to forget.

He undressed in the same feverish way he had in the past—slipping his shirt, fully buttoned, over his head, pulling off his pants and briefs at the same time, kicking off his shoes, no socks to bother with.

He dropped down beside her, already pulling her to him before even landing. Kate felt almost giddy with arousal. She kissed him hard on the mouth, darting her tongue past his lips, his teeth, until it tangled with his. They made love with their tongues. A prelude.

Adrian held her tight, her naked body pressed against his. So that they fused together, dissolving into each other. Like old times. The good times. Times full of magical promise.

He forced himself into the present. Those times were long gone; false promises long broken; good times replaced by hard times. Time enough now only to fill the moment. What was this about, then? An exorcism?

Again that voice in his head echoed danger. For once in his life he knew he should play it safe. He would catch that flight back to London as scheduled, he vowed, even as he draped her leg up over his thigh and began kissing her eyes, her cheeks, her throat, the side of her neck, his hands weaving through her hair. Yes, that's what he would do....

"Yes, yes, yes..." Kate was murmuring against his ear, fluttering sighs more than words.

He rolled her over on her back, pinning her arms high above her head. Suddenly, a gust of cold fury for all those lost, hurting years rushed through his veins like adrenaline, mixing with the lust and the love and the heartache. *Damn you, Katie. Damn you. Damn you...*

His hands clamped her wrists tightly as he leaned fully over her, leveling himself between her thighs. Kate could feel his breath, hot and hard, fanning her face. His eyes were dark with intensity. She could feel the rage emanating from him. She was suddenly afraid, sensing the potential for violence in him. Insane as she knew it was, it in no way diminished her desire. *This is what it's like to be out of control. Anything can happen. Anything...* The insanity was, she was game.

Roughly, he drove her thighs apart, his fingers digging into the tender skin of her wrists. Her arms were stretched to full extension, forcing her to arch her back.

His mouth swooped down to her breasts, gnawing on her nipples until she cried out. Her cry was cut off by his savage kiss. She could taste blood, but she kissed him back with equal ferocity. Maybe she wanted the pain. Maybe, she thought, enough pain would obliterate all of the other feelings she had for this man. *Hurt me. Make me hate you....*

Even as the plea ran through her mind, he released her, then fell away from her, disgusted with himself. He shut his eyes, sweeping his arm across them. Tears slid past his closed lids.

"Damn you, Katie," he whispered in a heartbreakingly doomed fashion.

Kate rolled onto her side, facing him, not quite touching him. She had to pause a few moments to catch her breath, then she reached out her hand and gently pried his arm away from his face. She leaned closer, her fingers gently wiping away his tears.

He opened his eyes. He watched her slip her fingers past her lips, tasting the salty wetness of his tears. The sight was at once both wrenching and erotic. He thought he had never wanted her more than he wanted her now. Fear held him immobile. He had come close to hurting her. That driving, fearful surge of anger had passed, but he couldn't trust it not to resurface, sneak up on him, catch him unawares.

He knew he should get up, throw on his clothes and get out of there. This wasn't safe for either of them.

She was stroking his arm, his chest, then lower still, letting her fingertips run ever so lightly over his penis, which was ramrod hard—an organ with a bloody mind of its own.

He looked into her eyes. *What is this, Katie? Absolution?*

She smiled tremulously as though she'd read his mind. She wrapped her arms around him, drawing him back over her, spreading her legs and lifting them, her ankles locking at the small of his back.

Now he was her captive. He gave a short, breathless laugh. She laughed, too. For the life of them, neither knew why. All they knew was that it felt good.

When he entered her a moment later it felt even better. Like they had found their way home again at last.

Ten

Sylver had been moved that evening from the emergency room to a six-bed ward on the seventh floor. Her condition had stabilized, but the attending doc had diagnosed her as being malnourished, anemic and suffering from clinical depression. He told Riley that he'd arranged for a psychiatrist to see her the next morning.

Sam Hibbs stuck around for a while after they'd gotten Sylver settled in, but decided she wouldn't be in any condition to talk long-term treatment for at least a couple of days.

"You gonna hang around awhile longer?" Sam asked Riley.

Riley nodded.

Sam looked down at Sylver. "Be careful, pal. I know you want to pull her up from the abyss, but my bet is she's stronger than she looks." The drug counselor shifted his gaze to Riley. "She could pull you down with her if you lower your guard."

Riley shook his head slowly. "Naw. It was an interesting place to visit, but I wouldn't want to live there. She's hit bottom, Sam. I think she's ready for a move up."

Sam gave Riley's shoulder a reassuring squeeze, told him he'd be back, and shoved off.

Riley pulled up a chair and sat beside Sylver's bed as she drifted in and out of consciousness. He didn't want her to wake up, scared and bewildered, and find herself all alone in a hospital ward. Anyway, he'd promised her he'd stick around, although he did wonder if there was anyone she'd want him to call. A friend? A family member? One person he wouldn't contact, though, was Sylver's scummy boyfriend, Nash Walker. Even if she wanted him to. She would have to do that herself, and for now, there wasn't much of anything she could do for herself. He believed that once he got her into a treatment center, she'd come to her senses and realize that Walker would only keep her down.

Riley knew plenty of guys like Walker—selfish, narcissistic bastards who thought the world owed them something just for being so damn good-looking; guys who got their kicks out of alternately demeaning women and charming the pants and the money off them. Walker was one of the users. Riley knew. Once upon a time he'd been one himself.

His eyes rested on Sylver. He leaned a little closer to her, smoothed her damp, tangled hair away from her face, exposing her delicate neck and perfectly shaped ears—the kind a master sculptor might have created. She looked so small and fragile, yet for all she'd been through, he knew what Sam had meant about her being stronger than she looked. What was her story? She had to have a story. They all did. He did. The stories were what drew him; what had made him realize awhile back that what he needed to do was get those stories down. His, hers, all the lost souls'. It was in the writing that he believed his real freedom lay. Who knew? Maybe it would free Sylver if she could share her story with him.

He stared at her. Her face was etched with pain. Nothing, though, could quite obliterate her beauty, even though she'd certainly given it her best shot. For Riley, she was a tragic figure who tore at his heart in a way that continued to confound him. And fascinate him.

He'd been off the booze for two years now. Clean. Straight. A model citizen. What he hadn't been until Sylver walked into his life yesterday was truly alive. He'd just been going through all the right motions. Tonight, he felt life flowing through his veins. It felt good.

Sylver's eyes fluttered open. She looked beyond him at first, trying to sort out where she was, then raised her eyes to him as if it didn't really matter. "Hi," she croaked.

He smiled. "Hi."

"So, I'm still among…the living." She tried to sound flip, but she was shivering too hard to pull it off.

"Cold?" He unfolded another blanket and threw it over the two already covering her.

She closed her eyes again, opening them a few minutes later. This time she gave him a closer scrutiny. "I know you, right?"

He smiled, made a typing motion with his fingers.

At first she was puzzled, then the light dawned. "The writer. Next door."

He felt a ridiculous sense of joy seeing the flicker of recognition come into her blue eyes. "Really Riley."

"Riley Quinn."

She began shivering some more and grabbed onto his shirt sleeve. "Can you...get me...something...Riley Quinn?"

"What you want, sweetheart, is what got you here in the first place." He put his hand over hers. "It was just a matter of luck that it wasn't the *last* place," he added pointedly.

Sylver got the point. She just didn't care. She felt awful, hurt everywhere, and she couldn't stop shivering. "You call it...luck. I'd rather...be dead."

"I know the feeling," he said.

Sylver wasn't in the mood for empathy. She wanted something to stop the pain. She wanted to be numb again. "Please, Riley. I feel so...sick." Tears began to roll down her cheeks. She didn't have to manufacture them, but she could have if it had been necessary. She always had been able to cry on cue. The problem was, she couldn't always stop crying.

He bundled her in the blankets, then stroked her cheek. "You're gonna have to ride this one out on your lonesome, Sylver."

She felt desperate. "Please, Riley."

Her words were a cry of agony, a cry for help. How could he make her see that he couldn't help her in the way she wanted because that would be no help at all? She'd tossed aside the blankets when she pleaded with him. He went to cover her up again, but she swatted away his hand. "Where's...Nash? Nash will...help me. Get...Nash down here."

"Nash can't help you, Sylver. He can't help himself."

She wanted to scream at this self-righteous bastard who'd popped into her life out of nowhere, but she didn't have the strength. She wanted to tell him to get out of her sight if he wasn't going to help her, but she felt terrified of being alone.

"Here, drink this." He gently cupped the back of her head and eased her up slightly as he placed a glass to her lips. "It's only water, so don't get your hopes up for nothing," he said softly.

She gave him as rueful a look as she could muster, but she did take a few sips. It hurt to swallow, but once she got the water past her throat, it felt almost good.

He eased her head back on the pillow. She still had a weak grip on his shirt. "Does Nash know... I'm here?"

Riley shook his head. "Is there anyone other than Nash you want me to call? Someone in your family?"

Sylver's grip tightened on his sleeve, panic suffusing her features. "No. No. Don't let her... know. Promise me. Promise me."

"Who?" Riley asked. "Who don't you want me to let know?"

"My... mother." She started to cry in earnest, pulling at him. "Don't let her... lock me up, Riley. I'm not crazy, but I'll go crazy... if she puts me in a loony bin."

Riley put his arms around her, holding her against his chest, rubbing her back lightly with his palm. It had been a long time since he'd held a woman simply to offer comfort. He'd spent so much of his life fleeing at the vaguest hint of someone wanting anything from him but momentary physical pleasure, feeling like he had so little of himself to give.

After two years of sobriety, he was beginning to honestly face himself. A lot of what he saw about how he'd lived his life up to now he didn't like. He'd been hard-nosed and stubborn just like his father, inheriting the old man's rotten temper, as well. He'd gone through a marriage that had been so brief it was over before he knew what hit him. He'd been one hell of a cop, though. At least for a while. Until that day four years back, when Lilli was four years old, staying with him for the weekend—the first weekend in months because he'd been locked into an undercover assignment. They were going to spend the day at Disneyland. They were walking out of his apartment house, heading for his beat-up Ford, when a black sedan came whizzing by. Bullets flew. Lilli fell... The bastard who killed her died in a high-speed chase a month later.

Police work and booze became his whole life after that. As big a lush as he was, he never drank on duty. He never needed to. Being a cop was a natural high for him. It was a place to put all that pent-up rage, all that fierce energy. No one was better than him in an interrogation room. Alone in that box with a suspect, he could clamp on the lid and let the pressure build to the breaking point. He could play any game, any role; be their friend, their confessor. He got off on that war of wills. He was brilliant, but as arrogant as hell. And always a loner, although his partner, Al, had managed over seven years of banging at the walls, to make a few dents.

On duty, he was driven, hardened, as wily as they came. It was when he was off duty that he lost his anchor; when the loss and the loneliness began crowding in on him; when he had time to think about his baby, about being one of the unloved; when the questions about where his life was going and where it had been, started to surface. Riley had one solution—booze.

He'd closed himself off long ago. A survival mechanism that got to be habit. By the time he was twelve, he could suffer his father's regular-as-clockwork beatings without even batting an eye. His mother would stand by, crying, too scared of her husband herself to intervene, and he wouldn't even feel pity for her. Or rage for abandoning him. He was tough. He didn't let himself feel anything. That was his safety net. Only Lilli had gotten through it. Only Lilli had moved him. After she died, that part of him just shriveled up.

If he hadn't joined the L.A.P.D. Riley knew he could easily have ended up on the wrong side of the law just like most of the guys in his West L.A. neighborhood. As it was, he'd screwed up royally anyway. He might have been one of the good guys, but he hadn't been a very nice guy. He wasn't proud of that, but he couldn't change the past. He could only live in the present and work toward a future that held some meaning and purpose.

Riley saw that meaning and purpose in the woman enclosed in his arms. Sylver was weeping quietly now as he held her against his chest, and he realized he was gently rocking her. It felt okay. It felt better than okay. It felt good. For once in his life, he didn't want to run away. He didn't try to understand these new feelings that were starting to surface, afraid he'd grasp more than he could handle. One step at a time. He was traversing new terrain. He'd take it nice and slow. There might be land mines and one of them could blow up in his face if he wasn't real careful.

A nurse came in. The instant Sylver spotted her, she pushed away from Riley. "Nurse, please. You've got to give me something. I'm in so much pain."

The nurse was heading for one of the other patients, but she nodded in Sylver's direction as she passed by.

Sylver brightened, rubbing away the tears rolling down her cheeks. "Thanks. Thank you so much."

She gave Riley a challenging look as she sank back down on her pillow. Her high spirits lasted until the nurse stopped by a few minutes later with two aspirin tablets.

Sylver threw them at her. "This isn't going to do anything," she screamed as the nurse walked off without a backward glance.

Riley looked down at her. "Sylver, you're a drug addict. You've just had your stomach pumped because you OD'd. They're not going to give you more drugs."

"You're crazy. I'm not a drug addict. That was an accident. My nerves were shot. I just wanted to take something to calm me down, that's all."

She held out her arms for inspection. "Do you see any tracks? No, because there aren't any. Okay, so sometimes I snort a little coke or have a couple of drinks. God, I'm not a saint or anything. That doesn't make me an addict."

"You use booze, pills, coke to escape whatever it is you're terrified to face," Riley said calmly. "You're hooked, Sylver. You're dependent on drugs to get you through each day."

"I thought you were a writer. What are you? A preacher on the side, Riley?"

"I'm not preaching to you, Sylver. I've been in your shoes. I've been in that bed you're lying in. I'm not telling you anything you don't already know. Including that you either have the courage to face your demons, or they're going to do you in."

She rolled over on her side, turning from him. "Go away."

A minute later, she looked over her shoulder. "You're still here."

"I wrote you off for dead," he said quietly. "In the novel I'm writing."

Sylver rolled onto her back, eyeing him suspiciously. "I'm in your book?"

He nodded. "You kind of creeped into it without my knowing."

"I did?"

"Now I'll have to do some rewriting."

She smiled crookedly. "Maybe not. I could still oblige. Especially the way I'm feeling."

"I'd rather rewrite. Can't do much with a dead character. A lot more options if you stick around."

She was getting interested. And getting interested was getting her mind off how miserable she was feeling. "Like what?"

Riley considered her question carefully. Or, more to the point, considered his answers carefully. "Well, you could get your act together and hop a bus for Yuma...."

She made a face.

"Chicago?"

She shook her head.

"Where to? The sky's the limit."

Sylver chewed on her bottom lip. "I'd like to go...up in the mountains somewhere. Someplace...rustic. No smog, no noise, no hassles. You know what I mean."

"Sounds good. I can work with that."

"And snow. Lots of snow. I've hardly ever seen snow."

"Snow you want, snow you'll get."

Sylver let herself drift into the fantasy. "It does sound good. Snow, fresh mountain air, everything around me...so clean."

Maybe it didn't have to be a fantasy. She gave her new friend a hopeful look. "I could really pull myself together if I could just get away to a place like that, Riley. I really could."

For a minute Sylver thought about Kate. A short time ago, she'd believed that she needed Kate to help her pull herself out of the hell she'd created. Now she decided she didn't need Kate—or anyone else, for that matter. "If I could get out of this whole rat race, I could do it," she repeated to Riley, the hope in her voice tinged with desperation.

Riley smoothed the covers back over her. "Only if I were writing a fantasy novel, Sylver. I never did go in for fantasies. I'm into writing books based on realism. No holds barred. The nitty-gritty. The way it really is."

"No, I don't mean in your book, Riley. I mean in real life. If I could get away...from everyone...I could get myself straightened out. I'd quit the booze, the coke, the uppers, the downers. I admit I've gotten a little caught up on that junk, but if I had a fresh start, I wouldn't need any of it. I really believe that, Riley."

"You *want* to believe it. You want me to believe it. Wanting it won't make it happen. It wouldn't work. You can't do it yourself. You need help."

She started to protest, but he placed a finger to her lips. "Not now, Sylver. We'll put it on hold until after you've had some sleep." He fought back a yawn. He was dead on his feet himself, even though it was only a little past eight. He remembered then that he hadn't slept in close to twenty-four hours. Too busy keeping the midnight oil burning while his fingers flew over his typewriter keys. He hadn't written with that kind of a creative fervor since he'd bought that used typewriter nearly two years ago. He wondered if he'd have the energy to hit the keys when he got home that night. As exhausted as he was, he knew he'd have to rewrite that last scene with the dead girl that was still stuck in his typewriter. He couldn't go to sleep until he'd brought her back to life.

Sylver became fearful at the thought of Riley leaving. He kept her mind occupied. And for all his obnoxious preaching and refusal to get her something for what ailed her, he seemed like a decent enough sort.

He'd started to rise.

"Riley?"

"Yeah?"

"Could you...stay with me just until I fall asleep? I don't know what it is about you, Riley, but I feel...safer with you here. Just stay for a little while."

He sat back down, folding his hands in his lap. "I'll stay. And I'll be back tomorrow."

She looked at him in confusion. And with more than a little suspicion. What was in it for this total stranger playing the Good Samaritan? Everyone had an angle. Sylver had learned that a long time ago. Still, she couldn't figure Riley out. He knew she was stone-broke, so he wasn't in it for the money. Her star had faded long ago, so he couldn't be in it for the notoriety. And he couldn't want her body. Only someone who was warped or blind or both could find her even mildly attractive in the state she was in. She knew Riley wasn't blind, and he didn't seem warped. On the contrary. He seemed solid and put-together. Even in her condition, she had also not failed to notice that Riley Quinn was very attractive. More than that, his face had substance and depth. A face that had seen a lot, been through a lot and reflected it all.

"Why are you doing this, Riley? I'm not worth it, believe me."

"Only time will tell."

She smiled. "Good answer."

He smiled back. "There's more."

She gave him a curious look. Was that a blush she saw on the ex-cop's cheeks? Riley Quinn kept surprising her. "Tell me."

"I haven't stopped writing on my great American novel since I met you. I wrote all through the night, all day today. I guess you could say you've become my...inspiration."

Sylver stared at him in silence for a minute, trying to figure out if he was serious or putting her on. He reached over
and gently closed her eyelids. She let herself begin to drift
off, Riley's words and his warm, tender smile staying with
her. For the first time in a long time, she felt almost as if she
might be worth saving.

Nash kicked a pile of unfolded laundry out of his path as
he walked into the bathroom. He was in a foul mood. For
one thing, he was broke and some creeps were on his case to
cough up the dough he owed them for his last few hits. For
another thing, his goddamn agent, who'd refused to take his
calls or return any of them for weeks, finally had his secretary tell him when he called that morning that, "Mr. Lester
Barton is limiting his clientele and will no longer be able to
represent you."

"Limiting his clientele, my ass," he'd screamed into the
phone, but the line had already gone dead. Without an
agent, he'd never stand a chance in hell of getting an audition for that flick at Avalon he might have had a real shot at.
And getting another agent to take him on, given his long dry
spell, was going to be a real bitch.

He'd been so mad after he hung up the phone, he'd
kicked his foot right through the glass door of the phone
booth on Sunset. Now, on top of everything else, he had a
long, bloody gash running down the side of his leg.

He flipped the toilet seat down in the bathroom and
hoisted his foot up on it, pulling up his trousers to examine
the damage. He flinched at the sight. It wasn't the blood
that bothered him; it was seeing his otherwise-perfect leg
marred. Damaged goods.

He shoved open the medicine cabinet. Not much there but
some empty pill vials without renewal dates. "Sylver, get
your ass in here and help me. I'm bleeding to death. Where
the hell are the bandages?"

When he got no response, he got even angrier. "Damn it,
Sylver. If I have to come in there and drag you out of that
bed, you're gonna be one unhappy broad. I mean it,
Sylver."

He snatched the roll of toilet paper off the tank lid of the toilet and began winding it around his leg, all the while shouting curses in the direction of the bedroom. When his leg was fully swathed, he stormed out of the bathroom. He'd never struck Sylver—never struck any woman, for that matter—but he could feel himself wanting to take his rage and frustration out on someone. And Sylver was such a perfect target. Hell, she'd probably welcome a few punches. Let her know she was still alive.

When he got to the open door of the bedroom, he came to an abrupt stop. The room was empty. He didn't get it. Where was she? She never went out at night without him. Hell, she hardly ever went out *with* him. She was usually too stoned to get out of bed and get dressed.

He looked around for a note, something, a clue as to where she might have gone. His rage dissipated. This wasn't like Sylver. Was she pissed because he hadn't come home last night? Why would she be any more pissed than all the other nights he hadn't come home? She knew he always showed up again. "Like a bad penny," she'd tease.

He was about to head out again—one thing he couldn't stand was being alone—when he saw the flashing light on the answering machine. Sylver could have called to leave him a message.

He rewound the tape and listened. The message wasn't from Sylver. It was for her. From her mother.

Nash sat down woodenly on the bed. Was that the solution to the mystery of Sylver's disappearance? Had Nancy Cassidy showed up with white-jacketed goons wielding a straitjacket and carted Sylver off to the loony bin?

He dropped his head into his hands. He should have come home last night. He should have been there today. That old bitch wouldn't have been able to pull this off if he'd been around.

He got up. He had to get out of there. He was starting to come down. He needed a hit. For it all, it hurt to lose her. As bad off as she was, Sylver had been the one constant in his life. She owed him, and she knew it. He hardly ever had to remind her. In a crazy kind of way, he really loved her.

He was crossing the living room when the front door opened. "Sylver?" Man, he'd let her have it for putting him through so much grief.

Only it wasn't Sylver who walked in. It was Nancy Cassidy with a young, muscle-bound dude standing behind her at the open door. What were they doing back here?

Nash backed away nervously. Sylver's mother had never liked him.

"Where is she?" Nancy demanded without preamble.

That threw Nash. He squinted in her direction. "I was gonna ask you the same thing."

"Don't play games with me, Nash," Nancy warned, then nodded to her companion. "Pete, see if you can get this bastard to be serious."

Nash felt sick as Pete stepped around her and started into the room. This goon could bash his face in. His career would really be over, then. His looks were his fortune. His only shot at one, anyway. He held his hands up in front of his face as Pete, smiling like he was really going to enjoy this, swaggered toward him.

Nash broke into a sweat. "Please.... I swear...I'm telling the truth, Nancy. I don't know where Sylver is. I just got home. She was gone. I heard the message on the machine. She must have...bolted. Look, she'll be back. I...I know she will. She can't make it on her own...."

Pete was nose to nose with Nash now, but he glanced back at Nancy for the go-ahead. To Nash's great relief, she motioned the goon to step aside and she walked up to him herself, her eyes flashing like blue ice. "Now, you listen to me, Nash. You find Sylver and you bring her back to Malibu." She reached into her purse and pulled out a fifty-dollar bill, stuffing it into his hand. "That's for the cab. You use it for anything else and I'm going to have Pete here grind you up into meat loaf. Do you understand?"

Nash nodded anxiously.

Nancy doubted she had ever hated anyone in her life more than she hated Nash Walker. "I hold you fully responsible for the mess Sylver's made of her life. If you hadn't butted in back when I still had some ability to talk sense into that child, she wouldn't need to be institutionalized now."

Nash kept shifting his gaze nervously between Nancy and Pete. "It wasn't my fault," he whined defensively. "Sylver was in bad shape when she came to me, pleading with me to help her. I could have turned my back on her like everyone else, but I didn't."

"Shut up," Nancy said between clenched teeth.

Nash was so jiggy at this point he couldn't stop himself from going on. "Christ, was it my fault she was raped? Was it my fault she got pregnant?"

"You don't know what you're talking about," Nancy hissed, all the color draining from her face. "She wasn't raped. She got drunk. She'd never gotten drunk before in her whole life. She only did it because she was so depressed over not winning the Oscar. We were all upset. She should have won. Everyone knew it. What a birthday celebration that was going to be."

Nancy shut her eyes. Sylver's eighteenth birthday. Right on the eve of the Academy Awards, her baby up for the biggest award of them all—Best Actress for *Glory Girl*. It was going to be so perfect. She'd been so sure Sylver would win. None of the other actresses were even in the same ballpark—certainly not that simpy, middle-aged ham, Lynn Parnell, who walked off with the Oscar. The only reason those bastards hadn't picked Sylver was that she was so much younger than any of the other nominees. Plenty of other chances to win Oscars in her future. Her future...

"She made a mistake. A big mistake. That's all it was," Nancy muttered, more to herself than Nash. "She got tipsy and had a stupid little fling with her director. Sure, Nicky Kramer should have known better, but what man ever knows better when he's horny and some beautiful young thing is falling all over him. She must have inflated his ego until it was about to burst. The next morning Sylver panicked, was all. She just let it get blown out of proportion. Thanks to you. And Kate Paley, too. I was the only voice of reason."

"I tried to do the decent thing," Nash countered, some of his own guilt surfacing. Sylver had been his date that long-ago night, but he'd gotten plastered, too. When he'd seen Kramer lure Sylver out of Spago he had a pretty good idea what was going to happen. And an even better idea that the inebriated birthday girl didn't. What was worse, she was still a virgin then. Not for want of Nash's trying, either. It pissed him off that he wasn't going to be her first lover. Drunk as he was, he might have stopped Sylver, but he was up for the lead in Kramer's next movie. Nash wasn't about to bite the hand that might feed him. Later, though, he tried to make it up to Sylver; make it right.

"Maybe it would have worked out for us if you hadn't arranged that annulment," he muttered. "She could have had the baby. Plenty of girls get married and have babies at eighteen. We could have been ... good parents."

Nancy laughed harshly. "Good parents? In your dreams, Nash. You destroy everything you touch. You destroyed her, putting crazy ideas in her head. I had to ... take care of things. Sylver knew it was for the best. If you'd stayed away from her, I'd have had my baby back on the right track a few months after the abortion. All she needed was some therapy and a little rest. It would have all been fine, damn it, if you had just left her alone." Her voice cracked. She was trembling. There was nothing she detested more than being reminded of those terrible days that had triggered the collapse of her glorious world.

Nancy stared at Nash Walker in disgust and revulsion. Although she believed at this point that he didn't know where Sylver had gone, she was tempted to have her play-mate pummel away at that Adonis face of his, anyway. She might have given Pete the okay if she hadn't heard some-one out in the hallway opening a nearby door.

Riley could barely get his key in the lock. He'd heard enough of the conversation next door between Nash Walker and the woman he presumed was Sylver's mother to make him feel physically sick.

As soon as he stepped into his apartment, he sagged against his closed door, his fists clenching, his breathing shallow. Christ, no wonder Sylver Cassidy was so royally screwed up. Rape. Abortion. A mother with the maternal instincts of a viper. A bright, beautiful, talented girl's eighteenth birthday turned into one of those nightmares there was no waking up from.

What really threw Riley over the edge, though, was learning the name of the man who had raped Sylver. The celebrated director, Nick Kramer. Riley knew Nick Kramer.

About a year before he was booted off the force, he and his partner, Al, had picked Kramer up as a suspect in the murder of a West Hollywood hooker. Kramer had been identified by the hooker's pimp as her last "john" the night she was strangled to death and unceremoniously dumped in a vacant lot behind her apartment.

Riley could still recall that unique smell of fear reeking from Kramer as they squared off in the interrogation room. Al Borgini played good cop, he played bad cop. After a couple of hours they had Kramer so he didn't know if he was coming or going. Riley was sure he was guilty, convinced he could have gotten a confession out of him if Kramer's hotshot Beverly Hills lawyer hadn't pulled some strings and gotten him out of there just when he was about to hit pay dirt.

They never did gather enough hard evidence to bring Kramer to trial for the hooker's murder. There was some justice, though. Not three weeks after he'd strutted out of the police station, having literally gotten away with murder, Kramer was involved in a head-on crash with a catering van on the Pacific Coast Highway. They'd had to pry him out of his nifty Mercedes with the Jaws of Life. No life left in him, though. Good thing, too, Riley thought, knowing what he knew now.

He was thinking the scumbag would never leave. He hates him now not only for what he's done to Sylver, but for making him endure all these excruciating hours in a hospital. He hates everything about the place—the smells, the echoing moans from the patients, the tight-assed nurses in their prissy white uniforms who don't give a damn about anything but what time their shift's up; the smart-alecky young docs with their stethoscopes around their necks like badges of honor strutting up and down the halls like they're gods.

He has to see his princess; let her know that she isn't alone, that he hasn't abandoned her. What if she didn't pull through the night? The very thought of never seeing her again fills him with a pain too devastatingly awful even to contemplate. He will not let her die. She will feel his presence. He alone can give her the will to live.

The problem is getting into her room. What if someone stops him? Questions him? What would he say? Another of Sylver's brothers? No, he doesn't want to generate any suspicions. Best to get into her room unobserved. But how?

He steps out of the waiting room and looks up and down the hall. An orderly in hospital whites is coming out of a nearby room. None of the nurses at the desk gives him so much as a glance as he walks by.

He follows the orderly down the hall, sees him enter another room. As the door swings open, he catches a glimpse of a row of lockers. He smiles, his hand slipping inside his pocket, making contact with the snub-nosed barrel of his .22, as he, too, steps inside the locker room.

As soon as he enters the room, the orderly turns around and looks at him. His hand grips the handle of the gun.

"Hey, pal. Just coming on duty? Not a bad night. Not too many screamers. Only watch out for the old bag in 608. Thinks she's Cleopatra and kept bugging me to show her my asp."

He flinches as the orderly cackles while pulling off his uniform and tossing it into a nearby laundry basket. While the orderly dresses, he slips around to the next row of lockers, pretending to be working on the combination lock on one of them. All the while, one hand remains in his pocket. If the orderly comes around the corner and starts asking questions . . .

He jumps as the orderly, dressed now in crisp khaki slacks and a tight black T-shirt, slams the palm of his hand on one of the end lockers. "I am out of here, man. Got myself a hot date tonight and I am going to treat her so-o-o nice, there won't be anything she won't do for me."

He gives the orderly a thumbs-up sign, keeping his face averted. Beads of sweat ring his brow. He wipes them off on his shirtsleeve after the orderly leaves. The panic that had been pounding in his chest abates. He lets his hand slip out of his pocket. His palm's all sweaty. He rubs it against his pant leg. Then, wasting no more time, he hurries over to the laundry bin and plucks out the orderly's discarded uniform.

As he steps out of the locker room he realizes he needs one more thing. He frowns, checking the time. The hospital flower shop is very likely closed. Where the hell's he going to find a red rose?

He finds one in room 612. A haggard, middle-aged woman attached to a respirator has a whole bouquet of red roses on her bedside table. He would have preferred buying Sylver a rose rather than swiping one. He never could abide stealing.

And something else troubles him. For a brief instant, when he looks at the frail, shrunken woman in that bed, he's reminded of his mother. Even this woman's shallow breathing, her smell, the way her mousy brown hair mats on her cheeks...

He shuts his eyes to block out the memory of his last visit to his mother as she lay dying in a hospital bed so like this one, but that only brings her into sharper view. He can see her looking up at him, hatred radiating from her eyes. She blamed him. She blamed him for her being sick; she blamed him for never having made anything of himself; she blamed him for her whole miserable life. Those eyes, those fearful eyes, condemning him, defying him to ever know even the slightest joy or happiness. He feels a scream rise in his throat.

His eyes shoot open. What's the matter with him? Is he losing control of his senses? His mother was dead and gone. She had lost her power over him. Sylver was proof of that. Sylver had brought him the happiness and joy his mother had never wanted him to know. Slipping the stolen red rose underneath his white top, he hurries out of the room.

He's very careful to make sure she's asleep before he approaches her bed. He doesn't want to disturb her. God only knows she needs her rest.

He feels instantly better the moment he's able to get a closer look at her. While she's very pale and drawn, there's a faint smile on her lips. *Are you dreaming about me, princess? Can you feel me here with you?*

Then something strikes him with momentous force. This is the closest he has ever been to his precious darling. Years of longing crowd in on him as he stares down at her. He aches with the desire to lie down beside her, cradle her in his arms, stroke her damp forehead. He can picture himself brushing her tangled hair until it shines as it did when she was a child. She is still so young, so innocent.

He leans a fraction closer, so he can feel her breath. He opens his mouth, taking in her breath, swallowing it, capturing it inside him. She is inside him. She is part of him. They are united.

Feeling himself grow hard, he is instantly disgusted by the way his body betrays him against his will. This isn't about sex. He would never violate his princess's purity. Never.

He has to leave. The hardness will not go away. Now demon thoughts and desires are infiltrating his brain. If he isn't careful they will consume him.

It's all the stress and worry over Sylver's condition— that's all it is. Look at her. Beautiful as ever. That sweet, sweet smile. All she needs is a little rest. And something to hold on to.

Gently, he lays the red rose on the pillow beside her. *I'm here, princess.*

Eleven

Kate picked up the private line on her office phone on the first ring, hoping it was Adrian. After they'd made love last night, he'd left her place with hardly a word. If it hadn't been for her crumpled sheets, she might have imagined it had all been some kind of strange but certainly torrid silent-movie dream.

It wasn't Adrian on the line. It was Marianne Spars.

"I'm very angry at you, Kate."

"Marianne, I'm sorry I didn't make it to the opening."

"You must have had a pretty good reason."

Kate hesitated, a faint smile playing on her lips. "I did."

"When do I get to find out what it is?"

Kate laughed. "When can we do lunch?"

"How about today? I have other plans, but I'm sure our lunch will be so much more fun."

Kate actually glanced at her calendar, forgetting for a flash that this was D day. Her lunchtime meeting with Windham. One night of passion and she was already getting her priorities out of whack. "I can't today. How about...?"

"I have an idea," Marianne interrupted. "How about cocktails at my place this evening and then you can join me and Maury Deitz for the benefit dinner at Century Plaza? Rose Fried was supposed to join us, but she came down with the flu."

"What benefit?"

"'Feast or Famine.'"

"Oh. That benefit."

"They're honoring one of their largest contributors to the cause." There was a small pause. "Adrian Needham."

"Yes," Kate said softly. "I know."

"Yes, dear. I thought you would."

Kate smiled. "Tell me, Marianne, does anything ever get past you?"

"Not anymore, Kate. Not anymore."

Kate was swamped with calls and meetings that morning, but she managed to get away from the studio and arrive back at her house a half hour before Charlie Windham pulled up behind the wheel of a silver Porsche. Usually the CEO of Paradine was squired around in a chauffeured Rolls. Then again, this wasn't business as usual. Kate felt a tremor go down her spine as she peeked out at the formidable ruler of Paradine through her bedroom window, watching with her breath held as he stepped out of the sports coupé.

On the surface, Charlie Windham was not a prepossessing figure. He was a small, compact man in his late sixties with thinning gray hair that he combed straight back from an overly broad forehead. He wore thick bifocals and sported an unfashionable mustache that drooped down over his top lip. Even his pin-striped suit, while custom-tailored and *très* expensive, had an old-fashioned forties look. He wasn't at all stylish or physically attractive. Kate doubted he had ever been a handsome man, nor did she think he'd ever given two hoots about his appearance. He was one of those old-time, no-nonsense movie moguls with the instincts of a born hustler who had struck it big many more times than he'd struck out. He had never run Paradine the way the baby moguls were taught in business school—balancing short-term gains and losses with long-term plans and projections. He knew, as did Kate, that to win you had to gamble. The big question was, Would Charlie Windham gamble on her?

Kate opened the door for him herself. She'd given Lucia the afternoon off, the housekeeper having prepared a couple of cold lunch plates before taking off—simple fare since Windham had a heart condition and kept to a strict nonfat, low-cholesterol diet. He'd even cut down on the stogies he used to puff on nonstop.

Inviting the CEO of Paradine into her home was a heady experience for Kate. Whatever the outcome, there was no taking away the fact that he had considered her an important enough player to pay this personal call. She showed him into her stylishly redone living room, hoping to elicit at least a flicker of approval from the great man. He appeared oblivious to his surroundings, however.

"Sit down, Kate." He motioned to her sofa.

"Would you like something . . . ?"

"Please. Sit down. This won't take long."

She sat down, her heart starting to pound so loudly in her chest she was sure Windham could hear it. She could almost feel the ax start to fall. *Oh, God, don't let me break down. If I'm on my way out, let me go with style.*

The CEO remained standing, hands clasped together in front of him. "I'll get right to the point, Kate. I'm making some changes."

She looked up at him, but her vision was clouded, and she couldn't quite bring him into focus. Not that she really wanted to. Changes. This wasn't sounding good. In a flash she saw herself packing up her office, pounding the pavement. Sure, every studio in town wanted her while she was on top, but they'd lose interest fast, once word spread that she'd gotten the old heave-ho. *Nobody wants you when you're down and out.* Hollywood's anthem. By forty, she could end up with her gorgeous Bel Air house on the market, a has-been who'd never quite had it.

Kate tried to comfort herself by remembering the passion she'd felt last night in Adrian's arms. Maybe she had her priorities all mixed-up, just as Adrian had so often told her. He hadn't told her that last night, though. He hadn't told her much of anything last night. If only he had....

"I'm moving you into Ritchie's position. As of tomorrow morning, you'll be President of the Motion Picture Division."

Had she heard right? The CEO came into sharp focus. "President?"

Windham nodded.

As the reality sank in, Kate quickly relocated her temporarily misplaced sanity. "President," she repeated, feeling almost giddy with relief.

This was it. This was what she wanted, what she'd dreamed of, what she'd busted her chops for all these years. Real recognition at last. Her shot at being a major-league player. How could she even have thought for a fleeting moment that Windham had come here to fire her? Still, she was baffled by his reason for making the appointment so...furtive.

Windham observed her closely. "I assume you're pleased."

Kate rose. "Pleased? Oh, Mr. Windham, you are a master of understatement."

"Charlie."

She grinned. *Welcome to the old-boys' network.* "Charlie."

He gave her a shrewd look. "You better sit down again, Kate."

Uh-oh. There were strings. Naturally. Her smile vanished. She sat back down.

Charlie Windham, poker-faced as always, folded his arms across his chest. "I'm a blunt man, Kate. It's no secret that I haven't been very pleased with my son-in-law's performance of late. To be kind, let's say his management of the feature-film division has been ineffectual at best. He tries too hard. He's become too cautious. He's lost whatever killer instincts he once had. Then there's that nasty business with Ritchie. Luckily, I've squelched that lawsuit, but it cost me a pretty penny. Which my son-in-law is going to have to pay for."

He gave her a conspiratorial look. "Between you and me, my plan is to phase Doug out of the loop. Ostensibly, he'll still be the studio chief, but I'm going to limit his...shall we say, freedom of choice. Doug will take on carefully delineated administrative responsibilities and he'll take a more active hand in our overseas interests. Obviously, I can't get rid of him, so I'll give him more money, more stocks, a bigger office, but I can't have him running the show any longer or he'll run Paradine into the ground. I need people like you, Kate, to bring the guts and the glory back to Paradine.''

No hint of her feelings showed on her face, but inwardly Kate was caught between mind-blowing elation at her own good fortune and sympathy for Doug, who would inevitably feel humiliated by being relegated to the role of figurehead. On the other hand, maybe it would be a relief to him not to have to constantly carry around the weight of so many make-or-break decisions. Regardless of how Doug took the news of his change of status, she couldn't let his situation cast a shadow on her happiness. Besides, Windham's—Charlie's—assessment of Doug was, unfortunately, right on the mark. Sad as it was, Doug Garrison had become a relic. He was out of step; out of touch with the times. It happened to the best of them. It could happen to her. Not yet, though. Not by a long shot. She was just getting into her stride. And maybe she'd be one of that rare breed who pulled it off, made it all the way to the top....

"We'll move ahead in stages," Windham went on. "Let you test the waters. And let me test you."

If Doug wasn't going to be making the decisions, that meant she could go straight to Charlie Windham for a green light on *Mortal Sin*. Would he trust her with what would be the studio's biggest-budget picture to date? Talk about a test!

"I understand," Kate said solemnly, trying to decide whether this was the time to make her pitch.

"You don't understand yet," Windham countered, "but you will. I'm giving you the authority to personally greenlight anywhere from two to three projects over the next year, depending on the size of your budgets. We're talking in the ballpark of fifty mil at your disposal. It'll be your call." He paused for effect. "Also your ass on the line."

It took a few moments for the full impact of Windham's words to sink in. He was giving her direct authority. Full decision-making power. No groveling at Doug's feet or his to get what she wanted. This was incredible; absolute financial and creative control. Now it came down to the proverbial crapshoot. Was she going to play it safe—make two or three moderate budget flicks and bring in some nice, solid

figures—or let everything she had ride on a single roll of the
dice? Like Charlie said, it was her ass on the line.

"You don't have to decide this instant. Think about it,"
he suggested.

She knew there was nothing to think about. "Make it one
project. One big-budget project—A list all the way."

The shrewd CEO raised his eyebrows. "The Lerner
script?"

"Doug told you?"

Windham didn't answer her question. Instead, he asked,
"Thirty mil on *Mortal Sin?*" They both knew this was a
high-risk venture, to say the least.

"Forty," Kate said, not missing a beat.

Windham smiled for the first time. That smile would re-
main indelibly imprinted on Kate's mind.

He stretched a gray pin-striped arm in her direction. Kate
rose for the second time and clasped his hand. She couldn't
believe it. Forty million dollars and Charlie Windham,
without blinking an eye, was willing to shake on it.

The CEO's grip was firm. "I don't subscribe to the one-
hit-makes-you-a-genius philosophy."

"How many hits will I need, then?" was Kate's quick
comeback, her own grip equally solid.

"You know the old adage—you're only as good as your
last picture. If *Mortal Sin* falls short of your expectations..."

"It won't, Charlie." She simply wouldn't accept any other
possibility.

The CEO didn't stay for lunch. Their business was settled in under ten minutes and he was out the door, mission
accomplished. Kate walked into the kitchen in a daze,
picked up her plate of salad and grilled chicken, then put it
back on the counter untouched. She couldn't eat a thing.
She was flying.

That evening Kate was seated to the right of Marianne
Spars at a round banquet table with eight other Hollywood
dignitaries in a banquet hall at the Century Plaza. Marianne's date, Maury Deitz, an international financier whose
hobby was investing in vintage airplanes, was sitting on

Marianne's left, chatting with Ken Bragman, celebrated biographer of the stars and mountaineer extraordinaire. At least eight hundred guests—film people, society types, politicians, even L.A.'s new chief of police—were seated at a hundred other round tables crowded into the space. A large rectangular dais at the front of the room was reserved for the founders and special honored guests of the Feast or Famine charity. Adrian Needham held the seat of honor.

The hum of conversation in the room blended with African music resonating from the speaker system.

"You haven't touched your food," Marianne Spars murmured to Kate.

"I'm not particularly hungry," Kate replied, staring absently at the five-hundred-dollar-a-plate dinner of rice and beans, a side of seaweed and a soft drink courtesy of the company that was opening up plants in a number of Third World countries. Given the nature of the function—a benefit affair to raise money for starving people as well as to honor Adrian Needham as a major contributor to the cause—the dinner was a back-to-basics, dress-down affair. Kate was wearing a simple gray linen blazer over a black silk shirt and slim black-and-gray pin-striped slacks. The outrageously attractive six-foot-tall, fifty-three-year-old Marianne had chosen a striking silk-and-linen blend African floral-print tunic over bright lime Lycra stretch pants.

Kate's eyes strayed from her dinner plate over to the man of the hour seated at the head table about twenty yards away. He was chatting with Leonore Remington, founder of the Feast or Famine organization.

Kate looked away, feeling vexed. Other than a brief greeting earlier in the evening, she and Adrian hadn't exchanged so much as a glance. He seemed to be deliberately avoiding her. Was he annoyed that she'd shown up at the banquet? Did he think she was trying to crowd him?

Kate was sorry now that she'd come tonight. This should have been her night to celebrate. She had just been promoted to the job of her dreams. As of tomorrow morning she was president of the motion-picture division of Paradine studios. Better still, she was being given free rein from the head man himself—and more than enough rope to hang

herself—to make *Mortal Sin* with a forty-million-dollar
budget. First thing tomorrow, she'd phone Lerner's agent,
Artie Matthews, and give him the news. Artie would positively flip out. She was sure the agent never dreamed she
could actually pull this off with a major budget. Naturally
he'd try to worm the million for Lerner out of her that she
herself had offered, but Kate figured she could talk him
down to seven hundred and fifty thousand. Now the next
step was securing the director.

Again Kate's eyes shifted in Adrian's direction. Had he
even read the script? Was she going to have to chase him for
an answer? At this point she was desperate enough to let him
have the satisfaction of seeing her sweat a little. As long as
he came around in the end.

If worse came to worst, she told herself, she could go with
Dan Mills. She frowned. The outcome of this film in the
marketplace could literally make or break her. Hollywood
would forgive all nature of crimes and misdemeanors per-
petrated by their own, but one thing they never forgave was
failure—especially one of the magnitude she was taking on.
Charlie had been quick to remind her of that. To turn *Mortal Sin* into a box-office coup, Kate had to have the best.
And there was no getting away from it—Adrian Needham
was the best. She needed him in more ways than she was
willing to admit.

"Adrian does look delicious," Marianne murmured,
following Kate's gaze. "Too bad he's not on the menu. Or
is he?"

Kate shot her friend a disapproving look, then checked
around the table to make sure no one had overheard Marianne's remark. Fortunately, they were all engaged in their
own conversations.

Marianne gave Kate a little nudge a minute later. "My,
my, did you realize Douglas Garrison and his lovely wife,
Julia, were here?" Marianne smiled impishly. Kate had
confided in Marianne earlier that evening about her extraordinary luncheon meeting with Charlie Windham.
Marianne was thrilled for her, but she had cautioned Kate
not to expect many other honest well-wishers. Topping her

list of those who would be out for blood was Douglas Garrison.

Kate surreptitiously glanced Doug's way. Surely Charlie had to have told him about her promotion by now. Had Charlie also informed him that he'd given her the okay to drop forty mil on *Mortal Sin?* If Doug knew that, he'd also be quick enough to surmise that his father-in-law had already begun edging him out of the loop. Just as she was being let in. If appearances were the yardstick, the studio chief either didn't know what was up yet, or was putting on a good show of concealing his upset. He seemed perfectly at ease and in high spirits as he chatted animatedly with Flo Ingram, a rich, young socialite and ex-senator's wife, whose name was associated with all the "in" charitable organizations.

"Are you finished with your dinner?" a pretty young waitress asked Kate, who nodded distractedly. The dinner plate was replaced with a gelatinous crimson dessert with white flecks in it. Neither Kate nor any of the others at her table gave the concoction a try.

Adrian was given his award by the charity's founder after the dessert dishes were cleared away. He stepped over to the podium reluctantly to receive his plaque. Kate couldn't help but think that he looked very dashing in his English tweed jacket over black jeans and a black T-shirt, his bare feet encased in scruffy maroon loafers. He gave the embossed mahogany wood plaque a brief scan, smiled awkwardly, and looked out at the audience. He caught Kate's eye for a brief moment as he played the room.

"Giving is relatively easy when you've got plenty to give, so I really don't feel that I've done anything extraordinary here," he said modestly. "It's only when the giving's hard, when it hurts, when it really means sacrifice that the giver deserves the spotlight. To have very little and to risk it all for something beyond yourself—that's what true giving is all about in my book."

He smiled sheepishly, which only heightened his irresistible appeal. "Still," he added—cut to rogue charmer—"I'll find a place of honor for this fine plaque as soon as I get back home to London tomorrow night."

It was at that moment that Adrian's eyes met Kate's again. Nothing on her face revealed even a hint of her disappointment, anger or hurt at his final words. She wouldn't give him the satisfaction. Inwardly—that was another story altogether. His announcement that he was, indeed, leaving L.A. tomorrow as planned, tossed her about in its undertow, pulling her down, making it hard for her to catch her breath. Had he even planned on calling her tomorrow before he took off? Was he even going to personally turn her offer down to direct *Mortal Sin?* Was he going to leave without a mention of what had happened between them last night?

Ta, love. Thanks for the roll in the hay. See you around.

The whole picture was coming into sharper focus now. She'd been had. Adrian hadn't made love to her last night, he'd gotten even with her. What an idiot she'd been to let herself be ruled by her hormones even for a few brief hours. A worse idiot still to imagine that there had been more than lust involved; to allow herself the fantasy that they could have it all again. Maybe even do it right this time.

Last night hadn't been a beginning at all. It had been an end. Now Adrian could blithely go off, having had the last laugh. She hated him. He was no different from all the others—as vain, vindictive, cruel, callous as the rest of them. What was so devastating was that she'd let herself be duped into believing Adrian Needham was the one man who was above all that. Now she knew that when it came to the opposite sex, there were no exceptions. A lesson learned the hard way, but one she wouldn't forget.

She retrieved her purse and started to rise as soon as the brief speeches by some of the others at the dais were concluded. Marianne took hold of her hand.

"Aren't you going to stay for the dancing?"

"I'm not in a dancing mood," Kate muttered.

Marianne gave her a sympathetic look. "Don't let anyone rain on your parade, darling. Not a one of them is worth it."

Kate thoroughly agreed, but nonetheless she felt like she was being deluged by a thunderstorm. All she could think about was running for cover. Making a quick getaway from the room, however, was impossible. Waves, nods and brief stops at selected tables along the way were necessary, or else suspicions would be raised and rumors would start flying.

Once she made it out to the lobby, Kate thought she was home free. Until she felt a hand clamp down on her shoulder halfway to the hotel exit. She turned, expecting—okay, hoping—to see Adrian. So much for having learned her lesson. Were there some lessons you simply never got down?

She swallowed her disappointment when she saw it was Doug.

"Leaving so soon?" The studio chief made no attempt to camouflage the edge in his voice as he fixed his gaze on her.

Kate had difficulty meeting his eyes. So, he did know something was up. How much, though? "Yes. I'm tired."

"You still haven't given me your answer about Tahoe." He spoke in measured tones, like a man fighting for control of each word.

Kate looked around nervously. They had always been very discreet about their personal relationship. "Do you really think this is the place . . . ?"

She started to walk away, but he caught hold of her arm. "Tell me, Kate. When is a good time to stab a friend, a lover, a mentor, in the back?"

It wasn't even his words that took her aback, it was the undercurrent of fury behind them. "You know I deserved that promotion, Doug. I assumed you'd been the one who'd encouraged Charlie. . . ."

He smiled slyly. "So it's Charlie now. How cozy."

"Let's not get into this now. We'll both end up saying things we'll be sorry for later. Besides, there are a lot of people around. Including your wife."

One of the rules Douglas Garrison had always played by was never to cause Julia any public embarrassment because of his extracurricular activities. Tonight, however, he seemed bent on disregarding that rule. He stood his ground, his face masklike for a moment before disgust swept over his features. "I know what you think, baby. You think I'm done for. You think you've got it made."

Kate kept looking nervously around. It was obvious Doug was itching to make a scene, which would put them both in jeopardy. He was being completely irrational.

"Doug...please."

He wagged a finger at her like a principal scolding an errant schoolgirl. "You have never needed me more on your side, baby, than you do now." He slurred his words, indicating to Kate that he'd had more than his usual two martinis. No wonder he was behaving this way. He was obviously drunk.

"We're on the same side, Doug. We always have been," Kate said placatingly. "I've got to go now. Look, we'll—"

"You don't know Charlie like I do. You think he's handed you the world on a fourteen-karat gold platter, but one or two slips and he'll smash that platter right over your beautiful head."

"Doug, this isn't the time...."

"You need help, Kate. Without me on your side, you could fall flat on your face. You could get yourself in a mess of trouble."

She gave him a sharp look. "Are you threatening me?"

"I'm the man who made you what you are today, baby. And I can make you what you'll be tomorrow. Don't ever forget that, Kate."

He leaned toward her to kiss her, but she turned away before his lips landed. He swayed, but managed to right himself.

"This is beneath you, Doug. We'll talk tomorrow when you're...thinking more clearly."

Doug smiled contemptuously. "Right. Have your secretary call my secretary. Or am I supposed to have my secretary call your secretary now?"

"Really, Doug..."

"You've got a lot to learn, Kate. You think I've taught you all I know, but you're wrong. I've got plenty more lessons in store for you." The malice in his voice was palpable.

Kate was far more angry than frightened. "Good night, Doug," she said firmly.

Doug grabbed her arm, stopping her retreat. "I'll book our flight for Tahoe. Our usual suite at Caesar's? No. Something more lavish. After all, it's a celebration, isn't it, Madam President?" He released her with a taunting smile.

Kate decided this was no time to tell Doug that she wasn't going to Tahoe with him this weekend or any other weekend. If only she'd broken it off with him before her meeting with Charlie. Now he was bound to misinterpret her motives for ending the affair.

Well, she decided, that couldn't be helped. If Doug couldn't see that she'd merely been going through the motions for years now, there was nothing she could do about it. Besides, he didn't have such a big beef. Even if he was out of the loop at Paradine, he'd still garner all the pomp and circumstance as the studio chief. And as long as he stayed married to Julia, he had guaranteed job security. Which was more than she had.

The next evening, Adrian queued up at the end of a huge line in front of the British Airways check-in counter at LAX. He was wearing the same outfit he'd had on the previous night at the benefit, his few other possessions tucked away in a battered brown leather overnighter at his side. Besides the plaque, the only other item he had on him that he hadn't brought from London was the script of *Mortal Sin*, which was tucked under his arm in a Manila envelope addressed to Kate Paley. Attached to the cover page was a brief note: "Great script. I'm sure it will be a hit. Sorry I can't take it on. Best of luck. Adrian."

He edged up in the line, taking hold of the Manila envelope and staring at it. He still hadn't sealed it. The note he'd written—the last of about a dozen—troubled him. It was a crummy response—not just to the script but to Kate. He was so damn conflicted about her. His little visit to her place last night hadn't settled anything for him. What a bloody idiot to think that was the way to get her out of his system. All he'd succeeded in doing was wedging her solidly inside him now. His only hope was that once he was back in London, he'd figure a way to pry her out.

He slipped the script from the envelope, scanning the note and frowning. He should at least have congratulated her. The word of her promotion had spread like wildfire that day. He'd lost count of the calls to his hotel room, everyone wanting to be the first to give him the news.

Lucky Katie. The power, the money, the glory, at last. Everything she'd always wanted. Hell, she didn't need his congratulations. Besides, she'd see right through them. She knew better than anyone how he felt about life at the top in Hollywood. The ultimate sellout. Danté's hell revisited.

Oh, Katie, what's going to become of you?

The haggard young woman with her toddler in tow nudged him in the small of his back. "Could you please move up?"

"Sorry." He started to step forward and then, muttering to himself, slipped out of the line altogether.

After pacing the terminal for twenty minutes, giving himself silent lectures, even rejoining the end of the line at the British Airways counter twice, and twice stepping back out, Adrian ended up at a phone booth dialing Kate's number.

When the call came in, Kate was stretched out, face-down, on a masseur's table at her health club, her masseur having one hell of a time loosening the knots coiling down her spine. He paused to hand over her portable phone.

"Kate Paley," she said wearily.

"Carte blanche" were Adrian's first words.

Kate rolled over onto her back, the knots in her muscles giving way like magic. "Yes."

"It's going to be hell working together. Very likely worse than *Deadline,* you being such a bloody big shot now."

She felt so giddy, a schoolgirl laugh escaped. "We lived through it once. Some things get better over time. Or so I've heard."

There was a long pause. Neither of them knew what to say next.

"That's it, then," Adrian said.

"Seems that way."

They both clicked off at the same time. They were both smiling. And both wondering how long their smiles would last.

Twelve

During her first three days in detox at the Westwood Drug Treatment Center, Sylver refused to speak to anyone. She spent her days pacing up and down the halls; her nights twitching, sweating and cursing as she suffered through withdrawal. Riley showed up each day, but she seemed to hardly notice him most of the time. The few instances when she did register his presence, she glared at him as though her misery was all his fault.

She did blame him. He was the one who'd talked her into voluntarily signing herself into the detox program. She must have been out of her mind. She *was* out of her mind. What woman in her right mind tries to commit suicide?

No. No, she was getting confused again. She hadn't tried to off herself. That wasn't the way it had happened. It was an accident. She'd explained that to Riley back at the hospital. Only he hadn't looked convinced. She knew what he thought. He thought that deep down she wanted to die. He thought she hated herself, hated her life, hated what she'd become, hated her inability to do anything about it. And she hated Riley for being right. Hating him was a welcome breather from hating herself.

On her fourth day in the program, Sylver was moved into a double room. Her roommate, Jill, a free-lance photographer in her mid-thirties, bone thin with short, curly hair, had been hooked on amphetamines for nearly ten years. This was her third shot at trying to clean up her act and she was feeling very upbeat about her latest "cure." Jill's cheery, effervescent manner only added to Sylver's agitation. Why couldn't everyone just leave her alone? On top of being stuck with a bouncy roommate, Sam Hibbs, the director of the treatment program, had informed her that morning that she was going to be starting group therapy the next day. The very thought of sitting around with a bunch of druggies crying and whining about their lives made Sylver cringe.

The thing to do was bolt. She wasn't a prisoner here. Hibbs had told her himself that she was free to go. So, what was she waiting for? She stood at the open door to her room. Her roommate was in a session with her shrink, so she wouldn't even know she'd left. All she had to do was walk herself right down the brightly painted yellow corridor, turn right at the beach-scene mural painted by a grateful ex-cocaine artist, and head straight out the door to freedom.

Freedom. Freedom meant taking up residence again in her scuzzy three-room apartment in West Hollywood. Freedom meant getting back together with Nash. Freedom meant coping with her domineering mother. Freedom meant that never-ending search for numbness. Freedom was nowhere.

Being in rehab was hell, but it was somewhere. Sylver retreated back to her small but tidy—regulations—twin-bedded room. Soft flowery wallpaper and matching curtains and bedspreads gave the space a warm, sunny look. The tangerine-colored wall-to-wall carpet enhanced the brightness. There were two matching desks on either side of the room, two bureaus and one shared closet. The space reminded Sylver of a moderately priced motel room except that there was no TV. Jill had told her they weren't allowed in the rooms because the druggies tended to "spaz out" on TV, given half the chance. There was one television in the lounge at the end of the hall, but times for watching were scheduled. More regulations.

Sylver walked over to the mirror above her bureau. With her three days in the hospital and her four days here, she'd been stone-cold sober for a whole week. She frowned in disgust at her reflection, her golden hair falling limply down around her pale, drawn face. Her eyes were bloodshot and she had a twitch at the right corner of her mouth.

She stepped back and smiled cynically at her woebegone reflection. "And this year's winner of the Most Washed-out

Druggie of the Year goes to—envelope please, Don—well, I'm not surprised, folks. The winner is the *Glory Girl* herself, the one and only—thank God—Sylver Cassidy.''

She jumped as she heard a soft round of applause at the door, turning scarlet as she saw Riley Quinn standing there. Embarrassment and something else—something she wasn't ready to define—made her scowl at him.

"Go away," she snapped.

Riley crossed his arms over his chest. "At least you're talking to me, now."

She scowled. "No, I'm not."

"Come on. Let's go for a walk."

She was thrown by his suggestion. "A walk? Where?"

"There's a park across the street. It's a bright, sunny day...."

She shook her head vehemently. Only a couple of minutes ago she was feeling like the walls of this place were closing in on her and all she wanted to do was escape. Now, suddenly, the idea of leaving, even for a little stroll in the park, terrified her. Inside she was safe. This was her haven, even though, in the same breath, it was her hell.

Riley understood. "Okay, let's walk down to the lounge."

She didn't move. She just kept staring at him. "Does anyone know I'm here?"

"I sent a note to your mother that you'd voluntarily committed yourself to a rehab program, but I didn't say which one. Or even which state. I only did it because I thought she might report you to the police as a missing person."

"Anyone...else?" she asked guardedly.

He gave her a long, steady scrutiny, much to her discomfort. She turned away from him, unable to bear it any longer. "I'm not in love with Nash Walker, if that's what you're thinking. How can you love someone when you don't love yourself? It's only that I wouldn't want him to...worry about me. For all his faults, he—"

"Cut the acting crap, Sylver. Turn around and talk to me. Real talk. Do you even know what real talk is?"

She spun around. "How dare you?"

"No, no, no. That's just a line. A tired one, at that."

Her whole body started to twitch. She felt like an infestation of hornets had taken up residence inside her. Her skin was stinging everywhere. Her hair felt like it was weighing down on her. Her hands flew up to her face. "Stop it, stop it, stop it, stop...."

She could feel herself crumbling to the ground, but then Riley was grabbing her, keeping her up, holding her against his warm, solid body. Riley to the rescue one more time. She let him hold her, ironically finding his itchy beat-up red wool crew-neck sweater soothing to her skin. She liked his smell—sweat, laundry detergent, soap. No macho after-shave lotions or fancy men's colognes. Riley smelled real.

"My hair," she muttered, pushing strands away from her face. "My hair is driving me crazy."

"I can brush it for you."

"No. Cut it. Cut it off for me."

Riley edged back and looked down at her to see if she was serious.

"Please, Riley. I hate my hair."

"I could take you to a beauty parlor."

She shook her head.

"A barber?"

"No. I want you to do it."

"Maybe you'd better think about it for a couple of days."

"Damn it, just get me scissors and I'll do it myself. They won't give us scissors. We can't be trusted."

Riley sighed. "Okay, I'll do it."

Two minutes later he was back with scissors. Sylver was standing in front of the mirror above her bureau as Riley came up behind her.

"How much do you want me to take off?" he asked nervously. He'd never cut anyone's hair in his life.

"Cut it all off," she said firmly.

Riley hesitated.

She smiled at his reflection. "I trust you."

"You say that now." Sucking in a deep breath, he grabbed a hunk of Sylver's hair and snipped it off right at the nape of her neck, his eyes anxiously studying her expression. She was still smiling. He exhaled deeply, grabbed another hunk.

"Is Nash at the apartment?" she asked quietly.

Nash Walker was not Riley's favorite topic of discussion. Then again, at least Sylver was talking. If he started deciding what was okay and not okay for her to talk about—or who—she might clam up again.

"He's in and out." He hesitated. "If he doesn't come up with the rent money in five days, he's out permanently."

Sylver frowned. "He'll never come up with the money."

"How do *you* come up with it?" he asked quietly, snipping off another hank of hair at the back of her head.

Sylver didn't answer.

"Sorry," Riley said softly. "It's none of my business."

"I made a movie about a year ago. Nothing that I'd win an Oscar for. It has paid the rent for a while." She felt her face heat up, her eyes start to sting. Her lips compressed.

Nice going, Riley. You really know how to boost a gal's spirits.

He smiled gently. "We do what we have to do," he murmured, working his scissors around to the right side of her face. He kept his eyes on the particular hank of hair he was cutting, not relishing the moment when he'd have to look at the inevitable disaster his hacking away had wrought.

"And I have this one...friend," Sylver faltered, "who helps me out."

"A friend?" *That's it, Riley. Don't just stick your foot in your mouth, swallow it!*

Sylver looked at him in the mirror. "It's not what you think, Riley. Her name's Kate Paley. She's a big shot at Paradine Studios. She was the one that got me my start in movies. Did you know I was once a movie star?"

"Yeah. I know."

Sylver was pleased that he sounded less than impressed. The adulation, envy, and star treatment had never sat well with her. "Anyway, Kate was working at Paradine and she brought me to meet Douglas Garrison and somehow managed to convince him to give me a small part in this comedy he was making. And the rest is...history." She smiled wanly.

Riley was cutting the last hank of her hair, leaving a sea of golden strands gathered at their feet. Now that the haircut was done he was afraid to check out Sylver's reaction, certain that she'd be horrified at having been practically scalped. Instead, he heard her laugh.

"Riley, you're a genius. I love it."

He looked at her in the mirror, aghast. She looked like a refugee from a prison camp; as if her hair had been hacked off with a dull saw. Her laughter convinced him that she was further off the edge than he'd thought.

She spun around and impulsively hugged him. Then she ran her fingers through her now very short, spiky hair, shaking her head vigorously, the smile of pleasure still on her face.

To his surprise, Riley found himself reassessing his opinion of his handiwork. Her hair really didn't look all that bad. The new "do" gave Sylver a kind of winsome, gamine look. Made those incredible aquamarine eyes of hers look like giant beacons. Those eyes were fixed on him now, drawing him in.

Riley was rattled as he stared at her. With her hair chopped off, the long, graceful line of her neck was accentuated. She was wearing a detox-issued cherry red T-shirt and he noticed not only how much the bright color contrasted with her ivory skin, but how the material pulled slightly at her breasts. He flashed on that day he'd found her naked in her bedroom, ashamed then as now at finding himself aroused by her. And not merely sexually aroused. He felt a sharp tug in his chest as he backed away. She was really getting to him. He was starting to feel *responsible* for her. He'd never done well with responsibility. He was afraid if she got too reliant on him, he'd end up disappointing her badly.

Or was it the other way around? Was he scared because he was getting too reliant on her?

He crossed his arms over his chest, rubbing his shoulders like he'd caught a chill. The opposite was true. He was burning up. "So, tell me more about your friend. What was her name again?"

She tilted her head back, picking up on Riley's discomfort, but not understanding it. *Who are you, Riley Quinn? What makes you tick?*

"Kate. Her name is Kate Paley."

"Would you...like her to know...you're here?" Riley asked. "She could...come and visit you." He tapped the closed scissors nervously in the palm of his hand.

Sylver stared at Riley, but she wasn't seeing him now. She was seeing into her past. Feelings and realizations she'd been assiduously avoiding for years through booze and dope suddenly began crashing down on her like she'd stepped right under an avalanche. Tears glinted in her eyes.

Riley set the scissors down on the bureau, walked over to her and placed his hands lightly on her shoulders. "What is it, Sylver? It's not your hair?"

She shook her head, trying to fight back the tears, but she had no luck. "I lied, Riley. Kate's not my friend. Not... anymore. I just like to...pretend she is. She always gives me a generous handout whenever I ask, but I know she doesn't do it because she cares about me. She just feels sorry for me. And maybe...a little guilty. Not that she has any real reason to feel guilty, because...because what happened wasn't her doing. I had no right to expect Kate to save me...."

Riley's memory was suddenly jogged. He'd thought the name Kate Paley rang a bell. Now he knew why. That heated conversation in Sylver's apartment between her mother and Nash the day he'd come back from having admitted Sylver to the hospital. The incensed woman's words—"The next morning Sylver panicked, was all. She just let it get blown out of proportion. Thanks to you. And Kate Paley, too. I was the only voice of reason."

Riley's eyes fell on Sylver. He started fitting the pieces together like the detective he'd once been. *The next morning Sylver panicked.* The morning after she was raped. *She just let it get blown out of proportion. Thanks to you. And Kate Paley, too.* Sylver must have told Nash Walker and Kate Paley what had happened. So Kate and Nash knew Sylver had been raped. And very likely by whom. They must have been as upset and distraught as Sylver was. Had they wanted her to press charges against Nick Kramer? What was it Kate felt guilty about? Not being able to convince Sylver to take action? Sylver's mother had clearly wanted to sweep the incident under the rug, turn it into some innocuous "fling." Riley had no difficulty figuring out why. Sylver's mother wouldn't want the publicity, the scandal that would ensue, the risk to her daughter's reputation. Riley knew one thing. Sylver had never pressed the rape charge, or he would have picked it up on Nick Kramer's record when he was investigating him for the murder of that hooker.

Sylver, lost in her own thoughts, walked shakily across the room and sank down onto her bed, dropping her head into her hands. "When I was a kid I could tell Kate anything. I could always trust her. I don't know what happened. I just thought... she'd always be there for me. I don't know why she pulled away. I don't know if it was something I did. Was it my fault? All I know is things changed between us. I lost her...." Her sentence trailed off.

Sylver felt suddenly drained; the adrenaline lift she'd gotten thanks to the haircut was short-lived. So much for that brief happy-go-loopy feeling, replaced now by feelings that were far more grim and weighty. She felt scared, alone, disconnected. There was no place she felt that she belonged. She was an outcast. She had always been an outcast.

Riley came over and sat down beside her on the bed. He took her hand in his. It was cold and clammy. "What can I do for you, Sylver?"

She swallowed hard. Her lips parted, but no sound came out at first. "I...don't...know. I guess...you could...just drop Kate...a note." She turned to him, her expression so desperate it hurt to look at her. "Only make sure she knows I don't want money—that I'm not asking for any money at all—just that... I thought maybe she'd... I don't know... maybe she'd send me a...a get-well card. Something goofy. Something that would make me laugh. Kate always used to send me funny cards on my birthdays—never any of those syrupy ones everyone else always sent."

Sylver was thinking in particular about the birthday card that used to arrive each year in a red envelope, the front of every card picturing red roses, and inside, some sappy, flowery message. Each one was signed the same. "From your everlasting fan." Those cards and the gifts from her anonymous fan—always something red, often a red rose—

had lasted until she'd dropped out of the world after her eighteenth birthday. Then just a few weeks ago, the red roses had started arriving at her West Hollywood apartment. At first they'd perked her up a bit. Nice to know she still had one fan out there who'd tracked her down and still cared. Only now she wasn't so sure. It had spooked her, finding that rose on her pillow that first morning she woke up in the hospital last week. How had it gotten there? Was it from her fan? Had he asked a nurse to deliver it to her room? Or had he been there, himself, in her hospital room, watching her as she slept, maybe even touching her? Was he some pathetic, star-struck, innocuous fan or was he one of those obsessed stalkers drawn to celebrities? Was he dangerous...?

"Sylver? You're off somewhere. Tell me where you are," Riley prodded softly.

His voice startled her. She'd forgotten he was even there. She smiled crookedly. "This detox crap isn't the belly laughs you made it out to be, Riley."

He ruffled her mangled hair. "You don't know it, but you're making a lot of progress."

"I'm glad one of us thinks so."

Later that afternoon, Riley bluffed his way through the gate at Paradine and all the way into the outer office of the president of the motion-picture division, Kate Paley.

Kate's secretary, Eileen, whom Kate had brought with her when she got bumped upstairs, gave Riley a disdainful glance. "I'm sorry," she said archly, "but Ms. Paley can't see anyone without an appointment."

When Riley burst into Kate's office only seconds after her secretary's frantic buzz, the new president was ensconced behind a red-lacquered Victorian desk in the vast, new office that she had managed to put her stamp on in less than a week with the help of her overjoyed decorator, Jarrett Craft.

Riley was unimpressed by the lavish space with its Picasso etchings on the wall, posh antique furnishings and pricey Oriental rug on the floor.

Kate didn't bat an eyelash as she pressed the button on her intercom. "Get security up here immediately, Eileen." Her voice was clipped, giving no sign of any fear or concern. Inside, however, her stomach was churning. Who was this madman? Some irate filmmaker? A desperate actor? A wacko screenwriter?

"I'm Detective Riley Quinn with the L.A.P.D. I'm here about Sylver Cassidy."

Kate went white.

Riley stepped farther into her office. "I think you ought to call off your dogs."

Kate clutched her hands together. "Sylver? Is she . . . all right?"

Riley did a quick reassessment of the motion-picture executive. Sylver was wrong. Kate Paley did care. Her concern was no act, Riley was sure of it. He felt a wave of relief. This would make things easier.

"That depends on your definition of 'all right,'" he answered.

"Then she's not . . . dead." Kate could hardly get the word out.

"She's not dead," Riley confirmed, deciding not to waste time telling her how close Sylver had actually come to dying.

"Is she in jail? Does she need bail money?" Kate was already opening her desk drawer, reaching for her checkbook.

"She's not looking for a handout."

Kate flushed. "I just . . . I thought . . ."

"I'd like to take you to see her," Riley said quietly.

Kate gave him a puzzled look. "When?"

He smiled. "Right now."

Her door burst open and two large, beefy men in security-guard uniforms rushed into the office. They were just about to strong-arm Riley when Kate waved them off. "I'm sorry. It's okay. You can go."

The two security guards eyed Kate quizzically, then Riley, then Kate again. "You sure?" one of them asked.

Kate nodded. She wasn't about to tell them that this man who had burst into her office was a policeman. Rumors of

every variety would instantly start circulating. She waited for
the guards to exit.

"Look, I can't just leave work in the middle of the day.
I'm booked solid here till six and then I've got a meeting
across town...."

"You're a very busy and important executive, Kate. I can
certainly see that. But you impress me as a woman who's
never too busy for a friend in need."

Kate narrowed her gaze on her intruder. Something was
off about him. He didn't act like your standard-issue police
detective. Not that she'd ever actually met one before, but
she'd certainly seen enough movies....

"I'd like to see some identification, Detective." Now she
was sorry she'd so impetuously dismissed those guards. And
more than a little scared.

He smiled pleasantly, slipping his hand inside his gray
blazer like he was reaching for his ID. Only it wasn't his
badge that he pulled out. It was a gun.

Kate went from white to gray. For a moment, she thought
she might pass out. So did Riley.

"I'm not going to hurt you, Kate. I just want to impress
upon you how important it is that you reschedule a couple
of meetings and come with me now to see Sylver. Because I
know how it is with busy people. You'll want to find the
time, but you won't be able to. Something will always come
up."

Kate forced herself to stay calm. "How do I know you're
going to take me to see her? Where is she, anyway?"

"She's at the Westwood Drug Treatment Center. The
number's 555-3682. Go ahead. Call now. Ask if there's a
Sylvie Quinn registered there."

"Sylvie Quinn?"

Riley smiled. "I thought it best that the tabloids didn't get
wind of Sylver's...present circumstances. Not that she's big
news anymore, but my guess is she'd still sell copy."

Ten minutes later, Riley opened the passenger door of his
car for Kate. When she hesitated, he nudged her with the
gun, which was concealed inside his jacket pocket. Kate got
in. Once she was settled—or more to the point, unsettled—

in Riley's car and he'd pulled out of the visitors' space, he tossed the gun onto her lap.

"Just so you know it isn't loaded."

Sylver thought she must be dreaming when she saw Kate Paley walk into her room at the detox center that afternoon.

Kate thought she must have entered a nightmare when she saw Sylver. She looked like a Holocaust victim. And her hair—what had they done to her beautiful hair? Kate's hand instinctively sprang up to her mouth. "Oh, my God..."

Sylver rose from her desk chair, so ecstatic to realize her friend really was there that she didn't register the shock and horror on the woman's face. "Kate. It really is you. But how...?" She broke into a wide smile. "Riley told you, didn't he?"

Kate nodded dumbly. She remained speechless.

"And you came here to see me? I was just... hoping for a card. Remember those funny cards? I was telling Riley about how you'd always send... Oh, what am I babbling about? I'm so surprised to see you. I'm so... pleased. Except for Riley, well, there hasn't been anyone.... Not that I wanted anyone to come.... I mean... I don't mean you, Kate. I'm really glad to see you. Would you like to sit down? Jill's out for the afternoon so I've got the room all to myself. Or, we can go out if you want to. We have to sign this paper—regulations. God, we're practically drowned in regulations here. Not that it's bad. Well, sometimes it is. I start group therapy tomorrow. They say it really helps. But I'm better already. I'm really making progress. Riley says so, and Riley must know."

Kate kept staring in anguish at Sylver, watching her wring her hands as she ran off at the mouth like a runaway freight train.

"I really am glad to see you. It's been so long. How long has it been? God, about the money, Kate. I want you to know I intend to pay back every penny. Really. Every last cent."

"It's okay, Sylver," Kate said softly, finding her voice at last.

"No, no, I don't want you to think—" Sylver stopped, chewing on her bottom lip, her hand going nervously to her hair. "The way you're staring at me, Kate... It's my hair, isn't it?" She gave a forced laugh. "Riley did it."

Kate was aghast. The man really was crazy.

"No, I asked him to. God, I had to beg him. I hated my hair. I kind of got it into my head that my hair was...alive. Strangling me. It was like...there was so much of it. It'll grow back, though." She clutched the back of her chair, closing her eyes. "I'm such a mess. You're probably sorry you came."

Kate was sorry, all right, but not that she'd come. All of the regrets she'd been fighting and denying all these years, filled her now almost to the breaking point. If she had done things differently... If she had protected Sylver more, put her interests first, would Sylver be here now?

Kate thought about Riley Quinn, the man who had brought her here at gunpoint, waiting out in the hall—keeping guard to make sure she not only went in to see Sylver, but spent some quality time with her. Riley may have been the reason she'd come, but she knew that wild horses couldn't pull her away, now that she was here.

As Kate crossed the room and enfolded Sylver in her arms, she felt something come alive inside her that had been in a deep freeze for a long, long time. She felt the thumping, pumping, tumbling beat of her heart. It felt good. She felt good. And grateful to a perfect stranger who'd helped her reconnect with her soul.

When Riley walked by Sylver's room, he saw the two women holding on to each other, both of them crying softly. He stood there for a moment watching them, smiling, tears spilling down his cheeks, too. A mild tremor spread through him. It was at that moment that he knew, if he wasn't very, very careful, he could end up falling in love with Sylver Cassidy. And that was the last thing either of them needed.

Someone is shaking him. He jerks awake, confused and disoriented. Terror grips him when he sees the cop staring down at him, eyeing him suspiciously.

"You got some place to live, buddy?"

"Yes. Yes, I was just... I must have dozed off."

He sees the cop look across the street. "You from the detox center over there?"

He swallows hard. "No. No, I don't have a...a drug problem. I don't have any problem."

"It's after ten. Any reason you're hanging around here at this particular hour?"

"No. No, just sitting in the park, that's all."

"Not a smart place to be sitting at this time of night."

"Right." He rises abruptly, eager to get away.

"Hey, you forgot this," the cop calls out.

He turns to see the cop holding a red rose. He was so nervous, he left it behind.

"Oh, that isn't...mine." He hurries off. So much for waiting until lights-out at the center so he could cross the street and leave the rose outside on Sylver's windowsill. Oh, well, there's always tomorrow night.

He harangues himself all the way back to his apartment for having been so stupid as to have dozed off. From here on out, he'll have to be more careful, especially now that he's begun to set his new plan in motion.

Thinking about his plan boosts his spirits, makes him forget about the cop and his aborted mission. Soon, there'll be no problem showering her with roses every day. There'll be no furtive deliveries.

A month ago, he cashed in his life-insurance policy and last week he used it for a down payment on a real cute, bright and sunny one-bedroom condo over in Encino in the San Fernando Valley. When Sylver is released from the center, she won't have to go back to that dreadful apartment in West Hollywood; back to her old life. He'll be giving her a fresh start.

It took him weeks of looking to find just the right place in just the right location. He didn't have a fortune to spend, but he wanted the very best he could get for his money. It had to be the sort of place that, when he finally brings Sylver here, she'll step inside and immediately feel like she is home.

A week ago, he found the ideal place. Thinking about his princess living in that clean, cheery condo with its big picture windows and big, bright rooms, away from all the scumbags and creeps—he will see to that—makes him feel so good inside, he feels like he's floating. The best part is, he's finally taking action. He's finally going to take care of Sylver with the love and devotion only he can lavish on her.

He expects that she may be wary at first, feel obliged to him for all he is doing for her. He will make it absolutely clear to her that he expects nothing in return from her. He will tell her he simply wants to make her happy, protect her, look after her.

Still, maybe someday she will come to feel just a fraction of the love for him that he feels for her. Just a fraction. It would be enough to satisfy him. More than enough.

Thirteen

"We need Tom to be more...out of touch. I think that's where we're going wrong here," Kate offered. "He's still too connected."

"In the last rewrite, we all agreed he needed to feel connected to Liz," Ted Lerner complained.

"To Liz, yes," Adrian agreed, flipping through the script and folding it open at about the halfway mark. "This scene at the power plant on page forty-eight is very strong between Tom and Liz. It works. A bloody beautiful seduction right before everything explodes. The problem is that from that point on we need to see Tom losing hold, more and more. Liz becomes his last, fragile connection to reality; to anything good and decent in his life. He bloody well knows if he loses that, he's done for. Which, of course, he is, or the movie falls flat on its face."

Ted Lerner ran his hand slowly up and down the side of his face as the threesome sat around an eighteenth-century Venetian table in a corner of Kate's spacious office, going over his latest draft of the script. Kate could tell the screenwriter of *Mortal Sin* was losing patience, and she was sympathetic. Two drafts in two months put a lot of pressure on a man who tended to work slowly. Everything about the thirty-two-year-old Lerner was lumbering—the way he worked, the way he carried himself, even his speech. He was a huge man, tipping the scales at well over three hundred pounds, and even though he'd lived in L.A. for close to fifteen years, he still spoke with a lazy Louisiana drawl.

"I think we almost have it, Ted," Kate said, reaching across and giving the screenwriter's darkly tanned flabby forearm a supportive pat. "What we're talking about here only requires changes in a couple of scenes."

"Give or take a few," Adrian said with a wry smile.

Kate gave Adrian a sharp look. She'd lectured him a dozen times about not overwhelming Ted or he might freeze up. Then she checked her watch and saw that she was running late. "Well, I've got to go. Why don't you two hash it out some more and, say, we get back together after the holidays and see where we're at?" She gathered up her things and dashed out of the room.

Adrian was hot on her heels as she stepped into her outer office. "Where are you in such a hurry to get to, love?"

"I told Sylver I'd have lunch with her today." She dropped off a few papers on Eileen's desk, then turned and wagged a finger at him. "Will you please go easy on Lerner? We have an almost-perfect script. You know it as well as I do. Just guide him gently through the changes." She waved to Eileen and started for the door.

Adrian continued after her, putting Lerner on hold. No harm in giving the screenwriter some time to think about the changes. They stepped outside the sprawling stucco bungalow that housed Paradine's top officials. It was mid-December and the temperature was in the eighties.

Adrian never failed to be both jarred and amused by the fantasy-world aura of the holiday season in Hollywood. Strings of colored lights on the exotic palm trees lining the drive. Christmas wreaths hanging on the outside doors of all the stucco bungalows. Beyond the movie lot, Santas standing on street corners in shorts, their fake beards dripping with sweat in the sweltering tropical sunshine; holiday sales advertised on surfboards in store windows. Christmas in L.A. was like a movie production gone awry—a loopy mix-up of seasons on the set.

Keeping pace with Kate, Adrian asked, "How's Sylver doing?"

"Actually, she's great," Kate said with a smile that quickly vanished. "Or she would be if Nancy would get off her case." About six weeks earlier, Nancy had finally tracked Sylver down at the center. Kate had visited Sylver shortly after her mother's first visit, and Sylver had been a wreck. Now that Sylver had cleaned up her act, her mother could focus on nothing else but her daughter's triumphant comeback.

"I thought you told me Sylver's ex-cop pal, Riley, read Nancy the riot act," Adrian said, "threatening to spread the word to the trades that Sylver was drying out in detox, if she showed up at the center again without an invitation from her daughter."

Kate smiled. It was a great ploy. The last thing in the world Nancy wanted was bad publicity for Sylver. Since she didn't know Riley, Nancy had no way of knowing he'd be the last person in the world to carry out such a threat.

"Nancy's still waiting for the invitation," Kate said, "but that hasn't stopped her from sending Sylver little notes and clippings reminding her of the 'good old days.' Poor Sylver. Getting those on top of the red roses . . ."

"What red roses?" Adrian asked.

"Every morning Sylver finds a red rose on her window-sill left by some secret admirer. Years back, there was this fan who used to send her red roses. Then just before she signed herself into the center, she started getting them again at her place in West Hollywood. Now, it seems he's tracked her down to the center."

"How touching to have such a long-standing, devoted fan."

"Not really," Kate said, scowling. "This character's got her kind of spooked."

"He sounds harmless enough."

"I suppose."

"When's Sylver getting out of the center?" he asked as they headed for the almost-empty VIP parking lot. The whole movie lot was like a ghost town with so many people off for the holiday season.

"She can leave any time," Kate said, digging her keys out of her purse. "Her drug counselor says she's ready, but she's scared of getting out until after the first of the year. Holiday blues. Afraid she might slip up."

Kate knew all about holiday blues. She wasn't looking forward to the upcoming holiday with good cheer herself. Oh, there were plenty of parties to go to, and she had dates lined up for all of them. The problem was, none of the men falling over themselves to be her escort meant anything to her. Nor was she naive enough to think she meant anything to them on any personal level. She was a very important and powerful woman. Being seen with her enhanced the status of the men who courted her. It was all a game. None of these involvements had any substance. She had everything she wanted—money, power, authority—but there was no getting around it: Clichéd as it was, it was damn lonely at the top.

The one person in her life who could change all that was Adrian Needham. Adrian, however, would be gone for the holidays. He was going back to London to spend Christmas and New Year's with his elderly father who lived with Adrian's younger sister and brother-in-law and their two kids.

Not that Kate could delude herself into thinking it would have much mattered if he'd stayed in town. Following their one brief but glorious night of passion two months back, shortly after which Adrian had officially signed on to direct *Mortal Sin,* they had mutually agreed not to mix pleasure with business this time around. Both of them were afraid it would muddy the waters as well as reopen too many old wounds.

Logically, Kate knew it was the right decision, but emotionally she was having a tough time living with it. Not only was she fending off almost constant sexual frustration, she was also frustrated by never knowing whether Adrian felt any regrets about their business-only arrangement. He gave no hint of any personal feelings for her—not even a hint that he was as horny as she was. They didn't even fight the way they used to. Kate knew that it had nothing to do with either of them mellowing. She suspected Adrian was deliberately avoiding hassles with her as a way of keeping her at arm's length. The man was driving her bloody crazy!

"You'd better get back to Ted or he'll feel deserted," Kate said when they got to her car. She was sure the only reason Adrian was out there was to avoid having to deal with the screenwriter. While she knew the two men respected each other's talents enormously, their styles and energy levels were so different that they often had difficulty communicating. Still, they were almost there. A final polish on the script and they'd be ready for principal shooting by February. Casting was already under way, with Jack West and Laura Shelly lined up for the leads. They just needed to work out some minor contract differences.

Kate checked her watch again. "Damn, I'm really running late. I've still got to stop and pick up some barbecued chicken and the trimmings. I promised Sylver a picnic in the park."

"Lovely," Adrian said.

Kate smiled conspiratorially as she unlocked her car door. "I've got an early Christmas present for her."

"What's that?" he asked, opening her door for her.

"The key to my cabin up at Running Springs. Riley told me it's kind of a fantasy of Sylver's to spend some time in a snowy mountain retreat. She might even change her mind and leave the center before Christmas, if she could spend the holidays up there."

"Far from the madding crowd?"

Kate smiled. "Far from drug pushers and liquor stores, as well."

"Will you go with her?"

"Me? No. My calendar's booked solid for the next few weeks," Kate said, determined not to let Adrian think for a moment that she'd be pining away for him while he was off in London surrounded by a big, loving family.

She felt compelled to click off her schedule of activities. "There's Charlie Windham's must-attend Christmas party, and Marianne Spars is throwing a big New Year's Eve bash at her restaurant, Stars and Spars. Then there's an endless round of holiday brunches, cocktail parties.... Well, you know the scene."

Adrian grimaced. It wasn't a scene he relished. Which was why he was escaping L.A. for the holidays. One of the reasons, anyway. His eyes skidded off Kate. Could she tell? Did she have an inkling of the battle raging inside of him? How many times these past few weeks had he been tempted to invite her to join him in London? Sure, like she'd give up all those bloody glamorous Hollywood galas for a chance to be holed up in a crowded flat in the East End with a pair of screeching kids racing about, his old man snoring in his chair after Sunday supper, his sister Freda asking Kate, the president of the motion-picture division of a big Hollywood movie studio, if she'd like to pitch in with the dishes. He could just imagine it.

No, the problem was, he couldn't imagine it. Not for the life of him.

"Riley said he'd be glad to spend a few weeks up there with Sylver, if it's what she wants," Kate was saying.

Adrian pushed aside his pointless meanderings. "What gives with Sylver and this ex-cop?"

Kate smiled. "I think they're crazy about each other and it's a toss-up which of them is more afraid to admit it."

Adrian grinned, tapping his index finger against his lips as he observed her.

Kate gave him a guarded look. "What's so amusing?"

"Nothing. Just that I never pictured you as the matchmaker type."

"Oh, really, Adrian."

"No, no. It adds a whole new dimension to your personality. I find it very charming."

Both embarrassed and ridiculously pleased by Adrian's remark, Kate waved him off and was about to get into her car when she saw Douglas Garrison heading in her direction. She frowned. Adrian followed her gaze. He frowned, too.

"Should I stick around and punch the bloke silly?"

Kate gave him a little shove. "No. You can't go around punching the studio chief, even if he is becoming a royal pain in the ass. I'll deal with Doug. You go back inside and cope with Lerner."

Adrian reluctantly walked off, mostly because he knew if he stuck around he just might start swinging at Garrison, who seemed hell-bent on doing everything in his power to throw a monkey wrench into the making of *Mortal Sin*.

For a moment, Kate considered dashing into her car and pulling out before Doug got to her. She didn't do it because he'd only track her down later. Ever since their disturbing encounter in the lobby of the Century Plaza two months ago at that Feast or Famine benefit, things had gone from bad to worse to positively crazy between them. One day he'd storm into her office accusing her of having single-handedly destroyed his career and turning him into a laughingstock; a few nights later he'd show up on her doorstep, weeping, begging her to take him back, swearing that he couldn't live without her; then the very next day, he'd do something deliberately underhanded to try to sabotage her picture, like starting rumors that the script was in terrible trouble, or that Adrian and Lerner were constantly at loggerheads and each was threatening a walkout. Doug had even had the gall to demand a check of the books to see if money was being skimmed from the movie budget for her or Adrian's personal use. On top of all that, he was wildly jealous of the ongoing love affair he imagined she was having with Adrian. Several times, she was sure she'd spotted his Lamborghini cruising down her street late at night, like he was checking to see if Adrian's car—a recently purchased mint condition 1968 white Volkswagen Beetle—was parked in her driveway.

Kate's frustrations as to what to do about Doug were compounded by the fact that he had managed to raise doubts in Charlie Windham's mind about his decision to have put so much power and so much money in her hands. She'd had to have several meetings with the CEO to assure him that none of the rumors filtering up to him—thanks to Doug—were true. The last time they'd met, Charlie had virtually demanded smooth sailing on this project. Fine, she'd thought to herself, as long as she could figure out some way to toss Doug off the sailboat.

Doug approached her with a swagger. "Lover boy took off in a hurry."

Kate worked hard to keep her cool. "What do you want, Doug? I'm late."

"What do I want? I want to know exactly what you've been telling Nancy Cassidy. That's what I want."

"What are you talking about?"

"Nancy Cassidy dropped in to see me this morning. She seems to think you've promised her daughter the second lead in *Mortal Sin.*"

Kate looked at Doug, astonished. "What? Nancy's crazy. I never even mentioned it as a possibility to Sylver. She's not ready to get back into acting. I don't even know if she plans to, in the future."

"Actually, I think Sylver could bring something to the part of Beth."

"Maybe so, but . . ."

"I admit I was against the idea at first, but Nancy can be very persuasive. Besides, you know I've always had a soft spot in my heart for her kid. And Nancy insists Sylver's in top form now. So as not to make a liar of you, darling, I said okay."

Kate's expression went from astonished to dumbfounded. "You said what?"

"Sylver's got the part of Beth in *Mortal Sin.*" There was no missing the challenge in Doug's gaze. Nor did Kate have any doubts about his motive for wanting Sylver to have the part. He wasn't counting on Sylver's success, but her failure. Another chance for him to sabotage the production.

"This is my movie, Doug. You have no authority—"

He gripped her arm hard, his eyes narrowing to slits. "That's where you're wrong, Kate. That's the mistake you keep making."

Kate flinched, from the pain, the icy tone in his voice, and the eerie blankness in his eyes. "Let go of me, Doug."

"I don't ever intend to let go of you, Kate. Until I'm finished with you."

"Doug," Kate said through clenched teeth, "I think you'd better switch from your psychic back to your psychiatrist. You need help."

He released her then—so abruptly she had to grab onto her open car door for support.

A flicker of madness flashed across his features. "You'd like that, wouldn't you? Well, let me tell you something, baby. When all's said and done, I'll be right back in the power seat and you'll be the one who'll need to be stretched out on a shrink's couch."

Angry as she was at Doug, she did understand some of what he was going through. What she resented was that he seemed to be taking it all out on her. She hadn't been the one to limit his authority at the studio. And as far as her having broken off their affair, she was sure that it was his ego that was wounded, not his heart. Douglas Garrison simply didn't like losing anything that he thought he owned. Well, he didn't own her, and he never had.

She attempted to reason with him. "Trying to undermine my movie isn't going to help your situation, Doug. If *Mortal Sin* is the hit I predict, it will give Paradine back the competitive edge it once had. Can't you see we all stand to gain?"

His features softened. This was what threw her the most about Doug lately—the swift mood swings. "Can't you see how hard this is on me, Kate? I always thought you were the one person I could always count on."

"You *can* count on me," she said carefully. "Our friendship means a lot to me, Doug, but it's hard to be sympathetic when you . . ."

His features instantly hardened. "Sympathetic? Is that what you think I want? Your sympathy?"

Frustration welled up inside her. He could twist everything she said and felt for him, turning whatever kind words she had for him into assaults. If he kept this up much longer, there would be no good feelings left.

"Doug, we can't go around and around like this. I've got to go." Before he could grab her again, she quickly slipped inside her car, slammed the door and flicked the switch for the electric locks.

As she sped away, she looked back at Douglas in her rearview mirror. The lines of hatred etched into his features were chilling.

Kate spread out a blanket in the park and began pulling items out of a wicker basket—colorful rainbow paper plates, matching napkins, a tub of freshly made coleslaw. Sylver smiled with delight when she saw Kate unwrap the aluminum foil from the barbecued chicken.

"My favorite. You remembered," Sylver said softly.

Kate grinned, pulling out a large bottle of raspberry soda. "I hope this is still a favorite, too."

Sylver laughed. "We must have gone through a half-dozen bottles of the stuff at that slumber party years back."

"Make that a dozen. The next morning every one of you had a purple tongue."

Sylver's expression turned wistful as she picked up a crispy brown chicken leg and began nibbling on it. "You are a special friend, Kate. What have I done to deserve you?"

Kate busied herself with pouring the soda into paper cups. Each time she visited Sylver, she felt this weight in her chest. She knew what it was, just as she knew there was only one way to get rid of it. Slowly, she looked over at Sylver who was watching her quietly with those intense azure eyes.

Kate was struck afresh by Sylver's incandescent beauty. What a transformation in her appearance since their first encounter at the center two months ago. Sylver's complexion was now glowing with healthy color, thanks to spending a couple of hours each day outside in the sunshine. She'd also put on some desperately needed pounds and had joined an exercise class at the center, so that her figure now looked trim and athletic. Even her spiky hairstyle had a unique appeal now that it had grown out a few inches and the golden luster had been restored.

"What is it, Kate?" Sylver asked anxiously, her beauty touched by melancholy. "Every time you come to see me, there's always something so... sad in your eyes."

Kate tried to swallow down the huge knot in her throat. She wasn't successful. "What you see is... guilt."

Sylver reached across the blanket and gripped Kate's hand. "What do you have to feel guilty about? I thought I'd cornered the market on that particular emotion. I'm the drug addict, the alcoholic. I'm the complete screwup. You're this dazzlingly bright, successful, got-it-all-together..."

The anguish inside Kate threatened to explode. "Stop, Sylver. Please stop. You're only making it worse." Seeing the stricken look on Sylver's face caused by her outburst, Kate instantly regretted her words. She pressed her clenched fists against her closed eyes. "Oh, God, I'm making a complete botch of this."

Sylver sat very still, her heart pounding, the chicken leg feeling leaden in her hand. "We don't... have to talk... about it."

Kate dropped her hands from her face. "Yes, we do. I do. I need to talk about it. What I'm trying to tell you, Sylver, is that I never should have forced you to finish *Glory Girl*. None of what happened to you would have happened if I'd let you off that picture."

Sylver leaned forward, as if she wasn't able to get close enough to see her clearly. "Kate, that's crazy. You didn't force me to finish it. You just gave me your best advice. You thought it was the right thing for me—"

"No!" Kate shouted. "I thought it was the right thing for Paradine. Don't you get it, Sylver? I was worried about the disastrous effect letting you out of the picture would have on the studio. I wasn't thinking about *your* best interests. Damn it, I was thinking about *mine*."

"Hey, come on, I understand that, Kate," Sylver said softly. "You worked for Paradine. Why, you could have lost your job if I didn't finish the picture. I don't blame you for what happened to me. Anyway, finishing the picture or not, I had no business getting drunk the night of my birthday party...."

Kate grabbed hold of Sylver's shoulders and shook her. "Never, never think for one instant that what that bastard, Nick Kramer, did to you was in any way your fault. He raped you. It doesn't matter if you were drunk or sober. Nothing you did or didn't do matters. You told him to stop and he wouldn't. Oh, Sylver, I should have made you press charges against him. I should have." There, it was out. *Give it a minute. Absorb it. Face the guilt. The self-hatred.*

"Kate..." Sylver began distraughtly.

Kate slowly shook her head. "I knew it was the right thing to do—that bringing Kramer up on charges was the only way for you to fight back having been victimized."

"You didn't talk me out of pressing charges. It was my mother. All she cared about was what a scandal like that would do to my career." Sylver laughed dryly. "My precious career. I showed her, didn't I?"

"Don't you see? I was no better than Nancy." Kate shut her eyes, the pain of her admission making her cringe. "Oh, sure, at first, when I got that call from you and then saw you at Kramer's place.... God, it almost felt like it had happened to me."

"You wanted me to press charges, Kate. Don't you remember? So did Nash. You both wanted—"

"Right. At first. Then we backed down. Nash started realizing that he'd never get a crack at the lead he wanted in Kramer's next picture if word got out he'd been instrumental in getting you to report the rape."

"I never had any illusions about Nash," Sylver said, looking away, rubbing her arms, feeling a chill despite the warm, sunny weather. She lifted her gaze back to Kate.

Kate sighed wearily. "Your mother, Nash, me... When push came to shove we all started calculating our personal losses. We all put ourselves first."

Kate had to stop for a moment to compose herself before she could go on. "I was the worst, because I betrayed your trust. And all it took was a bit of persuasion from Doug. I went to see him that evening. Oh, I was boiling mad, ready to rip Kramer's heart out with my bare hands for what he'd done to you. I told Doug that Nancy was giving you grief about pressing charges, but that I was sure that with my support, you'd have the courage—" Kate stopped. "Courage. That's a laugh. I was worried about your courage when I was the one who was the miserable coward. As soon as Doug pointed out that I would be committing professional suicide if a scandal broke..."

"So Douglas Garrison knew about the... about me and Kramer?" Sylver still couldn't say the word *rape* out loud.

"Yes," Kate said quietly. "I didn't go to him only because he was the executive producer on *Glory Girl*. Doug and I were... lovers at the time."

"You and Garrison?" Sylver echoed, stunned. "I wouldn't have seen you two as a matchup. Sorry. To each his own. Go on. He told you you'd be committing professional suicide...."

"To be fair to Doug, when I first told him what had happened to you, he was terribly upset. Actually, I was surprised at how upset he was. He really was fond of you, Sylver.'' Kate was reminded of her conversation with Doug a short while ago. Did he still have a soft spot in his heart for Sylver, as he claimed, or was he merely trying to use her as a pawn in his effort to sabotage *Mortal Sin* as she suspected? In any case, Kate decided this wasn't the time to mention to Sylver that Doug had told her mother—without authority—that she could have the part of Beth in the film. Actually, despite Doug's suspect motives for wanting Sylver to have the part, Kate was beginning to think that it might be a good idea at that. They wouldn't start principal shooting until next month. Would Sylver be ready by then? Would she want the part?

"I never was quite sure how Douglas felt about me,'' Sylver said softly. "There always seemed to be this strange push and pull between us. He never felt quite comfortable around me, never knew what to say. I suppose it's because he never had any kids of his own. I can't picture him as a father, can you?''

Kate shook her head. There had been a time, though, many years before, when she had not only pictured Douglas Garrison as a father, but the father of her children—the children she'd never got around to having.

"My mother never had very flattering things to say about Douglas,'' Sylver went on. "Oh, of course she was always kissing up to him whenever she saw him, but behind his back she used to call him a conniving, coldhearted bastard....'' She flushed. "Sorry. I guess you felt differently about him.''

"We all make errors in judgment,'' Kate said wryly.

Sylver reached out and lightly rested her hand on Kate's arm. "One thing being in group has taught me is you have to let go of the past and not beat yourself over the head with it.''

Kate nodded. "Easier said than done.''

Sylver smiled. "I will admit I didn't shed a tear when Kramer died in that car crash. The truth is, I felt like getting blitzed and dancing on his grave.'' She sighed. "I got blitzed anyway. I always had an excuse for that. Although you've got to admit, that was one of my better excuses.''

Kate easily saw through Sylver's glibness. She pulled her close and hugged her tightly. "Let's be done with excuses. Okay?"

Locked in Kate's secure embrace, tears spilled from Sylver's eyes. Suddenly, the stark reality of the trauma she'd suffered that long-ago night came crashing in on her. "Oh, God, Kate. He raped me. Nicky Kramer raped me. He was the one we should have been hating. Instead, we've both wasted all these years hating ourselves. I'm tired of hating, Kate. I don't have the strength for it anymore. I don't want to destroy myself anymore." She wrapped her arms around Kate's neck, burying her face against her breast. "Just be my friend. Just love me, Kate. Please."

Kate nodded as she rocked Sylver in her arms, stroking her hair. "I do love you, Sylver."

It was the first time in her life Kate had openly admitted loving someone. No hedging, no couching her feelings in "safer" expressions, no modifiers. *I do love you, only... but... What I mean is...* None of that. Just a simple, unqualified *I do love you.* She found herself smiling. Damned if it didn't feel amazingly good. Good to know, after all those years of angst, that it could be so easy to say. And even more stunning, so easy to feel. Now, if it could only be that easy with Adrian Needham.

Right. Next, she'd start believing there really was a Santa Claus.

Which reminded Kate. Her early Christmas present for Sylver.

PART TWO

Winter 1992-93

Fourteen

Riley stood outside the center feeling like a schoolboy waiting for his first date. Nervously, he glanced inside the back of his rented Ford Mustang—courtesy of Kate Paley—at his suitcase and typewriter in the back seat. Was he nuts? Had he gone over the edge? Three weeks in a secluded cabin in the mountains alone with Sylver and he was going to keep things between them strictly platonic? He wasn't going to take advantage of her? He was going to ignore his over-heated hormones? He was going to help her reclaim her faith in herself and others, especially him? And while he was being so noble and self-sacrificing, he'd be in a perfect state to finish off his Great American Detective Novel?

Get real, Riley.

"Hi, Riley."

He jumped as he saw Sylver spring up in front of him out of nowhere. "Oh, you're... out."

Sylver gave him a crooked smile. "Yeah. Da boys sprang me. Dis da getaway car?"

He grinned.

Sylver winked. "Den let's blow dis joint, fella."

It was close to a three-hour trek up to Running Springs. While Riley drove, Sylver acted as navigator with the help of Kate's map and detailed written instructions, directing him on and off the freeway, up and over the winding mountain roads. They didn't really talk about anything much on the drive, but neither of them felt troubled by the quiet. There was something about putting more and more distance between themselves and Hollywood that they both found comforting. Riley was even beginning to think com-

ing out here with Sylver was a good idea. After all, even if
his hormones did get juiced up every now and then, Sylver
had never given him any reason to believe she felt anything
more toward him than gratitude and friendship. Friends.
He'd never had a woman friend before.

"We make a right turn at the next fork," Sylver said excitedly, "and then, according to Kate's map, the cabin's two
and a quarter miles up the road on the right."

"Aye, aye, captain," Riley said, full of good cheer and
optimism.

"Oh, Riley, look. It's starting to snow. It's going to be a
white Christmas. My very first."

Riley smiled as he looked across at her. Sylver had never
seemed so young and innocent to him. Unfortunately, also
never so appealing. She'd come a long distance in two
months. So, he realized, had he.

His heart began thumping, doubts settling back in. Could
a beautiful, desirable young woman and a horny, no-ac-
count ex-cop really carry off a platonic relationship?

He almost missed the cutoff at the fork.

Sylver shifted in her seat so she was half facing him.
"What's going through your head, Riley?"

"My head? Oh . . . just stuff. About my book."

"Remember that you promised I could read it while we're
up here," Sylver said.

"Remember that you promised not to have very high expectations," he countered nervously. No one had read a
single page of his unfinished manuscript yet. He knew the
main reason wasn't his fear of criticism or disappointment.
It was that so much of himself came through on those pages.
He had revealed himself in print as he had never revealed
himself in person. In reading his book, whether she thought
much of it or not, Sylver would get to know more about him
than he was sure he wanted her—or anyone who was close
to him—to know.

Anyone who was close to him. That was a funny thought.
Other than his old partner, Al Borgini, Sylver was the only
other person that he had ever felt close to. The difference
was, in his relationship with Al, Al had done most of the
work while he'd ducked and dodged, trying to no avail—

thank God—to fend him off. With Sylver it was different. He'd let himself voluntarily get close to her. If anything, she'd been more ambivalent than him—warm and teasing one day, wary and cautious the next. He wasn't sure that Sylver really knew how she felt about him. Or how she felt about that creep, Nash Walker, now that she was out of that life. Walker, however, wasn't completely out of Sylver's life. A couple of weeks ago, she'd dropped him a line, letting him know where she was and how well she was doing.

"Sam Hibbs told me your pal, Nash, stopped by the clinic to see you the other day," Riley said offhandedly.

Sylver's position shifted, her body turning away from him. "I saw him for a few minutes. He...got himself a place over on...La Cienega." Riley had paid up Sylver's rent, but had the locks changed so that Walker couldn't make himself at home there any longer.

"How's he doing?" Not that Riley didn't know he was still up to his old tricks. He wanted to see if Sylver could see through him yet; see him for what he really was.

"Okay, I guess. He's auditioning for a small part in a Mario Vega movie." Sylver shrugged. "He won't get it."

"Because he's a lousy actor or because he's too spaced-out to show up for the audition?"

Sylver smiled crookedly at him. "You don't like Nash much, do you?"

"Do you?" The words just slipped out. Too late to grab them back. He kept his eyes straight ahead on the road. His hands gripped the wheel tighter.

"We have a history," Sylver said quietly, knowing that was a vague answer at best, but not sure how else to respond.

Riley shot her a look. "Wartime buddies, huh?"

"Nash is still in the trenches. When he came down to see me at the center, I did try to get him to sign himself in. He looked at me like I was crazy. 'I'm no addict,' he says. 'I just mess around a little.' Sounded mighty familiar. Was I as transparent as Nash?"

"It's not how transparent you are that matters, Sylver. It's what shows through."

"Don't blame Nash for my debacle, Riley. He didn't make me do anything I didn't really want to do."

He glanced across at her, their eyes meeting and holding for a few seconds. That was when it hit Sylver. She was about to spend three weeks alone with this man she hardly knew in an isolated mountain cabin. The kicker was she was going to do it stone-cold sober.

She looked away edgily. Would Riley try to make a move on her? Why should she think for one minute he was different from every other man? Especially now that she looked half decent again. Why else would he have offered to come up here with her? And didn't she owe him? He had saved her life. Even though she wasn't always that sure he'd done her a favor.

"There's the painted yellow mailbox," Sylver said, pointing off to the right. "We turn up the driveway just past it."

Riley made the turn, driving up a narrow, twisting snow-covered path. Kate's getaway retreat was a hundred yards up the hill. As the place came into view, Riley let out a low whistle as he got his first gander at the huge cedar-clad three-story A-frame chalet, with one-story wings affixed to each side.

He shot Sylver a look. "This is a *cabin?*"

Sylver grinned. "That's Hollywoodese for a small palace."

Well, he thought, at least they wouldn't have to be stepping over each other every time they turned around. They might not even find each other!

He follows them all the way to Running Springs, driving slowly past the driveway they've turned onto. He's sweating, even though the heater's busted in his car. Nervous energy.

He pulls over to the side of the road a little ways past their driveway. He should have known that creep, Quinn, would be waiting outside the center for her. What had he been thinking?

He knows what he was thinking. Only about how he'd go springing out of his parked car as soon as she stepped out of that center, finally introduce himself as her secret lifelong fan, usher her over to his car and joyfully announce that he was taking her to her beautiful new home. Even if Quinn hadn't been there and he'd gotten the opportunity, he realizes now that she would probably have thought he was nuts. Certainly, he'd have been the first one to teach his princess never to go off with strangers. Only he wasn't a stranger. He was her soul mate. They had been together for a long time—in a unique sort of way. Once he explained to her... Once he made her see...

Sometimes he does wonder if he has all his marbles—blowing twenty thousand bucks on a down payment for a condo he might never be able to convince Sylver to move into. He's sane enough to know she might refuse even after he told her everything that was in his heart. Then what? Kidnap her and move her in against her will? Hope that, in time, she would realize what a great and generous guy he really was, and be eternally grateful? He slams his hand hard against the steering wheel, tempted to turn right around, go back to the city, put the condo on the market and forget this madness.

No, it isn't madness. What he feels for Sylver is the sanest feeling he has ever known. How could he even think about deserting her? Leave her alone out here in the wilderness with that scumbag, Quinn? Anything could happen to her. He has to stay; keep an eye on her; protect her.

He reaches across to the glove compartment and pulls out his gun, slipping it inside his raincoat pocket. The snow's starting to come down heavily now and he flicks on his windshield wipers to fast speed. As the window clears, he catches sight of a small cottage up a little ways on the left.

He drives up to the cottage, noting that there are no tire tracks, no car parked in the drive, no lights on in the house, no smoke coming out of the chimney.

Engine running, he sits in his car for a long while, debating. He's never broken into a house before. Not that it would be all that difficult. And it isn't as if he were a criminal, out to steal anything. All he needs is some shelter. And a place close enough to his princess so he can look out for her welfare.

He gets out of the car, turning and looking across the road. From here he can see the large chalet where they were staying. The lights are going on in one room after another. He goes around to his trunk, pops it open, and retrieves a small leather case.

He opens the case, taking out a pair of binoculars. He stands outside the deserted cottage for several minutes, watching them through the binoculars, mindless of the chill and the snow falling down on him. Sylver is in the kitchen, opening cupboards. Quinn is in the living room, throwing logs into the fireplace.

Finally he turns to the house, tests the door, then all the windows. The place is locked up solid. He ends up breaking the small pane of glass over the back door, reaching in and unlocking it, letting himself into a pleasant, knotty-pine kitchen. He flicks the light switch by the door. No lights come on. The electricity is off. A good sign. It probably meant no one was staying up here. It's still light enough to see around the room and he gives it a quick check. A few canned goods in the cupboards, dishes, pots and pans, silverware. He finds a working flashlight in one of the drawers, a few candles in another.

He walks through the kitchen into the cozy living room whose small-paned New England-style windows offer a perfect vantage point for watching the chalet across the road. He lifts the binoculars to his eyes and looks out. If he can't spend the holidays with Sylver, at least he will be close by her. Watching over her. That's enough for him. He has never asked for much.

Riley stopped at the open doorway of the master bedroom—a large airy space that had a cool, crafted elegance with a cherry canopy bed, a generous oak armoire, fine lithographs on the butter cream walls. The room was romantic and feminine without a lot of froufrou. It fit his image of Kate.

The sumptuous room—the whole chalet with its pure pricey comfort and country warmth straight out of the pages of a glossy decorating magazine—intimidated Riley. The only times he'd ever been in digs like these was when he was on the job as a cop. He usually never made it past the front hall, the occupants of those lavish homes no doubt afraid he might leave scuff marks on their bleached oak floors.

Sylver didn't spot him at first and he had a chance to study her getting settled in. Unlike him, she seemed right at home in these posh surroundings. A few years on the skids hadn't erased her memories of once having lived like this.

"How's it going?" he asked, his voice strained.

Sylver was pulling out a soft white challis nightgown from one of the bureau drawers, along with a note. She turned to Riley, her face awash with astonishment.

"I can't believe this. Kate not only had the kitchen stocked with enough food to feed an army for a year, she's insisted on outfitting me in everything from nightgowns to snowshoes."

She looked down at the note, shaking her head. "Everything in these drawers and closets is for me. She must have bought out Neiman's. She's gone completely nuts."

Riley smiled. "I have to admit, I wasn't all that wild about Kate Paley at first, but she grows on you once you scrape away that VIP veneer and get a peek at the real woman behind it."

Sylver held the nightgown up in front of her. "What do you think?"

Her smile was radiant. He could feel the warmth of it all the way across the room. He could also feel another kind of heat rising in him as he started imagining just how beautiful and desirable Sylver would look in that nightgown.

Careful, Quinn. You haven't even been here with her for twenty minutes and already you're veering off the straight and narrow. Get a grip on yourself. It's a good thing you're bunking down in that bedroom all the way over in the other wing.

Sylver took his silence for disapproval. "You don't like it."

"No. No, I mean, yes. I like it. It's nice. Very...nice." He rubbed his hands together. "Say, are you hungry?"

Sylver turned away, folding the nightie and carefully placing it back in the drawer. "Sure."

She cleared her throat, trying to swallow down her disappointment at his less-than-enthusiastic response. Okay, so he wasn't attracted to her. Wasn't that a relief? At last, a guy who wouldn't hit on her?

She shut the drawer firmly, turning back to him, her smile again in place, but not, Riley noticed, quite so luminous as a few moments ago.

"Now that I think about it," she said, determined to be upbeat, "I'm starved."

Riley was getting to know her, though. When she struck a false note, he picked it up faster than a symphony conductor. "Sylver, I didn't mean to hurt your feelings."

She looked at him, startled. "You didn't, Riley. You just said what you felt. I want you to be honest with me. I'm . . . counting on it."

Honest. That was a laugh. That was the last thing he was being.

Neither of them slept much that night. New surroundings, so much silence, each of them more aware than they wanted to be of the other sleeping in the opposite wing. Sylver was down in the kitchen at the crack of dawn, wrapped in a soft pale yellow challis bathrobe and sheepskin-lined moccasins. She opened the well-stocked refrigerator, feeling overwhelmed as she stared inside. Cooking had never been her strong point. Most kids learned how to cook watching their moms. All Sylver had ever seen her mom do was make reservations. Eating, like everything else in the Cassidy home, had been connected to her career. You didn't eat at home because no one would see you. You didn't choose a restaurant because of the cuisine but because of who dined there. You didn't even pick items from the menu that you liked. Her mother gave the adage, You Are What You Eat, new meaning.

"Reporters," Nancy would tell her regularly, "will make judgments about everything you say and do, including what food you put into your mouth, Sylver. You don't want to eat too little or gossip will spread that you're anorexic. You don't want to eat too much or they'll suspect you might be bulimic." This also meant she was never allowed to go to the bathroom in a restaurant lest it lend credence to the possibility that she was in there sticking her finger down her throat. Sometimes she wanted to pin a sign on her chest. I Am Naturally Thin. I Was Just Made That Way. Kill Me!

Later, when she and Nash were together, she didn't advance her culinary skills any. Eating meant grabbing a hot dog or a pizza on the way to scoring a hit, or opening a can of spaghetti at home and swallowing it down with tumblers of J&B. Half the time, she was too high or too sick from coming down to eat much of anything. It was only since she'd been at the center that the act of dining had taken on any semblance of normalcy. Three square meals a day. People sitting down together, chatting, eating, no one worrying about who'd see them put what in their mouths. Sylver had actually begun to enjoy mealtime.

Cooking meals, though, was another story.

"Morning."

Sylver jumped, whirling around to see Riley standing right behind her. He was dressed in black jeans and a navy turtleneck, his hair still damp from his shower, smelling of soap and shampoo. Looking at him in the postdawn stillness in this idyllic mountain retreat, Sylver felt a little giddy and light-headed. It seemed so unreal, all of it. Maybe none of this was happening. Maybe she was so high on whatever Nash had copped for her, that she was delusional.

She had this incredible urge to reach out and touch Riley, so that she could reassure herself that he was truly there. Because if he was there, she had to be there.

Riley was fending off a similar urge to reach out and touch Sylver, but for different reasons. He'd spent a miserable night, alternately fending off erotic fantasies about her and running vitriolic lectures through his mind about behaving himself. When dawn broke, he thought he had gotten himself in hand. Now, here she was, wrapped in that soft, sunny yellow robe, no makeup, her big, thickly lashed azure eyes staring up at him with far more trust than he deserved, and all he could think about was scooping her up in his arms and carrying her off to the nearest bedroom.

"What are you doing up at this hour?" he asked gruffly, to cover up his real thoughts.

Sylver was taken aback by his tone. "I was...about to make breakfast," she muttered, quickly pivoting around to the refrigerator, but not really seeing anything inside it.

"How about cheese-and-tomato omelets?" His tone was a little softer. He was getting himself under control.

She glanced back at him, her expression wan. "Omelets?" She didn't know the first thing about making omelets.

Riley grinned. "How about you give mine a try? Nobody's died yet from my cooking."

Sylver laughed. "You might die from mine."

"Not after you have a few of Chef Riley's culinary lessons."

Twenty minutes later, with piping-hot golden omelets and buttered toast on their plates and freshly brewed coffee in their mugs, they sat together in the curved banquette built into the large bay window at the southern end of the kitchen, which looked out over snow-capped mountains. Outside the snow was still falling, more lightly now than the night before.

Riley waited for Sylver to take the first bite, which she did, chewing with relish. "This is great. Really great," she said enthusiastically.

She sampled the coffee next. "Mmm. Perfect." A bright smile lit her face. "Tomorrow, it'll be my turn to make the breakfast. I never thought cooking could be so much fun." *Fun.* The whole concept of *fun* boggled her mind, it seemed such an alien one. She could count the number of times she'd truly had fun in her life on one hand. Four fingers for Kate. And now one for Riley.

This emotion thing was new to her. She was surprised to find herself feeling a little choked up. "Thanks, Riley," she muttered.

He grinned. "Don't thank me yet. See how you do after you go solo."

Sylver hesitated. "Not just for the cooking lesson. For everything. I guess I never really did thank you."

"That's okay," he said awkwardly, not exactly a whiz when it came to handling emotions himself, especially someone else's gratitude. He dug into his breakfast, focusing more attention on it than was necessary.

"So, can I start reading your novel after breakfast?" Sylver asked after several minutes of silent chewing and swallowing.

Riley set down his coffee mug and furrowed his eyebrows.

"You promised, Riley," Sylver said, guessing that he was having second thoughts.

He leaned forward a little, locking eyes with her. "This isn't altogether easy for me, Sylver."

"I won't judge you, Riley."

"Yes, you will," he said softly. He picked up his mug again, but set it down without taking another sip. "You don't know anything about me."

"Give me a chance to know more. You know plenty about me—plenty that I'm not proud of."

"So, what are you saying? You want to make it even? Learn all the things that I'm not proud of?"

Sylver turned to him as she sat on the brightly patterned banquette cushion. She tucked her knees under her chin, curling her arms around her legs. "What aren't you proud of, Riley?"

He laughed dryly. "That could fill a book. It *has* filled a book."

"Still, the book's fiction. Give me the straight scoop."

He could feel himself grow hot under the turtleneck of his sweater. Sylver was really putting him on the spot. He'd never taken well to being cornered. Yet, oddly enough, there was a part of him that wanted to open up to her. There was this feeling of warmth and acceptance radiating from her that was melting down his resistance.

Go on, Riley. Show a little courage. Show her that, compared to you, she's an angel. "Three innocent people almost died because of me."

Sylver's heart lurched. She focused on the "almost." "How did it happen?"

He didn't answer right away. Confessing didn't come easily to him. The only other time he'd talked about this was with Sam Hibbs at the center. And even then, he'd only shared the facts, never the feelings—feelings so powerful that they had all but consumed him.

With a scowl, he swallowed down another sip of coffee, then sat there holding the mug between his hands, mainly to keep Sylver from detecting the tremor in them.

"I was off duty, a few blocks from my house. I'd been at a bar. Had had a few too many." He stopped, shot her a look. She merely nodded, waiting patiently for him to go on, sensing as did he, that not only was this hard for him but it also marked an essential shift in their relationship.

Riley's grip on the mug tightened. "Suddenly this character darts out of an alley, literally knocks me down. Not that I was all that steady on my feet. Anyway, as I go down hard, I hear someone screaming. That kind of sobers me up. I look over and see this hooker I knew . . . staggering out of the alley, covered in blood. She's screaming, 'I'll get you, Frisco, you bastard!'"

He set the mug down on the table, afraid the pressure of his grip might actually shatter it. Instead, he clasped his hands together. A bead of sweat broke out across his brow.

"Frisco. I knew the name. A local drug dealer in the neighborhood that my partner and I'd been trying to get the goods on for months. I'm up on my feet in a flash. I figure I have him now. I can bring him in for assault on the hooker, hopefully find some dope on him to tag on a charge of possession, maybe even dealing if he's got enough on him. He's racing across the street at this point. I'm not really thinking all that straight, but I think I am. I think I'm almost sober, that I can deal with this without a problem. I pull out my gun, order him to stop. I don't identify myself, nothing. He doesn't stop and I start shooting."

His mouth went dry, his pulse pounding against his temples. He was sweating profusely now. *What's the matter with me? Why'd I even get started? What good will it do to talk about this?*

Sylver leaned over and pressed her hand to his cheek. He looked at her, a shaky smile curling his lips. He'd come this far. *Finish it.*

"There was this family coming out of a shop across the way. I think it was a gift shop. They had...packages. Probably tourists."

He rubbed his hand across his chest. He could feel his heart pounding.

"A mother, a father, a little...girl." He closed his eyes. "The mother screamed. The father grabbed the little girl to him, trying to shield her. Frisco started running right toward them. I was...shooting. He was blocking them from view at first, so I didn't see them." He was having difficulty catching his breath.

"Did any of them get hit?"

He shook his head, not trusting his voice. The little girl was blond. Like Lilli. Not much older than Lilli....

"And Frisco?" she asked.

He swallowed, trying to pull himself back from the memory. "I winged him. A patrol car was coming along and pulled over. They brought us both down to the station."

"Didn't you tell them you were a cop?"

He hadn't told them anything. Seeing that little girl, knowing how close he'd come to shooting her, he'd completely lost it. That little girl and Lilli—they got tangled up in his mind. All he could see was a lifeless child's body sinking to the pavement. His Lilli. An innocent victim of some vindictive criminal. Was he any better? If he'd wounded that child, or worse... That little girl had been lucky. Unlike Lilli. By the time the police came over to him, he was bent over on the sidewalk, racked by sobs. He was sure those two young cops who carted him off with the drug dealer didn't know whether to take him down to the station house or to the nearest psycho ward.

"Riley?"

Sylver's voice reoriented him. "Yeah, yeah, I told them. I went in to make a report," he said offhandedly. He simply couldn't tell Sylver the part about him breaking down. It wasn't so much because he was ashamed as that it would open up an even bigger, more painful kettle of fish.

Sylver sensed that there was more to the story, but she was sensitive enough to realize even telling this much was a major breakthrough for Riley.

"Was that why you got thrown off the force?" she prodded gently. "Because of that incident?"

He took a sip of his now-lukewarm coffee. "Yeah. There
were no hard feelings, though. I was in no shape to stay on
the force and I knew it. It was really pretty much a mutual
decision."

"Do you miss it?"

He was slowly coming back from the abyss. The pain was
beginning to ebb, his heart rate starting to even out.

"It's still with me," he said, sounding more like his normal self. "I just write about it now."

"What pays the bills?" Sylver asked tentatively. For all
she knew, Riley could have a rich female patron who took
care of him. She found herself hoping she was wrong. The
idea of Riley being a kept man was thoroughly disturbing.
And completely alien to the way she saw him—troubled but
independent, tough but capable of great tenderness,
guarded yet struggling to open up. She saw them as having
a lot in common.

"I withdrew my pension. Didn't make me quite a mil-
lionaire," he said facetiously, "but I pretty much like living the simple life. I figure I've got enough dough to tide me
over for about three or four more months. Then, I either
finish this book and sell it or take some scrounge job as a
night watchman or a private cop, and stop kidding myself."

"How about letting me be the judge, Riley?" Sylver
asked softly.

Sylver began reading Riley's manuscript after breakfast,
making herself comfortable on the woven Navaho rug in
front of the stone fireplace in the spacious living room with
its enormous arched window, its pine posts, beams, panel-
ing and mantelpieces. Even if there had been any question
in her mind about whether Riley's novel, *Obsession*, was
going to be good, by the end of the first chapter she knew it
was more than good. It was brilliant.

At the same time she found the story itself deeply troubling. Of all things, he had chosen to write a crime novel

about an obsessed fan stalking a movie star, and the detective who tracks him down.

She didn't realize her agitation was so transparent—although misinterpreted—until Riley put aside some notes he was taking in long hand on a legal pad, rose from one of the cozy blue print wing chairs that flanked the fireplace, came over and placed the flat of his hand on the page she was reading. "I told you not to have any expectations. Look, just forget about it," he said gruffly.

She knew this was the time to tell him what it was about his book that was troubling her—not the writing by a long shot, but rather, how much her life seemed to be imitating his art.

Something held her back. The comparison seemed foolish. It wasn't as if her fan was stalking her. Who was ever harmed by a red rose? It was ridiculous. Besides, she didn't want to think about her faithful fan because it reminded her too much of who she had once been. Her days of being a movie star were long over, despite her mother's fantasies about her snagging a major role in a new Paradine movie. Nash had told her he'd read about her landing the part in a *Variety* article. Sylver had assured Nash it was nothing but a rumor instigated by her mother. Nash didn't believe her. He thought she was holding out on him. He was living in a dreamworld, just like her mother.

She shifted her focus back to Riley, gently but firmly lifting his hand off the page. The last thing she wanted was to in any way give the sensitive, insecure novice author the wrong impression.

"Even if I'd had expectations, Riley," she said, taking his hand firmly in hers, "I never would have expected this."

"Meaning?" he asked cautiously.

She smiled. A radiant smile. "Meaning you can write, Riley Quinn. Meaning you're a writer with a capital *W.* Meaning you'd better get your ass back to the typewriter this instant and finish your book."

Riley felt a whoosh of relief. So much for telling himself it didn't matter what anyone thought. Besides, Sylver wasn't anyone. "You really think it's that good?"

She gave him a friendly little shove. "Yeah. It's really that good."

He was so elated by her response that before he could think about what he was doing, he kissed her. Lightly, gratefully. At first. Until her lips responded to his. Then the kiss turned into something tender, intimate; taking on a will of its own.

A voice inside Riley's head was telling him he was taking a step from which there would be no retreat, but the incredible warmth and softness of Sylver's sweet lips was drowning out the warning. He wanted her. He wanted her so desperately it hurt.

Riley's kiss, so sudden and unexpected, unlocked a desire within Sylver akin to a drug rush. Her insides constricted, then expanded till she was floating, moving into the experience, letting it take over her whole body.

When the initial rush passed, instead of leaving her with that all-too-familiar dreaded letdown, her head cleared and she became sharply conscious of what was happening. Wanting it to happen. Not like she'd wanted drugs or booze. Now she didn't want her senses numbed. For the first time in what felt like a lifetime—maybe it was—she wanted to be immersed in feeling. Passion. Excitement. Need. Desire. Tenderness. Connection.

Her arms wrapped around Riley's neck, her lips parting, her tongue eagerly receiving his, new and powerful feelings consuming her. She felt like, until that moment, she'd drifted through life without any mooring. And now Riley Quinn, with his marvelous lips, his fine, strong body, his gentleness and soul, was providing her with an anchor. *Would wonders never cease? She was actually getting high on life. Or was it, on love?*

His mouth never leaving hers, he dipped her lower until they were both stretched out on the Navaho rug in front of the fire. She was still in her bathrobe. His fingers clumsily undid the tie. Under the robe she was wearing that delicate white nightgown that she'd held up for his approval the day before. Approval he hadn't trusted himself to give fully, for fear of what would happen. Of what *was* happening.

Sylver's eyes were closed, but her hands slipped beneath Riley's sweater. The first time she'd touched his warm, firm flesh. Another rush. Better than any drug. Her eyes opened, meeting his, electric emotion transforming their faces.

He saw the tiny tremor in her temple. He pressed his lips to it, absorbing the beat of her pulse. She slid closer against his body, her hands moving up his bare back. Her whole body trembled with the pent-up emotions and sensations breaking through all her carefully erected barriers.

She felt both vulnerable and without will. Riley had been her friend. After this, what would happen to their relationship? Without this, what would happen to her?

She tugged at his sweater, her lithe body undulating, urging him to undress her at the same time. She wanted to be flesh against flesh.

"Please, Riley," she whispered plaintively.

He let her tug the sweater over his head, Sylver thrilling to the sight of him bare-chested. Before this, she'd only been with two men. As for Nick Kramer, she'd succeeded in obliterating all memory of what he'd looked like naked. Then there was Nash. She supposed if a men's beauty contest were held, Riley's body wouldn't stand a chance against Nash's. Nash, with his perfect proportions, fine muscles, flawless skin; a body miraculously undiminished despite all the abuse he'd put it through. Nash was like Dorian Gray, the fictional character who never aged, but whose self-portrait bore the ravages of time and his debauchery.

There was nothing perfect about Riley's body. Scars marred his rough flesh; his muscles weren't finely honed; he wasn't perfectly proportioned. Yet she could imagine no physique ever seeming more desirable or beautiful to her. Riley was real, earthy, not ruled by vanity.

For a moment, as Riley began to lift up Sylver's nightgown, he hesitated. This was the point of no return. He might not be able to stop himself, but Sylver might come to her senses. She might stop him. When he looked down at her, though, he saw only yearning in her expression.

He undressed her, almost weeping with pleasure at the sight of her taut, firm body. The transformation from that painfully thin, wasted creature he'd found lying unconscious on a bedroom floor only two months ago into this sultry, sensual goddess made him incredulous.

Again, his lips met hers, this time their kiss full of heat and hunger, their hands all over each other's bodies, stroking, exploring, caressing. Riley still had on his jeans and Sylver impatiently fumbled with the snap. He reached down to help her when a figure fleeting past the window caught his eye.

He froze for an instant, then quickly rolled off her.

"Get your things on," he barked.

Sylver was so stunned by this bizarre turnaround, she couldn't move.

Riley had sprung to his feet. "Now, Sylver."

Awash with confusion, humiliation, rejection and shame, she snatched up her robe and quickly threw it on. He was racing across the room bare-chested, his jeans unsnapped.

Sylver was speechless as he raced out the front door. She sat there on the rug, staring after him. *Now this was taking coitus interruptus to new heights!*

Minutes later, when he reappeared, Sylver was seated demurely on the couch, once again clad in her nightgown and robe.

She cast him a wry look. "Wouldn't a cold shower have done the trick well enough?"

He smiled, but only barely. "I saw someone outside."

Sylver stared at Riley, incredulous. "What?"

He crossed his arms over his chest, rubbing his chilled skin. He was shivering. "It could have just been a hunter who got . . . sidetracked. Gone now."

Other more disturbing possibilities flew through Sylver's mind, but she urged them away. "Maybe it's deer season," she muttered, rising.

He started toward her, but they both knew whatever those moments of passion might have brought them a few minutes ago, they couldn't be recaptured now.

He stopped. She managed a weak smile, tossing him his sweater. "I'll go get dressed. You'd better get back to work."

He caught the sweater in midair, hesitated for a moment before slipping it back on.

As she started to leave the room, Riley called out her name. She stopped, but didn't turn back to face him.

He stared after her. Her head was slightly bowed, accentuating her long, graceful neck. "I'm sorry," he murmured.

Sylver nodded, taking in the words, but not knowing how to interpret them. Did Riley mean he was sorry they had almost made love or sorry they hadn't? She didn't ask. She wasn't sure she was ready to hear the answer.

It was two days before Christmas when Riley finally told Sylver about Lilli. Sylver had gotten to the part in his manuscript that involved his hero, Detective Michael O'Malley, fighting a custody battle in court for his little girl, Bridget.

They were in the living room. Sylver, dressed in jeans and a heather gray long-sleeved polo shirt, was curled up, cross-legged, on the colorful woven Navaho rug in front of the stone fireplace, while Riley sat with the sleeves of his frayed olive sweatshirt pulled up over his elbows, working at his typewriter at a small pine table near the Christmas tree they'd bought in town the day before along with two huge bags of ornaments they were going to hang on the tree that evening.

He looked up from the keys, smoothing his hair back from his face, and glanced over at Sylver. He saw her turn the page and brush away an errant tear. He got up slowly and walked over, kneeling behind her.

Sylver stopped reading, a chilling premonition clutching at her. "Something terrible happens to Bridget, doesn't it, Riley?"

He stared into the fire, its flickering flames dancing to a silent, mournful rhythm. "Yes. She . . . dies."

She leaned back into him. "Oh, Riley," she whispered with such tender sympathy that tears stung his eyes.

He tried to fight back the emotions that came with those tears—the old retreat-into-himself routine. It didn't work this time. He couldn't make his mind go blank.

Sylver twisted her head around and looked up at him. His face had gone pale and his eyes . . . She thought she had never seen such anguish in anyone's eyes. That was when she knew.

Her hand lifted to his damp cheek. "There was a real little girl, wasn't there, Riley?"

He looked down at her, but he wasn't really seeing her. Beads of sweat had broken out across his upper lip.

"Her name was Lilli." He didn't so much say the words as exhale them in a pained gasp.

As his daughter's name hung in the air, his head filled with the sound of screams. His own screams. Screams of shock and horror as those gunshots rang out and Lilli, without even a whimper, never knowing what hit her, crumpled to the ground. The whole time, he was holding her little hand....

He stared into the fire now. "She was born on Thanksgiving Day, eight years ago. A squealing, red-skinned, pinched-face little bit of a thing. To me, she was the most beautiful being God had ever created. That first time I lifted her into my arms...I was afraid she'd break. She was so tiny, my pinkie finger was twice the size of her whole hand."

He compressed his lips, tears streaming unchecked down his face. He told himself to stop now, knowing that if he went on he would be revealing the full sum of the pain and anguish, the recriminations and regrets he'd kept locked up inside him all these years, keeping him a prisoner. Was he ready for pardon? Or, at least, parole?

He looked down at the top of Sylver's golden head, which was pressed against his chest, surprised to see his own hand stroking her hair. He was so lost in himself, he had no idea he was touching her. She kept very still. He couldn't even hear her breathing. He could hear his own raspy breath, though.

"Her name was Lilli Anne Quinn and she was murdered three days after her fourth birthday."

As Sylver listened to his words and the background melody of agony, her heart felt weighted down by a terrible grief. She shifted around to face him so that she, too, was kneeling, her own features reflecting his sorrow.

"I loved her more than anything, and it was my fault she died," he said.

"No. I can't believe that." Not just words meant to soothe. Sylver knew it couldn't be true. She could see the deep, unabiding love he felt for his child woven through the very fiber of his being.

Riley felt himself being compelled back in time, no longer having the strength to keep it from happening. "I remember everything about that day as if someone had come along and filmed it in smell-o-vision Technicolor and then sealed the reel inside my head. For years, I ran the strip of film over and over in my mind. Lilli in her lavender-and-peach striped T-shirt with a little white daisy embroidered on the pocket over her heart, the royal blue running pants that didn't match, the new white high-top sneakers without a smudge on them. She'd dressed herself that morning, so excited that I was letting her pick out her own outfit. Her mother never let her do that.

"Tanya was a real stickler for things always matching. She bought everything for Lilli in sets. It drove Lilli nuts. Everything about Tanya drove me nuts. Then again, everything about me drove her nuts. That was why we split up when Lilli was only six months old. I tried to get custody, but I lost. Instead, I got to have her every other weekend and one month every summer.

"I don't know who looked forward to those weekends more—Lilli or me. It was funny. That morning, after she was dressed, she dragged me back into her bedroom to show me the mismatched outfit she'd set out to wear the next day. We laughed—" His voice broke. He squeezed his eyes shut. He had to go on, get it all out.

"Crazy, the things people fight about even when they're drowning in grief. Tanya and I had a huge battle because I insisted Lilli be . . . buried in that very outfit she'd planned on wearing that Sunday."

His lips were quivering. He dropped his head. A sob escaped his lips. Sylver put her arms around him and held him tightly. Her tender, loving embrace gave him the strength to go on.

"It was bright and sunny that Saturday morning. Lilli was so excited, she refused to eat breakfast. She wanted to wait until we got to Disneyland. Tanya and her boyfriend had taken her there once before when she was around two and a half, but she had no real memory of the place. She put her little hand in mine as we walked down the two flights of stairs of my apartment building, going on and on about Mickey Mouse and Cinderella. Those were her two favorites. She wanted to ride in Cinderella's big orange pumpkin coach and she wanted me to take a picture of her in Mickey's lap.

"I remember there was the smell of bacon cooking in the building. Lilli made this funny face, crinkling her nose and puckering her lips. She didn't like the smell. And someone in her nursery school had told her they kill pigs to make bacon, which really horrified her. She thought it was really terrible to kill anything that was alive. She said she'd never eat bacon as long . . . as long as she lived."

Sylver tightened her grip on him, Riley feeling like she was literally holding him together. "I remember how her ponytail bobbed as she insisted on jumping down the last three steps to the bottom of the landing. She almost fell, but I scooped her up just in time." He squeezed his eyes shut again. "Just in time."

Haltingly he told her the rest, the drive-by sniper-shooting by a vengeful dealer he'd sent up the river who was out on parole, the race in the ambulance to the hospital only to have Lilli pronounced dead less than an hour after they got there, his refusal to believe she was truly gone until Tanya burst into the hospital waiting room where he'd been sitting for hours waiting for a miracle that would not, could not, alter the grim reality.

"Tanya was sobbing and screaming. She rushed up to me and began pummeling me in the chest, slapping my face over and over. A couple of orderlies had to pry her off me. I didn't want them to stop her. I wanted those blows. More than anything, I wanted that bullet that had struck my little girl. Why? Why Lilli? I was the one who should have died. I wish to God I had."

He began sobbing in earnest, then, as Sylver cradled him in her arms, stroking him, soothing him, feeling the stinging grief of his loss as if it were her own. And then, suddenly, she knew why. In all the years since she'd had her abortion, she had never once mourned the loss of that baby she might have had. She'd blocked it out, just like she'd blocked out the rape from which that baby had been conceived. They clung to each other, both weeping for all that was lost and all that might have been.

When their eyes met again, they were huge with pain, but with something else, as well: longing.

"Riley," Sylver whispered, still in his embrace. She could feel his resistance. "Don't you...want me? Even just a little?"

A small sound of anguish strangled in his throat and he pulled her roughly against him. "A little? Don't you know, Sylver? Don't you know how much I want you?"

She pressed her face into the front of his soft sweatshirt. "No, Riley. Show me. Please..."

Guilt warred with his desire. "Are you sure this is what you want, Sylver? This isn't out of gratitude? Or pity?"

She lifted her head, her eyes meeting his. "Is that what you see, Riley? Pity? Gratitude?"

He looked searchingly, then smiled timorously. Her face was luminescent, strong with the same yearning he knew she saw in his face.

Still he hesitated, telling himself she wasn't prepared, when really he wasn't sure if he was. "I thought you needed more time. I don't want to take advantage...."

She quieted him with her lips. Lips so soft and yielding, Riley could feel what was left of his resistance crumbling. He lifted her in his arms and carried her into her bedroom, where he undressed her with an almost-reverential delight and then allowed her to do the same for him. They fell together naked on the big canopied bed.

Sylver smiled, but her lower lip trembled. "You know what's crazy, Riley? I feel like...a virgin. Like this is...my first time." How could she explain to him that, in a way, it *was* her first time. The first time she was ever truly *making love;* the first time she wanted to give herself fully and completely; the first time she understood what loving was all about.

He drew her to him, stroking her hair, then gently gliding his hand down her back, tracing the outline of her spine. He smiled as he brushed her lips, but a shudder passed through his body. "It isn't crazy, Sylver. This is a first for me, too."

He kissed her deeply then—a sloppy, noisy, delicious kiss. Sylver shifted her body closer to his, so close that not a speck of light could pass between them. It was like she couldn't get close enough, like she wanted to crawl under his skin.

When he gently but firmly drew her from him, she started to protest.

"I want to look at you," he said softly. "I want to see your beautiful face, your glorious body. Let me look, Sylver."

She felt shy and nervous under his tender gaze, afraid that close scrutiny would reveal all of the emotional scars crisscrossing her body. Slowly, his loving, honest smile, his gentle but seductive caresses stilled her fears, filling her with an unaccustomed feeling of pride, finally overwhelming her with the roller-coaster rush of her own desire.

Riley thrilled to the sight, the touch, the feel of Sylver. Her beauty cleansed and rejuvenated him. He felt filled with a new vitality, a zest for life he hadn't felt in a long, long time.

His mouth grazed her lips, but she held him fast, kissing him back with a need that was too powerful to contain. She wrapped her legs around him, all shyness gone. With a boldness that surprised her, she expressed her eagerness in moist, fiery kisses, and provocative caresses.

Her hips arched beneath him. "Let's disappear, Riley. Please. Please . . ."

"Oh, yes, Sylver. Yes. . . ."

Their hips collided until they found their rhythm. When they did, it was like magic; like every first time that existed on earth rolled into one. When they reached orgasm, they cried out unabashedly.

Afterward, wrapped in each other's arms, they lay on that big bed in that luxurious mountain retreat, filled with a topsy-turvy blend of rapturous contentment and anxiety. Was there really a chance for them? Could it ever work? They'd both screwed up their lives royally. Together, would they do any better?

Fifteen

"Don't sulk, Nash. You really aren't very attractive when you're down in the dumps."

Nash lit a joint and took a long, deep drag. The young redhead lying next to him on the bed leaned across him, snatching up the glass of bourbon from the cluttered bedside table. When she settled back against the pillows, she demurely pulled the sheet up over her naked, voluptuous breasts.

She threw him a look. "Not much of a talker, are ya?"

He glanced at her, realizing he didn't even remember her name. He'd picked her up at a pool hall down on Melrose a few hours ago.

"So, what are ya so bummed-out about?" she prodded. "A while ago you were really flying. I mean, I'd be flying too, if I stood a shot at a part in a legit movie."

"It's not just legit," he snapped. "It's A list all the way. A Lerner script directed by Adrian Needham. Man, it doesn't get any better."

"Yeah, well . . . So, like, when do you audition?"

That was the question, all right. The answer was—as soon as Sylver got finished with her vanishing act and he weaseled his way back into her heart. With Sylver snagging a supporting role in *Mortal Sin*, Nash was hoping he could get her to wield her influence to get him a reading. He didn't buy for one instant her story that her part in *Mortal Sin* was strictly a rumor being spread by her mother. Now that she was on her rise to the top again, she thought she could just cast her loving boyfriend aside like an old, worn shoe. Well, she thought wrong. He'd stuck by her through the bad times, and he damn well was going to be around for the good times.

Nash wasn't real worried, though. He knew the way back to Sylver's heart. Sure, she was on her soapbox now, but it only took one small misstep to fall off it. With a little nudge from a friend. And some fine blow.

Kate sat across the table from Artie Matthews in a small eatery with a Scandinavian motif near the ICA agency on Sunset. She was doing her best to conceal her foul mood, but Artie had known her a long time and he could see beneath her cool facade.

"I'm not blaming you, Kate. Or Needham. Laura's just not sure this is the right part for her at this time."

"She was sure three weeks ago. You told me yourself...."

Artie, a lean, balding, thirty-something man who favored Armani suits, cut Kate off at the pass. "I'm still working on her."

"And Jack West? You said he was in the bag. That as soon as he got back from Munich after the holidays he'd be ready to sign on the dotted line."

Artie took a bite of his roast-beef-and-Havarti-cheese sandwich.

Kate sat there waiting for him to chew and swallow.

He dabbed the corners of his mouth with his blue-and-white-striped linen napkin. "Right. Right. West is still looking good."

Kate raised an eyebrow, pushing aside the chef's salad she'd hardly touched. "Looking good? That doesn't sound like 'in the bag,' Artie. Level with me."

He took a swallow of his mineral water laced with lime. "How about we do something totally anti-Hollywood and level with each other. The buzz is this picture's already in trouble. What I'm hearing is that this is a real high-stakes poker game and you might be holding the wrong hand."

"I'm not getting dumped, Artie. And I've got solid backing from Charlie Windham on this movie."

Artie lifted up one of the pieces of rye bread from the half sandwich that remained on his plate and slathered extra mustard on it. "Solid?"

Kate gritted her teeth. "Okay, okay. I read the trades, too. Let's just say that someone over at Paradine's got a grudge."

Artie grinned. "Do I get to make three guesses?"

"No," she said sharply.

"Only need one."

Kate's expression turned grim. This was all Doug's doing. He'd managed to leak word to the trades through his lackeys that the making of *Mortal Sin* was in jeopardy. He'd even gone on record as saying that he, for one, thought it a big mistake to put so much money into the Lerner project, and that it would bring in far greater profits were it to be made with a modest budget. When a studio chief made a remark like that, most people in the business translated that to mean there was a good chance the budget could start getting chopped drastically.

Kate was sure that Artie Matthews, concerned about his own reputation and standing with his mega-box-office stars, Laura Shelly and Jack West, had advised them to hold off on signing for *Mortal Sin* and let him see what was really going down. Both actors were up for other big-budget movies and it was Artie's job to make sure they made the right choice. Otherwise he might not have a job.

Kate understood all that, but right now she was behind the eight ball herself. If she didn't bring in Shelly and West for the leads, Doug's lies would turn into truths. Once word got out that her two stars had backed off, every other A-list actor would start to get nervous. What was so infuriating was that, were it not for Doug's deliberate fabrications, every element would be in place by now and this picture would be moving along without a snag. If she kept running into brick walls, she was going to have an increasingly harder time convincing Windham that her ship wasn't heading for very rocky waters.

Over dessert—apple tart for Artie, black coffee for her—Kate tried to allay the agent's anxieties. By the time the check came—she raced him for it and won—she thought she'd done a good job of damage control. They walked out of the restaurant together, Artie giving her his assurance that he felt satisfied and would convey his confidence in the project to Shelly and West.

They exchanged a light peck on the lips at her car and made little ''everything's gonna be great'' noises. Then Artie trotted off down the street to his office and Kate slid behind the wheel, started her BMW up, and flicked the air-conditioning onto high. She needed to cool down and give her stomach a couple of minutes to unknot.

She looked at her watch. Two-fifteen. She added eight hours to it. Ten-fifteen at night in London. Adrian was due to arrive at Heathrow in an hour. She wanted to fill him in on her meeting with Matthews, if for no other reason than to have someone to commiserate with over all the hoops she was having to jump through in order to get their movie made. What was so frustrating and nerve-racking was that every time she successfully cleared one hoop, she didn't even have time to pat herself on the back before Doug rolled another one out in what was becoming an endlessly obstacle-strewn path.

Kate considered the idea of phoning Adrian around four her time, which would make it midnight in London. She knew he was a night owl and would certainly be awake, but his family might not be, nor might they appreciate him getting a call at that late hour.

His family. The words stirred feelings of envy and sorrow in Kate, especially with the holidays around the corner. Her sense of aloneness, heightened by Adrian's departure and Doug's escalating attempts at sabotage, were hitting her hard. She thought about Sylver, up there in that romantic cabin in the mountains with Riley Quinn. If things were different, Kate could imagine herself there with Adrian, their naked bodies stretched out on her king-size bed or on the floor in front of a blazing hearth....

She shot out from the curb with a vengeance, ordering herself to stop mooning over Adrian like some lovesick adolescent. She was just down because she was having all this grief over *Mortal Sin*. Somehow, she was going to have to convince Doug that this had to stop; get him to see that in ruining this movie, he was not only destroying her career, but keeping Paradine Studios on a downward course. Surely, once he got it through his head that he was trying to cut off the very hand that kept him fed in beluga caviar and Dom Pérignon, he'd cease and desist.

She called Doug's private number from her car phone. He picked up on the fourth ring, sounding irritated and slightly winded.

"Are you okay?" Kate asked.

"Your concern is touching," Doug said dryly. "To what do I deserve this honor?" His voice was cutting and brisk, like he had someone on hold.

"I'd like to talk to you, Doug. I thought I could come by your office in . . . say, twenty minutes."

"I'm not at the office. I'm home."

That stopped Kate for a moment. Home. In the middle of the day. She quickly concluded that Doug's jet-setting wife, Julia, must be out of town. She just as quickly concluded that Doug wasn't home alone.

"When can we talk?" she asked bluntly.

"I'll stop by your place around four."

"I won't be—"

He hung up before she could finish.

Damn. The idea of having a tête-à-tête with Doug Garrison at home, given the shift in their relationship, made her decidedly uneasy. She'd wanted to keep their meetings in relatively public places. In case Doug got out of hand, she'd be in shouting distance of help.

After driving for a few minutes, she decided she was being overly paranoid. She could handle Doug. Hadn't she always? Besides, her housekeeper, Lucia, would be around. Doug would find it too humiliating to lose control in earshot of a "servant."

"So, do you like these better than the old ones?" she cooed seductively as he buried his face in her firm, voluptuous breasts.

Doug Garrison grunted, but the truth was he didn't really remember Nancy Cassidy's old breasts. A lot of years had gone by since he'd seen them, nuzzled them, sucked and caressed them. How many times had they been together?

Once? Twice? He wasn't sure. What the hell. Out with the old, in with the new. It seemed almost providential. Wasn't the New Year just around the corner? Anyway, he was horny and the new wasn't half bad, especially when viewed in the dim light with the curtains drawn. So, Nancy Cassidy wasn't a spring chicken. She did have better boobs than he'd seen on many a twenty-five-year-old. And she was working awfully hard at pleasing him.

As Doug attended to Nancy's breasts, she kept busy stroking him to an erection with slow, rhythmic motions while he groaned with pleasure. She smiled. She still remembered that he'd been quick on the trigger. He'd gotten even quicker with age.

He was panting heavily as he moved on top of her. Nancy breathed in the rich scent of his woodsy cologne as well as the heady aroma of wealth that emanated from the luxurious bedroom of his tony Beverly Hills mansion.

He entered her roughly, greedily. She wasn't exactly ready, but she didn't mind. Her hands cupped his buttocks. "Still the same ole bucking bronco. Ride 'er, cowboy. Just like the good old times."

When he came, she faked an orgasm. Not that she thought he'd really give a damn one way or the other, but it gave her a chance to do a little acting. If things had turned out differently years back, she might have been the star instead of Sylver. That had been the angle she'd been working on that hot summer night she'd shown up in Doug Garrison's Paradine office for an after-hours "interview." Things hadn't turned out as she'd expected, but then things rarely did in her book. Still, being the mother of the hottest female child star to hit Hollywood in decades had had more than its share of pleasures. And there were distinct advantages to being backstage and in clear control of things. She'd had respect. Studio heads, directors, producers, agents—they'd all stood in line waiting to kiss her ass.

If only Sylver hadn't gone off that night with Nicky Kramer and gotten herself knocked up. Nancy had seen Sylver heading down the same path to oblivion she'd taken. She wasn't about to let that happen. She'd thought she had it all under control....

Sweating and panting, Doug rolled off her, gave her a pat on her rump and told her offhandedly that he had another appointment, so she'd better get herself dressed and out of there.

Nancy pouted, not inclined to be so summarily dismissed. Especially not before she'd gotten what she'd really come here for, which was a guarantee in writing that Sylver had the part of Beth in *Mortal Sin.* The trades had run the story, but the buzz was that it was merely a rumor, which had only served to stir up lots of unpleasant old rumors about Sylver—rumors Nancy meant to put to rest.

Thank God, no word had gotten out about Sylver's most recent trials. While Nancy hated Sylver's new take-charge boyfriend, Riley Quinn, she was grateful to him for having kept her daughter's true identity under wraps at the hospital and then at the treatment center. The only other people who knew the truth were Kate Paley and Nash Walker. Neither of them was likely to go blabbing it—Kate because it would merely create more negative rumors about *Mortal Sin,* and Nash because Nancy was confident that he was hoping to ride back into stardom on her baby's coattails.

Doug was already getting out of bed. Nancy popped up, draping her arms around him, pressing her big, perfect, silicone breasts into his back.

"Come on, honeybuns. We were just getting warmed up." Her hands slinked down to his groin, her fingers playfully stroking him. "Don't tell me I've worn you out already?"

He glanced back at her, a cocksman's grin spread across his face. "Okay, but we got to make it quick."

Nancy smiled. She had a feeling he'd rise to the challenge. The question was, Would he rise to the bait? If sex didn't work, she could go another tack. One way or another, Doug wasn't going to renege on giving her baby a second chance at stardom. If it came to it, she could make things mighty uncomfortable for Douglas Garrison.

She'd kept their little secret for a long time—twenty-four years, to be exact. Not that Doug hadn't kept his part of the bargain for as long as she'd kept her daughter in line. Without Doug always there on the sidelines, Nancy knew Sylver might never have achieved the degree of success she had as a child. Now it was time for Doug to come through for Sylver again. He owed her. He owed them both.

Nancy drew Doug back onto the bed, slowly caressing his body with her moist lips. He guided her head lower until he had her where he wanted her. She willingly obliged. Once he was in her mouth, he clasped the sides of her head, setting the rhythm and the pace, Nancy adding a few moves of her own. He groaned loudly, growing very quickly with her ministrations, his thrusts increasingly rapid as he neared climax. Afterward he reached for a tissue, bestowing a smile of contentment on her. She hoped she'd be leaving with a smile on her face as well, and that it wouldn't come to her having to resort to veiled threats. But desperate times might require desperate measures.

"Lucia, I'm home," Kate called out as she stepped into her house. There was no answer from her housekeeper.

Kate frowned, only then remembering she had given Lucia the afternoon off to do Christmas shopping. She set her briefcase and pocketbook down on her hall table, checking her watch. Three forty-five. She actually gave some thought as to whom she might call to come over and act as referee, bouncer, or stabilizing force. There was always Eliot Reid, the celebrated Hollywood attorney who was escorting her to the annual Gifts for Tots charity holiday ball that evening. He wasn't due to pick her up until seven, but maybe she could invite him over earlier for cocktails. Say, five o'clock. The expected appearance of a renowned figure—an attorney, no less—would certainly keep Doug in line.

She went so far as to start dialing Eliot's number, but aborted the call before the first ring. Dropping the receiver back into the cradle, she told herself she was being ridiculous. As long as she kept the conversation civil and pleasant, she was sure things wouldn't get out of hand with Doug. After all, she wasn't looking to challenge him or pick a fight. She was intent on winning him over to her side. She was damn good at manipulation. One of the keys to her success.

It was close to five before Doug arrived. Not that anyone with any position in Hollywood was ever on time for an ap-

pointment—it would have been considered terribly dé-
classé. Still, Kate had begun to think maybe he wouldn't
show. Which wouldn't have boded well for her plan to get
him to stop spreading the bevy of lies he was deliberately
leaking about *Mortal Sin*.

She greeted him at the door with a martini in hand. He
took it without comment, walking past her so that he ended
up leading the way down the wide hallway into her living
room.

"So what's up?" he asked, taking a sip and glancing idly
around the room. He turned slowly to face her, sizing her up
coolly, the look of sheer disdain on his face taking her
aback.

"Sit down, Doug."

"Giving orders to the top brass now, Ms. Paley?"

Kate sighed. "Can't we even talk anymore, Doug? Are
things really that bad between us?"

Doug's posture, his whole manner, was defiant and bel-
ligerent. "Things are exactly the way you made them,
Kate."

"This isn't all about my breaking off our affair...."

"So, tell me. Is Needham really that good in the sack?"

"Don't be crude, Doug. It isn't you."

He smiled blandly, finishing off his martini in one long
swallow. Kate didn't intend to give him a refill. Doug, sober, was proving difficult enough to handle. Doug, drunk,
might prove too big for her to tackle.

She sat down on one of her tropical-print club chairs,
looking more composed and at ease than she felt by far. She
told him something she was sure he already knew. "We
could lose Laura Shelly and Jack West as the leads for
Mortal Sin. If that happens, we've got problems. Not that
there aren't a few other stars who could—" She stopped as
he turned and walked over to the bar, pouring himself a refill. She cursed herself for being dumb enough to leave the
martini pitcher out.

"Pour me one, too." She didn't want a cocktail, but she
figured that was one way to limit how much he consumed.

He glanced over his shoulder at her. "Say please."

She grit her teeth. "Please."

He laughed. "Doesn't come easy, does it, Kate." He finished off his second drink, then used the same glass to pour out one for her. He brought it over to where she was sitting. When she reached for it, he snatched hold of her wrist with his free hand. There was a frantic energy radiating from Doug. He got that way sometimes. After sex. Kate wondered whom he'd been with at his house before coming over here. Someone who'd held his interest long enough for him to arrive very late.

Kate could feel her patience already wearing thin. She could also feel a stirring of anxiety, but she was careful not to show it.

"We're not on opposing sides, Doug. I'm not your enemy."

"What are you, then?" His fingers tightened on her wrist.

"Let go of me, Doug. I don't appreciate these strong-arm tactics."

"You used to like it when I got physical. Or was that just an act? Were you just biding your time?"

"I'd like my drink," she said evenly.

"Say please." He smiled innocuously, but there was nothing innocuous in his tone.

Her pulse began beating like a drum against her temples. "Doug..."

Still clutching her wrist, he held the martini just out of reach. "Say please, Kate." His gaze was implacable.

Kate glared at him. "You're acting like a spoiled child, Doug."

"I'm just trying to teach you some manners, Kate. Didn't I tell you there were still some things I could teach you? Like humility? Gratitude? Loyalty?" He was looming over her now, forcing her arm up and then behind her neck.

Fear gathered in her eyes. She saw now that Doug really was on the edge. For the first time, she believed him capable of true physical violence. It chilled and thoroughly unnerved her.

"Say please, Kate." No smile now. His glazed eyes were menacing. What was more, she could see that he was enjoying himself.

Kate knew one thing. Whatever had gone before between them—the caring, the tenderness, the camaraderie, the mutual support—all of those fond memories would be forever tainted by these moments.

"All right," she relented, seeing no other choice. "Please." She spoke softly, wearily.

He laughed dryly. "There, it's getting a little easier, isn't it?"

To her dismay, instead of releasing his hold on her, Doug put the glass to her mouth. She refused to part her lips, finding this whole situation utterly humiliating, then realizing with alarm that this was exactly what Doug intended. He wanted to be in control, and he wanted her dependent on him. As long as he'd seen their relationship that way, he was fine. Once he viewed her as having the upper hand, it was simply intolerable.

He was tipping the drink so that it began running down her chin. She struck the glass away with her free hand, sending it flying across the room. Doug took the opportunity to snatch up her other wrist, pulling her roughly to her feet before she could offer any resistance.

"Eliot Reid will be here any minute, Doug." She knew there was no point in pretending Lucia was around since, if the housekeeper were there, she would have been the one to have opened the door when he arrived.

His eyes swept down over her clearly daytime persimmon-colored jersey Bill Blass shift. He smiled patronizingly. "And you're not even dressed."

Kate cursed herself for coming up with such a transparent lie. Better to deal straight from the top of the deck. "Doug, can't we sit down and talk like two rational adults? All I want is to make a great movie. I haven't stepped on your toes to make it. I came to you with it first. Okay, so you thought the budget was too steep, and your father-in-law decided to gamble . . ."

Doug wasn't listening. "I've missed you, Kate. I've tried 'em younger and I've tried 'em older, but you're still up there with the best of 'em."

Kate felt sickened. "Can't you see you're cheapening everything we once felt for each other?"

"My feelings for you haven't changed, Kate."

She gazed at him in amazement. "How can you say that? You've been running a nonstop campaign to ruin my movie, you come into my home and browbeat me, manhandle me...."

"I just want things to be the way they used to be." He pulled her closer to him, imprisoning her hands behind her back.

The inside of Kate's mouth went dryer than the desert sands. "This isn't the way...."

His gray eyes darkened as they flickered over her face. "I want you back, Kate. I need you."

He pressed her hard against him and she could feel the outline of his erection. Panic set in. He wouldn't...he couldn't mean to take her against her will. *Rape.* A horrible pressure expanded in her chest, making it hard to catch her breath.

"Doug, don't." She took a quick gasp of breath, fear seizing her heart. "Please."

The sharp ring of the telephone punctuated her plea. Doug seemed startled. He let her go abruptly, stepping back, giving her a scathing look. Now that she was released, her fear shifted to fury. She wanted to throw something at him, vent her rage on him.

Another ring. Kate hesitated, then crossed the room to answer the phone, if only to cry for help. As she picked it up, she turned back to Doug, wanting to ensure that he didn't make another move on her. To her relief, she saw him heading out of the room. She didn't say a word until she heard the front door slam shut.

She held the phone to her ear, her breathing raspy and shallow.

"Katie? Katie, is that you? Are you okay?"

Relief washed over her as the voice on the other end of the line penetrated. "Adrian?" Her own voice threatened to break as she whispered his name.

"What's wrong, Katie?"

Clasping the receiver like a lifeline, she crumpled into the nearest chair and covered her eyes with her hand. "Nothing...now."

"Katie. I miss you."

Her hand dropped from her eyes. "What?"

He laughed softly. "Bad connection? That would be my bloody luck."

"No. No, it isn't a bad connection. Where are you?"

"At Heathrow."

"And you called to say you miss me?"

There was a brief pause. "I don't suppose the feeling's mutual, Katie?"

Tears slipped down Kate's cheeks. She wasn't sure if she could handle the abrupt shift from sheer terror to sheer joy. "The feeling's more mutual than I can say."

"I've been a jerk, Katie. The truth of it is, I'm bloody scared."

Kate choked back a sob. "I'm scared, too."

"What would you say if I asked you to ditch all those glamorous parties and fetes, catch the next flight out to London and spend the holidays with me and the rest of the rowdy Needham clan?"

Kate could hardly believe her ears. She was so surprised, she was rendered temporarily speechless.

"I know you've got a whirlwind schedule and it's a lot to give up...."

Kate found her voice. "Do you mean it, Adrian? You...want me?"

He laughed softly, seductively. "Get over here, love, and I'll prove it to you."

"Oh, Adrian..." She couldn't say any more. She was overcome. So this was what it came down to? Here she was, one of the most successful and revered career women in Hollywood—at least for the time being—and a man at the other end of the universe calls and tells her he wants her and she's reduced to quivering ecstasy. Was this what it was really all about? Wanting to be wanted? Wanting to be loved? That, she quickly concluded, very much depended on who the man was that was doing the wanting.

"You're not crying, are you, Katie?"

The tears that had welled in her eyes spilled down her cheeks. "No. Of course, I'm not crying."

"Well, then, don't just stand there 'not crying,'" he teased. "You'd better hurry up and pack. Your flight leaves in one hour and fifteen minutes. A limo will be picking you up in forty-five minutes. You'll catch a 6:00 a.m. flight out of Kennedy and I'll be at Heathrow to pick you up tomorrow afternoon."

She laughed giddily through her tears. "You were awfully sure of my answer."

"No, love. I was just willing to risk looking an awful fool."

"Adrian?"

"Yes, Katie?"

There was so much she wanted to say, so many feelings swirling around inside her. She took in a raggedly drawn breath. Yet, in the end, all she said was, "See you soon."

Sixteen

Sylver woke on Christmas morning to the wonderful aroma of freshly brewed coffee and pancakes sizzling on the griddle. She stretched languidly, looking over at the clock to see that it was just past seven. For so many years, mornings had been nothing more than a blur to her, her usual waking time well into the late afternoon. Sometimes, it was well past dusk.

Whenever she did wake up, it was invariably with the accompanying wish that she hadn't. Her head always throbbed, her body ached and trembled, and all she could think about was how she was going to make it through the day without feeling even worse.

Now, she woke with a smile. Sylver Cassidy reborn. No aching limbs, no pounding migraine, no quick grab for whatever dregs might be left in the bottle of booze on her bureau.

How incredible it was to wake up clearheaded; even more incredible to wake up actually looking forward to the day ahead. A special day. How long had it been since Christmas morning had held any special meaning for her? Not since before she became a child star. After that, Christmas had become not a holiday but a media event produced by her mother, to be milked for all the publicity she could garner. Sylver still remembered with sadness and anger the shaggy cocker spaniel puppy her mother had given her one Christmas. She must have been eleven or twelve. The tiny puppy lay nestled in her arms that holiday morning, trembling, burrowing its wet nose into the crook of her arm, frightened by the constant flare of the paparazzo's flashbulbs. Sylver had adored the puppy. She called him Dodger.

Less than three months after she'd gotten him, she came home from a long day at the studio to find him gone. Nancy had given him to their gardener, telling her that it just wasn't fair to the dog to have to be left alone so many hours of the day. When she cried bitterly, arguing with her mother that she could have brought Dodger to the studio with her, Nancy had called her selfish and uncaring. How could a child of eleven understand that the shoe belonged on her mother's foot!

There was a light rap on her door. "Hey, sleepyhead. Don't you want to see if Santa came down our chimney last night?"

Sylver threw aside her sad memories of Christmases past. This was Christmas present and she'd allow no ghosts to mar the day. Leaping out of bed, she raced across her bedroom and threw open her bedroom door. "Hi."

The instant he saw her in her salmon-colored silk nightshirt, her flaxen hair seductively tousled, those azure eyes glinting with excitement and anticipation, Riley was overcome with a rush of arousal that he quickly hid behind what he hoped looked like a platonic smile. "You're up."

Sylver wagged a finger at him. "I was going to make breakfast this morning. You beat me to it." She grinned. "Smells great. Time to dig in?"

"It's kind of chilly in the kitchen. Better throw on a robe. And don't forget your slippers."

Sylver eyed him ruefully. "Don't go paternalistic on me, Riley."

Riley was feeling anything but fatherly toward Sylver, but he was bound and determined to keep his real feelings from getting out of hand again. He went over the litany in his head for what must have been the thousandth time—Sylver was still too vulnerable. She was just beginning to find herself again. There was no way she could know what she wanted yet; how she really felt about him. And, besides all that, she was way too young for him. He had to pull back. He couldn't let this become a full-blown affair. Or even allow the fantasy that it could be more than that.

He was feeling hot under his turtleneck. "I'll go...flip the pancakes while you...wash up. Don't forget your slippers."

He pulled her door closed, leaving Sylver to once again ponder the enigma that was Riley Quinn. Where did she stand with him? How did he really feel about her? One of these days she'd have to have a woman-to-man talk with him. Not today, though. She wasn't going to take any chances of anything happening to mar this special Christmas.

Sylver slipped on her soft off-white challis robe and obediently stepped into her slippers. As she walked into the living room she saw with delight that Riley had spread out their breakfast on the rug right beside the gaily decorated tree, under which were several gift-wrapped boxes. When they were in town a few days before, they'd split up to buy each other gifts, agreeing to make inexpensive choices since neither of them was exactly swimming in dough.

Sylver felt like a little kid as she gobbled down her pancakes, eager to get to unwrapping the gifts. Riley was only half through with his breakfast when she thrust a gold-foil-wrapped package in his lap.

"You first. Go on. Open it," she said. "It isn't much, of course, but I think it's something you'll like. I hope it is. You can certainly use it...."

He tossed a napkin at her. "Relax. I love it already."

She grinned. "Okay, okay. I'm nervous."

He started to undo the wrapping with painstaking care. Sylver leaned across him and ripped it off impatiently. Riley grinned at her as he lifted up the lid of the box, folded back the tissue paper and extracted a lovely burnt umber leather folder for holding papers. His initials were embossed in gold on the lower right.

Sylver watched nervously as he stared down silently at the gift, not saying anything. Did he hate it? Did he think it was useless? Silly?

"I thought... When you're taking notes for your novel...or for...whatever..." she stammered. "I only had them put R.Q. on it because...I didn't know if you had...a middle initial."

Slowly, Riley looked over at her. She let out a long breath when he finally smiled. "It's the most thoughtful gift anyone's ever given me," he murmured huskily.

Sylver flushed. "It was on sale. I didn't even have to pay extra for the initials."

He leaned across and kissed her lightly, chastely, on the lips. It took all of his willpower to pull back. It took all of Sylver's to allow his retreat.

Riley quickly handed her a small silver-foil-wrapped box. Sylver took it tremulously from him. As eager as she'd been to hurry him unwrapping her gift, she took her time with his, savoring the anticipation.

Now it was Riley's turn to get nervous. "It isn't much, Sylver. You probably..."

"Shh," she ordered. Riley clammed up.

Under the wrapping was a white velvet jewelry box. Sylver's heart was hammering as she lifted the lid. Inside, on a bed of deep blue velvet was a delicate white pearl on a silver chain.

Sylver's gaze shifted from the necklace to Riley and then back to the necklace again, carefully lifting it from the box. "Would you...put it on...for me?"

She turned away from Riley, dropping her head so that he would have an easier time with the clasp.

It took him a few tries. He was all thumbs and he couldn't stop thinking about what an exquisitely long and graceful neck Sylver had.

"There," he said finally.

Sylver looked down at the pearl. "It's beautiful, Riley."

Riley cleared his throat. "I'm happy you think so."

There was a long, pregnant pause as their eyes met and held.

"This is the best Christmas," she whispered.

Riley was having the same thought. Only one thing would make it better. He vigorously shook off the thought, determined to put sex out of his mind. He gestured to the rest of the gifts under the tree. "What should I open next?"

Sylver handed him the other two boxes. One contained a ream of typing paper. The other was a book of poetry by

Walt Whitman because Riley had once mentioned to her that he particularly liked the poet.

Riley had two more gifts for Sylver, as well. As she opened the first box she let out a gasp of delight. It was his finished manuscript.

"When?" she asked excitedly. As of yesterday he was still struggling with the final chapters.

"Last night."

"Oh, Riley, I can't wait to finish it. You know..." She hesitated.

Riley frowned. "What?"

She regarded him cautiously. "*Obsession* isn't just a fantastic book. It would make a...great movie."

"I don't know...." He shook his head. Then he squinted at Sylver. "You think so?"

"How about if you let Kate read it when we get back and ask her opinion?"

"I don't know. I'll have to think about it. I've got these two publishers to send the manuscript to. I sent them the first few chapters about a month ago and they were both interested. Neither of them would give me any definite word, though, until they saw the completed manuscript."

"You might be able to work a book and movie deal at the same time. This could be a huge across-the-board break for you, Riley. Why, you could make a mint—"

"Whoa. Slow down. I've seen what Hollywood's done to some novels. Those poor authors must have been cringing in their seats, tearing their hair out, wanting to—"

"Okay, okay. I get the message. Just think about it."

Riley nodded. "All right. I'll think about it," he lied, only because he didn't want anything to upset their day. "You still have one more gift to open."

Sylver stared down at the nine-by-eleven Manila envelope decorated with an assortment of Christmas stickers. She gave him a curious look. He smiled awkwardly.

She opened the envelope, sensing something momentous, and pulled out the single sheet of paper inside.

It was the dedication page to his novel. On the center of the sheet, neatly typed out, were the words: "To Lilli Anne for having once been the light of my life. And to Sylver for bringing that light back into my life after so many dark years.''

Tears welled in Sylver's eyes. She was overwhelmed. She didn't know what to say.

Riley's hand moved over hers. "I could never have finished the book without you, Sylver."

"Oh, Riley. You'll never know...what this means to me." Having said that, she burst into tears.

Riley smiled as he held her in his arms. "Or to me, Sylver. Or to me."

"More eggnog, Katie?" Frank Needham, a large, ruddy-faced man with a swath of gray hair, was already pouring a third refill into her glass before Kate could protest.

"You'll get her tipsy, Da," Adrian's sister, Freda, said with a bright laugh as she plucked her own glass of the spiked eggnog from her eleven-year-old son Francis's hand. "What are you trying to do? Give Katie here the impression that I'm raising a juvenile delinquent?" She gave the boy a playful swat on his behind as he left the dinner table to go merrily off to play with his new baseball glove that Kate had picked up for him at Kennedy airport. His sister, Diana, had already been excused from the table to play with her Christmas cache.

Kate smiled as Francis took off. Never had she bought so many gifts in such a short space of time, worrying the whole while she madly rushed about the air-terminal shopping area that she was buying all the wrong things.

As it turned out, she seemed to have done just fine. Francis adored his real American baseball mitt; his seven-year-old sister, Diana, seemed utterly taken with Barney, the stuffed dinosaur so popular in the States. The elder Needhams all seemed pleased by her selections, as well—Freda with her woven silk-and-linen scarf and sheepskin-lined leather gloves, her husband, Andrew, with the New York Knicks running suit, Frank with the carved African-figurine chess set—thank God she'd remembered Adrian having once mentioned his dad was an avid chess player. The toughest person to buy for had been Adrian. She'd felt at a complete loss as to what to get him. Finally, frantically wandering through a bookstore minutes before she had to board, she spied a beautifully illustrated edition of *A Child's Christmas in Wales* by Dylan Thomas. It wasn't much, but Adrian had seemed surprisingly touched when he opened it that Christmas morning, and had even read it aloud to the whole family later in the day.

Kate was deeply moved by the presents waiting for her under the tree that morning as well, knowing that they'd had to be, of necessity, last minute purchases. There was a lovely Lenox bone-china floral-patterned cup and saucer from Freda and Andrew, and a beautiful antique silver hair comb from Frank. Adrian's gift was a true delight—an exquisitely detailed fourteen-karat gold charm in the shape of a movie camera. Freda had dug up a thin strip of black velvet from her sewing kit so that she could wear it around her neck.

"More mincemeat pie, Katie?" Freda asked, rising from the table. She moved slowly, being close to seven months pregnant with twins.

"Oh, no, thanks. It was fantastic," Kate said, "but I couldn't eat another bite. I don't think I've eaten this much in . . . Well, I don't think I've ever eaten this much."

They all laughed. Adrian's dad, who was sitting on her right, gave her a hearty pat on the back. "Do it some more. You could use a little meat on your bones, lass."

Adrian, sitting to her left, came immediately to her defense. "She's fine just the way she is, Da."

Francis and Andrew shared a grin. Adrian flushed. Kate quickly rose to help Freda clear the table.

"Now you don't have to do a thing," Freda protested. "You're our guest. Besides, Adrian told us—" She clammed up abruptly, catching her brother's scathing look.

Kate looked from Freda to Adrian. "What? What did you tell her?"

Adrian shrugged. "Nothing."

Freda grinned. "Doesn't matter. Come to think of it, I could use a hand with this cleanup, Katie."

"What you could use," Kate said firmly, "is a nice rest. Adrian and I will do the cleaning up."

All eyes shot to Adrian. It was obvious to Kate from their expressions that none of them saw him as the domestic type. Kate's eyes were on him, too. Challenging.

With a laugh, he rose from the table. Freda raised an eyebrow. "Now you be careful, Adrian. This here's my good china and crystal."

"I'll be very gentle," he said solemnly.

"Wouldn't expect anything less of you, lad," Frank teased with a wink at Kate.

"Right, Adrian," Andrew piped in with a grin. "Mind you, same with the lass."

Freda gave her husband a swipe on the back of his head as she waddled toward the worn brown corduroy easy chair in the living room.

Adrian was smiling as he followed Kate into the tiny kitchen with its waist-high refrigerator, old-fashioned sink resting on stout pedestal legs, and the narrow four-burner stove that the Needham's referred to as the "cooker." Speckled Formica lined the small counter space and a similar pattern in linoleum covered the floor.

Kate carefully placed the dirty dishes on the counter. "Do you want to wash or dry?" she asked, snatching up one of two dish towels hanging from a hook above the sink.

When he didn't respond, she glanced over at him. He was still smiling.

"What's so amusing?" Her tone turned instantly defensive. Was he mocking her? Did he think she was making a fool of herself, trying so hard to fit in? Was it obvious that she stood out like a sore thumb in this warm, demonstrative, boisterous household?

He took the dish towel from her hand, swept it around her waist and drew her to him, holding on to both ends of the cloth. "You're something, Katie."

"Define 'something.'" Her tone was still a touch cautious, but she could see the pleasure glinting from his aquamarine eyes.

His thick brows knitted together contemplatively. "I don't know if I can. Would you settle for delightful? Surprising? Alluring?"

With each word, he drew her closer to him. By the time he got to "alluring," their lips were a mere fraction of an inch apart.

"Your family," she whispered.

He smiled devilishly. "They adore you."

"No. I mean...someone could walk in. One of...the children."

"Do you or don't you want to be kissed this very minute, Katie?"

Her body swayed into him, her lips already meeting his by the time she murmured, "Oh...yes." This was what she'd traveled across the Atlantic for.

Their kiss was openmouthed and full of urgency, Kate forgetting all about the Needham family gathered beyond the kitchen.

"How fast do you think we can get these dishes done?" Adrian whispered as they broke apart.

She smiled slyly. "What do you have in mind when we're done?"

"A visit to a lovely little room over The Fox and Goose."

"The Fox and...?"

"The pub just down the street."

They washed, dried and put the dishes away in record time. As Adrian hurried Kate out of the house, he called out to his family that he was going to take her down to the pub for a couple of pints. Andrew started to suggest going along with them, but Freda nudged him with her elbow. Titters followed them out the door, but neither of them noticed. They were too eager to get to that pub!

The room Adrian had reserved for their tryst was up a narrow flight of stairs to the side of the pub. Holding Kate's hand, he led the way.

"Come here often, do you?" she quipped.

"I only hope my other lovelies have cleared out before we get upstairs," he teased, with a wink back in her direction.

All teasing stopped as they stepped into the small, low-ceilinged guest room fitted with little more than a double bed covered with a puffy white down-filled duvet, a wooden bureau and a small floral-chintz boudoir chair that had seen better days. There was nothing quaint or charming about the space, but as Adrian shut the door and reached for her, Kate thought it nothing short of heaven.

Neither of them uttered a word as they quickly and efficiently dispensed with their clothes, leaving them in a pool on the floor by the door. A narrow window curtained in sheer muslin admitted a soft glow from a streetlight, bathing them in pale shadows.

Adrian wrapped his arms around Kate's naked body, once again marveling at how taut and firm she felt. With athletic ease, he hoisted her up, cupping her buttocks, and she circled her legs around his thighs.

He pressed her up against the closed door, entering her without any preliminaries. Kate was not only ready but desperate to receive him. She arched her head back, her eyes fluttering closed. Adrian watched the play of emotions on her face, taking a greedy delight in her mounting pleasure and excitement.

He, too, was immersed in a swirl of erotic intoxication. He had never stopped wanting her, dreaming about her. Kate Paley stirred a relentless craving inside him that he couldn't temper, no matter how hard he tried.

With each of his thrusts, her back thumped against the door and for a moment he worried that he might be hurting her. When he started to move her away, she clung to him, urging him on, begging him not to stop.

Kate could feel her heartbeat in her throat, gasping as he plunged deeper and deeper, wanting him to fill her completely. For once, she wanted to hold nothing back. *Just love me and let me love you. Is it possible it isn't really so hard for me to do? Have I gone and wasted years, terrified of something that really never existed?*

Later, he carried her to the bed, the downy soft duvet enveloping them as they stretched out alongside each other. He kissed her softly, tenderly, his tongue teasing her lips, sliding along her teeth, finding her tongue. Kate's hands moved languidly over his sweat-dampened body with loving strokes.

They made love again, this time neither of them hurrying. Kate loved Adrian's gentleness, the way his knowing hands stroked and caressed her body in all the right ways, in all the right places. He was making love to her, caring about her pleasure, all of his attention focused on arousing and delighting her. It was more than she'd had in a long time; more than she expected. More than she deserved?

Adrian was immediately aware of the shift in her feelings. He kissed her softly on her lips, her throat, her breasts. He pressed his mouth to her ear and told her how much he wanted her, how beautiful she was, how good it was to be together again.

"It's always been you and me, Katie," he murmured. "Always will be."

She gave a shuddering sigh, then her mouth covered his in a deep, passionate kiss, urging him on top of her, her need for him expanding so rapidly within her she felt she might explode. When he entered her again, she cried aloud, shameless in her passion, not wanting—no, unable—to hold anything back. She felt whole and complete for the first time in ages. Adrian filled her, body and soul. He wasn't Doug—selfish, needy, insensitive. Adrian was his own man. He was generous and he made lovemaking a two-way partnership. It was only now that Kate realized the emotional anguish she'd been suffering in silence for so long, trying so desperately to deny its existence.

"This is the very best Christmas I've ever spent," Kate murmured euphorically, snuggling into him afterward. It was all the more wonderful for how unexpected it was. She'd just about given up all hope that they would ever again be together like this.

"Even though you had to miss all those fancy balls?" he queried softly, that cockney lilt of his sounding sexy and irresistible as he nuzzled her neck.

Kate stretched against him, her back arching balletically. "With a bunch of boring, self-absorbed moguls and mogulettes. You saved me from utter tedium." She hesitated. "You saved me from more than you know."

Adrian was immediately alert to the hint of disturbance in her tone and the faint tremor of tension in the muscles beneath her flesh.

He lifted himself on his elbow, looking down at her. "What do you mean?"

Kate immediately regretted having given Adrian anything to question. She'd decided on the flight over not to ruin their time together by making any reference to her last troubling encounter with Doug from which, thanks to Adrian's phone call, she'd been literally saved by the bell.

"Nothing." She lifted her eyes to meet his, having difficulty when she arrived there. "Really."

"You're a bloody lousy liar, Kate."

So it was Kate now. He only called her Kate when he was in a very serious, no-nonsense state of mind.

She kissed him lightly, teasingly on the lips, compelled to lighten his mood, hating to see their rapturous moments together ruined.

"I'm usually a very good liar. See what's become of me?" It was a vain attempt to procure so much as a half smile from those lips she still hungered for.

"The more you dodge the issue, the more momentous you make it," he argued logically.

She adored him for many reasons, but being logical—at least right now—wasn't one of them.

"It will only make you angry. It certainly did me," Kate admitted reluctantly. "And I don't want either of us to feel anger now."

"That means it has to do with Doug Garrison."

Sublime logic. She did have to admire it. "Yes, all right. We had another one of our...confrontations." She decided it would be best not to tell him where they had it or how "intense" it had gotten.

Backtracking, she told him first about her luncheon meeting with Artie Matthews. Adrian was furious when he learned that Jack West and Laura Shelly might not sign on after all. Like Kate, he knew exactly who was responsible for their ambivalence.

"I tried to talk to Doug, make him see that he was only hurting himself and the studio by being so spiteful, but he was completely unreasonable," Kate went on as Adrian scrutinized her, mining her face for any sign of deception.

"We'll pull it off in the end," she went on, her tone determinedly upbeat. "I'm sure of it. Doug will come around in time." Too late, she realized she'd infused her voice with too much confidence. Adrian drew her away from him, his hands firmly gripping her shoulders.

"You're scared," he said.

"Not scared." Not now that she was safe in Adrian's arms, she thought. "Just worried. Hey, headaches go with the territory."

"You're holding back on me, Katie. I can see it in your eyes, feel it in your body." He squinted at her searchingly and then his eyes widened. "Jesus, he was there. He was there when I called you. I remember, your voice sounded . . . funny. Like something was wrong. Like you were...scared. Were you scared, Katie?"

The question hung in the air like an unpleasant odor.

Kate could feel her eyes smart with tears. They came on her so suddenly, she couldn't stop them. She wasn't even sure if her tears were a reaction to the terror and anger she'd felt at Doug for sexually harassing her, or if it was a reaction to Adrian pressuring her. Or maybe what it really had to do with was her need to unburden herself, even though it meant revealing the core of vulnerability she was always trying so hard to hide. No man had ever made it more difficult to conceal than Adrian.

Haltingly, lying together in the little room that minutes before had pulsated with a warm and cozy afterglow only to give way to a melancholy drabness, Kate told Adrian the whole story. He didn't say a word when she finished. He just lay there, not moving a muscle, like he'd become rooted to the spot. When she looked into his eyes, though, she could see the emotions gathering there like a storm.

"Nothing actually did happen," she said shakily.

"I could kill the bloody bastard," Adrian said huskily, each word punctuating the air like a sharp stab of rage.

Kate had felt much the same way during her encounter with Doug—when she wasn't being too frightened to be angry—but time and distance had tempered her rage. Now, she saw that she'd have to temper Adrian's.

"Let's get dressed and go downstairs to the pub," she pleaded softly. "I'd love a pint. I know—we'll play a game of darts and whoever wins buys the first round." She was trying so desperately to bring him around, but she could see that she was unlikely to make any progress.

Riley was so nervous while Sylver settled down in the living room to finish reading his novel, that she suggested he take a late-afternoon stroll. After he left, she stoked the fire and curled up on the rug with the last few chapters of his manuscript.

She must have been reading for about forty-five minutes, so absorbed in the story that at first she didn't register the knock at her front door. A second knock made her look up from the page. Damn, she was right at the most exciting part—the stalker himself being stalked by Holly Blake, the actress who had joined forces with Detective Michael O'Malley. They were closing in on him....

A third rap made her reluctantly set the page down. She rose and started for the door, thinking Riley must have accidentally locked himself out and forgotten to take the key.

"You're too early. I'm not finished," she was saying as she swung open the door.

Riley wasn't standing there. No one was in sight. A low gasp escaped her lips as she lowered her gaze. Something had been left just outside the door. A long white box tied with a luxurious satin bow. A *red* satin bow. Sylver immediately flashed on it looking like a coffin, but she knew what it really was. A florist's box.

She stared down at it. Another Christmas gift from Riley? An extra surprise? She rubbed her hands together nervously, a new, frightening thought streaking through her mind. She tried to shake herself free of it. Okay, what if Riley had arranged to have a bouquet of flowers delivered to her? Instead of standing there panicked, thinking there was something sinister here, she should see it for what it was—a lovely romantic gesture.

Just as long as what was inside that box wasn't a bouquet of red roses. Anything—daisies, daffodils, chrysanthemums. Anything but red roses. Because if they were red roses, that would mean Riley could be... She shut her eyes, chastising herself for her runaway imagination.

She knelt down and began to slowly, cautiously lift off the lid of the box. She peeled aside the green tissue paper. A guttural sob escaped her lips as she stared down at the bouquet. Wishing hadn't changed the reality. A dozen red roses lay nestled on the bed of green. And a note. "I will watch over you always. Your everlasting fan...."

She jumped back with alarm as she saw Riley coming up the path to the front door. He was smiling nervously, his expression filled with expectation. When he got to her, her eyes were wild with rage and panic. She literally sprang for him, feeling out of control.

"Did you buy me these? Did you? Tell me, damn it. Has it been you all along? Watching me? Following me? Stalking me? Is that why you wrote that book? Letting me think you were the detective when all along you were the obsessed stalker? God, Riley, I trusted you. Why me?"

Suddenly her knees went soft. Black dots began swimming before her eyes. Riley caught her up in his arms and carried her inside the house. She was still clasping the note in her hand. He pried it from her fingers, read it, then kneeled down in front of her. She stared at him, but her eyes had gone blank and dead. It was too much. To finally have trusted someone...

"Listen to me, Sylver," Riley said softly but persuasively. "I didn't buy those flowers. Do you hear me? I am not your fan. I haven't been stalking you. Since we've been up here, though, I've had the feeling that someone might be. Remember that other day..."

Her eyes took on some life. She knew immediately which day Riley meant. The day they'd come within a hair's breadth of making love. The day he'd stopped so abruptly and flown out of the house. The day he'd seen something—no, someone—lurking outside.

"You said...you thought it was...a hunter," she stammered.

"I didn't want to scare you. Now, I see you've been scared for a while. How long has this been going on?"

She lowered her head, feeling drained. "A long time."

He cupped her chin, tilting her head back up so that their eyes met. He smoothed her hair back from her face. "I want you to tell me everything about this, Sylver, but only when you're ready. Only when you're absolutely sure, in your heart of hearts, that you can fully trust me."

She stared at him in silence for several moments, searching his face for some sign of obsession; some hint of madness. All that she saw was tenderness, concern, compassion, a tinge of sorrow. What she saw was the face of the man she had grown to love. A man who was now asking for her complete trust.

Her voice was whisper soft, but there was no hesitation in it as she began to tell Riley about her "everlasting fan." She started at the beginning, and he listened with rapt attention the whole time, never once interrupting her. When she was done, having told him all that she knew—which was sadly very little—he enfolded her in his arms and pressed his lips against her hair.

Sylver buried her face into his shoulder. "I'm sorry, Riley. I'm sorry for what I said before. How could I think, even for one minute..."

"Shh. Don't be sorry, Sylver. Just know one thing. I'm here for you and I'm not going to let any stalker—anyone at all—ever harm you. You're not alone anymore. Do you believe that?"

She lifted her head and looked into his eyes. A smile trembled on her lips. "Yes, Riley. I do believe that."

Seventeen

"I've had it, Katie," Adrian said, throwing up his hands as he paced back and forth across her studio office. He stopped at her desk, placing his hands palms down on its glossy wood surface, and eyeballed her. "Don't you see that your vision—my vision—it doesn't mean anything to Windham? It's the studio system with its connect-the-dots mentality. They just can't escape the dead zone of mediocrity. The stakes are too high, their hands clenched around those fistfuls of dollars. If Windham has his way—and why won't he, since it's his fists?—this movie will be unrecognizable from the one we intended to make. They'll keep sucking the fire out of it to make it more 'commercial.' It'll be mucked up completely."

Adrian had been ranting nonstop for several minutes. When he finally paused for a breath, Kate jumped in. "I know you're frustrated. So am I. We both know that Charlie Windham wouldn't be butting in now with all of his 'suggestions' if it weren't for this relentless campaign of Doug's to discredit us." She didn't add that it hadn't helped matters any that, right after their return from London a few weeks ago, Adrian had barged into Doug's office threatening to do him serious bodily harm if he ever again so much as touched a hair on her head. Kate was sure the only reason Doug hadn't seen to it that Adrian was fired on the spot was because he couldn't afford to risk the details of his encounter with her getting back to his father-in-law. He knew neither Kate nor Adrian would let it out, either—for fear of more bad press surrounding *Mortal Sin*. Since his run-in with Adrian, however, Doug had escalated his crusade to kill the picture, which he would certainly succeed in doing if her director walked out. Since then, Kate had had to step up her attempts to cajole the CEO and assuage his fears. Unfortunately, as hard and as fast as she was working to boost Windham's confidence in the project, and especially in her, Doug was working even faster and harder at making his father-in-law suspect the worst.

Adrian lifted his hands from her desk and pressed them together as if in prayer, resting his chin on his fingertips. "The horse is already dead, Kate. You just don't want to face it. You're trying to kick a dead horse."

Kate shook her head vehemently. "No, it's not true. We aren't licked, Adrian. If we stick together..."

"That's exactly what I want, love. I want us to stick together. Only we can't as long as you're stuck to Paradine."

Kate expelled a sigh of exasperation. "Déjà vu all over again," she said dryly, but inwardly she was terrified at the thought of losing Adrian once more. She was in love with him. She'd finally gotten brave enough to admit it to herself. She was almost brave enough to admit it to him. Until he hit her in the solar plexus with this veiled ultimatum. Would it really boil down to the same issue again? Having to choose between Adrian and Paradine?

Adrian's eyes filled with sadness. "Power corrupts, Katie. It happens to even the best of us. And you're one of the best. If you stay, it will poison you. It will poison every movie you make."

"And what will happen if I don't stay?" Kate countered, trying to quell her own incipient fears that she had already been corrupted by the system. And that it was too late to jump off the bandwagon now. And far too scary. As long as she held on to her position, fought to hold on to the power, she was a player. Walk out and she was just another "once-was," a brief "has-been."

"How will I feel knowing that some jealous, vengeful bastard drove me to quit?" she went on, finding some comfort in taking the offensive. "How do you think I feel when I pick up the trades and read rumors about my tenure at the studio being shaky? I will not be run out of this studio. It's tantamount to being run out of town. I'm not a quitter, Adrian. I'm a fighter. I always have been."

Adrian walked around her desk, swiveled her chair so that she was facing him. He leaned over, resting his hands on the arms of the chair. "The question is—what are you fighting for, Katie? We all have just so much fight in us. We've got to use what we have for the fights that really matter."

"Making good movies—great movies—matters to me, Adrian."

"And to me," Adrian said emphatically.

"*Mortal Sin* is a great movie."

He shook his head sadly. "No, Katie. It's a great *script*. If we were independents, with even half the budget, we could make a great movie. There'll be other great movies for us to make. What we need to do is reclaim dominion over our art. It's the only way."

Kate wanted to argue that he was wrong, only deep down she was afraid he might be right. Windham wanted all kinds of changes. And he was talking of cutting the budget now that Laura Shelly had definitely turned down the lead and Jack West was still vacillating. A smaller budget would mean Kate could all but forget about getting A-list actors, which she needed for *Mortal Sin* to have a serious shot as a box-office smash. Everything revolved around the grosses they could bring in during that first weekend release. Big-name stars were essential to draw in the early crowds and get a good word of mouth going so that *Mortal Sin* would develop staying power.

Adrian's hands moved from the arms of the chair to gently cup Kate's face. "Let it go, love. For the very reason we both got into this game to begin with. We're moviemakers."

Kate closed her eyes. "I don't think I can," she said in a pained whisper, knowing all that her words meant.

Her eyes opened as Adrian rose and stepped away. She wanted to reach out for him, pull him back, wrap her arms around him, wrap her whole body around him. She didn't because she knew that no matter how hard she clung to him, she could not span the invisible, ever-widening gap between them.

He walked over to the curved hunter green leather settee where he'd left his attaché case. She expected him to pick it up and walk out of her office without a word or a backward glance. Instead, he bent down, opened his case and retrieved a thick Manila envelope from it. He brought it over and set it down on her desk.

She gave it a curious look.

"It's Riley Quinn's novel," he said.

Kate nodded. Sylver had given it to her a couple of weeks ago, asking her to read it. Kate had passed it on to Adrian, planning to get around to it herself when she found the time.

"How was it?" she asked.

He smoothed back his dark, unruly hair. "I would say...extraordinary."

"Extraordinary?" Kate knew Adrian was not a man to throw praise like that around casually.

"I gave Quinn a call last night. He told me the two publishers he'd sent it to were both hot to buy it. He was flying out to New York today to meet with them. I suggested he get himself a literary agent." He paused briefly. "And a film agent."

Kate's eyes fell on the Manila envelope. "You think it would make a good movie?"

"No," Adrian whispered, a hint of a smile curving his lips. "I think it would make a great movie." He turned and started for the door, picking up his attaché case en route.

When he got to the door, he glanced back at her. "I told Quinn he ought to try his hand at writing the screenplay."

Kate's eyes met his. "What did he say?"

Adrian smiled fully now. "Some very derogatory things about Hollywood. All of which I told him I readily agreed with."

He turned away and reached for the doorknob.

"Adrian?"

He made no move, waiting for her to go on.

Kate hung back from the question as long as she could, finally asking, "Are you walking off the picture?"

"Eight years ago we parted precipitously," he said quietly, his back to her. "I don't want either of us to repeat the mistakes we made in the past. I won't do anything rash." He opened the door. "But I won't make you any promises I can't be sure I'll keep."

* * *

By any rational standards, Sylver knew her apartment was still shabby and woebegone, but since she and Riley had gotten back from Running Springs she'd set about doing her best to straighten the place up and make it cozy. Riley had helped her shop for curtains—she'd chosen bright red-and-white-checked gingham cafés for the living room and kitchenette, and soft, pale blue cotton drapes for the bedroom. She hung Modigliani and Van Gogh prints over the more serious cracks in the walls and even sprang for a woven rag rug to cancel the worst worn-out spots on the living room linoleum that was supposed to resemble wood planking.

She sat on her threadbare tweed sofa, admiring the redecoration, knowing she was merely putting off the depressing task of going through the want-ad listings in the newspaper. She had to find herself a job. At the moment her checking account was running on fumes. Kate had insisted on giving her another "loan" when she got out of the rehab center, but Sylver had adamantly told Kate it was the very last money she would take from her.

She returned to the listings, red pen in hand so she could circle all possibilities. As she started down the column where she'd left off, she could hear her mother talking to her as if she were sitting there right beside her on the sofa.

What a ridiculous waste, Sylver. Are you really going to take some pathetic, minimum-pay job as a waitress or a clerk, when you could be making a fortune in your real calling?

Sylver caught sight of the date on the top of the newspaper. January 18. Nancy had wangled her an audition for *Mortal Sin* on the 20th.

The tryout is strictly a formality, Sylver. Doug Garrison assures me the part is in the bag. The casting director simply wants to...get a look at you...make sure you're the right physical type. You know.

Sylver knew, all right. The casting director wanted to make sure she was sober, clean, and no longer looked wasted. Last night she'd talked it over with Riley. His view of Hollywood in general was less than glowing, and while he didn't spell it out in so many words, he made it clear enough that he thought she'd be nuts to get back on that treadmill again.

Nuts, but there was no denying it paid well. Then again, how did she assess the price she would have to pay if she went back into acting, a profession she hated? Plus there was her "fan" to think about. If she were in movies again, wouldn't that stir this fan's ardor even more? On the other hand, if she didn't go back, maybe he'd grow weary of chairing her one-man fan club. Not that she was even certain it was a man. She'd never seen him. That she knew of.

She glanced over at the coffee table where a business card lay in a clean ashtray. Riley had left it for her that morning before going off to LAX to catch his plane for New York. The card belonged to Riley's former partner on the L.A.P.D., Lieutenant Al Borgini, now the Beverly Hills homicide chief. Riley, who'd already touched base with him, had made her promise that if she spotted anyone lurking around the building or following her, she would call Borgini, tell him who she was, and he'd see to it that someone got out there on the double to investigate.

This "fan" of hers seemed to be freaking out Riley even more than he was her. Sylver chalked it up to Riley's overactive writer's imagination. After her outburst up at the chalet, she'd gone back to thinking her fan was harmless enough. There'd certainly been countless opportunities for him to have made a move on her had he wanted to; times when she'd been so wasted she wouldn't even have cared; times when she might have been grateful, had he put her out of her misery.

That had all changed. She wanted to live now. She wanted to feel that her life was vital, productive, meaningful. She wanted to make something of herself. Which meant finding something to do where she would be more than just a puppet on a string. It was finally time for her to pull her own strings.

Setting aside the newspaper, she decided to phone her mother with her decision not to go to that audition. Let Nancy deal with the casting director. She'd just started dialing when there was a knock on the door.

Sylver's eyes shot to the door. With Riley gone, and Kate unlikely to pay a visit to her humble abode, there were really no visitors that she particularly welcomed.

"Who is it?" There was a slight tremor in her voice.

"It's me, baby. Nash."

Sylver frowned. Nash had called several times since she'd been back, but she'd managed to discourage him from coming over, offering a variety of excuses. She didn't know if she was ready to see him, and she did know that never would be soon enough as far as Riley was concerned.

"Hey, baby."

She saw the handle jiggle and reluctantly went to open the door.

He let out a long, low whistle when he saw her. "Jeez, you look great, Sylver. Man, I can't believe my eyes."

He stepped into the apartment, circling around her like a wolfhound. She was wearing a pair of khaki cuffed walking shorts that showed off her long, shapely legs, and a jaunty blue-and-white-striped sailor jersey cut low at the V-neck and high at the waist.

He was behind her now and she turned to face him. She smiled. "I've put on fifteen pounds. And I've been doing some of the Jane Fonda workout tapes."

"It's worked out very nicely," Nash said seductively, his voice carrying a touch of good-ol'-boy Southern lilt.

It had been a long time since Sylver had been the recipient of Nash Walker's provocative charm, and she was a little thrown by it. She tried to assess if he was high on anything, but she wasn't sure. He was good at covering up. She might have gotten a clue from the size of his pupils, but he was wearing his favorite wire-rimmed Armani sunglasses. His outfit—tight jeans and a formfitting navy T-shirt, indicated that he certainly hadn't let his body go to wrack and ruin since they'd been apart.

"Aren't you going to offer me a drink or something?" he asked with a teasing smile.

"I...uh...only have...lemonade. Or orange juice. Or...water," she said nervously.

He brushed her lips with his. "Maybe I could offer you something, then."

She stepped away from him. "No," she said firmly.

He ambled into the living room, looking around. "Say, you cleaned the place up. Looks almost livable."

Sylver ran her hands up and down her arms. "It's fine. I... I'm comfortable."

He slung his long, lanky frame down on the couch, draping one leg over the arm. "You don't look comfortable, baby. You look uptight."

"It's just that I'm... kind of busy right now."

He glanced over at the newspaper on the coffee table, reached over and lifted it up. "The want ads?"

"Gotta work to pay the bills," she said with a manufactured smile.

He sat up a little straighter. "What about *Mortal Sin?*"

"Didn't ya know? I'm off sin. I'm into salvation." A poor attempt at humor. Neither of them smiled. If anything, Nash's expression turned abruptly grim.

"You didn't get the part?" It wasn't so much a question as an accusation. "I thought it was a sure thing."

Sylver hesitated. "I'm not auditioning for it. I don't want it. I... I don't want to go back to acting."

He let out a harsh laugh. "Baby, you didn't get clean in that rehab joint. You lost your marbles there."

"I don't expect you to understand," Sylver said quietly. Why should he understand now, when he never had before? Acting was his life. Next to drugs, booze and women. Or maybe they all blended together for him—inseparable components.

Nash crouched low, as if taking it in, then he sprang up from the couch like a panther. "You're right. I don't understand. Did you read the script? There are like three decent parts I could do with my eyes closed. The pimp, the cop who gets killed in the final shoot-'em-up, the hustler who roughs up the sister. Not that I couldn't play the lead, but hey, I'm not asking for miracles. I'm willing to work my way back up, pay my dues again."

Sylver wasn't surprised that all Nash really cared about was his career, not hers. He was just hoping that if she got in, she'd use her influence to get him in, too. She wasn't angry or disappointed. She just felt sorry for him. "I did put a word in for you to Kate."

His mouth tightened, making him look not ugly but menacing. "Yeah, and what did she say?"

Sylver hesitated. She couldn't tell Nash what Kate really had said, which was that he had talent the size of a pea and an ego the size of the planet. "She says the director's pretty much got certain actors in mind for those parts already."

"Yeah, well, I could act the pants off of every one of them, given half a chance." He sneered, reaching into his pocket for a small sack and settling back down on the couch.

Sylver stiffened. "Nash, please . . ."

He looked up at her, smiling crookedly as he got ready to do a line of coke. "Sure, baby. You know me. I've always shared whatever I scored with you. We could both use—"

She held up her hands as if to ward off his offer. "No. No, I don't want any. I'm not using anymore. I'm never—"

"Never say never, baby. Come on. Just one hit to unwind." He was already sampling the merchandise, waxing ecstatic over it. "Oh man, yeah. Nice. Real mellow. Takes the edge right off."

He held out his hand to her, gesturing for her to come join him.

She would have been lying to herself to pretend she wasn't tempted. She was uptight. She would like to unwind. She could still remember singing the very praises Nash was singing.

He was setting up another line of coke. For her. Sylver's eyes were riveted to the thin strand of white powder, beads of sweat punctuating her upper lip. Her heart was racing. It wouldn't slow down. She began silently cursing Riley for deserting her. If he were here now . . .

Oh, God, don't let me slip up. One slip and it's over. I know it.

She tried to recapture her fervor for staying clean—begun after her first torturous weeks at the rehab center and then cemented during her idyllic mountain holiday with Riley. If she screwed up now, what would Riley think? She was sure he'd be disgusted with her. She desperately didn't want that. She wanted him to be proud of her. Hell, she wanted him to want her. Little chance of that, if she went back to using.

Then she remembered what Sam Hibbs had told her at the center. *You can't stay clean for someone else, no matter how much you care about them. You have to stay clean for yourself, because you care about yourself. You can't really care about anyone else until you care enough about yourself to stand on your own two feet.* And he said something else. *It all boils down to a battle between fear and loathing on one side and self-esteem on the other. You have the power to determine the outcome of that battle. Only you can decide who's gonna win.*

Sylver pulled her eyes away from that tantalizing powdery white line on the coffee table and stared down at her bare feet, planted firmly on her brand-new rag rug. The pounding in her heart started to even out.

"I think you'd better go now, Nash," she said quietly, firmly.

Nash heard the conviction in her voice and realized he was going to have to try a new approach. After snorting the line, he rose and started toward her, a puppy-dog smile on his face. "Sorry, Sylver. I just thought—one hit for old times. But you're right. You never were all that good at handling the stuff. I should have watched over you better. I will from now on."

He was right in front of her now and he went to put his arms around her. She jerked away. He looked disappointed, sad, hurt. She wasn't sure how much was real, how much was acting. Maybe he was a better actor than any of them thought. Or maybe she was just feeling very vulnerable.

"Please try to understand, Nash. That...that part of my life is over for me. We can't..."

"We can do anything as long as we're together, baby," he murmured seductively, his breath warm on her face.

She stepped back, arms folded protectively across her chest, conscious of the frantic beating of her heart—not from temptation now, but uneasiness. "I need time...by myself, Nash."

He smiled dismissively, undressing her with his eyes—one of his true talents. "You do look good, Sylver. I've missed you. Things were bad before. I know that. I know I didn't treat you right. But I've never stopped loving you, baby. I've never stopped dreaming about when we could be back together again."

He drew closer and closer. Sylver began shaking her head. "It's over, Nash. I need to start fresh."

"Sure you do. I can dig that. Hey, lookee what I found in my pocket." He held up a little blue capsule between his thumb and index finger. "I haven't forgotten what you like, baby."

Sylver pushed him away, the capsule slipping from his hand to the floor.

"No," she said sharply. She spotted the pill, grinding it with the heel of her foot.

Nash still didn't believe her. He was sure he could get her to change her mind. He just had to work on her a little. It wasn't so much that he wanted her back on dope again. What he really wanted was to have her dependent on him again, have her turn to him, need him. He knew once they were back together, he could talk her into auditioning for *Mortal Sin*. And once she was in the movie, she'd have the director's ear. Adrian Needham. They didn't come much better. With Needham in the driver's seat, Nash was convinced he could do the acting job of his life. He'd prove to everyone he was more than a pretty face; that he had what it took. Gibson, Cruise, Costner—they had nothing over him; nothing but the chances he'd never gotten.

He shifted to a new tack. "I know what you're thinking, but you're way off base. I'm not trying to get you hooked again, baby. God, that's the last thing I want to see happen to you. Sure, I know they brainwashed you in that joint to believe you could never touch the stuff again, but they're full of it, Sylver. It's all about moderation. Hell, we can do anything as long as we don't get carried away. I'll make sure you don't abuse the stuff this time. You've got my word on that, baby. Just a hit or two every now and then. A couple of beers with pizza. If you're dragging one day, then you take a little energy boost. You're having trouble sleeping once in a while, so you pop a little pill. Everybody does it, baby. You don't want to miss out on all the fun. Now that your head's on straight, you can really enjoy it."

"Please don't do this to me, Nash," she pleaded, feeling some of the fight going out of her.

Nash could see it, too. He breathed a silent sigh of relief—almost home free. He slipped his arm around her waist. "Remember how good it was to make love when we were high on coke, Sylver?" He really was turned on by her. He hadn't felt this way since *Glory Girl*.

She swallowed hard. "That was a long time ago."

He brushed his lips to her cheek, his fingers stroking up and down her spine. "Too long. Have one little hit, baby, and we'll fly to the moon together. We'll reach the stars. We'll soar right over them. Just like the old times, baby..."

The old times. Those words echoed in Sylver's head. She remembered the old times, but not the way Nash apparently did. She remembered them with shame, bitterness, sorrow. They were dark memories that had sucked her slowly but irrevocably down the drain. What she wanted wasn't to revive the old times, but to put them truly behind her. These were the new times. A time to find herself; to find happiness, even love. She closed her eyes and she could see Riley smiling at her, a smile of encouragement. He was there for her. He couldn't fight her battles for her—only she could do that—but he could do something almost as important: He could believe in her.

"The old times are over, Nash," she said with such finality that even he got the message.

"Is it that guy next door? The ex-cop? You making it with him, Sylver?"

"No. This has nothing to do with Riley."

"Are you in love with him?"

"No. I don't know. I'm working on trying to love myself right now." She walked to the door, opened it.

He didn't make a move. "I almost forgot."

She eyed him warily.

He dug his hand into his pocket and pulled out a small gift-wrapped box. "A belated Merry Christmas, Sylver."

Sylver stared at him, suddenly misty-eyed. "Oh, Nash. I . . . I didn't get you . . . anything."

"Hey, that's okay. Look, Syl, I hope, whatever happens, we're gonna still be friends. We've been through a hell of a lot together."

She nodded. "Yes. Yes, we have."

"I'm sorry, Sylver. I'm not proud of a lot of things I've done."

"That makes two of us," she said softly.

"So, are we friends, Sylver?" he asked timorously, his eyes moist.

Sylver let the door close and walked over to Nash. "Yeah, we're friends."

He deposited the tiny box in her hand. She just stared down at it.

"Don't worry," he teased. "It's not an engagement ring."

She laughed softly and opened the box, letting out a cry of delight as she lifted up a pair of dangling silver earrings in the shape of stars, with a diamond chip in the center of each one.

"You are a star, Sylver. On or off the screen," he said softly.

"Thanks, Nash. They're lovely." She slipped them right on and she could see by his smile that he was pleased.

"Well, I guess . . . I'd better be going."

Impulsively, she leaned over and kissed him lightly on the lips—a chaste, sisterly kiss. "I'll talk to Kate again, Nash."

Nash left the apartment smiling.

His mouth sets in a hard line as he sees her old boyfriend leave the building. He watches Walker strutting down the street with the air of a man who'd gotten what he'd come there for. He can feel the veins in his neck protruding, his fists clenching tightly. He thinks to go after him, wipe that smirk off his face. He wets his lips, feeling a rush of pleasure at the fantasy of making him regret his visit to Sylver.

Later. He'd deal with him later. And with Quinn. Poor Sylver, too innocent and naive to understand that these men just wanted to use her. She didn't realize she was being abused, like she'd been abused all her life. There was so little love in this world. Sometimes he felt like he had cornered the market on it. And it was all Sylver's for the taking. He would show her what it was like not to be taken for granted. She would blossom and flower under his tender, unselfish love.

His hand slips in his pocket, not to feel the comfort of his gun, which is nestled safely in his other pocket, but the key to the condo—soon to be Sylver's new home. This is the perfect day for the move. Quinn is gone. He saw him leave the building earlier that morning with an overnight case in hand, and get into a waiting cab. He brazenly walked right by it, catching Quinn bark "LAX" to the cabbie before slamming the door shut. With Quinn out of town and the old boyfriend on his way again, the coast is clear.

The question plaguing him is how to do it. Does he walk right up to her apartment, ring her doorbell, introduce himself, and invite her for a drive? Would she go with him? Would she look into his eyes and see the trust and love radiating from them and know that she would be in safe hands? The safest of hands?

It plays out beautifully in fantasy, but he's smart enough to realize that his plan might not work. He needs a backup. He has one. Only he isn't thrilled about the idea of resorting to it. He is not, and never has been, a violent man. He comforts himself with the belief that, in this case, the means, if necessary, would more than justify the end.

Eighteen

Stars and Spars looked a little like a nineteenth-century McDonald's with glorious sandwiches, salads, and homemade soups served up amid old-time movie posters and other movie star memorabilia. A funky eatery that was fast becoming one of the biggest "in" spots to hit the Hollywood restaurant scene in years.

The infamous "Spars" herself wedged her ample six-foot frame into a fuchsia-painted booth, one of about thirty that filled the large restaurant, sliding a bowl of her special Five-Alarm Texas Chili in front of Kate.

Kate gave the steaming plate a dubious look. "It's ten o'clock in the morning. I don't think . . ."

"Go on," Marianne ordered. "It'll perk you up. And, honey, you need perking up."

Marianne's voice boomed through the empty restaurant that didn't open until eleven. By eleven-fifteen, Kate knew the joint would be jumping, tourists rubbing elbows with truck drivers and movie people. It would keep up until the restaurant closed at two in the morning.

Kate took a taste of the chili and her eyes immediately started to tear.

Marianne grinned. "Told you."

Kate set her fork down. "I've been so wound up I started seeing a psychiatrist. Not that he's helping much."

Marianne's demeanor softened. "Rough times, huh? I read in the trades that Laura Shelly and Jack West both turned down the leads in *Mortal Sin*."

Kate rubbed her temples. Her head was pounding. "It's like I've got the Midas touch. Instead of everything turning to gold, though, it's turning to dust. Disintegrating in my hands. Now Windham's hedging on giving me final cut. What am I doing here?'' Kate muttered mournfully.

Marianne leaned forward and gave her friend a sympathetic pat on the hand. ''You're trying to ride a bucking bronco who's trying his damnedest to throw you off. You've just got to hold tight and ride him out.''

''I think Adrian's going to walk,'' Kate said, taking another bite of chili, this time welcoming the burning sensation. She'd been feeling numb ever since her encounter with him in her office the day before.

''He wouldn't,'' Marianne said, disbelieving. ''The guy's nuts about you. He had you meet his family in London, for chrissakes.''

Kate felt drained and exhausted. She hadn't slept more than a couple of hours last night and she'd actually canceled her morning appointment with her personal trainer. Right now, even the thought of her body going to pot didn't faze her. ''Oh, Marianne, I wouldn't blame him if he did walk out. Charlie Windham's driving us both nuts. He's getting cold feet about the project—or at least about my being in charge of it—all thanks to you-know-who.''

Marianne's violet eyes glinted with disgust. ''I'd like to wring you-know-who's neck.''

''Doug's off the wall,'' Kate said tightly. ''He's not going to be satisfied until he gets this movie shelved because no one will touch it with a ten-foot pole.'' She tried massaging her temples again. ''Word's out that my number may be up at Paradine. Last night I was at Spago after the opening of *Compelling Forces* and I bumped into Artie Matthews. He barely said hello. I had to practically plant myself in his path. Lovely getting snubbed by underlings. I'll bet you anything, Artie's already putting out feelers to shop Lerner's script elsewhere.''

''What are you going to do?'' Marianne asked with concern, sipping on a glass of spring water with a twist of lime.

Kate gave her a hapless look. ''Why do you think I'm sitting here with a bowl of chili in front of me at ten o'clock in the morning? I don't know what I'm going to do. What *should* I do?''

"Well," Marianne said philosophically, "what are your choices?"

Kate sighed. "Adrian wants me to quit Paradine and go independent."

Marianne puckered her full ruby lips. "Hmm" was all she said.

"I've grown very accustomed to...living well, Marianne. There's no telling what sacrifices I'd have to make if I struck out on my own at this point. I was poor and now I'm rich. And let me tell you, rich is better."

"If it gets you what you want," Marianne interjected with a knowing smile.

"You mean Adrian," Kate said glumly.

Marianne grinned. "No, honey. *You* mean Adrian."

"He's slipping through my fingers again. I can see the writing on the wall."

"Make a fist. Hold on to him."

"If I hold on to him, I've got to let go of...everything I've worked all these years for." Kate wasn't only thinking about the money and all the security it had bought her. She'd have been lying to herself to deny that she also got off on the power and the glory. Being on the top in Hollywood was being about as "top" as it got. If she could weather this storm and get *Mortal Sin* to the screen and it was the hit she was convinced it would be, all the rumors and worries would be forgotten. She'd be golden.

Marianne gave her friend a level look. "I've had love and I've been alone. And, honey, having love wins, hands down. You think about that."

Kate nodded solemnly. She had a lot to think about.

That afternoon, Kate canceled her meetings and told Eileen to hold all her calls. She kicked off her pumps, settled on the curved leather couch in her office, and began reading Riley Quinn's novel, *Obsession*.

She was held spellbound from the first page to the last, not even realizing, until she had finished the book in the one sitting, that her right foot had fallen asleep and her neck had a crick in it.

Once she got the crick out and her circulation going again, she reached for the phone. It was nearly five o'clock. She dialed and Sylver picked up on the first ring.

"Why didn't you tell me that ex-cop of yours was a writer?" Kate said without preamble.

Sylver laughed. "You read his book."

"Read it? I devoured it. It's fantastic. It would make a great movie."

"That makes two of us who think so."

"Three," Kate corrected. "Adrian thinks so, too."

"Now all we have to do is convince Riley," Sylver said. "He doesn't exactly have a glowing view of the movie industry."

"I can't imagine why," Kate said facetiously.

Sylver hesitated. "I've been turning something over in my mind for the past week or so...."

"Let me guess," Kate broke in. "You wouldn't mind playing the movie star in *Obsession*. I can't blame you. The part is tailor-made for you...."

"No. Oh, God, no," Sylver said so sharply that Kate was taken aback.

"Sorry. I know how ambivalent you feel about returning to acting. And I agree with you completely that you're certainly not ready at this point to get back in front of the camera. Believe me, Sylver, I haven't had any hand in this audition your mother and Doug arranged for you for *Mortal Sin*. If Charlie Windham hadn't gotten it in his head that it would be a brilliant idea to bring you back on board... Well, I just hope you don't let them push you into anything you don't feel you can handle."

There was a long silence on the other end of the line.

"Sylver? What's wrong? Are you upset about what I just said?"

"No. No, of course not, Kate. As for the audition, I've already decided not to go. I'm through having my mother or Doug Garrison or anyone making my decisions for me."

Kate smiled. "Good for you."

There was another pause. Kate's smile faded. Sylver wasn't sounding herself. Her new self, anyway. Oh, no, Kate thought with a rush of panic, was she using again?

"When's Riley due back?" Kate asked cautiously.

"Not until the day after tomorrow. At the earliest."

"So, you're . . . all alone?" Kate pressed.

"Nash stopped by about an hour ago."

Kate felt sick. "Nash?" She began to pray silently that her worst fears weren't true. Why the hell couldn't that bastard Walker stay out of Sylver's life?

"He brought me a beautiful pair of earrings for Christmas," Sylver said softly.

Yeah. And what else did he bring you? "Earrings," Kate repeated inanely.

"Shaped like stars. With little diamond chips in the centers."

Kate bit down on her lower lip. "They sound . . . lovely."

"I . . . I told him I'd try to wangle him an audition for *Mortal Sin.*"

Wangle him an audition? Kate wanted to wangle him a nice, long jail sentence. "I told you, Adrian's already—"

"Right," Sylver said. "It's just that I know how hard it's been for Nash to get another break. I guess I was hoping if he did get a . . . a second chance, maybe he'd clean up his act, too."

Kate gave pause, letting Sylver's last words filter into her brain. "Then he didn't . . . ? You didn't . . . ?"

Again Sylver hesitated. "Is that what you were afraid of? That Nash would get me hooked again?"

Kate felt ashamed of herself. How could she have so little faith in Sylver? If she couldn't believe in her, who would? "I guess . . . when you said Nash was there, I just . . . for a minute . . ."

"It's okay, Kate. You were right to be afraid. I was afraid, too," Sylver confessed. "Nash was more than eager to share his goodies with me. And I was tempted. Sorely tempted. Since I've been straight, I've been flooded with feelings— good and bad. Things from the past keep playing in my head. Nicky. My mother. Even my little dog, Dodger. Do you remember him, Kate?"

"Dodger? Oh, right. The puppy Nancy got you for Christmas when you were a kid." Then Kate remembered with a start what had happened to Dodger. She remembered comforting Sylver over the loss of that dog and hating Nancy for having been so typically callous.

"Sometimes," Sylver said, "I still think it's easier to be numb, but I never think it's better. I didn't take Nash up on any of his offers." She laughed dryly. "He made several."

"That's great. That's terrific, Sylver," Kate said enthusiastically.

"I'm not going any of the old routes again, Kate. I want to travel down new roads. I'm terrified, but excited. Do you know what I mean?"

"I think I do," Kate said quietly.

"What I was saying before... about turning something over in my mind...?"

Kate had almost forgotten. "Yes?" Obviously, whatever it was, it didn't have to do with acting.

"I was thinking... maybe we could get together for a bite and... I could talk to you about it?" Sylver asked haltingly.

"Sure. Absolutely," Kate said without hesitation.

"Tonight?"

Kate frowned. "Oh, Sylver, I'd love to, but I can't tonight. I've got this damn dinner...."

"Hey, I understand. You're incredibly busy. I don't know how you do it. And do it so well, besides," Sylver said.

Kate wanted to tell her that she wasn't doing it well at all, but she didn't want to burden Sylver with her problems when Sylver had enough of her own to cope with. She flipped through her datebook. "How about tomorrow night? No, no, I forgot I've got this cocktail party.... Thursday night? Thursday night looks good."

"Great. Fine. Thursday's good," Sylver said. "Where should we meet?"

Now Kate hesitated. "Depends. Are you ready to... go public?"

Sylver took a few moments to think about it. While she was thinking it over, Kate offered to make dinner at her place.

"No," Sylver said firmly. "I mean... not that I'd mind eating at your house. It's just... Well, I don't have any reason to hide away. So I get my picture snapped a few dozen times. After a while they'll find someone else to pester."

Kate was proud of Sylver. She was beginning to see her in a whole new light. Most significant, Kate was seeing Sylver as a grown-up for the first time. Maybe she was losing a kid sister, but she was beginning to think she was gaining a friend. An equal.

"I know just the place," Kate said. "Stars and Spars, my old friend Marianne's new joint. My treat," she quickly added.

"Okay," Sylver said, "but hopefully next time—or at least sometime in the foreseeable future—it'll be my treat."

"Don't sweat it," Kate said gently. "About tonight, I'm sorry. I know with Riley gone..."

"I'll be okay," Sylver said hurriedly. "I'll be fine. Just fine. No problem."

After they hung up, Kate was left with a disquieting feeling although she couldn't quite put her finger on the reason. Something in Sylver's voice off and on during their phone conversation. An edginess that she was trying to cover up. Kate sighed, deciding she had to start having more confidence in Sylver's ability to cope.

Sylver set the phone down and began pacing nervously around her living room. Just before Kate had phoned, there'd been a knock on her door. She'd hesitated in seeing who was there, afraid it would be Nash again with his bag of goodies. When she finally did open the door, no one was out there. On the doorstep, though, was a single red rose.

Sylver had picked it up as if it were contaminated and shoved it in her trash. She was trying to decide whether to phone Riley's cop friend when Kate's call had come in. Kate's opener about Riley's book had temporarily pushed her worries aside. She was so happy that Kate had loved the book and saw its fantastic film potential. It was exactly what she had hoped for.

In the silence of her empty apartment, Sylver's uneasiness resurfaced. She flashed on the red rose. Her fan was obviously in the neighborhood. He could be lurking in her hallway this very minute. Should she have said something to

Kate? What could Kate do? She was too busy to even get together with her until Thursday.

She tiptoed over to her door, pressing her ear against it. Was it just her imagination or was she picking up faint footsteps out in the hall? She edged away, jumping when she heard a car backfire outside. Her eyes fell on the phone, and then on the small white card beside it.

Detective Hank Salsky sat on Sylver's living room couch, the red rose he'd retrieved from her trash tucked into a plastic bag. He had a notepad flipped open and he looked across at Sylver standing by her window.

"Anything else you can tell me about this character?" he asked, glancing over the few notes he'd scribbled on the page.

Sylver shook her head. "I told you. I've never seen him. I have no idea what he looks like." She stared down at the street. "He could be that guy in the blue jean jacket. Or the man in the running suit crossing the street. Or..."

"I get the picture," Salsky said, then chuckled. "What I mean is... I get that there is no picture."

Sylver fabricated a smile. "Sorry. I wish I could be more helpful. I've wasted your time. I shouldn't have called...."

Salsky raised his large bulk from the couch. "No problem. This kind of thing can really get to you. The price of fame, I guess."

"I'm hardly famous, Detective Salsky."

"Yeah, but you were, Miss Cassidy. I saw all your pictures. You might say I'm a real fan." He saw the flicker of fear cloud her features and quickly added, "Bad choice of words."

Sylver blushed. "I'm just edgy. If only he'd stop sending me those roses. If only he'd just leave me alone."

Salsky lumbered toward the door, checking the locks. He'd already gone through each room and checked the windows. "Looks pretty secure. You say your...friend's due back day after tomorrow?"

"Yes," Sylver said, knowing that once Riley came home—even though home was next door—she'd feel safe again.

"Then I'd stay put, especially after sundown," Salsky said. "Lock up everything and sit tight. If you're out during the day, stick to populated spots. Don't go wandering off down deserted streets or go parking your car in underground lots. That sort of thing."

He opened the door, checking the hallway. He glanced back at her. "Looks quiet, but if you actually see or hear someone trying to pay an uninvited call, you've got my number."

Sylver walked over to the door. "Thanks, Detective Salsky. And please thank Lieutenant Borgini."

Hank Salsky smiled, gave a little salute and left. As soon as the door shut, Sylver locked it and set the chain in place. Then she went around the apartment and made sure all the windows were locked, even though the detective had already done a check.

He has a thing about cops. As soon as he sees that cruiser pull up in front of Sylver's apartment, he gets edgy. The edginess grows when the cop comes back out and starts giving the people on the street a slow study. The cop even stops and talks to a few shopkeepers.

He feels conspicuous sitting in his car across the street. What if someone in Sylver's building reported a robbery or something? Just his luck, somebody in the neighborhood would have noticed he'd been hanging around a lot, and he'd get tagged as the robber.

As soon as the cop steps into a small Spanish grocery store, he pulls out. His plan would have to wait for another day. Driving past her building, he gazes up at her windows on the third floor.

Don't worry, princess. I'll be back for you. You can count on that.

Nineteen

Kate stared at Charlie Windham in utter disbelief. "No, I am not on antidepressant medication. And I most certainly will not submit to an impartial psychological assessment of my current mental state." She bit off each word.

Paradine's CEO seemed unperturbed by Kate's outburst. He sat there with studied detachment, in his unstylish brown suit, an expensive Cuban cigar wedged into the corner of his mouth, behind his enormous Chesterfield desk. He was surrounded by original and very phallic African and Tibetan art pieces, mounted in specially lit display cases around his enormous sun-splashed office.

She would have said more, but Charlie's trim, efficient secretary, Margaret, interrupted. The svelte twenty-something redhead carried in a glass of raspberry-flavored spring water with a twist of lime and handed it to Kate although she hadn't asked for it.

Charlie nodded and Margaret smiled fetchingly back at him. "Don't forget your blood-pressure pill at three, Mr. Windham."

As she slipped out of the office, Charlie sighed. "See what I mean, Kate? None of us are immune."

Kate couldn't believe the gall of the man. "I am probably the sanest person at this studio," she snapped. She didn't say, "including you," but it was clearly implied. Screw diplomacy!

"It's all relative," Charlie said with a shrug. "The point is, things aren't going well with this Lerner project. You know it and I know it. As for the reasons . . ."

Kate set the untouched glass of water down on Charlie's desk, deliberately ignoring the quaint little hunting-scene

coaster set out to protect the perfect finish of the wood. Let
him cope with a wet ring. Something to remember her by.
Because she knew if she didn't shut up this very instant and
do some tricky backstepping, it was going to be sayonara.
Only she was too revved up to shut up.

"I'll tell you the reasons," she countered, looking him
square in the eye. "In two words. Douglas Garrison."

Charlie Windham's expression was warm with sympathy. "Can I give you some advice, Kate? Don't hold a
grudge. Whatever went on between you and Douglas..." He
paused, extending his hand out, palm facing her. "Of
which, believe me, I don't want to know any of the details.... You had to know it was bound to come to an end.
For all Douglas's faults, and no one knows them better than
I do—"

Kate could certainly disagree there.

"He has a very strong allegiance to Julia. He did the right
thing, breaking it off with you...."

Kate's eyes widened as she stared at the CEO, incredulous. "Doug told you he broke it off with me? That's a
complete lie."

Charlie shrugged dismissively and returned to the subject at hand. "I got a call from Mel Frankel at ICA this
morning. He tells you you practically bit off his boy Artie
Matthews's ear when he told you Jack West had opted to do
a Keenan Zel project instead of going with the Lerner pic."

"You're damn straight I almost bit his ear off. Artie
swore up and down that West was committed to the project. I even threw in an extra point. And then he has the gall
to tell me West changed his mind at the last minute and decided to do something else. Something else? He didn't even
have the courtesy to make up something specific."

Charlie removed the cigar from his mouth and inspected
it like it held some deep message. Slowly, his gaze shifted to
Kate. "Now I want you to listen to me, and I don't want you
to say a word until I finish. I'm not pulling you off the
Lerner pic. I think it's got everything you think it's got, and
we could turn over a nice profit. I also think maybe we were
being a little too grandiose as far as the budget was concerned. Jack West, Laura Shelly—they could as easily

bankrupt a picture as bring in a profit. Especially when there are already tensions developing on the project. For all his caution, in this particular instance I think Doug is right—"

"Charlie, if you start to tighten the strings on this one, you'd be ruining—"

The CEO waved her off dismissively. "Hear me out now, Kate," Charlie said. It wasn't a request. It was an order. "What it all boils down to is that I see *Mortal Sin* as basically a small, character-driven piece. Instead of throwing in big names, a lot of bucks, I say we rethink it. Paradine can't really handle a big box-office disappointment right now, Kate. If we play it closer to the cuff, we can't lose too much and we may even win the hand."

Kate stared at him. *Mortal Sin* was her shot into the big leagues. With Charlie Windham losing his nerve, letting himself be guided by his son-in-law's neurotic need to keep her in her place, she knew she would never get out from under their thumbs.

Doug had won. His latest fabrication about her had clinched it. Somehow he'd found out she was seeing a shrink, providing him with a convenient lie that she was on antidepressant medication. More proof that she was unstable; that she didn't have the mettle to play with the high rollers. Charlie Windham, for all his lip service about his ineffectual son-in-law, had bought his deceits about her, hook, line and sinker.

Windham leaned back in his chair, smiled benevolently, apparently done with his sermon.

Kate knew if she stayed and made *Mortal Sin* with all the restrictions and changes, the film might still be able to make a respectable showing and she would be able to salvage her reputation; possibly even outsmart Doug. If she pulled *Mortal Sin* out of the hat, she could regain Windham's trust. That being the case, she would then be able to bring in *Obsession,* which she was now thinking could be an even bigger smash hit than *Mortal Sin.* The film version of Riley's book could be the one to put her name on the map.

She'd get to best Doug. She'd finally have the clout she had been working for all these years. She'd get the last laugh. All it required was selling out. And losing Adrian.

She rose slowly from the sumptuous Hepplewhite chair, feeling a disorienting mix of revulsion and relief. Windham rose, too, ever the gentleman. He stretched his hand out to her, certain of her acquiescence. His hand hung out there, untouched, as she quietly but resolutely said, "You'll have my resignation on your desk in the morning."

Charlie Windham's mouth dropped open. Kate had to smile, even though her insides were doing triple somersaults. She'd gotten the last laugh, after all.

She was a little wobbly walking over to her car. People passed and greeted her on the lot and she could do little more than nod numbly. Here she was, a woman who all her life had planned and plotted, developed carefully considered strategies, and she had just impulsively quit the very job she'd focused all those efforts on.

When she drove through Paradine's gates a few minutes later, however, Kate noticed that her headache had finally lifted, her heart was beating rhythmically instead of pounding threateningly, and the day, which had started out smoggy and overcast, was fresh and warm.

After trying without success to get Adrian on her car phone, she canceled her dinner engagement and then phoned Sylver, telling her she'd had a change of plans and was free for dinner that evening, after all.

Sylver was delighted.

Kate was in no mood to be brushing elbows with the stars that evening, so she chose to drive down to Newport Beach to a quiet, out-of-the-way Moroccan restaurant replete with exotic music and intimate tents decorated with Persian rugs for private dining.

Sylver was just as happy to get as far away from West Hollywood as possible, although she couldn't completely shake her edginess that her "fan" might be following them. Only after they'd pulled into the restaurant's parking lot and she saw that no other car had driven in after them, did she start to relax.

Kate didn't tell Sylver the news of her resignation until they were comfortably seated on low cushioned sofas and had washed their hands, a tradition before being served what was something of a ritual Moroccan feast—eaten without benefit of silverware.

Sylver was entranced by the atmosphere, although bemused by Kate's mood. She couldn't quite describe it, perhaps because she'd never actually seen Kate like this before.

"This feels like a celebration," Sylver commented, sipping on a cup of delicate, aromatic tea.

Kate smiled enigmatically. "It *is* a celebration."

Sylver's eyes shot to Kate's ring hand. "Did Adrian propose?"

Kate's smile faded for an instant. A proposal from Adrian. Would he ask her now? Was she ready for marriage? She wasn't even certain she was ready for a relationship. It seemed to be developing in spite of herself.

"Kate?" Sylver prodded, baffled by her silence.

Kate's smile returned as she met Sylver's puzzled gaze. "I quit."

"Quit?" Sylver echoed, not comprehending.

Kate tapped her teacup against Sylver's. "I am, what they say in baseball—or is it football, or both?—anyway, I'm a free agent."

Sylver's eyes widened. "You quit the studio? You walked out?"

"My legs were a little shaky at first, but it's amazing how quickly you relearn things you used to know how to do once you put your mind to it."

Sylver was stunned. Kate and Paradine Studios had been synonymous in her mind since she was a child. Kate had reached the pinnacle there. It was what she'd always wanted, what she'd strived for. "I can't believe it. No, what I mean is, I can't believe you're smiling about it."

"I am smiling, aren't I? I'm not sure I believe it, either." Kate laughed softly. "I thought it would be the end of the world. I am giving up a lot," she added matter-of-factly.

Sylver grinned. "That's an understatement." She hesitated. "So now what?"

"I don't know yet," Kate said.

Sylver's whole demeanor changed. Excitement bubbled inside her. It was like everything was finally falling into place for her. She could barely contain herself. "I do."

Kate gave her a curious look. "You do?"

"In a way, it's what I wanted to talk to you about. What I've been tossing around now, really, I guess, since I read Riley's book. I listened to all of Riley's gripes about what a studio would do to his powerful story once it got in their hands, and I had to admit he was probably right."

"Probably?" Kate said dryly. "Make that *definitely*. They'd trash it."

Sylver was on the edge of the couch. "I thought to myself, this book deserves better. And I figured I owed it to Riley to see that it got better. That's when it all clicked."

"What all clicked?" Kate asked, but she was beginning to get a sense of where all this was leading.

Sylver put her answer on hold until after the server, a thin, elegant young man in a fitted white Nehru-style jacket, brought them two bowls of fragrant Moroccan soup. It smelled wonderful, but both women were too preoccupied to even sample it.

"I realized," Sylver said, a hint of a tremor in her voice, "that this was my chance to make it in Hollywood on my own terms. Instead of being the puppet on a string, why not be the one pulling the strings?"

Kate stared at Sylver with newfound respect. "You want to produce *Obsession*." As she said it, she had no idea if Sylver could really pull it off, but she admired her enormously for wanting to give it a shot.

"No," Sylver said. "I want *us* to produce it. I need you, Kate. Before you just dropped the bomb of the century, I was going to ask you if there was any way you could help me get started. If there was someone already in the business that you trusted that I might be able to team up with."

Kate stared at Sylver, startled by the change in her. There was an exuberance and effervescence she'd never before seen in her.

Sylver leaned forward and clasped Kate's hand. "I want us to be partners."

Kate started to speak, but Sylver silenced her. "Oh, Kate, I know it's a far cry from where you've been, but really, there's no telling how far we could go. I know one thing. We couldn't find a better first venture than *Obsession*. And we'd be able to do it our way. Of course, we still have to win Riley over, but I'm betting that if all three of us . . ."

"*Three* of us?"

Sylver's eyes sparkled. "I figure Adrian will want in."

Kate laughed. "I suppose . . . he will."

"And once we've got Riley to do the script, which I know he's secretly itching to do, especially after he learns that the two of us will be in the driver's seat, we'll be set. Hell, we'll be unstoppable," she added with absolute conviction.

Kate fell against the back of the sofa. She felt a little dizzy. Her whole life was changing right before her eyes. Things were definitely out of control.

Sylver gave her a worried look. "I'm sorry, Kate. I'm coming at you like a steamroller. God, you'll probably have glorious offers from every studio in town by tomorrow. Money, position . . ."

Kate's eyes misted over.

Sylver was stricken with guilt. "It's okay, Kate. You can turn me down. I'll understand. Honest, I will. You don't owe me, Kate. You've already done so much—more than I can ever repay. I don't mean the money—I'll pay you back the money someday. I mean . . . your friendship, your honesty."

Tears started rolling down Kate's cheeks, but to Sylver's astonishment she saw that she was smiling.

"Are you all right, Kate?"

Kate wasn't sure. She felt a little dizzy and light-headed, but she didn't mind the feeling at all. "Go figure. I've just walked out on a multimillion-dollar job. I'll probably have to put my fabulous Bel Air mansion up for sale. I may never again get a power table at Morton's or La Scala. And you know what?"

"What?" Sylver asked tremulously.

Kate threw her arms out expansively as if she could gather the whole world to her bosom. She made do with Sylver, giving the astonished young woman a huge bear hug. "I feel great." She laughed gaily. "Correction, I feel great, partner."

"Partner? Kate, you mean it?" Sylver hugged her back. "Oh, Kate, I knew you wouldn't let me down."

Both women held on tightly.

"I have let you down in the past, Sylver. You, Adrian...maybe myself most of all. I'm going to do my best, though, to make it up to all of us from here on out."

The server arrived with tangy Moroccan salads meant to be scooped up with hunks of bread. He was dismayed to find their soups untouched, but Kate and Sylver assured him the soup was perfect; he was perfect; everything was perfect.

After he left, the two women laughed like giddy schoolgirls.

"I may be crying in my soup tomorrow," Kate confessed in a pause between laughter.

Sylver shook her head. "You'll be too busy to cry. So what shall we call ourselves?"

Kate snapped her fingers. "I've got it. FeelGreat Productions."

Sylver grinned. "I love it. FeelGreat Productions."

The women shook on it, hugged again, and then, feeling suddenly ravenous, settled down to do their exotic Moroccan feast justice. After dinner, eager to start the ball rolling, Kate invited Sylver to bunk out at her place for the next couple of days so they could work on drawing up a game plan. Sylver accepted the offer without hesitation, thrilled not to have to return to her empty West Hollywood apartment and her "fan."

He is going out of his mind with worry. Where is she? He'd driven back to her street the night before just in time to see her driving off in a fancy gunmetal gray BMW sports car. He took off in pursuit, but got trapped at a red light. He would have run the light, but his lousy luck, a cruiser pulled up right beside him. Nothing for him but to return to her street and wait for her to get home. Only she never came home that night.

If only he'd gotten a glimpse of the person behind the wheel of that BMW. He isn't even sure if it was a man or a woman. By the time dawn rolls around and Sylver still hasn't returned, he becomes convinced it was a man; convinced Sylver has spent the night with him.

For the first time, he feels a rush of anger toward Sylver, but he's immediately filled with a paroxysms of guilt and shame. How could he think she'd gone off and spent the night with some man? That wasn't at all like Sylver. There had to be some other explanation. His heart nearly stops and he gets clammy all over. What if something terrible happened to Sylver? What if there was a car accident?

A newspaper. He has to pick up a newspaper and see if there've been any reports of a gunmetal gray BMW having been involved in an accident last night. Or, God forbid, a carjacking. He flashes on his beautiful princess sprawled on a roadside in a pool of blood....

Bile rises in his throat. Panic sucks at him. He tears at the door handle, his hand trembling. Gotta get a paper. There's a convenience store across the street. He can almost see the headlines. Again, he flashes on his love's lifeless body.

Oh God, oh God....

He springs across the street, never seeing the blue Ford Probe until it's too late. He throws up his hands, his eyes wide as a frightened doe's as the car comes barreling into him. He hears someone scream and then everything goes black.

He's floating and out of the blackness, a slender blond-haired woman comes into view. She walks up to him and gently strokes his forehead. "I'm here now. Everything's going to be all right."

And he knows it will be.

PART THREE

Spring 1993

Twenty

The FeelGreat Productions team had been trotting around town with *Obsession* for six weeks, testing the waters, only to discover they were not only going against the current, they were rowing upstream without a paddle in very turbulent waters. Stirring up that turbulence to fever pitch was none other than Douglas Garrison.

Kate's leaving Paradine had not satisfied her ex-lover/ex-mentor's thirst for revenge. Doug was far from through with his smear attack. On the contrary. It had gotten worse, his campaign spreading to Sylver, Adrian and Riley. He wanted to see them all ruined. No way was he going to take any chances on them outsmarting him and coming up with their own winning film. He'd hired a private detective who had managed to dig up dirt on all of them—including Sylver's stint that past fall in the detox center, a run-in Adrian had had with a British producer the summer before that had led to an all-out brawl, and Riley's quick-trigger finger that had nearly caused the lives of innocent bystanders and gotten him thrown off the L.A.P.D. Every studio in town was leery of backing a FeelGreat picture, even though there wasn't a one of them that didn't think *Obsession* had major hit written all over it.

Kate dropped wearily into her brown upholstered swivel chair in the cramped rented space on the sun-parched lot of what had once been the mighty Majesty Studios. When the studio went belly-up in the late eighties, the bank took it over and rented out a block of offices to independents.

FeelGreat Productions occupied two small rooms on the ground floor of a two-story bungalow. The quarters were starkly but tastefully furnished, although seriously lacking any sign of glitz or glitter. Kate had brought over a few original watercolors and a beautiful nineteenth-century Bessarabian rug to add an extra touch of class. A second lien on her Bel Air house was paying the rent on the offices and their secretary's salary. Riley was footing the rest of the bills with the generous advance—slowly but steadily dwindling—he'd received on his book, which was due out in the fall with a major promotional campaign. Adrian threw his meager savings into the pot, and Sylver, having no financial resources, paid her dues by putting in eighteen-hour days and by keeping all their spirits going. Once viewed by the others as the most fragile and vulnerable of the foursome, Kate, Adrian and Riley had grown steadily in awe of Sylver's refusal to buckle under, despite what was getting to feel like insurmountable odds to the rest of them.

Sylver walked in a few minutes after Kate. She looked glamorously businesslike in a jade green Nino Cerruti suit she'd picked up for a steal at one of those "second time around" boutiques. She set her cinnamon leather attaché case on her desk and glanced over at Kate, who was glumly going over a sheet of figures.

"No luck with Fielding?" Sylver asked, surmising the answer from Kate's demeanor.

Kate smiled wryly. "Let's just say, even if Doug hadn't poisoned him against us, Hal Fielding hasn't forgiven me for snatching *Mortal Sin* out from under his nose."

"I thought Greg Coffman told you Fielding had nixed the buy," Sylver said.

Kate slipped off her René Brunaud black-and-white windowpane jacket. L.A. was going through a March hot spell, but they were keeping the air-conditioning on low in the offices to conserve energy, not to mention costs.

Kate shrugged. "You expect logic? Reason? Anything give at Beekman?" Don Hunt at Beekman Pictures had been left to Sylver because of the mutual antipathy between Kate and Don that dated to way back when. Coupled with the current spate of lies Doug was spreading around about her—the latest buzz was that she might be bisexual—Kate knew she didn't stand a ghost of a chance getting anywhere with Hunt—anywhere that she wanted to get.

Sylver compressed her lips. "He says he'll consider a deal if..."

Kate rolled her eyes. "If. That word is fast becoming my most least favorite word in the English language." She frowned. "Does what I just said make any sense at all?"

Sylver laughed. "Perfect sense."

Kate waved her on. "Go ahead. If what?"

Sylver leaned against her desk and tapped her index finger to her chin. "Let's see. If we make major changes in the script, for starters. He'd like to see the stalker kill the little slut."

Kate arched a brow. "What little slut?"

"Oh, right. He thinks Riley's movie star isn't slutty enough."

"Hmm. What else?"

"Skipping the rest of the changes he'd like to see in the script, he wants Jim Harris to direct."

Kate clapped her hands together slowly. "I say we don't mention your meeting with Hunt to either Riley or Adrian. One or both of them might take it into their heads to go barging into his office and punch the little weasel out."

Sylver smiled mischievously. "Could we watch?"

The intercom buzzed. Kate motioned to Sylver to take it. Sylver flipped the switch.

"Yes, Lois?"

"Nash Walker on line two."

"Thanks, Lois. Ask him to hold for one minute," Sylver said, her gaze shooting across the room to Kate.

"It's a small role," Sylver said. "And even Adrian admits Nash's right for the part."

"What does Riley say?" Kate retorted bluntly.

Sylver stepped around that question. Riley had nothing good to say about Nash Walker. "Nash really has cleaned himself up. He hasn't used in three months."

Kate narrowed her eyes. "Sylver."

"Okay, maybe he's slipped up a few times. It isn't easy, Kate. Especially if you have no one on your side. No one to believe in you. No one to give you a chance to get back on your feet. No one to be there to..."

Kate held up her hands in surrender. "Stop, stop. I give."

Sylver smiled. "Funny. Riley said pretty much the same thing."

Still smiling, Sylver picked up the phone, pressing the button on two. "Nash? You're on. Come in to sign the contract on Tuesday." A short pause. "No, Nash, I can't. Really. The office. Tuesday. Around two." Another pause. "No, I can't do lunch that day." Sylver could feel Kate's knowing eyes on her even though she wasn't facing her. "That's right, Nash. Strictly business... Don't thank me. Just don't let me down."

Adrian picked Kate up at nine the following evening. He greeted her with a tired but tender kiss at the door. Like the rest of them, he'd been pounding the pavement, looking for financing for *Obsession,* calling in all favors owed him, but still coming up empty-handed. His discouragement showed in the lines at the corners of his eyes and mouth, but he was making an effort to be upbeat.

"Mmm, you smell good," he murmured.

"Infatuation."

"No. I'm way past infatuation, my sweet," he said with a teasing smile. He gave her another kiss, this one more animated. While their lips were mingling, his hand was meandering down her bare back, courtesy of the provocative cut of her black matte-jersey Byblos dress.

Kate wiggled out of his embrace as his caresses turned friskier. "Do you want a drink before we go?"

Adrian's eyes glinted with irreverence and lust. "A drink wasn't quite what I had in mind, love." He turned on his bad-little-boy smile that got her every time.

Kate draped her arms around Adrian's neck, her tongue darting out to moisten her lips, her fingers playing lazily with his hair, which edged well over the collar of his starched white shirt. He looked exceedingly handsome tonight, all dressed up in a black tux for the formal dinner party being hosted by Marianne Spars at her newest venture, Oceana, right on the beach just north of Malibu. Everyone who was anyone—meaning anyone who could finance *Obsession* if they chose—would be there. Marianne, the dear, was doing more than her part to help them get *Obsession* off the ground. She had also agreed to invest two million of her own hard-earned cash in the project. Now all they needed was about fifteen million more and they'd be off and running.

Adrian was planting moist little kisses down the side of her neck.

"You are incorrigible, Adrian," Kate murmured.

He drew her closer. "I would happily stay put and sniff you all night."

She gave a hank of his hair a tug. "You can sniff away to your heart's content after we get back from Marianne's do."

His hands caressed the silky cloth over her behind. "Do you know that I can get out of a tux faster than Houdini got out of a pair of handcuffs?"

Kate sighed, knowing she was going to give in to what was certainly mutual desire, even as she said, "Riley and Sylver will be wondering where we are."

Adrian laughed softly. "No, they won't."

As soon as Sylver opened her apartment door and saw Riley, she knew he was in a foul mood. She was pretty sure she knew why.

"I hate these monkey suits," he muttered grumpily, trying to loosen the stiffly starched white collar by tugging at it.

"You look terrific in a tux, Riley," Sylver said, meaning it completely, even though he was clearly miserable. Still, the tux was not the real issue here, and she figured they'd better clear the air before heading off for Marianne's private party at her new restaurant where they'd have to shift into a wheeling-and-dealing mode.

"Are you ready?" he asked curtly.

Riley didn't offer so much as a halfhearted compliment about her appearance. Even when she was clad in a pair of scruffy jeans and a worn T-shirt, he'd say something about how cute she looked, or how delectably her jeans hugged her "pert behind." Now, here she was, decked out to the nines, in a formfitting bright pink linen dress, slit up to the thigh, and Riley was mute. That wasn't like him at all.

This was serious. Maybe their first really serious clash. She nervously fingered the white pearl hanging on the silver chain around her neck—her Christmas present from Riley—one she never took off.

"Look, Riley, I know you didn't want Nash Walker in the picture, but—"

"I don't want to talk about it," he said, gruffly cutting her off.

Sylver folded her arms stubbornly across her chest. "Well, I do want to talk about it. And not in the middle of the hallway." She stepped aside so that he could come into her apartment and she could shut the door.

He made no move to enter. "We'll be late."

"That will make everyone already there think we're important. You're always late if you're important enough. It's expected."

He smiled ruefully. "Another piece of Hollywood logic. No wonder the movie business is so crazy."

"Please come in, Riley. I can't go until we settle this."

His smile winked out. "There's nothing to settle. This nutso fan finally fades into the woodwork and you saddle yourself with another loser."

"If you're worried that Nash'll be a bad influence... that he'll get me to start using again..."

"That's your worry, not mine."

Sylver felt like Riley had just struck a blow to her solar plexus. Never, in all the months she'd known him, had he ever been so callous. Was this the real Riley Quinn?

Riley cursed himself to beat the band. What the hell was the matter with him? He knew what it was. Jealousy. Nash Walker had once been Sylver's lover. Could he be again? Especially if he was clean and made a comeback? Walker was younger, better looking, and he shared a whole history with Sylver.

He walked into her apartment and shut the door behind him. Sylver just stood there, mute, hurting inside like she'd never hurt before.

She wore her pain like a shroud. It broke Riley up. He had hurt so many people in his life. He vowed it would be different with Sylver. Nothing was different. He'd called

Walker a loser, but *he* was the real loser. Because he really had something to lose.

"Sylver..."

She shook her head. "This isn't a ... good time ... to get into... anything. We've all been under a lot of pressure. Don't you think I know you could have had every studio in town eating out of your hand if Kate and I weren't the producers of *Obsession*. It's a brilliant script. Everyone knows that. Why Doug Garrison won't let up on Kate, and why he has it in for me, I don't even know. I guess he's just pissed because he went out on a limb for me, getting me that audition for *Mortal Sin* and then I canceled out. They're still going ahead with *Mortal Sin* with Doug in charge. The buzz is he's destroying the script. I didn't tell Kate, but I made an appointment to see him next week. If we can get Garrison to back off..."

Riley grabbed her so abruptly, she stopped midsentence, her hands flying up to her face as if to ward off a blow. It wasn't a deliberate movement; it was pure instinct.

Riley felt his heart wrench. That she could even think for an instant that he would ever physically harm her made him feel like a leper. He let her go as if he'd been burned and rubbed his face with his hands.

"What's going on here has nothing to do with my script or Doug Garrison or...even Nash Walker," Riley muttered, his voice rife with anguish. Slowly, he dropped his hands from his face and met her gaze. She no longer looked frightened, only deeply concerned. And despairing. "It has to do with you and me, Sylver."

"You and me?" she echoed quietly, all the while her heart pounding.

He crossed her living room, still tidy and clean since her return from Running Spring, and sank into the pine rocker they'd recently picked up at a secondhand store. Riley sat forward, elbows on his knees, his hands propping up his head.

"I've never been good at responsibility, Sylver. I let Tanya down. I let ... Lilli down. I let my partner, Al Borgini, down."

Sylver went to him, knelt before him, drew his hands from his face and held them tightly. "You haven't let me down, Riley."

She was inches from him, her beautiful face taut with worry, her large eyes burning into his. All he wanted to do in the whole world was pull her into his arms, kiss those exquisite, inviting lips and hold on to her, never let her go.

"I don't want to let you down, Sylver, but I'm scared out of my mind that I will. And if I do..."

Sylver pressed her lips to his. "We're all human, Riley. None of us is perfect." She laughed dryly. "I sure as hell wasn't perfect when you met me. When I think of all the times I cursed you out, called you every name in the book... What I'm saying is—" She stopped, shaking her head, determination firing up her eyes. "No, this is what I'm saying. I love you, Riley. You're not perfect, but you have soul, you have heart. And you can put it down on paper better than anyone on earth. You make words sing. You make me sing. No other man has ever—will ever—make me feel the way you make me feel, Riley. And no imperfection is going to change that."

Riley sat there motionless for a long moment, searching her face. "Did you say that... you love me?"

Sylver smiled tremulously. "Didn't you know? Riley, what did you think?"

He laughed. "I was trying not to think. Every time I started to think, I got...nervous." He scrutinized her more closely, rubbing the side of his face with his hand. "You do love me."

"You're the last one to know it," she said softly, expectantly.

Riley sank back against the chair. He closed his eyes. "This is it. This is what love feels like," he said in a low voice, almost as if he were talking to himself.

Sylver's whole body was trembling. Was he telling her that he loved her, too? She'd waited so many months, one day thinking he had to love her; the next, worrying that he didn't. A dizzying seesaw.

"What does it feel like, Riley?"

He opened his eyes and smiled at her. What a smile. A thousand-watt smile. It lit up the whole room; lit her up inside. She was glowing, blazing with light. Her pulse was galloping.

"I can't explain it." He laughed. "Some writer, huh? When I really need the words, they go and desert me." He took hold of her hand, pressed it against his chest, the pounding of his heart thumping against her palm. "Hear it, Sylver? That's what it's like. This old ticker pumped blood before, but it didn't really beat. Not until now."

The light inside her just grew and grew. She was incandescent.

He kissed her. It was more than lips meeting; it was souls touching, connecting. But even as each of them felt it, they recognized that the connection was fragile. Would it withstand the pressures still facing them?

"Did I tell you that you look beautiful in this dress?" he murmured, unzipping it.

"Then why are you taking it off me?" she asked with a teasing smile, her body vibrating with desire.

"Because you're even more beautiful naked," he said as he slipped the dress over her shoulders. She wore nothing underneath save for a pair of skimpy pink lace bikini panties.

"We're going to be awfully late for that gathering at Oceana, Riley," she said as she undid his bow tie and began unbuttoning the pearl buttons of his shirt.

He shrugged out of his jacket, grinning seductively. "See how Hollywood I'm getting."

"Sylver, you look absolutely glorious," Marianne Spars exclaimed as she greeted the late-arriving pair at the arched entry of her glitzy seaside restaurant. She slipped an arm through Riley's. "Whatever are you feeding her, darling?"

Riley blushed scarlet. Sylver's coloring was a close match.

"Where are Kate and Adrian?" Sylver asked, changing the topic.

Marianne trilled a laugh. "They only arrived a few minutes ago. Kate was looking absolutely glorious, too. I suppose it must be the joy of going independent," she added

with a salacious wink that only someone as good-hearted
and generous as Marianne could get away with without of-
fending.

"Some joy," Sylver muttered, coming back to earth with
a thud.

"Buck up, darling," Marianne soothed. "Are you ready
to face the hordes?"

Sylver and Riley shared a look. They both would have
preferred to have remained curled up naked in bed together. Sylver plastered on a bright smile. "Ready."

Marianne shepherded the once-celebrated actress and the
ex-cop-turned-hot-screenwriter into the restaurant proper—
a slick, colorful emporium done in bold primary colors,
sporting the mast of an old seafaring vessel jutting right out
of one wall, like it had gotten lost in a time warp and made
a disastrous detour during a bad fog. The entire west wall of
the restaurant opened onto a large terrace fitted with blue-
and-white-striped umbrellaed tables and chairs that faced
the blue Pacific.

Even though Sylver looked cool and confident, she was
unnerved by what felt very much like her coming-out party.
Riley was acutely aware of how the low buzz of genial conversation and business chatter—most of it focused on the
Oscars which were a little more than a week away—dropped
to a murmur as they made their entrance.

The tang of salty sea breezes blowing in from the terrace
mingled with Rodeo Drive's most expensive scents. People
stopped the pair continually as they threaded through the
crowd. There were the requisite oohs and aahs, kisses that
landed in midair, compliments tossed around like play
money, most of them having about as much worth. Riley
felt like he was drowning in phoniness. He was sorely re-
gretting this outing, having just as soon left the business end
of getting his movie made to Kate and Sylver. Especially as
so much business in Hollywood was done at chichi dinner
parties, charity balls, upscale restaurants—all arenas where
Riley felt decidedly out of place. A month ago, he wouldn't
have even been allowed entry to any of these high-roller
bashes. A few years ago, to get in, he would have had to
flash his badge. Hollywood!

Marianne gave their arms a tug. "See the short guy with the beard and glasses and the gray Armani suit? Over in the corner, with that statuesque brunette."

Sylver and Riley spotted the statuesque brunette first.

"Robert Locke," Marianne said, her voice tinged with awe. She saw the blank looks on her friends' faces. "Robert Locke Presents." Still nothing. "*Dangerous Curves, Running Against the Wind, Rift.* He likes to say he 'dabbles' in the movie business. The truth is, he's one of the movers and shakers behind the scenes. He's sitting on a billion dollars, and he doesn't mind spending some of it when a project takes his fancy." She turned to Sylver. "And he happens to be a fan of yours. He loved *Glory Girl* and still thinks you should have walked away with the Oscar for it. Oh, he's looking your way." She gave Sylver a little shove, keeping a hold on Riley. "I have someone else for you to butter up," she told him.

"Great," Riley muttered sardonically, reluctantly letting Marianne lead him away.

Meanwhile, in other areas of the vast restaurant, Kate and Adrian were also working the crowd. Adrian had cornered Ed Gordon, the number-two man at ICA—not bad going for a guy who never finished high school.

"With a few modest changes in the script," Adrian was saying, "I think the part of Detective Michael O'Malley would be tailor-made for Kelso." Adrian, as well as Gordon, knew FeelGreat Productions would be way ahead of the game with a star element firmly attached to their film. Bill Kelso, who'd landed a Best Actor nomination for *Calling the Shots,* had guaranteed bankability. With him on board, they immediately achieved more credibility. Hopefully, enough to counteract Douglas Garrison's dirty-tricks campaign, and get the financial backing they so sorely needed.

Gordon, a real glad-hander, nodded enthusiastically. "It's a terrific part. And you're right, Needham. Bill would be great in the role. Only problem is . . ."

Adrian smiled crookedly, already tuning out before Gordon gave him whatever excuse he was giving him for why he couldn't work a deal. While Gordon talked, Adrian was already cruising the crowd to see who his next target might be. Looking around, he spotted Kate, with her warrior-like stance, looking poised and elegant as she engaged in a subdued powwow with the savvy deal maker, Jack Bale, an attorney to the rich and famous. Kate's eye caught his for a moment, conveying the faintest downcast flicker. *Ah, well,* Adrian thought philosophically, *another one bites the bloody dust.* They all knew it wouldn't be easy. He ambled resolutely over to Phil Palmer, hatchet man at Marble Hill Pictures who reported directly to Marble Hill's head honcho, Steve Zimmer, on all matters financial.

Five minutes with the puffed-up, would-be seducer Robert Locke, and Sylver was convinced neither of them was going to get what they wanted. While she'd been trying to put a bite on his wallet, the spoiled billionaire was trying to put a bite on her tender flesh. Not wanting to accumulate any more powerful enemies, she sought to back out graciously.

"Producing is a full-time job, Mr. Locke...."

He slid his hand insolently over her hip. "Robert."

As an excuse to edge away from his touch, she reached for a glass of champagne from a passing waiter. It wasn't until the drink was in her hand that she realized this was the first time in six months that she'd been this close to booze. Terrific. Not only did she have to contend with her own temptation, but no doubt by tomorrow morning Hollywood tongues would be wagging that the rumors about her being off the wagon were obviously true.

As Locke sought to make contact again, she deposited the drink in his hand. He gave her an ironic smile.

"It was delightful meeting you, Mr. Locke...Robert, but I see someone I simply must say hello to. Would you excuse me?"

She didn't wait around for his response. Instead she started across the large dining room toward Riley, who was standing with a small cluster of blue suits from the Chris Blackman talent agency, looking like he was in the middle of a parole hearing. And from the drawn expression on his face, it didn't look likely that he'd get his parole. She decided she'd better rescue him.

Only she didn't make it over to him. A familiar and not particularly welcome figure was blocking her way.

"You've been avoiding me, Sylver."

A guarded look immediately shadowed Sylver's face. "I've been very busy, Mother. What are you doing here?" The implication was clear that Marianne Spars would never have invited Nancy to her shindig.

Sylver was surprised to see the flicker of what looked like honest hurt in her mother's eyes. Then again, she had to keep in mind that Nancy was a frustrated actress. Being frustrated seemed to be Nancy Cassidy's lot in life. For it all, Sylver felt a pang of pity for her mother. Behind the meticulously applied makeup, Nancy's face revealed the ravages of those frustrations. For the first time, Sylver was struck with the realization that her mother wasn't getting any younger. Nor, as they both grew older, were they getting any closer. Could there ever be a rapprochement between them?

Nancy quickly regained her bravado, flaunting it aggressively. "Frankie Erdman invited me. You remember Frankie."

Sylver managed a half nod. Frank Erdman had directed her in her first big box-office hit, *Crying Will Get You Anywhere.* Offscreen, he'd done the majority of his directing in her mother's bedroom. They were lovers all during the filming, and he was one of the few of Nancy's paramours who'd actually remained her friend afterward.

"I have to go, Mother...."

Nancy gripped her daughter's arm, holding her fast. "You look wonderful, Sylver."

The compliment, given so earnestly, was really what held Sylver in her tracks. How long had it been since her mother had praised her?

"Thanks," Sylver said awkwardly, her gaze taking in her mother's ruby red V-necked linen unitard. It was flashy, but the design was a step-up in sophistication from her mother's usual teenybopper wardrobe. *She almost looks her age,* Sylver thought. Was it really a crime to be forty-eight?

"You look nice, too, Mother."

"How's it going?" Nancy seemed honestly interested. Even though she had nothing to gain.

Could her mother be turning over a new leaf? "We're still pitching," Sylver answered.

"Any bites?"

Sylver smiled faintly. "Out of our hides."

Nancy scowled. "The bastard."

Sylver leaned a little closer to her mother. "Which one?"

Nancy looked at her daughter as if that was a ridiculous question. "There is only one. Douglas Garrison."

Nancy's grip on Sylver's arm tightened. "I'll make him sorry he ever tangled with either one of us." Her face filled with a hatred that took Sylver's breath away.

"Mother . . ."

"I was wrong. About so many things." Nancy's eyes fell on Sylver, the hatred that had glinted from them a moment before now reflecting sorrow. "I can't right the wrongs of the past, Sylver. I thought I knew what was best for you. Such an old excuse."

Nancy grimaced, a bead of sweat breaking out across her forehead.

Sylver gazed at her mother with alarm. "Are you sick?"

Nancy quickly smiled. "Sick? Old bitches don't get sick, darling. They just fade away." She patted Sylver's arm. It was the most maternal gesture Sylver could ever recall her mother making. "Don't worry about the smut Doug's spreading, Sylver. When I get through with him, I wouldn't be surprised if Charlie Windham himself didn't cough up the money for your movie."

Before Sylver could question her mother as to what she intended to do to get Douglas Garrison off their backs, Nancy had slipped away. When Sylver spotted her a few minutes later, Nancy had draped herself around Frank Erdman's arm. At first it looked like it was merely her mother's typical provocative stance, but then Sylver got the disturbingly unsettling feeling that Nancy was actually leaning on him for support—as if she couldn't manage to stand on her own.

For the rest of the evening, as Sylver, operating in concert with Adrian, Riley, and Kate, tried to mine the crowd for prospective backers for their film, her gaze kept drifting to her mother. Even though each subsequent time she observed her, Nancy seemed perfectly fit, Sylver couldn't shake the feeling that her mother was covering something up.

She was growing more and more convinced that her mother was ill. How ill? was the question. Along with several other questions that grew out of their brief but emotionally charged exchange.

By midnight, people were starting to clear out. The foursome had exchanged downcast looks, none of them having made any headway. Adrian went off to the men's room, Riley and Sylver stepped out on the terrace for a breath of fresh air, and Marianne stood off to the side of the restaurant entry, commiserating with Kate.

"The New England Clam Bake was terrific, anyway," Kate said despondently.

"They're all a bunch of wimps," Marianne muttered.

"The way they looked at me—like I'd just stepped out of a loony bin. What's so infuriating is that I'll lay you odds more than half of them are on the antidepressants or tranquillizers that they're so worried I'm taking," Kate sneered. "And thanks to Doug's warped insinuations about my 'broad-minded' sexual preferences, I actually had two women make overt passes at me tonight."

"Douglas Garrison is a complete swine," Marianne declared loud enough for those of her guests exiting the restaurant to hear. "I bet it's absolutely eating him up alive that the only major nomination Paradine got this year was for Kevin Hooper for best original screenplay for *Breaking Legs*. You were the one that discovered Hooper and shepherded that baby through."

"If Hooper wins the Oscar, I'd like to borrow it from him and personally clobber Doug over the head with it," Kate replied tartly. The same guests who'd overheard Marianne had no trouble overhearing Kate's retort. Several of them looked askance, but Kate merely tossed her hair back and smiled defiantly.

* * *

Adrian put his arm around Kate as they walked up the path to her front door. Their evening at Oceana had been a complete fiasco. "I think we've just about covered every base here, love. Between the four of us—not to mention your dear friend, Marianne—we haven't left a stone unturned."

"I truly hate him," Kate said in a low, hoarse voice. "It wasn't enough to drive me from Paradine. Doug is bound and determined to see to it that I never make another picture in this town. It's become a sickness with him. The man is warped."

"Pity you didn't see that a long time ago." No sooner had the words left Adrian's mouth than he regretted them.

Kate stopped dead in her tracks a few feet from her doorstep.

Adrian reached out for her, a contrite expression on his face. Damn his bloody jealousy. "Katie, I'm sorry. I'm just so damn frustrated at getting rejected at every turn."

"Well, here's another one," Kate said with surface cool, burning up inside. "Good night." She pulled out her house key and strode to her front door. Adrian hurried after her.

"Look, I said I was sorry," Adrian protested, wresting the key out of her hand.

"Give it back to me," she demanded, rigidly holding her hand out, palm up.

Adrian ignored her, slipping the key into her lock.

She shoved his arm aside. He grabbed her more roughly than he meant. The physical assault made her immediately flash on the night Doug had nearly assaulted her. Her hand flew across Adrian's face, but it really wasn't Adrian she was hitting; it was Douglas Garrison. All her pent-up rage seemed to explode inside her. She started pounding on Adrian's chest.

Adrian fought to gain hold of her wrists to stop her onslaught. She began struggling fiercely until he literally had to wrestle her to the ground.

"I hate you. I hate you. You bastard," she screamed, struggling against his considerable weight.

"It's not me you hate, Katie. It's not me," he soothed, imprisoning her wrists above her head.

She started to cry—loud, noisy, sloppy sobs. "It's all coming apart."

"What's coming apart, love?" he asked gently, his heart breaking for her.

"My...life. My whole...life."

Adrian sighed heavily and rolled off her. They both lay there on their backs stretched out on her front lawn, panting heavily, little sobs still escaping Kate's lips.

"You blame me, don't you?" Adrian said quietly.

"I blame Doug," she countered, swiping at the tears running down her face.

"I was the one that pressured you into leaving Paradine. You had it all and I made you give it up. I painted this wonderful romantic picture of what our life would be like as independents and you bought it. I forgot to mention the constant scrambling for money, the insecurity, the frustrations."

She glanced over at him. "We're going to get this movie made. Somehow, some way, we're going to get it made, Adrian. I won't be made a laughingstock in this town. Douglas Garrison will not get the last laugh. I'd rather...die than have that happen."

Twenty-One

Something has changed about him since his release from the rehabilitation hospital a couple of weeks ago. It isn't the limp. That really doesn't faze him, although many a night in that hospital bed he'd anguished over whether Sylver would find his deformity a turnoff. But then he'd chastise himself for thinking so little of his princess. Why, she would love him even more. His wounds would move her. After all, if he hadn't been so terrified that something had happened to her, he wouldn't have leapt out into the street like that and that car never would have rammed into him. Not that he blamed her. Not in the least little way.

So, what is different? There's a new pressure, a new resolve within him. He feels that time is running out. Yes, he's lost so much time these past lonely months in the hospital. No one came to visit him. He wrote endless notes to Sylver, sharing his feelings, pouring out his heart to her, even daring to ask her to come visit him. He mailed none of those notes. He has them still. Tied in a red ribbon in a shoe box in his bureau drawer. One day. One day he will show them to her.

He pulls up in front of her building in the early hours of the morning. The lights are out in all her windows. Is she tucked in bed fast asleep?

It would be best if she were asleep. He slips his hand in his jacket pocket where he keeps a freshly laundered linen handkerchief and a small vial of chloroform. Best if she didn't wake up until he had her back at his place. Not the beautiful condo he'd bought for her. During his long months in the hospital there'd been no one to pay his bills and the condo had gone into foreclosure. Still, he'd found a nice little garden apartment out in Toluca Park. Strictly temporary. Once the insurance money came through from his accident he'd buy her a new condo with the settlement. Or even a house. A sweet little cottage with a white picket fence.

He whistles as he gets out of his car and starts toward her building. After all these dark months, life is looking up at last. He steals up to her floor, feeling bolder than he ever has before. Like he can do anything; achieve anything. He knows beyond a doubt that he owes Sylver his life. He would never have pulled through if it weren't for her. She may not have been there with him in the flesh during those long and painful recuperative days, but she'd been there in spirit. Every minute of every day. He owed her his life; and every day for the rest of his life, he'd make it up to her.

It's even easier than he'd imagined, breaking into her apartment. He stands in her tiny vestibule, his heart thudding so loudly he's afraid the sound will wake her up. The place is dark and it takes a couple of minutes for his eyes to adjust. He needs the minutes to calm down. The rush of excitement and anticipation at being here in her apartment for the first time is overwhelming. He can pick up the scent of her fruity perfume. His hand strokes the brown suede jacket hanging on a hook by her door. He buries his face in the leather, inhaling her smell, taking it deep into his lungs. It gives him so much pleasure, almost too much. He feels himself begin to get aroused, and immediately releases his hold on her jacket.

Only when he gets to her closed bedroom door does he even allow himself the revolting thought that she might not be in that bed alone.

He closes his eyes for a moment, then takes a deep breath and carefully opens the door.

The one thing he hadn't counted on was that she wouldn't be there. When he sees that the bed is empty, all his strength and joy abandon him. He stares at her bed, the sheets all rumpled. Sheets didn't rumple like that from even a restless sleep.

She made love in that bed. He touches the sheets. Cool. It's been a while since she and her lover had been screwing there. He sinks down onto the floor, his chest heaving silently.

He loses track of time, but after a while he pulls himself together. Whoever it was she was with earlier doesn't matter. She would forget him in time. The bastard may even have taken her by force. Or got her doped up. Or drunk. Or she might have been so despairing—all these months without a single red rose to remind her that he hadn't forsaken her . . .

He drags himself to his feet. He limps over to her bureau. He touches her powders and jars of cosmetics. He sniffs her perfume. He opens her drawers slowly, one by one. He won't be able to leave with her tonight, but he can't leave her apartment empty-handed. He has to take something of hers with him. Kind of a deposit. Until he returns to collect her. And then their lives will really start.

Twenty-Two

Riley rolled over in bed and reached out for Sylver, only to find the other side of his bed empty. He sat up abruptly and called out to her, an edge of anxiety in his voice. Her head popped out of the bathroom. She was still damp from her shower, her body wrapped in a bath towel, a smaller towel wrapped turban-style around her head.

Riley squinted at his clock radio. It was nine forty-five a.m. They hadn't gotten home from Marianne's party until two and they hadn't actually gotten to sleep until close to four.

"What are you doing up so early?" he asked.

Sylver hesitated. "I'm going over to...Paradine Studios."

Riley sat up fully. "Why?"

"I want to talk to Doug Garrison," she said.

"I thought you didn't have an appointment with him until next week."

Sylver stepped back into the bathroom, but left the door ajar. "I decided there was no point in putting it off."

Riley appeared at the bathroom door. He was naked. Sylver avoided looking at him, knowing how tempted she'd be to climb back into bed with him and put aside the nagging thoughts that had kept her awake most of the night.

"I don't want you to see him alone," Riley said firmly. "I don't trust the bastard as far as I can throw him. And right now I'd like nothing better than to throw him to kingdom come."

Sylver slipped on Riley's terry robe, only then removing the towel draped around her body. She wished Riley would go put something on.

"No, Riley. I'll be fine. I need to speak with him alone." She tried to slip past him at the doorway, but he caught hold of her.

"What's this all about, Sylver? What are you holding back from me?" he probed.

"Nothing." She couldn't meet his searching eyes. "Please, Riley, I just want to talk to him, see if I can't get him to stop this smear campaign."

"And what makes you so special that he'll listen to you?" Riley demanded, the insinuation in his tone too obvious for either of them to deny.

Sylver wrested herself from his arms, glaring at him. "You want to know if we ever had something going between us? Go on. Ask me, Riley. Ask me."

"Did Kate tell you he tried to rape her?" Riley asked instead.

Sylver went white. She shook her head slowly. "No. No, she never . . . said."

"Now you know why I don't want you to see him alone," Riley said softly. He knew that Sylver could act as tough as nails, but he also knew how fragile she really was; how easy it was for her to get stomped on and abused.

Sylver wasn't listening. She felt a surge of fury rise up inside her. *Doug tried to rape Kate.* She started to shake. For the first time in a long time, she wanted a drink. Something to still the quaking spreading through her body.

Riley was worried about her. "Sylver, come back to bed. Just let me hold you."

"No. No, I've got to go next door and change." She gathered up her pink dress from last night, left the bedroom and hurried across the living room. Riley stopped her at his front door.

"Don't leave like this. I'm worried about you," he admitted.

Sylver's rage wouldn't abate. Instead it was spreading, touching everything in sight. She jerked her arm from Riley's grasp. "Say what you mean, Riley," she hissed. "Say you don't trust me. It's always going to be this way, isn't it? Isn't it?"

"Sylver... Look, I'll drive you over to Paradine. I won't go in with you. I'll wait in the car."

"Hey, if I'd wanted a keeper I could have let my mother lock me away in the loony bin like she'd wanted to," she said bitingly, wrenching the door open, hurrying out and slamming it behind her.

Nash did an incredible amount of drugs that night. He only vaguely remembered the pert little blonde, and only because she got so pissed at him for calling her Sylver several times in bed. Had they actually made it? He had the feeling he hadn't been able to perform and that had gotten her even more pissed.

He remembered something else. Doing his one big scene—his two-minute monologue from *Obsession*—for her. He thought that must have been earlier in the evening, before they'd gotten down to doing any of the hard stuff, because he'd been damn good. She'd applauded. Yeah, he definitely remembered that she'd really dug his acting. Okay, the part wasn't very big. Other than that one monologue early in the first act, he only had a few other lines, but that one bit could do it for him. He could feel it in his gut. This was his chance. His big chance to show them all; to get back on top—where he belonged.

It was just past dawn and he was walking on the beach. He didn't quite remember how he got there. That scared him a little. Having blackouts just when he was getting his career back in gear wasn't exactly smart. And now he wasn't feeling so hot. Really kind of lousy. Must have done some bad coke, he decided. From now on, he'd be more careful. Stick strictly to good blow. And only on weekends. His unwinding time. He'd sworn to Sylver he wouldn't use, but he'd keep it purely recreational. Hey, he knew how to keep it under wraps. One thing he sure as hell didn't want was another sermon from Sylver. Like he'd ever been as over the edge as she'd been. Like he needed to be stuck in detox with bona fide drug addicts. Drugs weren't his problem. Life was his problem. Now he was getting his life turned around.

He stepped on something sharp in the sand, and was bending down to inspect the damage to the sole of his foot, when he suddenly felt a huge weight leap on his back. At first, as he went facedown in the sand, he thought it was some wild beast. Then he heard the click of a gun being cocked.

He started to cry. His luck. Just when life was looking up, some goddamn trigger-happy mugger has to cross his path. He was so scared he wet his pants. Next thing he was being rolled over. Now the barrel of the gun was pointing right between his eyes. Still, he let out a whoosh of relief as he stared up at the handsome, dark-haired youth whose open shirt revealed a deeply tanned, hairless chest. The large gold medal that hung from a thick gold chain around his neck, dangled inches from Nash's face.

"Jeez, Remy. You scared me half to death. Cool it, man," Nash said, spitting out sand.

"The Nemo Boys want their dough, Walker. They're getting real impatient." Remy issued the threat without any inflection; like he didn't care one way or the other. Collect the money or shoot the junkie in the head. He'd get paid either way.

"Look, I just landed like a major role in a new movie, man. I'm gonna be rolling in dough in a...a few weeks." Sylver had promised him an advance against his salary, which wasn't exactly major bucks but it wasn't peanuts, either, as soon as they signed a deal.

"They don't want to wait a few weeks, man," Remy said nonchalantly, the barrel pressing into Nash's forehead, right above the bridge of his nose.

Nash began to sweat. "Look, I can show them my contract. I'm good for the money. I swear. Why, by next year, I'll be strictly A list. They'll all be down on their knees pleading with me...."

Remy shrugged, a lock of his slicked-back hair falling vampishly over one hooded eye. "You got one week, man. Then it's either..." He paused, an insidious smile curling his lips and revealing a gold tooth. "Your money or your life. You got that, man?"

Nash nodded glumly. One week. He'd never come up with all the money he owed, but he'd have to give them some good-faith cash.

Remy rose to his feet, brushing the sand off his skintight black leather trousers. He looked down at Nash, who hadn't moved an inch. He grinned as he saw the wet patch on the actor's jeans. "You stink, man. And I gotta tell you. From what I see, man, you're a lousy actor. But then, hell, I'm not paid to be a critic."

As Remy ambled off down the beach, all Nash could think about was where he was gonna get another hit. And some cash.

Tully, the guard at the Paradine gate was an old-timer who used to give Sylver penny candies when she was a child star working at the studio. He beamed at her as she drove up, greeting her warmly and waving her right in. Sylver was driving past the large bungalow that housed the executive suites on her way to the visitors' parking area when she saw a familiar pink Mercedes coupé peeling out of the lot. Sylver braked, watching the car whiz past. She frowned. What was her mother doing here? And what had made her drive off like a bat out of hell?

After Sylver parked, she stayed put for a couple of minutes to steady her nerves. She ran a comb through her hair, now grown back to shoulder length. She wore it loose on one side, clipped back from her face with a barrette on the other side. Stepping out of the car, she smoothed down the skirt of her canary yellow cotton shift. She left the matching jacket on her seat—the temperature that late-March day was soaring up to the eighties.

Douglas Garrison's secretary, a doe-eyed brunette, looked up from her word processor as Sylver announced herself.

"I don't have an appointment, but—"

Sylver didn't get to finish the sentence.

"Oh, you can't," the secretary said, her voice filled with agitation.

"Please," Sylver said, her own agitation growing. "I must see him. Couldn't you just see—?"

Suddenly the ornately paneled door to Douglas Garrison's office jerked open. The studio chief himself stepped out. He was red-faced and looked fit to be tied. Then he saw her.

He stopped short, staring at her with such a look of utter contempt that Sylver felt a terrible chill crawl up her spine. Doug and her mother must have had one humdinger of an argument. Over what, though?

"I'm sorry, Mr. Garrison," the doe-eyed secretary said nervously. "I was just telling Miss Cassidy that you couldn't see her...."

Doug waved her off. He motioned to Sylver, gesturing toward his office, a grim smile on his face.

Sylver hesitated now, uneasy. No. Scared.

"Are you coming?" It was a demand.

She had to know what was going on. That suddenly took precedence over what she'd come here for—namely, to beg Doug to stop spreading those awful lies about them.

"Shut the door," he ordered as she followed him into his office. As soon as she'd closed it he swung around to face her. They were only a few feet apart. His eyes bore into her with rage and scorn.

"She won't get away with it, the cheap little slut. She can't prove a thing. She knows it. I know it. And you know it," he spat at her like she was so much dirt.

Sylver felt her own fury mount. "I certainly hope you're not referring to my mother," she said tightly.

He laughed harshly. "And you're just like her. Even worse. A junkie and a slut. You both got what was coming to you. I don't owe either of you a thing. I did more than I should have for you. You just threw it all away like it was garbage."

He was ranting now, working himself up into a frenzy. Sylver could see the veins in his neck protruding like ropes. "Your mother sure knows how to pull out all the stops. I've got to hand that to her. First hopping in the sack with me, then threatening to blackmail me, and when she knows she hasn't got a leg to stand on, she starts crying those big crocodile tears, giving me some cock-and-bull story about being sick and wanting me to look after you."

Sylver sprang at him. "Sick? My mother told you she was sick?"

He shoved her away. "You're a good actress, sweetheart, but you're not that good. Don't you think I know the two of you are in cahoots. She shows up first, giving me the business. And then you come prancing in, all innocence and light, like you don't know the name of the game. Well, let me tell you something, honey..."

Sylver was at him again, her mind reeling. He couldn't shake her off. "What's wrong with my mother, damn it? And why the hell would she want you of all people to look after me?"

"Like you don't know why," he hissed, his smile mocking. "Like she didn't tell you I'm your daddy."

Sylver went pale. She could only stare at him, numb, disbelieving.

He laughed dryly. "She actually thought I'd marry her. Hell, I did the next best thing. I gave her the money for the abortion. Only she didn't go through with it. Kept thinking once you were born, that I'd be swayed. The stupid little slut—"

She slapped him so hard across the face that her palm went numb. Not that she intended to let that stop her from slapping him again. The next time, though, he caught hold of her wrist and twisted her arm behind her back, forcing her to arch into him. Before she realized what was happening, he kissed her hard on the mouth.

"You bastard. You sick, disgusting bastard. I could kill you!" she shouted, feeling a surge of rage so great it seemed capable of crippling her.

The door had sprung open, and his secretary stood there, looking panicked and terrified.

"Call the security guards," Doug barked at her.

A minute later she was literally carried, kicking and screaming, from the studio chief's office. A janitor washing down the tile floor in the outer vestibule got shoved out of the way as the security guards dragged Sylver, still trying to fend them off, out of the building. The shove made the janitor lose his balance. He fell against the wall with a painful thud. It took him a minute to catch his breath. When he was able to gather himself together, he limped over to the open door.

The two security guards stood like sentinels on the path, their backs to him, making sure that Sylver got into her car

and drove off. Had either of them turned at that instant and
seen the janitor, they would have been dumbfounded by the
look of sheer hatred and wrath etched in the workman's
features and his white-knuckled fists as he turned away from
the street and fixed his steely gaze on the closed office door
of Douglas Garrison.

Sylver was shaking badly by the time she got home and
had made it up to her floor. She stopped at the top step,
clutching her stomach, afraid she might heave. She still
couldn't take it in. Douglas Garrison was her father. How
could her mother never have told her? Why had she kept it
from her?

Sylver could guess why. Nancy and Doug had long ago
struck a deal that suited them both nicely. Doug had been
the driving force behind Nancy's little girl becoming a movie
star. He had even agreed to give her a part in *Mortal Sin.*
Only when she'd refused and then joined forces with Kate,
had he turned against her. Turned against his own child.

Her hand went to her mouth. She rubbed violently at her
lips as if to somehow erase the sensation of that far-from-
paternal kiss Doug had given her. There was no amount of
rubbing that would wipe it away. The sensation was indeli-
ble. She would never forget it.

And her poor mother. What horrible abuse must Doug
have hurled at her? Sylver was sure he'd done whatever he
could to degrade and humiliate her mother, and her fury was
even greater for the hurt he'd caused Nancy than for anything he'd said or done to her.

Nancy had told Doug that she was ill. The callous bastard had believed it was nothing more than a ploy to win his
sympathies. How naive could her mother be to imagine that
monster capable of compassion? Sylver knew that illness
was one ploy her mother would never use. She would never
want anyone to think she was sick. Nancy found illness de-
grading. Unless it was very grave, she would deny it at all
costs.

Sylver heard footsteps below. Not wanting to encounter
any of her neighbors, she hurried on to her apartment. She
passed Riley's door, not ready to face him yet, either. There

was no way she could pretend with Riley that nothing had happened at Doug's office. Her emotions from the horrendous encounter were all too raw. He'd see right through her. She needed some time to take it all in. She needed time to get a grip on herself. Then she would go out and see her mother. Somehow, she had to convince Nancy to tell her what was wrong with her; how serious it was; what she could do to help her. For all the devastating emotions she was grappling with, Sylver felt a newly tender connection to her mother. Maybe it wasn't too late for them. *Oh, God, make it not be too late.*

She was so upset and distracted, it didn't even dawn on her to be surprised by the fact that her door was unlocked. She just walked in, letting out a stunned gasp of alarm as a figure burst out of her bedroom.

"Sylver. Where the hell were you?"

"Nash? What are you doing here?"

He was sweating, jittery, rubbing his hands together. "Man, I've been waiting here for hours. Baby, listen. Listen to me, baby. I know you haven't closed a deal yet on the picture, but here's the thing. I just need a few bucks. You know... nothing major. Just like maybe a couple of grand. I know you don't have that kind of dough, but Kate would lend it to you. If you don't say it's for me."

Sylver felt sick inside. He'd promised her. "No, Nash...."

He was having trouble with his balance, and his eyes were all over the room, unable to focus on any one object, especially her face, for too long. "It's not what you think, baby. I know what you're thinking, but I'm through with that crap. All of it. Sure... Okay... I had one last fling. Just to get it out of my system. You know how it is. Like it was the last time. Only there are these old debts...."

It was too much for Sylver. She walked past him into her bedroom to check her machine, hoping her mother might have called. There was one message. It was from Kate. She sounded excited. Wanted her to call or come right down to the office.

Sylver couldn't deal with business now. She was on overload. Nash was at her bedroom door, leaning against the jamb, trying to keep himself erect. She swung around to face him, seething.

"I've had it with you, Nash. You're never going to get your head straightened out. Riley was right. You're a loser. You're off the picture, Nash. I want you out of here, out of my life. I don't ever want to see you again."

His body jerked convulsively. "You don't mean that, baby."

"I mean every word," Sylver said vehemently.

Nash managed to pull himself together a little. This wasn't happening to him. It couldn't happen. "You can't throw me off the picture. I signed a contract."

Sylver eyed him stonily. "You didn't read the fine print. The contract can be terminated if you're using drugs."

"I told you, I'm not . . . using. Not anymore."

"Okay, then go leave a urine sample in a cup in my bathroom. If you check out clean, I'll give you one last chance."

He started for her, swaying unsteadily on his feet. "Don't do this to me, Sylver. This is my big chance. You can't . . ."

Sylver stood there, arms pinioned across her chest. She could feel her whole life descending into mayhem and confusion. "Get out, Nash. I mean it. I've had it. With you, with Doug Garrison, with every other bastard who's ever taken advantage of me."

Nash shook his head, like somehow that would clear it. Then he wagged a finger at her. "I know the bastard who's to blame for everything. Nicky Kramer. Yeah, it's all Nicky's fault. I shoulda stopped him when he walked off with you that night of your party. The dirty old man. I knew just what he had up his sleeve. That leer on his face was like a big, neon sign."

Sylver sank down onto the edge of the bed, gripping the footboard with whitened knuckles. She stared at Nash, incredulous. "You knew what was going to happen to me? You knew that bastard was going to rape me? You knew yet you did nothing? And you said you loved me." The realization that even back then Nash had never really cared about her felt like a physical assault. "What kind of love was it, Nash? What kind of love did you have for me that you could stand by and . . . and . . ."

He went to her, fell on his knees before her. "Sylver, please. I'm sorry. Hey, my hands were tied, baby. I honestly thought I was a shoo-in for the lead in Kramer's next flick. The bastard screwed me over, too. Kramer screwed up both our lives. Don't you see, Sylver... ?"

"Get out of here!" she screamed in his face, slapping blindly at him as he reached out for her.

She didn't think she'd hit him that hard—not that she didn't want to, she just didn't have the strength—but the next thing she knew, Nash literally flew back from her. And then Sylver saw the real reason why. Riley had burst into her bedroom, come up behind Nash, grabbed him up from the floor by the neck and had him pinioned in a viselike stranglehold. Nash had gone stark white, all the color draining from his face. He was gagging, struggling against Riley's steely grasp.

Sylver sprang off the bed. She was afraid Riley would break Nash's neck. "No, Riley. No. Just let him go. I just want him out of my sight. Please, Riley. Please."

Riley was so blinded by rage, it took several moments for Sylver's impassioned entreaties to penetrate. When he finally was able to focus in on the terror and anguish on her face, Riley came to his senses and released Nash. Nash dropped to the floor, gasping for breath, clutching his reddened neck.

"Get out before I change my mind and break every bone in your body," Riley said hoarsely, his whole body trembling with rage and fear—fear that he was capable of carrying out that threat. So much for having put violence behind him. He'd honestly thought that by getting it all out on paper, he could somehow exorcise those demons inside him.

Nash was equally convinced that Riley would make minced meat of him. He stumbled to his feet and staggered out of the apartment without a backward glance. As soon as she heard the door slam, Sylver flew into Riley's arms. Her safe harbor. Her shelter against the fierce storm of her turbulent emotions.

She told him everything. She poured out all the monsters in her heart to him. He held her close, stroked her and lis-

tened. Finally, exhausted and drained, she let him undress
her and tuck her into bed. Within minutes she was sound
asleep.

Douglas Garrison was lunching with his father-in-law and
Mel Frankel, head honcho at ICA, in the paneled halls of
the select Hollywood Athletic Club. The three men were
heavily into negotiations, now that Doug had persuaded
Charlie to let him tackle the *Mortal Sin* production—his
way.

"Paley was really into the moral issues in the script,"
Doug was saying, looking perfectly cool and composed in
an impeccably tailored navy suit only a couple of hours after his dual incendiary encounters with the Cassidy women.
"Personally, I see *Mortal Sin* as a traditional whodunit with
a lot of sex. We get down and dirty and we'll have a hit on
our hands. We want you to find us a hot little starlet in your
harem who's not afraid to show some T&A—a real brazen
'material girl,' if you get my drift."

Mel Frankel, a trim, effete man in his early fifties, incredibly well groomed, wearing a French monogrammed
shirt under an Italian-cut gray suit, smiled broadly. "You
mean someone who doesn't mind going at it naked in front
of a whole camera crew. And can be underpaid."

Charlie Windham, unlit cigar wedged between his lips,
chuckled. Doug, dutiful son-in-law puppet that he was, immediately followed suit. The laugh, however, died in his
throat as his attention, as well as that of his luncheon partners, was drawn by a commotion going on at the entrance
to the dining room.

The maître d' was trying to block the way of a tall, broad-
shouldered man inappropriately dressed in a T-shirt and
jeans. "I'm sorry, sir, but you can't go in without a jacket.
And you don't have a reservation. . . ."

Riley Quinn brushed the maître d' aside. "I have an appointment with Douglas Garrison. It's real urgent," he said
in a booming, menacing voice, his eyes surveying the diners. Riley had never met Garrison face-to-face, but he'd seen
plenty of pictures of him in the trades. After a couple of
seconds he spotted him at a table for three off to the right.

Every diner in the large room watched with hushed curiosity, fascination and apprehension as Riley stormed over to Doug's table while the maître d' rushed to get some reinforcements before all hell broke loose, which seemed imminent from the gate-crasher's demeanor.

Placing his hands flat on the pristine linen-covered table right across from Doug, Riley gave him a fiendish smile. "Well, if it isn't *Daddy dearest?*"

Charlie Windham stared from Riley to Doug, irritation and astonishment on his face. "Douglas, who is this character?"

Doug shook his head, but his face registered unmitigated panic. "Some crackpot."

Mel Frankel slid unobtrusively out of his seat. While he was as curious as the next guy as to what this was all about—probably more so—he was not about to get caught in the middle of a *family* feud and risk some unpleasant publicity. "Sorry, folks, but I have to get back to the office for..." He was walking briskly across the dining room toward the entrance without finishing his sentence, nearly colliding with two large parking attendants being hurried in by a nearly hyperventilating maître d'.

The two young uniformed men—both good-looking studs—moved to either side of Riley.

"Let's not make a scene, sir," the larger and blonder of the two actor wannabes murmured discreetly. "If you'll please come with us..."

"Sure," Riley said amiably, much to the relief of all concerned, none more so than Douglas Garrison.

Their relief, however, was short-lived. Before anyone could make a move to stop him, Riley's arm shot across the table, his hand grabbing hold of Doug by his red striped power tie. He yanked and Doug went flying across the table, facedown, dishes, glasses, silverware flying everywhere.

Riley held him fast in a position at once humiliating and debilitating. "I've seen 'em all, Garrison, but you take the cake. You're just about as low and dirty as they come."

The two valets/bouncers grabbed Riley, one on each side, and began dragging him forcibly from the restaurant.

Riley's eyes, glinting with fury, never left Doug's face. "You touch Sylver again, pal, and it'll be the last time you touch anyone. You hear me, Garrison...."

Sylver was pale and drawn when she walked into the office the next day. Kate, already at her desk, sprang up and ran over to her partner. Just as she was about to give Sylver a giant bear hug, she stopped short, giving her a closer scrutiny instead.

"God, you look awful. What's wrong? I left a half-dozen messages on your machine yesterday. Where were you?" A rush of panic made Kate's breath catch in her throat. Was Sylver on something? Had she become so depressed by not getting a single bite on *Obsession* that she'd resorted to burying her misery in drugs? Now? Of all times? Just when their luck had finally changed.

"I had a run-in with Doug yesterday," Sylver said solemnly. "Then Riley went ballistic when I told him about it. He tracked Doug down and practically strangled him at the Hollywood Athletic Club."

Kate smiled. "I wish I could have been there."

Sylver managed a faint smile herself. "So do I." The smile didn't last. Tears sprang from her eyes. Kate became immediately alarmed, putting her own news on hold. She drew Sylver over to the small white batik sofa against the wall.

"Maybe you'd better tell me about this run-in you had with Doug," Kate said softly.

Sylver stared down at her lap, yesterday's encounter with Doug—with her father—playing over and over in her head. She didn't say anything for several moments, a new, disturbing thought hitting her. Finally, she said in a bare whisper of a voice, "There's something you've got to tell me, Kate. Did you know? Did you know all along?"

Kate took hold of Sylver's hand. It was ice-cold. "Know what?"

Slowly, Sylver tipped her head to the side and glanced at Kate. "That Doug's my father?"

The news hit Kate like a bolt of lightning. She'd never even known that Doug and Nancy had ever slept together.

Some of the tension bled from Sylver's face. "You didn't know."

Kate shook her head dumbly. Then she fixed her gaze on Sylver. "Are you sure?"

"My mother got there before me. She threatened to expose the truth unless he got off our case, but I gather he told her, as he later assured me, there was no way she could prove paternity. But he admitted it to me."

Kate shivered with disgust. To think she had been his lover; had once hoped to be his wife. "You're his only child and not only has he never claimed you as his own, he's dragged your reputation through the mud just so he could destroy me. How could any human being be so utterly callous?"

"I've never hated anyone the way I hate him," Sylver said tightly. "Not just for what he's done to me, and to you. We can fight back. My mother . . . can't. She's sick, Kate."

"Nancy? Sick?" It seemed inconceivable to Kate. They didn't come any tougher than Nancy Cassidy. Surely, she could scare any illness off.

"I don't know how serious it is yet," Sylver went on plaintively. "I've been trying to reach her, but her 'boy toy,' Pete, keeps answering the phone and says she's not in. First she's shopping, then she's at a meeting—he can't remember who she's meeting with or where—and when I called first thing this morning before coming into the office, he said she was going to be out of town for the week. At a spa."

"Well, that makes sense. If she's under the weather, spending a few days at a spa is probably just what the doctor ordered," Kate said, infusing optimism into her voice.

Sylver wasn't comforted. "It's serious. I know it, Kate." She sighed deeply. "I'm so mixed-up about my mother. I'm angry as hell at her for never telling me the truth about Doug. I had a right to know."

Kate nodded her agreement. She, too, thought Nancy should have told her. Kate wondered, if she had known the truth about Doug's fathering Sylver and then heartlessly disowning her, how it would have affected her own long-term relationship with him. Would she ever have let herself get involved with a man who would deny his own child's birthright? She didn't think so. A sadness and loathing filled her for all those wasted years.

"Still," Sylver was saying, anxiety and concern heavy in her voice, "I'm desperately worried about her. I'm scared that . . . that she might die. We've never been exactly a loving mother-daughter duo, but . . . but I do love her, Kate. It had to have taken a lot out of her to tell Doug she was ill. . . ."

Kate's eyes widened. "Did she tell him what was wrong with her?"

Sylver shook her head. "No. But after the awful things he said to her, I'm sure it didn't make her condition any better. Oh, I hate him, Kate. I hate that he's my flesh and blood. I feel tainted."

Kate put a comforting arm around Sylver. "You're nothing like him. And you don't even have a single one of his features, thank God." She stroked Sylver's cheek. "How about a piece of good news. Would that perk your spirits at all?"

Sylver's eyes shot to Kate. "Good news?"

Kate broke out in a smile. "We've got our money, Sylver. Fifteen million bucks. Plus Marianne's two. Seventeen million dollars to make *Obsession*. Our way. No interference. We'll run the whole show." She paused for effect. "And it's all your doing."

Sylver regarded Kate as though she might have lost some of her marbles. "My doing? How?"

Kate's smile broadened into a grin. "Do you know that next to Jerry Lewis you are probably the most enduring star ever to have hit France?"

Sylver gave her partner a blank look. "I am?"

"Plans are in the works for a retrospective of your movies."

Sylver flushed. "God, I hope not every one of them." A while back, she'd finally mustered the nerve to confess to Kate about her appearance in the soft-porn movie. "Anyway, what does any of that have to do with being handed fifteen million bucks? And by who?''

"By whom?" Kate corrected, pinching Sylver's cheek affectionately, relieved to see some of her color return.

Sylver grinned. "Okay, you can still teach me a thing or two. So *whom* is it?"

Both women laughed.

"A French production company by the name of Ciné Métropole with a lot of bucks and a hankering to break into the Hollywood mainstream," Kate said excitedly. "They believe they can do it with *Obsession*. Their head honcho, Pierre Allegret, actually came to me with the deal. One of his people out here got his hands on the script, apparently flipped out over it, and sent it to him. Allegret called right after he'd read it and. . . and the rest, as they say, is history. He's flying in for the Academy Awards on Monday. Literally arriving like a couple of hours before it starts. His film, *Avec Vous* is up for Best Foreign Picture. With all the hype over the German entry, he isn't likely to walk off with an Oscar, but. . ." Kate paused, her eyes sparkling. "Maybe he'll walk off with a Best Picture Oscar in a couple of years for *Obsession*. Now that we're bankrolled, we should be able to cast by June and start principal shooting sometime this summer. Allegret's prepared to meet with us Tuesday morning and close the deal before he flies back to Paris."

Sylver felt as if her emotions were on a roller-coaster ride. She didn't know whether to laugh or cry, wave her hands wildly in the air or throw them affectionately around Kate's neck. She sort of did a combination of all four.

"Does Riley know yet? Or Adrian?" Sylver asked, popping up from the couch after the two women hugged.

Kate's eyes sparkled. "Adrian knows, but I thought you might like to give Riley the news yourself," she said with a knowing smile.

Sylver started to dash for the phone on the desk, stopped midway and turned back to Kate. "No, I'll tell him in person."

Kate was still smiling. "Good idea."

Sylver grabbed up her purse and started for the door. Again she stopped, this time staring straight ahead of her. "What's to stop Doug from poisoning this Frenchman against us?"

When Kate didn't answer, Sylver pivoted around and looked at her. Neither woman said a word. What could either of them say?

Twenty-Three

The day started off poorly for Douglas Garrison and went from bad to worse.

It was the big day. The day of days in Hollywood. The day Hollywood honored its own. The Academy Awards. Over at the Dorothy Chandler Pavilion, security was already well in place, and throngs of star seekers were gathered outside the auditorium, herded together in a large penlike structure, just to get a glimpse or a snapshot of their favorite movie stars. And, of course, to get to see what they were wearing. Especially in recent years, the Oscars had taken on the added glitz of a celebrated fashion show. Every major designer—and a few unknowns praying for the exposure that would shift them into the limelight—would be on display on some of the most beautiful bodies in the world. Provocative gowns, period tuxes, wild jumpsuits—the costumes of the stars would run the gamut from the refined to the repellent, the worst outfits making as much if not more of a splash in the news than the glamorous ones.

Douglas Garrison was strictly a traditionalist when it came to what he wore to the Academy Awards. A conservatively tailored black Cerruti tux, white shirt, red bow tie. A new tux each year, tailored to accommodate the middle-aged spread that seemed to be getting the upper hand more and more as the years passed.

He was nearly dressed, anxious to get out of the house and make it over to the Beverly Hilton for his little tête-à-tête with Pierre Allegret before hustling over to the Oscars. His ulcer was acting up and he was on edge, thanks to his fight with Julia first thing that morning. Ever since that phone call she'd gotten a week ago from Nancy Cassidy,

Julia had been stewing. Of course, Doug denied up and down that there was even the remotest possibility that Sylver was his child. How could she be, he'd lied bald-facedly, when he had never even slept with Nancy? There'd been tension in the house ever since, and that morning, Julia had blown up, called him a liar, and stormed out of the house.

And now he had this to cope with.

He stepped into his bedroom to slip on his tux jacket, only to be followed in there by his uninvited guest.

"Look," Doug said impatiently, "I want you out of my house now or I'm calling the cops. You've got nothing I want or need. I'm holding all the cards. The whole lot of you are going to be history before the sun comes up tomorrow. You can come crawling to me on your knees and I wouldn't give you the time of day."

As his guest started to come back with a retort, Doug stepped over to the phone, lifting the receiver. He'd already pressed the 9 of 911 when Doug saw his guest making a hasty retreat.

Doug smiled. He replaced the phone, pulled down the cuffs of his sleeves, adjusted his bow tie. It was nearly four o'clock. Still enough time to make it over to the Hilton for his meeting. His smile deepened. Now, more than ever, he was determined to screw the deal FeelGreat Productions was about to make with Ciné Métropole.

FeelGreat. He laughed aloud, the sound ricocheting off the walls of his lavish bedroom. Those bimbos wouldn't be feeling too great tomorrow when Allegret didn't show up to close.

He heard a door open and shut. Then light footsteps. A wave of relief washed over him. "Julia? Julia, baby, is that you?" He knew she'd show up before he took off. Daddy wouldn't have been too happy with her if she didn't play the dutiful wife and show up on the arm of her eminent spouse as he walked down the red carpet into the Dorothy Chandler Pavilion. What would people think?

Doug frowned as he noticed a loose thread on the inner seam of his right trouser leg. Damn.

"Julia, honey. You'd better get your beautiful ass in gear. I've got to meet someone over at the Hilton, but I'll have the car come back for you in—say an hour—and then you'll swing back to the hotel for me and we'll head over to the Oscars."

He was on the edge of the bed, his back to the bedroom door, bent over as he attended to the errant thread on his trousers with tiny manicure scissors, and so, when the blow fell, he was taken completely by surprise.

Douglas Garrison literally never knew what hit him.

Shock waves rocketed through the gala post-Oscar parties just as the lavish affairs were shifting into high gear. What had everyone buzzing and a few of them reeling, was that one of their own was dead. Murdered.

Douglas Garrison's death was the primo topic of conversation and supposition. The buzz spread from Spago to the Biltmore to the Governor's Ball under a big tent adjacent to the Dorothy Chandler Pavilion. Some people were speechless when they learned of Garrison's murder, some were appalled, some were aghast, but no one was all that surprised. Ask those that knew the unscrupulous and vindictive studio chief who they thought had done him in, and they all would have come up with a short list of likely suspects. And their lists would have been remarkably similar. Kate Paley. Sylver Cassidy. Adrian Needham. Riley Quinn. Nancy Cassidy. A few of Julia Garrison's friends would have added his equally vindictive and unscrupulous wife to the list, as well. Motive was easy enough. They all hated him. With justification. So, it boiled down to means and opportunity.

It was close to ten at night. A hard rain was falling outside, with intermittent thunder and lightning that crackled and shimmered across the black sky. Kate was in her office going over the finishing touches of the contract she and Sylver would be signing the following day with Pierre Allegret. Beside her on the desk was a half-finished bottle of San Pellegrino mineral water and a barely touched smoked-turkey sandwich.

She was so absorbed, she didn't even hear the office door open. Only as the sound of approaching footsteps penetrated, did she look up with a start. Adrian stood before her, his hair plastered back from his face. His clothes—an old Irish-knit sweater and jeans—were soaking wet.

"What'd you do? Walk here?" Kate teased.

"Ran," Adrian said with a grim expression. He'd taken a small studio apartment a couple of blocks from the office. He stayed there on occasion—on any occasion when he wasn't spending the night at Kate's place.

Kate set her pen down and then she sat there perfectly still. "What is it?" Even as she asked the question, her lips hardly moved.

"Douglas Garrison is dead. It was on CNN about twenty minutes ago."

Kate stared at Adrian without seeing him. Without really seeing anything. Or feeling anything. It was like someone had turned off her light switch. She'd just have to patiently sit there and wait for it to get turned back on again.

Adrian stepped closer, placed both hands, palms down, on her desk. Water dripped from his hair and his face, some drops splattering on the contract. Neither of them took any notice.

"Katie."

She was still staring off where his head had been. He came around the desk, turned her chair to face him, forced her to look straight at him. "He was murdered. Somebody killed him." He swallowed hard, perspiration mixing with the rain.

Kate nodded.

"You know?" He paused briefly before adding, "You heard?"

His pause drew Kate out of her numb state into raw reality. She looked at him, horrified. "You think I...killed him?"

"No. No, of course not," Adrian said fiercely, grabbing her roughly to him, as if his denial and his embrace could convince either one of them that he had no doubts about her innocence.

Kate didn't fight his embrace, nor did she respond to it. She closed her eyes. "I'm not glad he's dead," she said in a hushed whisper, "but I'm not sorry, either. I don't think I feel anything about it at all."

Adrian held her close, stroking her, desperately trying to awaken a physical response from her. "Well, I'm glad. I hated the bloody bastard."

Kate pulled away. She looked him straight in the eye, her face expressionless. "You shouldn't go around saying that, Adrian. Someone might get the wrong idea."

Or the right idea, she means. Adrian released her, feeling as if all the life had suddenly been drained out of him, too. A terrible sense of loss engulfed him as he realized that Kate, the woman he loved and adored beyond all reason and whom he believed loved him equally, was no more convinced of his innocence than he was of hers. Even dead, Douglas Garrison was managing to destroy them.

While the news of Doug's murder was spreading like wildfire through the City of Angels, Sylver was driving down the Pacific Coast Highway heading for Malibu to see her mother. Having finally tracked down the spa Nancy had been staying at, Sylver learned that she'd checked out that morning. Guessing that Pete would have made up some lie about her mother still not being home, Sylver hadn't called first. The time had come for a showdown. Nancy couldn't avoid her forever. Anymore than she'd managed to avoid whatever was wrong with her. Heart trouble? Cancer? AIDS? One disease more gruesome and deadly than the next.

The roads were slick from the heavy downpour and the winds coming in off the ocean were buffeting her little car so that it took all her concentration to keep in her lane. Fortunately, there weren't many other vehicles on the road. Sylver imagined that most people had stayed home that night to watch the Academy Awards. Not her, though. As if things weren't chaotic enough, the red roses had started to arrive again. She hadn't told Riley. After hearing about what he'd done to Douglas at the Hollywood Athletic Club last week, and seeing what he'd done to Nash back at her apartment, Sylver was afraid that if she told him that her "fan" was back, his rage would explode. She wasn't nearly as worried about this stalker harming her as she was that Riley would harm the stalker. Or worse.

She flicked on the radio to get her mind off such disturbing thoughts. That's when she heard the news flash about Doug's murder. Her hands froze on the wheel and she shut her eyes for an instant. An instant was all it took....

The driver of a pickup truck about twenty yards behind Sylver's little blue sedan stayed at the scene and reported the accident to the police. He said the car was going along pretty smoothly, when suddenly the driver just lost control and started skidding all over the highway. What seemed strange to him was that she didn't even seem to be trying to regain control of the car. She hit the telephone pole off to the side of the highway head-on, and the car reared up the pole like a bucking bronco.

When the medics attended to Sylver after she was finally pried out of the car, they weren't too hopeful that she'd pull through.

It was funny. For almost a week now, Riley had been suffering from writer's block, struggling with a new novel he'd started about a month ago. Tonight he felt freed up. The words seemed to be flowing straight out of his unconscious onto the keys. His fingers were flying, as if they were operating on some powerful engine of their own. He had to stop to read each page as he pulled it out of the typewriter just to see what he'd actually written. It was like an out-of-body experience. What's more, what he'd written was damn good.

It was around ten-thirty at night. and he was going great guns when he was interrupted by the shrill peal of the telephone. Reluctantly, he lifted his fingers from the keys and picked up on the third ring.

"Yeah?" he said gruffly.

"Riley?"

He couldn't quite place the husky feminine voice. Someone who smoked, or who'd been crying a lot recently.

All of his senses heightened. "Who is this?"

"Nancy Cassidy. Don't...don't hang up on me."

"What's wrong?" Riley's voice was dead calm.

"It's...Sylver. There's been...an accident. Her...car... Oh, God, my baby..."

Riley felt boneless. "Is she . . . dead?"

Nancy was crying softly.

"Damn it, Nancy. Is she dead?"

"No. No, but the doctors don't think . . ."

"Where is she?" he barked, coming back to life.

"County Hospital. I'll be here, waiting for you."

He was about to hang up when she said, "You do know about Doug."

"I don't give a damn about that bastard right now," he snapped.

"He's dead, Riley. He was murdered this afternoon at his home. It was on the news."

Riley's tongue felt thick and his mouth sour, his head pounding like it used to when he had a bad hangover. Only now he was stone-cold sober. . . .

He whistles as he walks into his apartment. His mother used to get on his case for whistling in the house. Told him it was bad luck. He laughs out loud defiantly as he shrugs out of his raincoat. It's raining so hard out that his janitor's shirt is damp beneath. He starts to unbutton it as he walks over to the TV in his living room. He flicks to CNN, then goes into the kitchen to get a beer, having set the sound loud enough for him to hear the news.

He's pulling a Bud out of the fridge when he hears Douglas Garrison's name. He dashes back into the living room, a bright smile on his face as he sees a picture of the studio chief in the upper right-hand corner of the screen, a pretty brunette newscaster filling the rest of the screen, reporting the bludgeoning murder of the eminent chief of Paradine Studios. It's basically the same clip he saw on the TV down at Murphy's Bar about twenty minutes ago. But he doesn't get tired of seeing it.

The newscaster's saying that the murder is under investigation, but that so far no suspects have been named. She speaks with a nice melodic lilt. He likes her voice. Likes the way her lips curve into a faint smile. Like she's glad, too, that the scumbag has been offed.

He pops the tab on his beer can and is about to take a celebration slug when another image flashes on the TV, this one taking up the whole screen.

It's Sylver. His beautiful princess. The picture of her blinks off to be replaced by another. A shot of a strip of rain-drenched highway, a male newscaster in rain gear standing on the side of the road, being blown about by the wind. Behind him, a small blue car is mangled around a telephone pole. He recognizes the car. His heart stops, the beer can dropping from his hand, spilling all over his khaki work pants. All over the couch and the floor. He doesn't notice. He is burning up inside. Only three words of the newscaster's report are reverberating in his head.

In a coma. In a coma. In a coma...

He springs up from the couch. No. She cannot die. He will not let her die.

Twenty-Four

Riley ran through the corridors of County Hospital like a man possessed. It was still pouring outside, violent thunder crackling like the coming of doomsday. Clad only in a white cotton shirt and black jeans, Riley was soaked to the bone. When he got up to the ICU floor, a portly middle-aged nurse with kindly eyes intercepted him.

"Who are you here to see?" she asked gently.

Riley's mouth opened and closed, but no sound came out at first. His vocal cords had quit on him. The nurse nodded encouragingly. Mostly everyone who came to see newly admitted patients in ICU was in some stage of shock.

He had to place his hands on her desk to still the trembling and finally managed to say Sylver's name. His face stricken, he asked hesitantly, "She is . . . still . . ."

The nurse smiled reassuringly before he finished. "She's drifting in and out of consciousness. There's a team of doctors with her now. Are you her husband?"

Riley shook his head automatically, but then realized that only members of the immediate family would be allowed to see patients in ICU.

"I'm her fiancé." He thought to himself that it was almost the truth. He did want to marry Sylver. Suddenly all the fears of responsibility, commitment, possibly having a family again, seemed insignificant. He loved her. He wanted them to spend the rest of their lives together.

The rest of their lives . . . How much life did Sylver have left in her?

The nurse rose from her desk, grabbed a blanket from a shelf and threw it around Riley's shoulders. She patted his back. "You can go wait in the lounge at the end of the hall.

Sylver's mom is there. Have yourself a nice hot cup of coffee. I'll keep you updated.''

"When...when can I see her?" Riley asked, gripping the ends of the blanket with both hands.

"Soon," the nurse said noncommittally.

Riley walked down to the lounge, his vision blurry. He was living a recurring nightmare. This was the very same hospital—this very unit—where Lilli had died four years ago.

There was only one person in the small but incongruously cheerful lounge. It took Riley a couple of moments to realize the woman sitting there was Nancy Cassidy. She looked like she'd aged twenty years in the last few weeks. He walked over to her. She sat slumped in an orange tweed upholstered chair staring into a foam cup of black coffee clutched between both of her hands.

She glanced up as Riley gently touched her shoulder. He was shocked by her pallor, her hollowed cheeks streaked by mascara that had run from her lashes. Her eyes were red and swollen from crying. He remembered his last and only other encounter with Nancy back when Sylver was in detox. He hadn't liked her, yet he couldn't help but be impressed by her fighting spirit. Now, all the fight seemed to have gone out of her. She looked literally deflated, her body almost frail. Grief alone hadn't caused the ravaged changes; Sylver's fears that her mother was seriously ill hadn't been imagined. Riley sat down beside her. Separate from his own pain and anguish, he knew a parent's suffering. Knew it all too well. His heart went out to Nancy as he put aside all judgments. He gently pried the cup of cold, untouched coffee from her hands, then clasped one of her hands between his, letting the blanket fall from his shoulders.

Nancy didn't look at him, but she started to say something, only her lips quivered so much as they parted that she clenched them shut without a word.

They sat in silence for several minutes, Nancy's clasp tightening around Riley's hand, fresh tears falling down her cheeks.

"Have you seen her yet?" Riley asked finally.

Nancy nodded. Her lip still quivered, but she said in a hoarse voice, "They have...my baby...strapped to the bed. Tubes, wires ... everywhere. And those ... awful machines ... bleeping. I was so afraid ... they'd stop."

The nurse from the desk walked in. Both Riley and Nancy jumped, their eyes glued expectantly on her.

"The doctors are still with her," she said quickly, then looked at Riley. "There's a phone call. From Kate Paley. She asked if you were here."

Riley rose, but his balance was shaky and he had to grip the arm of the chair for a couple of seconds. The nurse approached him, but he waved her off. After taking a few moments to pull himself together, he followed the nurse back to her station and picked up the phone. He hesitated before bringing it to his ear.

"Hello, Kate," he said somberly.

A sob preceded Kate's voice. "Oh, Riley. I just heard on the news. Is it...that bad?"

"I don't know yet. The doctors are with her. Nancy's here, too. She's in pretty bad shape herself."

"What about you?" Kate asked, her voice husky from crying.

"I can't tell. It doesn't really matter. If Sylver doesn't pull through, nothing's ever going to matter for me again."

"I'm coming over," Kate said.

"They won't let you into ICU."

"I know. I'll wait down in the main lobby. Adrian'll be with me."

"I'll come down and tell you as soon as..."

"I know," Kate said softly. "Hold on, Riley. She's a fighter. She pulled through last time, didn't she? She's going to make it this time, too."

Riley's hand clenched around the receiver. "She's got to make it."

When he got off the phone and returned to the lounge, he saw a young doctor with frizzy Art Garfunkel hair, his wire-rimmed glasses resting on a large nose, sitting beside a sobbing Nancy.

Riley's breath caught in his throat at the sight, his eyes filling with tears of lost hopes, shattered dreams. *Oh, God, no, no. Don't let her be dead. You can't take everyone I love from me. It isn't fair.*

He stood there frozen until the doctor looked over at him and saw from the look on Riley's face what he was thinking.

"It's okay," the young doc said quickly. "She's coming around. Her prognosis looks a lot better than it did an hour ago."

Riley stared at the doctor, dazed. Was he hallucinating? Was the doc really telling him that Sylver had a chance of pulling through? So why was Nancy sobbing like that? Tears of relief? It didn't seem that way to Riley. And then he found out why.

"I'm afraid," the doctor said, "she lost the baby."

Riley blinked several times, as if that would help him take in what the doc had told him.

"The...baby?" Riley's gaze darted from the doctor to Nancy, who continued to cry quietly, her head in her hands.

"She was close to six weeks pregnant," the doctor said gently.

Riley staggered back against the wall. A baby. Their baby. Dead. Another lost child. He had to fight for breath. The doctor hurried over, eased him into a seat.

"Give yourselves a chance to settle down," the doctor said, "and then you can go in to see her one at a time. For a few minutes."

Nancy raised her head, dabbing at her eyes with a tissue as she looked over at Riley. "You go in first. I...I should fix myself up...a little. Sylver might go...unconscious again...if she sees me looking...like this." She tried for a faint smile, but it looked pained.

Riley set aside his own sorrow and helped the grieving mother get to her feet. He could feel, under the full sleeve of her pale yellow sweater, how bone thin she was. When she was standing, she swayed and Riley gathered her into his arms.

"How bad off are you, Nancy?" he asked, cutting right to the chase.

Nancy sighed. There was no hiding it anymore. "Pretty...bad. It's...cancer."

She looked up at him, misery and irony mirrored in her eyes. "Breast cancer. Can you beat that? Last year I go blow thousands on these brand-new knockers and now..." Her lips quivered again, but she fought back tears. "Don't tell Sylver. I'm not going under the knife for another couple of weeks. I fought it as long as I could." She hesitated. "Maybe too long." She shrugged. "Go to her, Riley. She loves you."

"I love her," Riley said, as much to comfort the mother as because it was true and it felt good to say it aloud.

Nancy wore a true smile now. "I know. She's a lucky girl."

He almost lost it when he went into Sylver's room and saw her lying there on that stark-white hospital bed, hooked up to those machines, the tubes up her nose, plugged into her arms. She was as white as the sheets, looking for all the world like she was fast slipping away. He fought back tears as he pulled a chair up to her bedside.

Her eyes were closed. Her breathing was raspy and shallow, so faint he had to lean very close to her face to be sure he was really hearing it. He whispered her name, expecting no response, feeling a sense of jubilation when her eyes fluttered open, her mouth curving into a weak smile. "Hi...Riley."

He felt like he'd been on death row, at the eleventh hour, and had just been handed a reprieve.

"Hi, Sylver."

Tears spilled over the lids of her eyes. "I'm sorry...about the baby, Riley," Sylver whispered weakly. "I...I only found out...this morning."

"Shh. Don't talk about it now."

"I was going to...surprise you. After we...closed on the movie...."

Riley stroked her clammy forehead, trying to tune out the tubes and the monitors, the pungent smell of sickness, Sylver's ashen coloring, the glassy look in her eyes. "Shh. It's okay, Sylver. It's you that matters to me. More than anything in the world. Just think about getting well." That was all he wanted to think about, too.

Sylver struggled for breath. "Oh, Riley, I wanted...that baby. It was my second chance. Yours...too." She began to sob quietly. A nurse hurried over, concerned that her patient not become more agitated. She wanted Riley to leave, but Sylver clung to him, begging him to stay.

"Once you're well, we'll make a new baby," he told Sylver softly. "Hell, we'll make one a year until you cry Uncle."

She managed a weak smile. The monitors registering her vital functions stabilized. The nurse backed off.

"Your mom's here," Riley said. "I'm going to wait out in the hall so she can come in. But I'll be back in as soon as the doc says it's okay." He started to rise.

She reached out and clutched his hand with what little strength she had. "Is Doug...really dead?"

He leaned down and lightly kissed her lips. "It isn't important. It has nothing to do with us."

Tears spiked her eyes again. "It does, Riley...."

Riley, Nancy, Kate and Adrian sat vigil at the hospital throughout the night and were still there late into the next day. The strain was showing on all of them, even though they were doing their best to stay optimistic. Sylver's progress was slow, but her doctor said if she continued as she was doing for another twenty-four hours, he'd be able to change her status from critical to serious. All they could do was hope and pray that she didn't take a turn for the worse—something the doctor had to caution them could happen.

At three that afternoon, the foursome was taking a much-needed break down at the hospital cafeteria. They were all picking at the food they'd ordered, no one saying much of anything. Nancy was the first to notice the two men threading their way around the tables in their direction.

"Damn," she muttered. "Reporters."

Riley craned his neck and looked back over at the two men. He recognized one of them. His ex-partner, Lieutenant Al Borgini, now Beverly Hills homicide chief.

He turned back to the others, his face expressionless. "No," he said. "Cops."

* * *

Lieutenant Al Borgini and Detective Hank Salsky lingered at the cafeteria table after they'd finished their initial questioning of the foursome. Salsky noshed on leftover french fries from Riley's barely touched hamburger platter plate while Borgini went over his notes, trying to tune out his underling's irritating eating habits—unavoidable when Salsky started waving a limp, greasy fry practically in his face.

"I don't know, Chief. None of them seems likely to be weeping over Garrison's grave. And none of them has an alibi worth a damn. Even your pal, Quinn." Salsky shoved the fry into his mouth, then reached over to Nancy Cassidy's turkey special, plucking a pickle spear from the plate.

Borgini couldn't hide his disgust. "Do you have to do that? If you want to eat, go get yourself your own damn food."

Salsky looked mystified by his boss's outburst. "What's wrong with this food? When I was a kid my mother was always on my case not to let good food go to waste. You know—the starving-kids-in-China routine."

Borgini shook his head wearily, and went back to studying his notes. "Let's see what we've got here. Nancy Cassidy says she was en route home from La Costa, a spa down near San Diego. Got home around six-fifteen last night."

"She could have easily detoured over into Beverly Hills on her way," Salksy pointed out, munching on the pickle.

Borgini kept his eyes on his pad to keep from watching Salsky eat. "She looks like she can hardly lift a fork, never mind wield a poker."

"You know the old saying, Hell Hath No Fury Like A Woman Scorned?" Salsky said, his eyes roaming the plates of food for his next selection. He opted for a handful of chips that accompanied Kate Paley's ham sandwich. "Even worse, is a mother's fury. I bet if she were steamed enough, she'd find the strength."

Borgini gave him a quizzical look. "What do you mean? A *mother's* fury?"

Salsky crunched down on a mouthful of chips, the sound making Borgini cringe. "You should read the trades and the tabloids more, Chief. Me, I've become a real Hollywood newshound. You can pick up a lot from the industry buzz, especially if you're a regular reader.''

While the detective methodically munched his way around the table, he gave his boss a detailed but concise overview of the motives for murdering Garrison for each and every one of the people they'd just interviewed, tossing in the one they couldn't interview because she was still in ICU. It was quite an earful.

When Salsky got around to Riley Quinn and the report from one of the tabloids that he'd been thrown out of the Hollywood Athletic Club after manhandling Garrison and threatening to kill him if he ever bothered his girlfriend, Sylver, again, Borgini slapped his pad on the table, a rosy hue rising up his neck.

''For chrissakes, Salsky. What kind of a cop uses sleaze rags for dope on someone in a murder case?'' He chucked his pad into his navy blazer pocket. ''Now if you're done pigging out on other people's leftover food, do you think we can get back to work?''

''Sure, Chief,'' Salsky said amiably, wiping his hands on a paper napkin, then adding knowingly, ''You really like that ex-partner of yours, huh?''

Borgini grunted and started off. The salty chips having made him thirsty, Salsky cuffed a can of cola from the table and started guzzling some of it down as he followed his boss out of the cafeteria. He chucked the can when Borgini turned and gave him one of his looks.

After leaving the cafeteria, Riley and Nancy hurried back up to ICU. Kate was ready to settle into one of the uncomfortable hospital-lobby chairs for the long wait, when Adrian gripped her by the arm. ''Reporters.''

This time the group heading toward them really were reporters.

Like two criminals on the lam, Kate and Adrian wound their way through the mazelike corridors, escaping into the street through an outpatient exit.

''Let's walk,'' Adrian said, once he saw they'd lost the media hounds. ''We could both use some fresh air after..." He let the rest of the sentence drop, but Kate knew he meant after the tense grilling by those two cops.

No, she thought. That wasn't fair. They hadn't "grilled" them. Nothing more than routine questions. It was the less-than-routine answers that were so troubling. None of them had an alibi worth a damn for the period of time during which Doug had been murdered. Riley had been home working on a new novel. She'd been at her office preparing the details of the budget for *Obsession*. Adrian had taken a drive up into the canyons for some hiking and meditation. Nancy was driving back from a spa. As for Sylver, Riley claimed she was next door in her apartment all afternoon, but he had to admit he hadn't actually seen her between the hours of three and five.

Kate was badly shaken. Being embroiled in a murder investigation was unsettling under any circumstances. Coupled with Sylver's accident, her condition still touch and go, it was exceedingly worse.

She started walking alongside Adrian, mainly because she lacked the energy to protest. She felt drained. And grubby—her gray linen jacket and slacks were covered in wrinkles, still slightly damp from last night's rain. As soon as she got the word that Sylver was truly out of the woods, the first thing she'd do was dash home for a quick shower and a change of clothes. She smoothed back her hair from her face as they walked down the street.

Yesterday's violent storms had given way to a tropical heat. The two palm trees on the hospital lawn swayed in the faint breeze. The skies were still overcast and smog hung over the city like a gray shroud.

Adrian, looking scruffy, tired and tense, turned to her. "Katie..."

She came to an abrupt stop. "I don't want to talk about Doug's murder, Adrian. Not now. Just...let it be."

"It's you and me I want to talk about," he said firmly, gripping her shoulders, forcing her to face him. "Okay, for a second in time back at your office last night—maybe a millisecond—we both had some doubts...."

"I don't want to talk about this," Kate said, struggling from his grasp, but he refused to let her go.

"Katie, I don't think you killed Douglas Garrison. Damn it, I love you. I would love you if you *had* killed the bastard...."

Kate opened her mouth to protest, but Adrian cut her off. "But I know you didn't do it."

"How...how do you know?" she asked cautiously.

He smiled at her. "Not because I killed him, love."

"I didn't mean—"

He pressed a finger to her lips. "I know you didn't mean that." He took hold of her hands, looking down at her long, slender, graceful fingers. "I know you're innocent because I can read your soul, Katie."

They had to move out of the path of a young couple with a squealing toddler hurrying up to the hospital. As the anxious family passed, Adrian took hold of Kate's hand and started to walk again, but Kate pulled him back.

"I'm not sorry he's dead," she said with a mixture of shame and anger. "He was hateful. A shameless liar, out for our blood. He was going to try to screw up our deal with Ciné Métropole. You heard what that policeman...Borgini...said. Doug had a four-thirty p.m. meeting with Allegret yesterday penciled in his appointment book."

"It shouldn't surprise you," Adrian said. "Anyway, he didn't get to see Allegret."

Kate sighed. "Neither did we." There was no way, under the circumstances, that she'd been in any condition to negotiate a close that morning. Allegret had flown back to Paris, with Kate promising to fly over there to tie up the deal as soon as she could.

There was a small inner-city park across from the hospital—not a spot you'd want to spend any time in after dark unless you were looking to score, but during the day it was safe enough. Kate and Adrian sat down on one of the graffiti-covered benches on a little patch of green grass.

"You're exhausted," Adrian said, knowing it was pointless to suggest she go home and take a nap. Kate wouldn't leave until she had some positive word about Sylver's condition. And he wouldn't leave until Kate did. So, they were there for the duration, however long it took; whatever the outcome. His own fondness for Sylver aside, he knew that if she didn't pull through, it would truly break Kate up.

She turned to him, searching his face as though she both thought and feared it held vital answers. "Who do you think killed him?"

Adrian eyed her ruefully. "I thought you didn't want to talk about Doug's murder."

Then she voiced what had been skirting the edges of both their minds; what they'd all feared back in the cafeteria was in the minds of those two cops from some of the questions they'd asked. A scenario right out of a B movie. Murder done in a moment of rage followed by guilt and remorse, leading to a failed attempt at suicide.

"It wasn't Sylver," Kate said emphatically. "She wouldn't. She couldn't. That car crash was an accident. She was worried about her mother. She was upset, the roads were slick...."

Adrian took hold of her hand. "It could have been a simple break and enter gone amok. Garrison walks in on the bloke, there's a struggle, and Garrison gets clobbered."

"Is that what you really think happened?" Kate pressed.

"It's what I'd like to think happened." He paused contemplatively, staring across at the hospital. "Then again, there's always the wronged wife."

"Julia?" Kate laughed harshly. "I seriously doubt it. If she'd wanted to make Doug suffer, a divorce would have done the trick nicely. I think Doug would have gladly chosen death over Julia throwing him out, because that would have meant instant expulsion from Paradine, utter disgrace."

Adrian stared out at the smog rolling in off the ocean. "Douglas Garrison is the epitome of everything that's wrong with Hollywood."

"You mean *was,*" Kate corrected somberly.

Riley sat at Sylver's bedside as she slept fitfully. He focused in on every shallow breath, his hearing attuned to any shift, no matter how faint, in the rhythmic beat of the monitors that were truly her lifeline. He stroked her hair, held her hand, smoothed down the thin white cotton sheet covering her body.

He nodded off, waking with a start when he felt a hand press down on his shoulder. It was Nancy, looking a bit better for the nap he'd finally convinced her to take.

"You go and lie down now," she whispered. "I'll sit with her. If she wakes up, I'll come get you."

Riley could barely keep his eyes open, but he was reluctant to leave Sylver's side. Still, he rose to give Nancy the chair. For a brief moment, his gaze fell on the woman's voluminous breasts, but he quickly looked away.

Nancy smiled wistfully, having caught his look. "It's funny how little everything else matters when you have a child fighting for her life."

"I lost my child," Riley said simply.

Nancy reached her hand up and he clasped it. They held on to each other for several minutes, both of them staring down at Sylver, knowing that every passing second mattered as none had ever mattered before.

Twenty-Five

Something kept nagging at the back of Detective Hank Salsky's mind. It was driving him nuts, but he couldn't put his finger on it. He pushed his wooden swivel chair back from his desk, rose wearily, and headed over to the coffee machine. It was Monday, two in the morning, two full weeks and miles and miles of legwork into the investigation of Douglas Garrison's murder. Two exhausting weeks filled with overtime in which he, Borgini and several other boys from homicide had interviewed dozens of people—everyone from major Hollywood moguls and celebrities to lowly parking attendants. Some of the interviewees had been open and forthcoming, others—especially those with any clout— had been everything from deprecating to circumspect to downright hostile. A few had insisted on having their high-priced lawyers present. One thing was for sure: Salsky could feel himself getting less and less star struck by the minute. Another thing for sure—this was the kind of high-profile murder case that got the media, the Hollywood honchos, the mayor and the D.A.'s office all worked up. Word had come down that the boys in Homicide had better bring in someone they could tie a noose around pronto.

Salsky was doing his best. He'd stayed late and had been going back over the pile of interviews since he went off duty at seven that evening, taking a quick break for a chili dog with a side of nachos from a Latino joint down the street. Now he had indigestion, but he hardly paid any attention to it. His wife, Liz, would have something to say, though. Since they'd moved out to sunny California she'd gotten into a real health kick. The other night she informed him she was thinking of quitting her job as a dental hygienist and taking night classes to become a licensed nutritionist. Actually, he blamed Liz for his indigestion. If she had decent food in the house for him to eat instead of all those sacks of bran and nuts and some crap she called "legumes," he wouldn't go around feeling so damned deprived. The chili dog would have been enough to satisfy him. He could have skipped the nachos.

He grabbed one of the mugs off the top of the file cabinet near the coffeemaker. There was a faint lipstick mark on the rim and muddy remnants at the bottom of the cup. He shrugged, then poured some fresh coffee into it. What the hell would a few more germs do to him?

He took a sip. The stuff tasted like sludge. He made a face, carrying the cup back to his desk. Lifting a page of his own notes off the pile of papers, he took another sip of coffee. This one didn't taste so bad.

He scanned his notes. One thing about this case. Instead of there being a dearth of suspects—which was usually the way it went in murder cases—there was a surfeit of them.

There were sworn statements by an assortment of witnesses who'd actually seen or overheard Garrison receiving direct death threats from at least five people. Garrison's secretary and several other people in his employ saw the director, Adrian Needham, barge into the studio chief's private office early in January. They overheard Needham threaten to do Garrison serious bodily harm if he ever again touched his girlfriend, Kate Paley, who also happened to be Garrison's ex-mistress. Those same staff of people also were witness to both Nancy Cassidy, and then her daughter, Sylver Cassidy, barging into Garrison's office practically in tandem less than a week before his death. Nancy had stormed out, after being overheard by one nosy clerk who must have had her ear pressed up against her boss's door, threatening to ruin Garrison by exposing the fact that Sylver was his daughter. Shortly thereafter, Sylver had her own confrontation with her alleged father that got so heated, Garrison had her forcibly evicted by two security guards. As if Garrison hadn't had enough for one day, that very afternoon the studio chief was threatened again, this time while he was having an upscale lunch at the posh Hollywood

Athletic Club. The police had statements from Charles Windham, the maître d' of the restaurant, two parking attendants and several other diners that Riley Quinn—his chief, Al Borgini's ex-partner, no less—had physically assaulted Garrison, and then threatened to break every bone in his body if he ever laid a hand on Sylver Cassidy again. Then there was the group from Oceana who'd overheard Kate Paley threaten to clobber Garrison with an Oscar. Maybe she'd settled for an andiron.

Salsky riffled through his papers looking for the private two-hour interview his chief had done with Kate Paley a couple of days ago. Now, talk about motive. Here was a broad who hated Garrison's guts, and made no bones about it. Not that it would have done her much good to conceal the truth. Just about everyone in La-La Land knew about the smear campaign Garrison was mounting against Paley shortly after they'd split up, stepping up his attacks after she'd quit Paradine. She'd dumped him. He'd dumped her. Salsky had heard it both ways. His cop's intuition told him Paley was the dumper. Why not? She had a hot thing going with that English stud director, Adrian Needham. Maybe the pair of them offed Garrison.

Of course, there was still the wife—the very classy, very uppity Julia Windham Garrison. Not what he'd describe as the loving, devoted spouse. The maid's statement was that the two of them were never more than cordial and for that whole week before his death, there'd been several fights. Still, Julia had a pretty solid alibi, was one of the only suspects in the case who did. She was getting a facial at an upscale Rodeo Drive salon—confirmed by the owner, several staff and clients.

Salsky picked up this week's *Variety*, lying amid the police papers. Like he'd told his chief, working the Beverly Hills beat, the trade newspaper was must reading. On page four was an update on Sylver Cassidy's condition. It was still listed as serious, but she'd been moved from County to a private suite at the posh Stillwater Hospital in Santa Monica. This was the kind of hospital where the patients' rooms resembled fancy hotel suites and were decorated with real antiques. If you were unfortunate enough to have to be hospitalized and you had a few million to spare, it was the place to be.

Salsky tipped his chair back and swallowed down some more coffee. His mind started to wander and he remembered his first encounter with Sylver Cassidy back at her tacky little apartment in West Hollywood. His chief, Al Borgini, had asked him to go over there as a special favor to Riley Quinn. Anyway, Borgini knew he was sort of star struck and would jump at the chance to see a real movie star. Not that Sylver Cassidy's name had been up in lights for a long time, and she certainly wasn't living like a glamorous movie star, but still, Salsky had to admit he'd gotten a charge out of meeting her. Thought she was damn pretty, too. Even though she was real edgy and upset that night. Some crazy fan was supposedly stalking her. She hadn't really used the word *stalking*. She described it more like he was always hanging around, watching her, leaving her red roses. His wife would probably think it was romantic. Anyway he hadn't seen anyone suspicious lurking about. He'd even talked to some of the shopkeepers on her street, but none of them had anything to say.

She sure was pretty. And what a body. He closed his eyes, picturing her in his mind, vividly recalling the way her tight worn blue jeans hugged her lovely butt and those long, shapely gams; how her pale blue soft cotton jersey outlined her pert breasts. He remembered thinking she had a real sparkle to her. . . .

He jerked upright in his chair, grunting so loudly that one of the cops at a nearby desk thought he was sick. Salsky leapt to his feet. That was it. That piece of the puzzle that had been nagging at him. He hurried into Borgini's office, pulled open the file drawer and withdrew the Manila envelope marked Garrison. He sat down at Borgini's neat-as-a-pin desk, opened the envelope and extracted a small plastic bag. He stared inside it, not knowing whether to be happy or feel rotten.

He dialed Borgini's home number, forgetting all about what time it was.

Borgini sounded less than thrilled to be woken up at two-fifteen in the morning.

"Sorry, Chief," Salsky said contritely, "but I got something here."

"It better be good," Borgini barked.

"Remember that earring we found on the scene? I know who it belongs to."

The last two weeks had been a nightmare. Sylver was finally on the mend, but she now had to come to grips with her mother's imminent surgery, which was scheduled to take place the following day in the same hospital. A double mastectomy. Nancy, wearing a nightgown and a blue hospital robe as she'd already been admitted for the required prep, was visiting her daughter's room. Although she was trying her best to hide her own fear behind her typical brash facade, Sylver could see through it. Still, it made it so hard for Sylver to show her caring and concern because Nancy refused to admit there was any real need for it.

"I'm going to be fine," Nancy was telling her that Monday as dusk was settling over the city. "I'm tired of these dumb boobs anyway. And who am I out to impress?" She picked up a brush and began to run it gently through Sylver's hair. "You look so much better, baby. And just think, Kate should be here any time now for your John Hancock on the deal with Ciné Métropole." She grinned. "My daughter, the hotshot producer."

Kate's flight from Paris via New York had landed a little over an hour ago. She'd called from the airport with the news that the negotiations with Ciné Métropole had gone like clockwork and she was going to pick up Adrian and head right over for the signing and a little celebration. Sylver had tried to sound upbeat on the phone, but she was worried about her mother. And there was still Doug Garrison's murder hanging over them all. And his murderer.

Nancy felt Sylver tense up as she continued brushing her hair. She was determined to be upbeat for both of them. "*Obsession's* going to be a terrific movie. And I think Adrian's absolutely right that you should film it in London, and set up your production company there. It will be good for all of you to get away from here. I'm going to get out myself. As soon as I get my clean bill of health. Being in this town's gotten old. I've gotten old. I think a change of scene is just what I need."

Sylver clasped her mother's wrist. "Where are you going?"

Nancy smiled conspiratorially. "I've sold the house in Malibu. For a very pretty penny. Most of it's yours, of course, since it was your earnings that bought it, but I thought—if you agreed—I'd take fifteen percent of the sale—say, a business manager's cut—and buy myself a nice little bungalow in New Mexico. I saw an ad for a place in Taos...."

"I don't want any of the money from the house. It's all yours. You can buy yourself a ranch, anything. You can travel. Maybe even come to visit us in London when we're filming. If you're up to it..."

"Of course I'll be up to it. You think women without boobs can't travel?" She continued brushing Sylver's hair. "I haven't done this since you were a kid."

Sylver smiled tenderly. "It feels nice." She didn't add, nicer than it ever felt when she was a kid. How tragic that it had taken a murder, a terrible disease and a car crash to bring out this new and cherished warmth and tenderness between them.

"Promise me you'll come to London," Sylver said, an unmasked urgency in her voice. As if somehow her mother's promise would be a promise to survive. Only how could Nancy make a promise, when keeping it was out of her control?

She did anyway. "Okay. I promise. But only for a few weeks. I don't want to start getting in anyone's hair."

"Looks like Sylver isn't much minding you getting in her hair at the moment" came a voice from the door.

Sylver's face lit up as she saw Riley standing there. Still, she scolded him lightly. "I thought we agreed you'd stay home and write today." He'd spent every single day at the hospital with her, letting everything else go by the wayside.

"And miss a party?" Riley returned with a smile as he ambled over and kissed Sylver tenderly on the lips. Then, to Sylver's delight, he gave Nancy an affectionate kiss on the cheek, and asked her how she was doing.

"I'm doing just fine. And so's this child of mine," Nancy said, quickly shifting the conversation away from herself. "Doesn't she look better and better every day? Her color is coming back. And I'm happy to report that she ate every last bite of her lunch."

"You heard from Kate?" Sylver asked Riley.

Riley smiled. "She and Adrian should be here any minute."

As if by magic, Kate and Adrian appeared at the door. Kate hurried over to Sylver. Her eyes danced and her whole body seemed suffused with a new vitality, despite the grueling plane trip. They hugged. A moment later, everyone else in the room got into the act.

After Sylver signed the contract, Adrian plucked a bottle of champagne out from under his jean jacket. "Nonalcoholic, of course," he said with a grin as Riley dug up five glasses.

Tears spiked Nancy's eyes. *Whatever happens to me tomorrow,* she thought, *sharing my daughter's joy and success like this, being welcomed at this celebration, is worth everything.*

Kate held up her glass to make the toast. "To FeelGreat Productions, and to all of us feeling great from here on out."

Glasses clinked, everyone hugged again, Sylver and Nancy's embrace taking on added meaning.

Their jubilation was interrupted by the sound of someone clearing his throat across the room. When they looked over at the open door and saw Homicide Chief Al Borgini and his sidekick, Hank Salsky, all of the joy drained from their faces.

Riley straightened and looked Borgini straight in the eye. He knew from the somber expression on his ex-partner's face that this wasn't another routine call.

Borgini shook his head sadly, then motioned to Salsky. The detective walked up to the side of Sylver's bed and took a small plastic bag out of his jacket pocket.

As Sylver saw the familiar star-shaped earring inside the bag, she gave a little start of alarm. Nancy clasped Sylver's hand. Kate and Adrian shared anxious looks. Riley's expression was grim.

"Have you ever seen this earring, Miss Cassidy?" Hank Salsky asked quietly.

Riley came up behind Salsky, snatched up the packet and eyeballed the earring. "Don't say anything, Sylver. Not without a lawyer."

"Riley," Al Borgini said sadly, "we know this earring belongs to Sylver. Hank here saw her wearing earrings just like this one the day he came out to her place after she reported some wacko fan was hanging around."

"There're probably hundreds, thousands of these earrings around town. You can't prove—"

"I can prove it, Riley. These are one of a kind. Made by a jeweler just off of Sunset Strip. Nash Walker bought them. We talked with him. He says he gave them to Sylver as a Christmas present."

Sylver began to tremble. Nancy, who was still clutching her daughter's hand, glared at the cops. "You bastards. Can't you see that you're putting my baby's health in jeopardy? I want you both out of here. This instant. Tell them, Riley. Throw them out of here. So what if that's Sylver's earring? What does that prove?"

"This earring was found at the scene of the crime, Mrs. Cassidy," Al Borgini said. "On the bed where Garrison lay, the back of his head busted open..."

"Stop it!" Sylver shrieked. "Okay, okay, it's my earring, but I don't know how it got...on that bed. I wasn't there that night. I swear." She gave Riley a desperate look. He put his arms around her. "I didn't kill Doug, Riley. I didn't. He was my father, for chrissakes."

"It's okay, Sylver. Just take it easy," he soothed, but he was pretty shaken up himself. So were the others. Nancy looked like death warmed over. Kate had collapsed into a chair and Adrian looked like he wanted to take on both cops for twelve rounds.

Sylver was terrified. "I...I haven't seen those earrings in weeks. Months. I never wear them. Never. Not since...since I finally got fed up with Nash. Wearing those earrings reminded me of him. And I didn't want to be reminded." She didn't add that it wasn't only anger and disappointment that made her want to block out memories of Nash Walker. There was also pain and even guilt. Could she have done something more? Was there some way she could have helped him climb out of the grave he was digging himself into?

"That's true," Riley was saying to Borgini. "I haven't seen her wear those earrings for ages." And then he remembered something Sylver had told him awhile back. He turned to her. "There was that locket...that gold locket you kept in a little tin in your bureau drawer. Remember, you told me awhile ago, that you couldn't find it and you thought maybe someone might have broken into your place and stolen it. Why not the earrings, too?"

Hank Salsky and Al Borgini shared less-than-credulous looks.

"Did you report a break-in, Miss Cassidy?" Borgini asked her.

Sylver shut her eyes and shook her head.

Borgini walked over to Riley, put a hand on his shoulder. "We've got to book her."

"You can't. She can't be taken from the hospital. She's still very sick!" Nancy shouted at them, nearly hysterical.

"We've already spoken with her doctor, Mrs. Cassidy," Borgini said, thinking there were times he really hated his job. This was one of those times. "He feels she's well enough to be moved to one of our secured medical facilities...."

Sylver let out a cry of terror. "You're going to lock me up? But I'm innocent. I didn't do it. I didn't...." She grabbed onto Riley. "Wait. What if—" She stopped, everything a jumble.

"What if what, Sylver?" Riley prodded.

"What if it was that crazed fan? We talked about it, Riley. He could have taken the locket and...and the earrings as...keepsakes. That's the word you used."

"Why would this wacko want to set you up as Garrison's murderer?" Salsky interjected.

"I don't think he did," Riley said, much to Sylver's and Nancy's dismay. "I think he kept these trinkets on him and the earring fell out of his pocket when he was leaning over Garrison, maybe checking to inspect his handiwork.''

Al Borgini didn't look convinced. "Why would he want to kill Garrison?''

"Because Garrison was hurting Sylver and he wasn't able to stand by and let that happen," Riley said. "I think this screwball's in love with her.''

Salsky rubbed his jaw. "I think we're stretching, here.''

"Al," Riley said, turning his back on the detective and eyeing his old friend and ex-partner. "Can I talk to you outside for a minute?''

Borgini jerked his thumb toward the door. As soon as they got outside, it was Borgini who got in the first word. "I know the two of you've got a thing going, but I've got to level with you. We think she did it, Riley. She had means, motive, opportunity. Her earring was found at the murder scene. Witnesses heard her threaten Garrison. I know how you feel about her, but you've got to take off your blinders, pal. This is an open-and-shut case. We'll get a conviction.''

Riley gripped the lapel of Borgini's tan jacket. "I'm telling you she didn't do it. What about this nut case?''

"Okay, who is this fan? What does he look like? What proof do you have that he even exists?''

"None," Riley admitted. "But I'll get it. Give me twenty-four hours. I've got a feeling about this, Al. You've got to...''

"Riley...''

"Sylver's not going anywhere. You have my word.'' He told Borgini about Nancy going under the knife the next morning. "I don't know how much more Sylver can handle right now. I'm begging you, Al. Just hold off booking her for twenty-four hours. Do it for me.''

"How're you going to find him?''

"I'm betting he's somewhere close by. I think he's keeping an eye on Sylver.''

"So you find him. Then what? What proof do you have that he did Garrison?''

"We'll deal with that in twenty-four hours," Riley said.

Borgini sighed. "Okay, Riley. I'm probably nuts myself, but you've got till tomorrow afternoon at—" He glanced at his watch. It was a little after three o'clock. "Hell, make it five o'clock. Then we book her."

"She didn't do it, Al."

"Look, I hope you're right." Borgini didn't have to add that he didn't think he was. They both knew that.

Twenty-Six

Finding an anonymous stalker without having anything at all to go on was like trying to find a needle in a haystack. Riley started by going down to Personnel at the hospital, checking to see if anyone had been hired on since Sylver had been admitted—only one female nurse, in her early twenties, a year younger than Sylver.

He walked out of the hospital, not really knowing what his next step should be. Then, as he was heading over to his car, it came to him. Red roses. Riley began to hit all the florists in the neighborhood around Fairwood Gardens. In each shop, he asked the same question. Could they recall anyone coming in on several occasions to buy a single red rose?

Six flower shops in the area and he'd reached a dead end. He checked his watch. It was almost five o'clock when he spotted another florist on a side street. A girl was already hanging up the Closed sign on the door.

Riley smiled roguishly and put his hands together in prayer. The girl, a pretty young clerk with long black hair that hung straight and a pale complexion offset by bright red lipstick, took pity on him and unlocked the door.

"Thanks a lot. I'd like to buy a red rose for my girl. She's in the hospital," Riley said.

"Gee, that's a shame. Is she gonna be okay?"

Riley broke into a real long sob story, none of it true, finishing it off by telling her how much his girlfriend liked roses, and how he'd buy her one red rose practically every day.

"Ya know, it's funny," she said.

"Funny?" Riley felt his whole body tense up in anticipation—or preparation for yet another disappointment.

"Oh, God, I don't mean your girl being in traction, or anything. I mean, there's this other guy who comes in here a lot to buy a red rose for his girl, too."

Riley felt an adrenaline rush. "No kidding. He wasn't in here today by any chance?"

The girl scraped at the peeling red polish on her thumbnail. "No. Come to think of it, he hasn't been in for a week or two. I usually didn't wait on him. Jack did. To tell ya the truth, the guy kinda gives me the creeps. Jack and I even joked about it. Like, what kind of a woman would ever go for somebody like that?"

"Bad-looking dude?" Riley prodded, hardly able to contain himself.

"Not ugly, really. Just sort of real skinny, with these sunken eyes. And he does that thing with his hair that I hate. You know, when a guy's going bald and he tries to cover it up by combing some long hairs from the side of his head over the top." She made a face.

"Doesn't sound like a winner to me."

"And downright rude, besides. We didn't see him around for months and then one day he shows up and like, he's limping real bad, so I says, gee, what happened to you? And he gives me one of those spooky-eyed looks and doesn't even have the courtesy to answer me."

"Does he . . . live around here?" Riley asked offhandedly.

"I don't think so. I always see him pull up in this beat-up green Chevy. My boyfriend's got the same car only his is in a lot better shape."

Riley smiled, paid for the rose, adding a hefty tip that brought a bright smile to the girl's lips.

The man at the convenience store next door to the Fairwood Gardens proved to be the jackpot. Not only did he inform Riley that he'd seen the guy in the beat-up green Chevy Riley described hanging around a lot a few months back, but he told him he'd witnessed the poor jerk getting hit by a car as he was crossing the street. Riley nodded. That explained why the roses had stopped coming for several months, the stalker's absence from the florist's shop and the newly acquired limp.

Riley hurried upstairs to his apartment. After a few phone calls, he was on his way to L.A. General. For a guy who hated hospitals, it felt like they were becoming his second home.

Hank Salsky was waiting for him down in the hospital lobby. Riley gave him a nod of greeting as Salsky ambled over.

"Borgini says you need a badge to have yourself a gander at some records. I'm your badge."

They headed over to the records office. After close to an hour of red tape and bureaucratic screwups, Salsky and Riley sat down in a cramped back office with a pile of admissions files—everyone who'd been admitted through Emergency on the day of Sylver's fan's hit-and-run accident.

Salsky pulled out two granola bars from his pocket and tossed one over to Riley as they were going through the files. "The wife swears by these things," Salsky said, tearing at the foil with his teeth. "Give me a Baby Ruth or a Heath bar, but I promised the old lady I'd go on the wagon," he added with a wink.

Riley smiled distractedly as he slapped down a file like it was a bad child, and opened another one, his seventh.

Lucky seven.

"This is it. Gary Browning. He lives over in Encino." Riley scribbled down the address. Salsky was already digging in his pants pocket for his car keys. They'd make it faster to Encino in his cruiser.

The maître d' led Kate and Adrian to a back table at an intimate little trattoria a couple of blocks from the hospital. A mural of gondolas on Venice's Grand Canal covered one wall; the other walls were white-painted brick. The tables were colorfully set with bright red tablecloths accented with hand-painted floral plates and large royal blue water goblets.

Kate didn't even bother to open her menu. Adrian scanned his briefly, then glanced over at her.

"How about spaghetti carbonara?" he suggested.

Kate nodded absently.

Adrian set his menu aside and reached across the table to capture Kate's hand. "It's going to be okay, Katie. If anyone can pull a rabbit out of a hat, Riley can."

"He's not looking for a rabbit," she said glumly. "And even if he manages to dig up this fan that's been hounding Sylver, who's to say he was the one who murdered Doug?"

"Katie..."

"If Sylver's arrested, Adrian, I...I can't go through with this movie. Not without her." She was beat. And she felt beaten. Beaten by a system that she'd fought so hard all these years to conquer. What hollow goals, she thought now. The emptiness and cutthroat ugliness of it all felt like a heavy weight bearing down on her. Douglas Garrison was a specter hanging over her. She felt cornered. No way out. Nowhere to turn.

A trim young waitress with a sandpaper voice, wearing a man-tailored white shirt and trim black trousers, took their order from Adrian—two spaghetti carbonaras and a half liter of Chianti.

After the waitress left, Kate stared hard at Adrian. "For a while there, I thought I was really going to have it all. That's what happens when you start to get greedy. When you start to feel you can have success, love, friendship...."

"You can have it, Katie. We can have it together. You're coming back to London with me. We're going to make *Obsession*. First, though, we're going to get married."

Kate looked at him like he was nuts. "Married?" She didn't know whether to laugh, cry or scream. She did none of them. Instead, she sprang up from her chair and fled from the restaurant.

Adrian caught up with her as she burst out the door onto the street. He had to practically tackle her to get her to listen to him.

"Okay, it wasn't much of a proposal. And maybe my timing was off...."

"I don't want to marry you," she said, struggling to free herself from his grasp.

"You're a bloody liar."

"I'm an emotional wreck. I don't know what I'm doing with my life. My best friend and partner is about to be sent up the river for a murder she didn't commit. And I'm..." Her breath caught in her throat. "I'm so scared."

He pulled her roughly into his arms and held her. Her whole body shuddered.

"If I hadn't been so driven by ambition, if I'd never had anything to do with Doug, none of this would have happened," she cried. "I'm as much to blame as if I'd wielded the blow that killed him."

He shook her. "That's not true, Katie. Douglas Garrison dug his own grave."

It would be rush hour. Even with Salsky driving, his red light flashing on the roof, they didn't make it to the condo complex until well after eight.

"Number 62," Riley said as he bolted out of the car and headed across a nicely manicured lawn to the strip of two-story Mediterranean-style stucco dwellings. Number 62 was an end unit.

Salsky, huffing and puffing, caught up with Riley at the door just as it was being opened by a cherubic little girl who was no more than four or five.

"Is your daddy home?" Riley asked, feeling sick to his stomach at the thought that this innocent little kid's father was Sylver's crazed fan turned murderer.

A young, overweight woman with streaked blond hair, holding a bowl of batter in her hand, came up behind the little girl.

"Cheryl," she said sharply, "what did I tell you about opening doors to strangers?"

"They wanna see my daddy," Cheryl said petulantly, looking unperturbed by her mother's scolding.

"Go get into your pajamas," Cheryl's mama ordered, pulling the child away from the door, which she then proceeded to start to slam, only Salsky's size-13 cordovans got in her way. He flashed a badge.

"We'd like to talk to your husband, Mrs. Browning."

She glared at him defiantly. "My name's Martin. Beverly Martin. And you can't talk to my husband cause I don't have one. And I don't know anyone named Browning."

"He gave this as his address when he was admitted to L.A. General three months ago," Riley broke in.

"Yeah, well I just moved in here the beginning of March. So your Mr. Browning musta moved."

Salsky looked at Riley, who looked anything but happy.

"I'm sorry, Mrs. Cassidy," the night nurse, an older woman with brown hair streaked with gray, said sympathetically, "but we've really got to tuck you in for the night. And your daughter needs her beauty rest, too."

Nancy and Sylver exchanged anguished looks. Neither of them wanted to be separated. Neither of them wanted that night to pass. Neither of them wanted to face what was in store for each of them and for each other the next day.

"What time is my mother's surgery?" Sylver asked the nurse.

"We'll be prepping her at eight. Surgery is scheduled for nine-fifteen."

"Can I see her before . . . before she gets . . . prepped?"

"Well, I don't think—"

"I'm sure Dr. Warner wants me as relaxed and comfortable as possible before he goes chopping off my boobs, nurse," Nancy said in her typically raunchy fashion. "And seeing my daughter for a couple of minutes would make me feel ever so much better."

The nurse raised her eyes to the ceiling. She'd been dealing with entitled celebs at Stillwater for nine years. One thing she'd learned early on—you might as well give in to them because, in the end, they were going to get their own way.

"Okay, I'll have an orderly wheel your daughter down to your room after she's had her breakfast. Around seven-thirty. But she'll only be allowed to stay for five minutes."

Nancy and Sylver both smiled appreciatively.

"Now, Mrs. Cassidy, how about letting me escort you down to your room? I've got a nice sleeping pill ready for you and you can be in dreamland within the hour."

"I'll be along in a minute," Nancy said. "I just want to say good-night to my daughter."

The nurse stepped outside into the hall.

Nancy hugged Sylver to her. "It's going to be all right, baby. We're both going to be A-okay."

"Right," Sylver said, no more convinced than her mother, but feeling as much of a need to verbalize something positive. Nothing, however, could lift the pall that hung in the air.

"There are so many things I want to say to you, Sylver. I've been such a lousy mother. That time I practically kidnapped you..."

"It doesn't matter now," Sylver said.

"Oh, you made me so mad. All I could see was that you were throwing your life away. I wanted to get you away from Nash. I put all the blame on him, but plenty of it was mine. I never gave you any choices. That awful night when Nicky Kramer—"

"Shh. We don't have to talk about that now. It's over with."

"I guess I thought if I denied what he did to you, then I could make you deny it, too. And then you found out you were pregnant...." Nancy couldn't go on. She began to cry softly.

So did Sylver.

"Funny," Nancy said through her tears, "but you know the one thing in the world I want more than anything?"

Mother and daughter's eyes met. "No. Tell me, Mom."

Nancy's lower lip quivered. She couldn't remember the last time Sylver had called her *Mom*. "I want to stick around long enough to see a grandchild. I want to be a grandmother. A real, regular, plain old granny. Ain't that a kick in the pants?"

Sylver nodded, unable to speak. A tall order, considering that Nancy had to beat the big C and Sylver had to beat a prison rap. And that was just for starters.

* * *

It took a couple of hours to track down Gary Browning's latest whereabouts. Riley and Salsky finally found out that the foreclosure papers on the condo had been mailed to a Toluca Park address.

They got to the tidy strip of garden apartments just before eleven that night. Definitely a step down from the condo out in Encino, but the neighborhood was quiet, the buildings were of recent vintage and kept up, although the thin strip of grassy lawn had gone to seed and was dotted with brown spots. Browning's apartment was number 3 on the second floor of one of the middle units.

Inside the little vestibule, Salsky nearly tripped over a tricycle. Riley shot him a look. Salsky raised up his hands in apology. Rock music drifted out into the hallway from the downstairs apartment on the right. There was a cloying smell of popcorn in the air.

They climbed the stairs. Riley knocked at Browning's door. Salsky eased his .45 out of his shoulder holster, put his hand behind his back to keep it out of sight.

No answer. Riley knocked a little louder. A middle-aged woman with a shopworn face in a worn blue terry robe opened the door across the hall.

"We're looking for Mr. Browning," Riley said. Salsky quickly stuck the gun away from the neighbor's view.

The woman shrugged. "He comes and goes at crazy hours."

"Thanks," Salsky said. "We'll ... just leave him a note. Sorry to disturb you."

The woman grunted and shut the door.

Salsky eyed Riley. "Now, you know we'd need a warrant to go inside."

"You mean *you'd* need a warrant," Riley said with a wry smile.

Salsky made a "be my guest" gesture toward the door. Riley pulled out a credit card from his wallet and a minute later they were in Gary Browning's living room.

The atmosphere was as drab and impersonal as one of those low-budget motel rooms. The furnishings were cheap but all new—matching neomodern blue-and-tan striped sofa and love seat, oak cubes that served as coffee table and end

tables, a pair of lamps whose brown shades sported an edging of blue fringe, a cheap white laminated entertainment
unit on the wall opposite the couch holding a TV, a VCR,
and a small stack of videos.

Riley walked across the room and took a look at the videos. His pulse picked up speed as he saw *Glory Girl* on the
top. The five other videos in the stack were all Sylver Cassidy movies. Pay dirt.

"In here," Salsky called out from the bedroom.

When Riley got to the open bedroom door, he gave a start
as he saw the bouquet of red roses in a glass vase on the side
of the bed. Salsky motioned him to step inside, then pointed
to the wall across from the bed.

What he saw really didn't take Riley by surprise, but that
in no way diminished the sick feeling in his gut at the sight.
The wall was plastered with pictures of Sylver—cutouts
from magazines and newspapers, photographs ranging from
when she was a kid of ten or eleven, all the way up to one of
her frolicking in the snow in front of Kate's chalet in Running Springs last Christmas. About two inches of the photo
had been cropped off. Riley guessed that had been him. So
he'd been right. The sicko had been up there with them,
spying on them, taking pictures.

Salsky was going through the drawers of a plain brown
bureau. Riley walked over to the louvered closet. Not much
hanging in there. Four shirts, a couple of pairs of trousers.
And a janitor's uniform. Riley took it out and held it up.

"Salsky."

The detective looked over.

Riley tapped the emblem on the shirt pocket. "It's the
Paradine logo. Browning works at Paradine."

Salsky nodded, then revealed what he'd dug up. A pile of
letters tied in a red ribbon. Each of the envelopes was addressed to Sylver. None of them bore any stamps.

Riley opened the top one.

Dear Princess,
I'm glad he's dead. Now he won't hurt you anymore....

* * *

The nurse had offered Sylver a sleeping pill, but except for those first days in the hospital when she had no say as to what was going into or out of her body, she'd refused all drugs of any sort—from painkillers to muscle relaxants to sleeping pills.

The room was dim and quiet. Another storm was blowing in over the ocean, the wind howling against the windows. She waited expectantly to hear the downpour start.

What she heard instead was her door opening. She closed her eyes, pretending to be asleep. If the nurse checked on her and saw she was still awake, she might try to persuade her to take something to help her drift off. Knowing she was unlikely to get any sleep that night, what with worrying about her mother's surgery, about getting charged with murder, about whether Riley would really be able to track down her obsessed fan, Sylver was afraid she might weaken and take a sleeping tablet after all.

She lay very still, trying not to let her eyelids flutter as the faint footsteps approached her bed. Her breathing was even and shallow. She smiled inwardly. She could still act if she had to.

"Hi, baby."

Sylver's eyes sprang open. The first thing she saw was a star-shaped earring—the mate of the one the police were holding as evidence. Her mouth started to open, but before she could say anything, Nash Walker's hand clamped down over it.

A memory flooded back into Sylver's mind. Her final confrontation with Nash. The day she'd thrown him off the picture; told him to get out of her life. She remembered now, walking into her apartment that day, in a stupor after her nauseating encounter with Doug. There was Nash coming out of her bedroom. Stoned out of his gourd. What had he been doing in her bedroom before she'd walked in? One thing he'd been doing, it dawned on her now, was swiping her earrings.

Nash was smiling down at her, his hair falling around his face. "I want you to know, Sylver, I did it for you," he whispered. "Oh, not the murder. Garrison just got me so ticked off. Kicking me out of that big, fancy house of his—

telling me—telling all of us—to take a flying hike. Who the
hell did he think he was? I came there trying to work a deal.
You see a pal of mine and that prissy wife of his were an
item for a while. I told him I'd keep quiet about their little
S&M games if he got off your case and didn't try to stick his
nose into this French deal you had in the works. I read about
the deal in the trades. I figured if you knew that I was the
one that made sure everything went like clockwork, you'd
put me back in the picture." He was talking like what he was
saying made perfect sense.

Sylver stared up at him, his hand still clamped tightly over
her mouth. She could see he was juiced up—coke, uppers.
And booze. She could smell whiskey on his breath. He was
staring down at her, but his eyes were vacant and glassy. As
he leaned closer, she could see that he was sweating profusely, which meant he was coming down. Nash was dangerous when he was in need of a hit.

"It didn't work out exactly the way I meant," he went on
in a raspy whisper. "I lost my temper. One thing I want you
to know, baby. I didn't set you up. That stupid earring must
have fallen out of my pocket. I kinda borrowed them. I
needed a little cash, but then we had that . . . misunderstand-
ing and I was so worked up I forgot all about them."

He laughed softly. "It turned out okay, though. These
dumb-ass guys on my case got themselves picked up by the
cops. Sweet, huh? I think my luck's changing, baby."

Sylver tugged at his hand, which was partially covering
her nose, as well. She could hardly breathe and she was still
very weak.

"I just want you to listen quietly, baby."

Sylver demonstrated with her eyes that she would. Nash
studied her contemplatively. Before lifting his hand from her
mouth, he exchanged the earring for a pocketknife, flick-
ing a little button so the blade popped out. He held the tip
right on the pulse beat of her throat.

"Nash . . ."

"Shh."

She felt the faint prick of the knife and clamped her lips
shut, terrified.

Nash nodded his approval. "Now the police have already come to talk to me, baby. And I told them I gave you the earrings. My guess is they're gonna arrest you for Garrison's murder. Unless..."

He smiled. A crazed, drugged-out smile. "Unless I tell the cops I remember you loaning those earrings to your pal, Kate Paley. Man, that's one broad who could use getting cut down a few notches. She's always hated my guts."

He stroked her hair. "Poor baby. I was really broken up when I heard about the crash. Just think, now we can be together."

She shook her head. "It's no use, Nash." Her voice didn't sound like her own. "The police won't believe you."

He was wild-eyed. "You shouldn't have canned me, baby. I'm a damn good actor." He grinned. "I sure as hell fooled Garrison. The jerk thought I'd merely walked out when he threatened to call the police. It was a real Oscar performance. When he heard me coming back in, I thought my goose was cooked. Only he thought it was that prissy wife of his... only she isn't so prissy, according to my pal. Likes being whipped. Likes pain." He dragged out the word, carving a light circle on her skin with the tip of his knife.

"Okay, Nash. I'll write you up a new contract. I lost my temper. I shouldn't have. I didn't understand."

He stared at her. "Man, you disappoint me, baby. This should be the acting job of your life, and you're blowing it. You're not believable."

"I'm telling you the truth, Nash. You're back on the picture. I don't know about the lead, but..."

Another circle at her throat. Sylver was afraid to swallow, the saliva was gathering in her mouth.

"It's got to be the lead, baby. Nash Walker doesn't take any two-bit parts. Not anymore."

Sylver felt clammy all over. She was between a rock and a hard place. If she told him he had the lead, no matter how persuasive she sounded, he wasn't going to believe her. If she said no...

"Nash, you're sick. You need help. I'll help you. I'll make the cops understand that you didn't know what you were doing when you struck out at Doug. I'll tell them...."

"You little bitch," he hissed, his acrid breath falling on her face, turning her stomach. "You're not gonna turn me in. No way. You've screwed my life up long enough. If it weren't for you, sweetheart, I coulda been a contender," he said in a poor excuse for a Marlon Brando impersonation.

She opened her mouth to scream, her last hope and a slim one at that, since she knew he'd be able to cut her throat long before someone could come running in. Still, she couldn't just lie there, submissive.

Before any sound came out of her mouth, though, Sylver was stunned to see a figure rush up behind Nash, a pair of hands circling the actor's neck.

It all happened so fast. One minute Nash was about to cut her throat, the next minute he was slumped on the floor in a heap.

Sylver's mind was reeling, grateful that her knight in shining armor had once again come to her rescue. "Riley..."

Only it wasn't Riley who approached her bed. She saw that the man walked with a slight limp. He was tall, gaunt, with thinning hair, a few long strands combed over his bald spot. There was something about him. He looked vaguely familiar, only she couldn't quite place him. He was one of those people who faded into the woodwork.

He smiled timidly. "Hello, princess. You don't know how long I've waited for this moment. I've come for you. I've come to take you home. Everything's going to be all right now. No one will ever hurt you again."

Sylver's lips moved, but no words came out. It was him. The stalker. She felt as if she were trapped in some hideous, never-ending nightmare.

"I brought you something, princess. Something red. It's my favorite color, too," he said brightly.

Her terrified eyes shot to the red scarf he was pulling out of his Windbreaker pocket.

"I've got a beautiful bouquet of red roses waiting for you at home, princess. Right by the side of the bed. So you can see them first thing when you wake up in the morning."

Sylver's eyes were riveted to the scarf in his had. She thought he meant to strangle her with it if she protested. She felt so weak and tired. "No. Please..."

"Don't be afraid, princess. I've tried so hard not to let any harm come to you. I'd give my life for you—"

The door burst open before he finished his sentence, as Riley rushed into the room, taking a flying leap for Browning and knocking him to the floor.

"No, Riley!" Sylver shouted. "Don't hurt him. He saved my life!"

Hank Salsky, gun drawn, followed Riley into the room and flicked on the light. Behind him was Al Borgini. Salsky had radioed his chief as he and Riley sped over to the hospital.

Gary Browning was pinned under Riley on the floor, looking utterly terrified. Close by, Nash Walker was starting to come to.

"It was Nash," Sylver said breathlessly. "He's got the other earring. He was the one that stole them from my apartment. He killed Doug. He would have killed me, too, if this . . . fan of mine hadn't stopped him."

It took Riley a few moments for what Sylver was saying to sink in. Finally, he looked over at Walker, then got off Gary Browning, even helped him to his feet. While Borgini cuffed Nash, who started babbling incoherently, Salsky frisked Browning, coming up with a small pistol and an old publicity shot of Sylver.

Salsky read Browning and Walker their rights. As the cops were about to cart the two men off, Browning gave Sylver a timid, forlorn smile.

"I don't suppose you'd . . . autograph your picture for me before I . . . go?"

Sylver looked over at Riley. "Do you have a pen?"

Riley tossed her one. Salsky brought over the photo.

"What's your name?" she asked softly.

"Gary. My name's Gary."

"To Gary," she wrote. "With everlasting gratitude, Sylver Cassidy."

Epilogue

Beverly Hills, California
Spring 1995

"Tell me, Deanna, have you ever seen so many stretch limos in your life?"

"Or so many stars, Alan? I have to say the women tonight look absolutely magnificent. Oh, look, there's Emily Chapman. Emily. Emily, over here. That gown is gorgeous. Whose is it?"

"Versace. Thanks."

"Well, Chapman walked away with the coveted statue two years ago for Best Actress, and now she's up for another one tonight for Lost Childhood. What do you think of her chances, Alan?"

"Emily's a great actress, but I gotta tell ya, Deanna, my bet's on the hot nominee tonight, Christine Tyler, for her star-turning performance as the young actress in Obsession."

"Obsession has certainly surprised everyone—a small independent picture walking off with five nominations, including Best Picture. You could say everyone around town's obsessed with Obsession."

"More and more, some of these classy little independent films are starting to get their due, Deanna."

"And none deserves it more than Obsession. Still, it's a real long shot for Best Picture. The odds makers say it's going to be the epic Da Vinci. And I'm going to have to go with them on this one, Alan."

"Okay, folks. You heard it here. Deanna Rubin's made her prediction. Now we all have to stay tuned for *the next three hours or so and find out if she was right.''*

''Oh, look, Alan. Coming up the red carpet. Riley Quinn, the author and screenwriter of Obsession, *and his gorgeous wife, Sylver Cassidy, who coproduced the film. Of course, a lot of us remember Sylver for her work in front of the cameras when she was a kid. I remember seeing her years back in* Glory Girl. *She was radiant.''*

''I don't think I've ever seen her look more radiant than she does tonight.''

''Her husband doesn't look half bad himself. I hear Sylver and her partner, Kate Paley, are about to start filming Quinn's latest opus, Shadow Boxing. *Could be another winner. What do you think?''*

''I'll tell ya, Deanna. I think they're on a roll.''

''Sylver. Sylver Cassidy. Over here,'' Deanna shouted. *''That gown is you, darling. Who designed it?''*

Hank Salsky let out a hoot when he spotted Riley and Sylver on TV as he sat on a barstool across the street from the station house. Al Borgini was perched on the stool next to him. Salsky, who had a handful of peanuts in one hand and a mug of beer in the other, used his elbow to nudge his chief in the ribs. "Hey, Quinn doesn't looked half bad in a monkey suit. And get a load of Sylver. She looks like a million bucks."

Al Borgini smiled. "Hell, she's worth at least that now."

Salsky popped some nuts into his mouth. "I gotta say, Chief, I'm real glad it worked out the way it did. I never really thought she did it. To tell ya the truth, for a minute or two there, I was scared it might be your buddy."

"My money was on the mother," Borgini admitted. "I thought she'd crack and confess as soon as I collared her daughter."

"That other twosome weren't exactly off the hook, either. Paley had more than enough reasons to off Garrison. And her boyfriend, Needham, struck me as a real hothead."

"Yeah. I wasn't writing them off the list completely, either. I have to say, I felt really relieved when it turned out to be that sleazeball junkie, Nash Walker."

"Say, isn't that Paley and Needham over there?"

"Where?"

"Over behind that broad with the dress cut down to her belly button."

Borgini smiled. "Yeah, that's them, all right."

A big grin spread across Salsky's mouth as the camera focused in on Kate and Adrian as they met up with Riley and Sylver, the foursome embracing. "Hollywood," Salsky said. "Don't ya love it?"

He sits on his sofa, a red rose in one hand, his autographed photo of Sylver pressed to his chest. She looks so beautiful tonight, even on his cheap thirteen-inch television screen. He can only imagine how much more beautiful she looks in person. For a while, he'd contemplated risking it. Who'd spot him amid all those crowds of movie fans? In the end, he decided he couldn't do it. The thought of spending time in prison—which was what the judge had said would happen if he didn't obey the strict restraining order forbidding him from getting anywhere near Sylver or sending her any more presents or notes—was more than he could bear.

Soon, she'd be heading back to London anyway, where she was now living. She had made a new life for herself. She looked happy. Truly happy. And that was all he'd ever wanted for her.

He would always be her "everlasting fan." And he would always be there if she needed him.

As she disappears from the screen, he draws the photo away from his heart. Tears mist his eyes as he reads the inscription for the millionth time—"To Gary. With everlasting gratitude, Sylver Cassidy."

Stay well, princess. I will always love you.

Sylver and Riley sat beside Kate and Adrian at their designated spots in the large auditorium of the Dorothy Chandler Pavilion. Because they were all up for the key awards— Sylver and Kate for Best Picture, Adrian for Best Director, and Riley for Best Adapted Screenplay, they had prominent seats.

The foursome were dressed to the nines tonight. Sylver's simple but glamorous Brunaud gown was a slim, ankle-length sheath the color of fine port wine. Around her neck she wore the pearl pendant Riley had given her on their first Christmas. On her wrist was a stunning gold-and-diamond bracelet he'd given her that morning for her twenty-sixth birthday.

Riley, still not crazy about dressing up, hadn't made too much of a fuss when Sylver had cajoled him into being fitted for a custom Ralph Lauren black tux, black striped trousers, gray-and-black pin-striped vest, and wing-collared shirt. Riley had insisted on a yellow bow tie for a touch of kitsch.

Kate's unique gown, a flowing coral silk with a scalloped neckline and Empire waist above a floor-length tapered skirt, was done by an as-yet-undiscovered—save for a select few—young London designer, Lisa Emory. One thing about Kate hadn't changed; she was still a trendsetter. There was no question but that by the next day every fashion maven from coast to coast would be buzzing about Kate's new find.

Even Adrian made a fashion statement that night. He looked dashingly antebellum in a tux that Clark Gable might have worn in *Gone With the Wind*, but when his gaze met Kate's as his name was announced as the winner for Best Director for *Obsession*, he wore anything but a "Frankly Scarlett, I don't give a damn" look. He smiled tenderly at his wife, who beamed back at him with pride and adoration. Sylver kissed him excitedly and Riley gave him a bear hug, not feeling at all disappointed that he hadn't won the screenplay Oscar. The way he saw it, he'd already won plenty, including the National Book Award for his new novel and soon-to-be film, *Shadow Boxing*, a story about an ex-cop who finally puts his demons behind him and finds love and redemption.

Adrian, looking dazed and uncomfortable, stood at the podium clutching his Oscar. He stared out at the crowd, but his gaze soon fell on Kate and he kept it there.

"I'm one lucky bloke. I not only got to direct a great movie, thanks to a great script by my good pal Riley Quinn, the terrific producing team of Sylver Cassidy and Kate Paley, and a wonderful cast—and I'm not going to name you all, because I'm so nervous I'll bloody well forget half your names and you'll all be pissed off—can I say that on the telly? Now, where was I? Oh, yes. About being a lucky bloke." He smiled broadly at his wife. "What really makes me the luckiest bloke around is that even though I was only the director, I got to get the girl of my dreams in the end. And I get to keep her long after *Obsession* is a rerun on the telly."

Adrian walked off the stage to a round of applause, with no one clapping louder than Kate.

After the next commercial, they arrived at the last and most prestigious award of the evening, the one everyone had been waiting for—Best Picture of the year. One of Hollywood's foremost actors, Jack West, was the presenter. He began naming each of the five movies up for the award, pausing in between for the showing of brief clips. *Obsession* was the last one on his list. After the clip, there was a huge round of applause. The independent film was a real crowd pleaser.

Jack West smiled into the camera and slowly, dramatically, opened the envelope, pulling the folded card out with a flourish.

Kate and Sylver sat side by side, their hands entwined. They both kept telling themselves they didn't have a chance in hell of winning the big one, and it didn't matter anyway, but they knew they were lying. It didn't mean everything—they'd both certainly learned that; the men beside them were all the proof they needed—but it meant a lot.

"And the winner is *Obsession*" came West's twangy voice. "Accepting the award for Best Picture will be the movie's two producers, Sylver Cassidy and Kate Paley."

Riley and Adrian gave their wives big, passionate kisses. Then Kate and Sylver turned to each other. A funny moment of awkwardness and incredulity overcame them. Was this really happening? Surely, dreams didn't come true. Not in Hollywood, of all places.

Kate laughed, breaking the tension. The two women clasped hands and started down the aisle together.

Everyone was applauding and congratulating them as they walked on wobbly legs up to the stage. They still couldn't fully take it in. They'd done it. They'd won. And what really counted was that, bucking all the odds, they'd won on their own terms.

When they got to the podium and turned to the audience, they were overwhelmed to discover they were receiving a standing ovation. Both women tried to fight back tears, but it was useless.

Finally, when the applause died down and everyone returned to their seats, Sylver nudged Kate forward.

Kate stood in front of the microphone, staring out at the sea of industry faces, trying to find the words. She glanced over at Sylver and smiled wryly. "I guess this means they like us. They really like us."

Sylver grinned and everyone in the audience laughed.

Kate turned back to them. "Seriously, folks. It's been one hell of a roller-coaster ride, but I wouldn't trade a minute of it. I've learned a lot, making this movie. I learned the power of words with honest feelings behind them from Riley Quinn. I learned the power of sticking to your ideals and believing in yourself from my loving husband, Adrian. And I learned—" she paused, taking hold of Sylver's hand, her eyes misting over as she turned to her "—the true meaning of friendship and forgiveness from a very special woman, Sylver Cassidy."

More applause, and then it was Sylver's turn to speak.

She looked at Kate and then she looked at her Oscar, her smile luminescent. "What a birthday present." She took a breath. "I—I owe so many people for this award," she said haltingly. "I wish I had Riley's words to tell him and Adrian, and Kate most of all, what this moment means to me." Again she paused, her eyes shimmering with happiness and pride. "I wouldn't be here now if it wasn't for all three of them." She tightened her hold on Kate's hand. Then she let her gaze fall on her husband. "What can I say, Riley? Except that you're brilliant, tender, a real...lifesaver. And that ain't no lie. I love you so much, Riley."

The cameras zeroed in on Riley, who was trying to fight back tears, but not doing a good job of it. He blew her a kiss.

Sylver looked straight at the camera. "And Skyler, I hope you're in your jammies, fast asleep. I love you, too, baby."

Tears streamed down her cheeks as she held the Oscar up high, gazing skyward. "Mom, I guess, most of all, this is for you. I know you're up there watching. And beaming. I only wish you could be here with us today. I miss you."

She started to turn from the podium, then leaned over to the mike for one final remark. "One more thing, Mom. Skyler saw your picture on the piano the other day and you know what he said?" Her voice caught, but she went on. "He said, 'That's my granny.' I thought you'd like to hear that."

As the applause filled the auditorium, Kate and Sylver, producing-team extraordinaire, stood there, side by side, Oscars in tow, their hands clasped together and held high in victory.

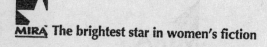

New York Times Bestselling Author

ELIZABETH LOWELL

Brings you another sweeping saga this January with

GRANITE MAN

He had determination of steel and a heart of stone....

Cash McQueen lived for the land and trusted no one.
So when Mariah MacKenzie blew into town asking too
many questions and digging around his property, he
knew there'd be trouble—for both of them. But Mariah
was a temptation too powerful to resist, and if she
wasn't careful, she just might uncover something too
hot for either of them to handle....

"Nobody does romance like Elizabeth Lowell."
—Jayne Ann Krentz

MIRA **The brightest star in women's fiction**

MEL1

New York Times Bestselling Author

Who can you trust when your life's on the line?
Find out this March in

Stevie Corbett is in jeopardy of losing everything—her career,
her future…her life. Her fate rests on keeping the truth a
secret, but there is one reporter who already knows too much.
She could lose everything…including her heart. All he has to
do is betray her trust….

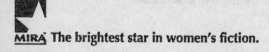

MIRA The brightest star in women's fiction.